DO NOT REMOVE
CARDS FROM POCKET

THE DAY
THAT
DUSTY DIED

PREVIOUS MYSTERIES BY LEE MARTIN:

Hacker
The Mensa Murders
Deficit Ending
Hal's Own Murder Case
Death Warmed Over
Murder at the Blue Owl
A Conspiracy of Strangers
Too Sane a Murder

THE DAY
THAT
DUSTY DIED

Lee Martin

ST. MARTIN'S PRESS   NEW YORK

Design by Basha Zapatka

ISBN 0-312-09779-4

First Edition: March

10 9 8 7 6 5 4 3 2 1

For Heather and you

Prologue

DUSTY MILLER DIED in the spring, on a day sweet with redbud and dogwood, blossoming with late daffodils and early daylilies, with the sky as soft and blue and innocent as a newborn baby's eyes.

I was there not as a member of the Major Case Squad, but just because a patrolman had radioed, his voice breaking with emotion, for the closest female officer—fast.

I was twelve blocks away, and I got there as fast as I could, with a flashing blue light magneted to my dash, my headlights flashing high, low, high, low, and my siren wailing. But I wasn't quite fast enough. When I pulled into the parking lot I could see the girl they told me later was Dusty Miller, perched on a high-rise windowsill, all alone, dusty blond hair flying about her face. But she could scarcely see me, down on the ground, and she probably couldn't hear me no matter how loudly I shouted. I needed to talk with her privately if I expected her to listen. It took me a while to get up the elevator and reach her apartment, and before I even found the right door standing open to the thick-carpeted hall I heard a patrolman yelling incoherently over the radio, screaming for an ambulance, as if that was going to do any good. I ran past the patrolman, who was still yelling into his radio, past a well-dressed, ashen-faced woman standing with her back to the wall with the knuckles of her left hand pressed into her mouth, past the young girl in pink who was standing alone in a hallway, and pushed at the closed bedroom door, reaching my arm above the head of another patrolman, who was working on the lock with a fingernail file.

"Move over," I said, and he did. It was an easy lock; I could only assume that this patrolman had not yet had any children lock themselves into the bathroom, as all toddlers do at least once. Seconds later, when the door sprang open under the blade of my pocketknife, I could see the dainty, white embroidered organdy curtains swaying gently in the breeze that came through the open window. But Dusty was no longer sitting on the windowsill. She had gone out the window.

Out the window, and fourteen stories down. Her pale pink sleeveless sweater and pale blue glacier-washed jeans now were a pastel blur, obscured with red—red—red. Her bare left arm bent where arms don't bend, and her head tilted much too far back, off the hood of the waxed blue Corvette where she lay. Already people, official and unofficial, were swarming around her, and EMTs were running toward her carrying the stretcher to get her into the ambulance that I knew would take her to the morgue, not the E-Room.

I turned back out of the bedroom, back to the living room, where the crying mother was being comforted by the patrolman who had been yelling into the radio. Andersen, his name tag said. The other, whose name tag said Woodall, was writing in his notebook, a great sadness visible on his face.

A man who must have been the victim's father came in then, yelling, "Where is that stupid little bitch? I'll teach her not to make threats like that. Get the police called in—"

The mother turned to look at him. "It wasn't a threat," she said dully. "She jumped. She's dead, Seth. Dusty's dead."

"Well, hell," the man said. "Why'd you let her do it, Ellen?" The only identifiable emotion in his voice was anger.

The young girl in pink—I'd guess her to have been about ten—continued to stand in the hallway. The mother went toward

· · · · ·

her and began to hug her, but the girl jerked away and ran down the hall. I could hear her door slam, hear the lock click.

The father sat down on the couch and said, "Damn it." The mother sat down then, too, on a chair about as far from him as she could get and still be in the living room.

In these few seconds I'd seen half a dozen reasons for suicide. But which one was the proximate cause? Which one was the trigger?

How at risk was the little girl in pink?

The Dusty Miller case started out as my own personal vendetta, to try to find out what could have caused a lovely, talented sixteen-year-old girl to volunteer for that long dive—to try to find out, and to do something about it.

But before it was over I had involved not only the Major Case Squad but a lot more people besides.

. . . . .

$\mathcal{O}n\varepsilon$
. . . .

"IT'S CLOSED," CAPTAIN Millner said to me. "Deb, I don't know what in the hell you expect to do about it. It was suicide. The girl jumped out the window. Nobody pushed her. Nobody helped her. Nobody talked her into it. A patrolman was in the apartment when it happened."

"Two patrolmen," I said.

"One patrolman, two patrolmen, what the hell difference does that make? They were there. So were her mother and sister. Standing right there inside the apartment."

"Condo. Not apartment. You don't expect people with that kind of money to live in a mere rented apartment, do you?" I knew I was totally unreasonable, arguing about trifles in hopes that continued anger would keep the sorrow at bay. But none of it was Captain Millner's fault.

"Whatever," he said.

I dumped the contents of my lap drawer into a cardboard box and hoped I would continue to manage not to cry. Dismantling a system it had taken me years to arrange exactly to my liking was depressing me even further, and I had a hunch I wasn't going to be able to put things back the same way when I got to Chandra's desk. "And the father came in right afterward. I wish you'd seen him, then you'd understand what I mean—"

"I understand well enough, and from what you tell me, if I'd have been there I'd have been tempted to knock his block off. But

. . . . .

my point is, it's *over*. The girl is dead. She killed herself. You know it, I know it. So what in the hell do you expect—"

"Quit asking me that," I said. "Quit asking me what I expect to do about it. I can't do anything about it. I know that. But don't you care *why*? There was something *wrong* there and I—"

"Of course there was something wrong," Millner said brusquely. "That jackass of a father made that clear, and anyway people don't kill themselves when there's nothing wrong. And of course I wonder why. You always wonder why, on something like this, especially when it's a kid. But I'm not going to indulge my curiosity on city time. And neither are you. You went there because that chowderhead started screaming for a detective. It wasn't a detective matter. It should have been handled by Uniform Division. Even if it was a detective matter it wouldn't call for the Major Case Squad. And even if it called for the Major Case Squad—"

"I'm out. I know." I folded the box flaps closed and started unloading another drawer into another box. "And he wasn't screaming for a detective, he was screaming for a woman. In case you haven't noticed, I'm a—"

"I've noticed, I've noticed," he said hastily. "Unless it's sexist to notice; in that case I haven't noticed. As for being out of the Major Case Squad, that's only temporary. You know—"

"You know I hate the Rape Squad!" I yelled. "I've done my time there. It's somebody else's turn!"

"We've got to have a woman in the Sex Crimes Unit," Millner said reasonably. "And with Chandra on maternity leave—"

"Haven't you got it through your head yet that I'm going out on sick leave, too?" I inquired, slamming the drawer shut and opening the next.

"You don't need to move everything you own," Millner said. "You probably won't be there over three months."

"I don't know what I'm going to need in three months. And quit changing the subject."

. . . . .

"If you need something, you can walk across the hall and get it. Nobody'll be using your desk. Quit packing everything you own. And yes, I know you're going out for foot surgery day after tomorrow. How long do you expect that to keep you out, for crying out loud? I mean, you already told me you won't even be spending the night in the hospital—"

"My doctor told me that it takes longer to recover completely from heel spur removal than it does from open-heart surgery."

"Bullshit," Millner said.

"That's what I said, or something like that. And he replied, 'You don't walk on your heart.' "

"All right, so you'll be out for a few days and then you'll be on crutches. So what if you can't get to the scene? You can still work in the office. And that's where we've got to have a woman. Deb, will you quit with the damned *boxes*? You aren't going to Timbuktu."

"I'll pack what I want to pack," I yelled. "I know there's got to be a woman there, but who said it had to be *me*? I'm not the only woman in the whole Detective Bureau."

"There was a time when you were," Millner pointed out. "And there was a time when you were glad of it."

"There was never a time," I said precisely and slightly viciously, carefully folding the sweater I keep draped over the back of my chair for use in summer when the air-conditioning freezes me out, "when I was glad I was the only woman in the Detective Bureau."

"You know what I mean," Millner said. "Will you please explain to me just what your objection is to the Sex Crimes Unit? I mean, women always say—"

"That there should be women on the Rape Squad. I know, but—"

"Quit calling it the Rape Squad!" Millner yelled. "It's the Sex Crimes Unit!"

"All right, all right, it's the Sex Crimes Unit! It just confuses me, that's all," I said less than truthfully. That was part of the reason.

. . . . .

It certainly was not all of the reason. "It seems like everybody's working on everything all the time. Not like—"

"The Major Case Squad," Millner concluded for me, his tone sardonic. "Where theoretically you've got one person, one case, only really everybody's working on everything all the time. Well, Deb, you know what? In the Sex Crimes Unit it's theoretically one person, one case, too."

"But I know what's going on here. I don't there." That was a lame excuse and I knew it, and I knew perfectly well he knew it, too. But I also knew that never in a million years was I going to explain to Captain Millner all the reasons why I hated working on the Sex Crimes Unit.

"I'll see to it," Millner said, "that you're adequately briefed on what's going on there. And you will leave this Dusty Miller thing *strictly alone.*"

"I won't spend any city time on it," I said.

He glared at me. He knows, as my family knows, that when I've got something on my mind I spend just about as much of my own time on it as I do city time. But he couldn't tell me how I could spend my own time, at least not unless he got an official complaint from a citizen that I was annoying him or her. So, probably wisely, he decided to change the subject. "Do you know everybody in the unit?"

"Yes," I said, and then realized that was, by now, a little less than completely true. Seven years ago, when I was in the unit myself, I knew everybody in it. Now the best I could say was that I knew them all by sight. Chandra Kay Randall, whose position I was temporarily filling, was a black woman in her early thirties, and I'd gone to lunch with her a few times. I liked her well enough, but that didn't matter, because while I was there she wouldn't be there. The whole rest of the squad was male, which I considered idiotic; logically, I figured, it should be at least half female. If not more. Most of the perps were male, to be sure, but most of the victims were female.

·   ·   ·   ·

7

At least most of the reported victims. And we couldn't do anything about the unreported ones.

It was headed by Sergeant Rafe Permut. I didn't really know him, but I liked what I knew. He reminded me of Captain Greco on the kids' television show "Mathnet," which I occasionally watch out of sheer ennui (as well as the fact that it's really pretty funny) when I am home at the right time. Roger Hales I knew but didn't like much, mainly because his sense of humor is a little wacky.

And that's saying a lot, because just about all cops have a grisly idea of what's funny. Despite the frequent citizen complaints about police laughing at murder scenes, it's not evidence of callousness. It's just the opposite; it's a drive for self-preservation. But Roger Hales laughs even at things most cops don't think are funny.

On top of that, he oughtn't, in my opinion, to be allowed anywhere near any victim of any crime, and especially not a sex crime. He doesn't quite believe in rape, unless the victim is bruised and banged around and cut up. He believes in the adage of the twig and the Coke bottle. You can't stick the twig in the Coke bottle unless the Coke bottle is holding still; therefore he figures the woman consented and then changed her mind afterward. He can't get it through his head that nobody was holding a knife to the Coke bottle's throat, or a gun to its head, or saying, "I'll kill your children if you don't cooperate."

Wayne Harris I didn't really know except by sight, and I wasn't sure anybody really knew him except by sight. He'd been brought into the Detective Bureau only a couple of months ago, and my overall impression of him was that on any possible topic of conversation he agreed with whoever was closest. Maybe he'd change, as he got to feeling more secure in the situation, and maybe he wouldn't. He reminded me of the joke about the town so blah there wasn't any there there. From all I could tell, the only him there was in him was a mirror.

Unfortunately, the closest desk to his was that of Roger Hales. I didn't really know Henry Tuckman. He was a fairly new

. . . . .

detective, too, within the last year, and he was the only black man in the Sex Crimes Unit. (Up until that time Chandra's presence had served two purposes: she was the only black *and* the only woman.) About the only thing I'd heard about him was that he takes his time in figuring anything out, but when he makes up his mind you can bet anything you want to name that he is right.

Manuel Rodriguez had come into the unit the same time Tuckman did, and in some ways he was Tuckman's opposite. He has these incredible leaps of intuition—he's like me, in that—but he's just as likely to be wrong as to be right, which come to think of it is also like me.

Six people, total, counting me as of tomorrow. Six people, to handle all the sex crimes occurring in the city of Fort Worth, Texas, population about five hundred thousand. Statisticians say that at least one out of every four American women is the victim of a sexual assault at least once in her life, as is at least one out of every six or seven American men, usually in childhood. Although the incidence of female sex offenders is increasing, it's still a predominantly male crime, which means that of the victims we see, most females are the victims of heterosexual attacks and most males are the victims of homosexual attacks. There are about four hundred and fifty reported and confirmed forcible rapes in Fort Worth per year, plus all the child molestations, statutory rapes (many of which are actually forcible but for various reasons aren't treated that way), sexual assaults on men and boys, and so forth. That's about seventy-five forcible rapes plus one-sixth of all the other reported sex crimes for each person on the squad to work per year—call it one hundred cases a year for each person, eight or so per month, slightly under two a week. And if you think six people can work that load adequately, I've got some nice oceanfront property in Arizona I'd like to sell you.

On top of that, you can bet your booties that fewer than ten percent of the sex crimes in any category ever get reported, here or anywhere else. So members of the Sex Crimes Unit, as well as

· · · · ·

9

public relations officers, go to schools and churches and give a lot of talks, trying to get it across to people that rape is real, that the victims really hurt, that it isn't funny, and that they really ought to report any sex crime that happens. I've found that when you're making a talk like that you can look out across the room at the frozen faces (usually female; I think male victims manage to avoid even showing up at that kind of talk) and know as well as you know you're standing there that you're looking at a woman who has been a victim of a sex crime that was never reported and will never be reported. And you can look at the self-satisfied, arrogant faces (usually male) and know who's a potential perp, or at least a predator who sees women as his lawful prey.

Not, of course, that most perps or potential perps are recognizable that way. Most of them look, and act, just like everyone else—which makes them that much more dangerous. Unfortunately, an awful lot of the sex crimes that are reported wind up "unfounded"—that is, there is inadequate evidence that a crime was committed. A lot of the time you unfound a case you know really happened, but you also know you'd never prove it to the court system. That's hard even for a cop to swallow. It's a lot harder for the victim.

And you know that for every sex offender you actually manage to convict, at least twenty walk. Most of them you never even hear of, because the cases don't get reported.

You also know that an awful lot of people (including, as I mentioned, at least one of the people in the Sex Crimes Unit) still don't quite believe rape exists, or else they believe it's a crime of passion. It's not. It's a crime of violence, hostility, usually hatred. Rape victims, just in the cases that I've personally worked or that have been worked by people I know, have been as old as ninety-two, as young as six weeks. Yes, that was *weeks,* and yes, of course the baby died.

I consider myself a professional police officer, but like most people I want to feel successful. That means I prefer to work cases

· · · · ·

I can clear. I prefer situations in which I can do some good. And I'd never—as much as I would like to be wrong—felt that I was doing any good in the Sex Crimes Unit.

Captain Millner persists in thinking I can do some good there, or anywhere else I'm placed. That actually means he trusts me, which usually I appreciate. "Sorry I'm so cross," I offered.

He shrugged. "Nobody likes suicides," he said. "Especially when it's kids."

"Yeah," I agreed. Let him assume that was the problem, because I had no intention of telling him the real problem. It was just too personal.

"Leave the boxes here," he said, obviously tired of leaning on Dutch's desk watching me pack. "I'll get somebody else to move them. Come on."

I followed him across the hall to the Sex Crimes Unit squad room, to be greeted by three interested faces (the other two men were out somewhere) and the realization that I was going to have to try to fit all my stuff into a desk that Chandra hadn't cleared out before she left. Not that I could blame her for that. The last month or so she'd hardly been able to fit behind it.

"Tell Deb what's going on," Millner said, "and then she's off the rest of the afternoon. She's got a lot of comp time coming, she might as well take some of it." He headed back toward his own office.

"Welcome," Rafe Permut said, knowing exactly how much I did not want to be there. He still looked like Captain Greco on "Mathnet." That means he was fairly short for a cop—about five seven—slender build, small mustache, mostly bald except for a little strip of short hair around the perimeter of his scalp, with very emphatic gestures and a slightly sarcastic demeanor. "And you want to know what's going on."

"It will sort of help," I said, feeling a little ashamed of myself for being so cross with Captain Millner. My personal feelings notwithstanding, this unit needed me. It has about the worst job in the city.

·   ·   ·   ·   ·

Look at it this way; the victim of a murder is already dead, but the victim of a sex crime is usually alive and freaking out, and your average male, even if he is a cop, tends to do a little freaking out himself when a woman won't stop crying.

Permut shrugged, waved his hands in the air resignedly. "Fellow named Morgan Powell," he said. "Served fifteen years of a hundred-and-twenty-year sentence. The courts turned him loose. He abducted and sodomized a twelve-year-old boy. I just put him back in jail. Roger's winding up the paperwork. He'd been on the street six days."

"How's the boy?"

"Your friend Susan Braun has taken charge of him."

Susan runs a private psychiatric hospital. That gave me a pretty good idea of the boy's condition. "What else?" I asked.

"We got a Super Glue rapist." I knew about that one; he'd been in the newspaper. The MO turns up every now and then, probably more often than it might if the tabloids didn't publicize it. "He's hit seven times now, all over town. Does the deed, glues the woman's eyes and mouth shut, and then guess where else he puts the glue."

"Shit," I said involuntarily.

"Agreed. Wayne and Manuel are on it. We aren't getting very far, very fast. We've got DNA—an accident; he uses a condom and takes it with him, but that time he dropped it outside—but DNA's no good until we get a suspect to match it to. No fingerprints. No description. No vehicle description. No pattern we can do anything with.

"We've got a rapist on the TCU campus. Jumps out from behind bushes and grabs coeds. The first time he hit was by the library. We put a stakeout outside the library. So he moved over to the Student Union Building."

"I don't know of any bushes by the Student Union Building," I said. I am vaguely familiar with the Texas Christian University

. . . . .

12

campus; they have a good campus police department, but they still need city help occasionally.

"Maybe he jumped out from behind a lamppost, maybe he landed on a flying saucer. Hell, I don't know, the victim said he came from nowhere, but we're pretty sure he came from somewhere. Henry's on that one. They've stepped up campus patrols, and we haven't heard from him in a week, so maybe he's gone. But I wouldn't hold my breath counting on it."

"Any description on that one?" I asked.

"Blue jeans. Sneakers. TCU sweatshirt. Brown hair, medium length. Brown eyes, or maybe they were blue. Two hands, two feet. DNA again, but again, what the hell good does that do right now? One day there'll be a nationwide file of DNA from convicted sex criminals."

"They're working on it," I said. In fact, the FBI expects to have the prototype up and running within four or five years. But that wouldn't do us any good today, and even then it would involve only convicted sex criminals. There are always a lot of amateurs, a lot of newcomers to the crime.

"Plus the usual run of date rapes, some of which are and some of which aren't. You know how that goes."

I know how that goes, and by now I felt I was a pretty good judge of whether or not the woman was telling the truth. I remember once, last time I was stuck in this squad, a known prostitute came in to report she'd been raped. The men—even the ones who were usually sympathetic to victims—pretended to her face to accept it, but behind her back they thought it was a scream. "You ought to call it theft of services," one jeered.

But I was the one who sat and talked with her behind a closed door as she told me about letting her little brother off by a movie theater, driving a block with an unlocked door, seeing a man opening the door at the next red light and getting in beside her. And she was shaking, her voice trembling, just as much as any other

. . . . .

13

woman does in that situation. Not that she denied her profession. "Just because I sells it don't give him the right to take it," she said to me the next day. But that was bravado. Her very breathing was frightened, and the skirt she was wearing—and very often the clothing the victim wears the next day is a completely unconscious signal of how deep the fear goes—was halfway to her ankles.

Then there was the woman who came in screaming, crying, seeming to faint with her head on any convenient desk. The men—even the ones who tend to be dubious at best—were falling all over themselves bringing her Cokes, bringing her Kleenex, bringing her aspirin. I was the one who sat with her and said, "Before you sign this statement, I want to explain to you the Texas laws on perjury."

She decided she didn't want to sign the statement right then. And the next day she came in wearing hot pants or whatever dress shorts were called then and confessed, shamefaced, that she'd made the whole thing up. She'd had a fight with her boyfriend, gone out and spent the night with another man, and was trying simultaneously to protect herself from possible accusations of infidelity and lay a guilt trip on her boyfriend.

And there was the woman who didn't report the rape until two weeks after it happened. She'd had a fight with her husband. To cool off, she went out to Trinity Park to sit by herself on the riverbank for a while. A man found her there . . . Even two weeks later, when she did report it, the marks of struggle were visible: bruised wrists, scraped knees. Her husband said he didn't believe it. He said it didn't happen. Furthermore, if it did happen, it was her own fault for being so stupid.

She was already under medical treatment for depression. Her personal physician was out of town, not due back until a 7:00 A.M. flight the next day, and she refused to be treated by the emergency room doctors. She wanted to wait until they could reach her own doctor. There wasn't any rape support team in town yet. After I went off duty that night, I went to the emergency room and sat in

. . . . .

14

the cubicle with her. I sat, and held her hands, and tried to talk her down, and watched her go insane. By the time her doctor arrived, twelve hours after she made the report, he had her immediately transported to a psychiatric lock-down.

She'd weathered the rape as well as anybody does, I thought then and still think now. It was her husband's reaction that brutalized her into madness.

And tomorrow, for the next three months at least—and knowing Chandra, I had a hunch that three months would stretch into five or six; not that I blamed her, I'd want to stay home with a new baby, too, if I could—I'd be back into coping with that kind of thing again. I was a lot older now than I had been the last time I'd had to cope with it, and I didn't know how I was going to manage. If I could just know I was helping . . .

But the prostitute I had talked with so long, in an interrogation room with the door shut, was dead now, murdered two years later by a drunken client in a motel room, and the rape case was still marked "uncleared." The woman I'd sat with in the emergency room had committed suicide two weeks after leaving the psychiatric unit. That case, too, was never cleared. We'd developed a suspect, but we had nothing to go on—neither physical evidence nor the victim's testimony—and my guess was he'd gone right on raping women on riverbanks. Oh, I remembered a few victories of sorts—victims vindicated, criminals sent off for twenty years—but anybody could have won those cases. I didn't see that I could claim any special credit for them.

On top of everything else, my mother was arriving today—not tomorrow, as I had hoped—to help me get ready for surgery. I love my mother, but I'd rather visit at her house. She always has to help me. I know my house is a mess more often than not, but I would rather clean it myself. When she puts things away it takes me a hundred years to find them. There was the time I had to pay a fifteen-dollar library fine because my mother, cleaning my house, had put four library books into my sewing box. Not my mending

· · · · ·

box, which I open several times a month, but my sewing box, which I open two or three times a year at best.

She was going to take my son Cameron to stay with her until I was on my feet again. I could see the point of that. I would be temporarily incapable of chasing an active three-year-old. But what was the point of her taking him on Wednesday? I wasn't going into surgery until Friday. She could take him Thursday night, I had said to Harry.

"She means well," he reminded me.

And of course she did. Her idea was that I could get a little rest before the surgery, and to be perfectly honest, I needed some rest.

But if my mother started cleaning my house and I was there, I wouldn't get any rest, because of course I'd have to go and help with whatever she was doing no matter how I happened to feel. That's my hang-up, not hers; she wouldn't mind at all if I went to lie down or read; in fact, she'd probably bring me a lemonade or something. But I'd feel like a rat.

The heck with it, I thought. Just because I got off work early didn't mean I had to go home right now. My mother is hyper-active; furthermore, in the last few years she has unexpectedly developed some of the personality traits of a drill sergeant. She would have the house clean, Harry straightening his computer stuff and putting the disks and printouts away properly, my teenager Hal terrorized into decent conduct, Cameron under control, and din-ner prepared by four-thirty, so we could eat as soon as I got home (never mind that we don't normally eat dinner until seven), and if I were there she would be giving me orders as if I were Cameron's age.

So I went out the front door of the police station, got in my car, and drove over to visit Matilda Greenwood, whom I refuse to call by her assumed name of Sister Eagle Feather. As usual, she was in her apartment upstairs above the spiritualist church she runs, with reference material all over the coffee table and her computer up and running; she writes books to supplement the semi-living she

· · · · ·

makes from her church (or else it's the other way around; I'm not quite sure, any more than I am sure why she doesn't officially practice as the psychologist she has trained to be). Right now she was doing research on genealogy for a new client she'd picked up who wanted a book written and didn't have time to write it himself. She took one look at me and said, "You need some Emperor's Choice tea."

"Why do I need that?" I asked wearily. Actually I like herbal tea most of the time, but every now and then Matilda has come up with some really strange ones.

"Good for PMS."

"How do you know I'm having PMS?"

"I know you, Deb, I know you. When you come in looking like the younger sister to a thundercloud you're having PMS."

At least she got a laugh out of me, which was more than anybody else had done all day, and before I knew it I was drinking hot, vaguely cinnamon-tasting tea and telling Matilda about Dusty Miller, and here, not having to be on guard, I did start to cry.

Unlike Captain Millner, she didn't get mad at me for crying. Unlike Harry, she didn't get panicky. Unlike Susan, she didn't start analyzing why I was crying. She didn't even point out to me the extreme illogic of my simultaneously insisting I wanted to work only cases in which I felt that I could do some good, and insisting on working an already concluded suicide. She just agreed that the whole situation was a bummer and if I thought something was wrong then something was wrong, let me cry, and brought me Kleenex and more hot tea, until finally I felt fortified enough to get up and go home in time that my family wouldn't realize I'd stopped on the way.

My son Hal, now a high school senior, and his girlfriend, Lori, who doesn't officially live with us although it seems like she's here all the time, were washing the windows in front of the house, and I stopped to admire them. "Grandma said I had to," Hal said grumpily. "She made Dad shampoo the carpets."

. . . . .

Pat, our caramel brown half pit bull–half Doberman, was lying morosely in the corner of the front yard and didn't even get up to greet me. By now he has figured out that when my mother is here, not only is he not allowed to go inside and kiss the baby, but furthermore the baby is not allowed to go outside and be kissed. And even worse than that, since we allow my mother to come inside the house, she is off limits for even being barked at, no matter how unwelcome he considers her to be. Both cats—our old calico, Margaret Scratcher, and Rags, the new one, who looks like a miniature Maine coon cat, bosses Margaret Scratcher unmercifully, and has turned into a mighty hunter before the Lord—were up in the mesquite tree where Pat couldn't chase them. Even if he could climb a tree, which he cannot, he was not about to brave the mesquite thorns. Pat was not a happy dog.

I went on in the house. The smell of beef Stroganoff vied for dominance with the smells of carpet cleaner and of lemon-scented furniture polish. The Stroganoff was clearly done, which as I guessed meant we would be eating before five. Eating this early would leave us all hungry again before bedtime. I was not about to go to bed hungry on a night when I needed to sleep, but for the sake of my waistline I was not delighted at the thought of a four-meal day.

The top of the coffee table was totally cleaned off for what was probably the first time in living memory; that meant that unless Harry had taken charge of them, all my unpaid bills were gone and therefore would not be paid until we got second (or third) notices. Cameron also was clean, which small boys usually are not at this time of day; he was wearing a little sailor suit I could not recall having seen before and which I considered utterly idiotic for a small child to wear to supper; and even he was working—he was scrubbing the front of the television set with some sort of disposable cleaning cloth with the cleanser built in. Mom had to have bought it; I never get those things.

Glancing at the front of the television set, I assured Cameron the

· · · · ·

screen looked wonderful. Mom grinned at me and assured him of the same thing. It didn't look wonderful, of course; it was horribly streaked, and as soon as Mom left with Cameron I would have to wash it over again. But he deserved credit for trying.

I stepped into the kitchen, or as far into it as I could get; it is an emphatically one-person kitchen, if that. I sometimes think it is a no-person kitchen.

"How are you feeling?" Mom asked.

"Fine," I said. "My surgery isn't until Friday morning, and it's just to remove heel spurs. I really appreciate your help, but I still don't see why you couldn't wait to—"

"Oh, well, you need some rest beforehand," she said, as I knew she'd say, bustling a bit unnecessarily. She was ill at ease about something, I could tell at once, and since she was never ill at ease about taking over somebody else's kitchen or house, I couldn't imagine what would be bothering her.

I didn't find out until shortly after dinner, with Harry fiddling around at his computer allegedly working on the paper due shortly for the very last course he was taking in his MBA program, Cameron asleep on the couch, Hal presumably walking Lori back to the aunt's house where she nominally lived, and me handing Mom the dishes so she could rinse them before she put them into the dishwasher. I'd told her twice that our dishwasher has a garbage disposal built in, and I saw no use in telling her again. "Rhonda's moving back home," Mom said abruptly.

Harry wasn't as absorbed in the computer as I thought he was. He threw down a book he'd had on the computer table and yelled, "Why the hell are you letting her do that?" He has not been terribly fond of my only sister for many years. Neither is anybody else in the family. Her habits, which include burglary with her relatives as victims, are sufficient reason, and she once stole several of Harry's guns along with a good many of our other possessions, which at the time were a bit sparse at best.

. . . . .

Cameron half woke, stirred, whimpered in his sleep at the shouting.

"She has to go *somewhere,*" Mom said.

"But why does she have to move in with you?" I demanded. "Mom, last time you let her go home she stole—"

"That doesn't matter now," Mom said. "I had to let her come home. I had to, Debra."

I waited. My mother, who does not fidget, was fidgeting; my mother, who is always totally self-possessed, sounded frightened.

"I had to, Debra," she repeated. "Rhonda has AIDS."

. . . . .

$\mathcal{T}wo$
. . . . .

IT WASN'T MUCH past six o'clock. My mother had departed, taking Cameron with her—and, naturally, leaving behind a clean kitchen, empty laundry baskets, clean laundry put away in straightened drawers, washed windows, and waxed or shampooed floors. I hadn't a thing to do except find my missing bills, which fortunately turned out to have been stuffed into the junk drawer in the kitchen. I'd worry later about where the usual contents of the junk drawer had gone; my guess was that the screwdrivers I keep in the kitchen to reattach loose pan handles had been taken to Harry's tool chest and the twist ties for garbage bags were now in the garbage. And the coupons? Heaven only knows, I thought. Probably in the garbage, too.

I returned the bills to the coffee table and then, considering how I would probably be feeling this weekend, wrote checks for all of them, thrust them into envelopes, stuck stamps on them, and put them out in the mailbox with the flag up. Now I *really* didn't have anything to do.

This is not a natural condition with me, and I found it somewhat odd. I wandered around trying to find small tasks to fill my time, so I wouldn't have to think about Rhonda. But of course I thought about Rhonda anyway. I had been asking myself for years why it was that I turned out all right—well, mostly all right—and Rhonda's always been such a mess. Because let's face it, when we were kids, Rhonda didn't have one whit more trouble than I did;

. . . . .

in fact, in some ways she had less. Because she was the younger girl in the family, she didn't have to baby-sit the way I, as the oldest child and older girl, did; because she was always so pretty, she was dating before I was, even though she was five years younger. She somehow managed even to get out of doing her share of the housework on the grounds that she was too frail, although she wasn't too frail to learn judo before I did (and more of it than I ever did).

But now I was the generally happy, generally healthy mother of four (three of them adopted, but that's all right) and grandmother of—I had to stop and count. Four, counting Jeffrey, who was originally Olead's brother but whom Olead and my daughter Becky had adopted. Becky had then given birth to two more—Jim and Laura—between the time my older daughter, Vicky, gave birth to Barry and the time she started on the forthcoming one. But then Becky and Olead could afford three, or four (I had a hunch Becky was pregnant again, although she hadn't mentioned it to me), or as many as they wanted. Olead was still in medical school, but he'd exhibited a rather odd talent for turning money into more money clear back when he was in his teens—and in a mental hospital being treated for schizophrenia that turned out to be a vitamin B deficiency. I wasn't sure how Vicky and Don would manage to pay for their forthcoming second child. Olead would gladly help them out, but Don—who was trying to be a solo attorney rather than a member of a partnership or corporation—would not gladly be helped out.

Anyhow, I was still thinking mostly about Rhonda and what a mess she was. Unlike her, I was generally happily employed in a job I liked most of the time (I don't suppose anybody likes her job all the time) and I was generally happily married to a husband I loved all the time and liked most of the time. Like any other married woman, I had times I could have joyfully strangled him. Now was one of those times.

Harry was huddled over the computer continuing to work on

.   .   .   .   .

his school paper. That was fine; he needed to finish it. My relief when he finally got through with that MBA, which I felt like he'd been working on for the last hundred years, would be indescribable. No, my problem was that he was banging and slamming things as if he were the only one affected by Rhonda's situation. I couldn't figure out whether he was angry because Rhonda existed, because she had been doing things that anybody with half a brain knew were likely to lead to AIDS, because she had AIDS, or because she had—let's face it—gone home to die.

He *said,* of course, that he was upset because of the situation's effect on me. But if that was what was bothering him, why was he slamming and banging around and upsetting me even more?

The front door opened, and I heard the clicking of dog nails on the vinyl flooring as the dog rushed in and began looking around for Cameron to kiss. "He isn't here, Pat," I said.

Pat manifestly did not believe me. He went on looking.

Pat was not supposed to be in the house to start with, but he ignored that semi-rule whenever possible, and at the moment nobody seemed inclined to evict him. That was fine with me. There are times when a nice, warm dog is kind of pleasant despite the doggy smell, especially when the cats are up in the mesquite tree, the baby is gone, the husband is acting like first cousin to a polecat, and I have nobody at all to hug. In fact, Harry and I had discussed allowing Pat to become a house dog. But that, since neither of us feel inclined to get up in the middle of the night to open doors, would have required the construction of a dog door, and a dog door big enough for Pat would have been big enough for Cameron. So we built a cat door instead, and even that had proved to be a mistake.

"Come 'ere, Pat," I said, and began to scratch his ears.

He submitted briefly to having his ears scratched, but then he struggled free and continued to look for the baby.

I should have known the semi-peace wouldn't last long. Hal and Lori arrived right behind Pat, which I should have expected, as the

· · · · ·

dog obviously couldn't open the front door himself. It turned out that Lori hadn't gone home yet after all, and it had, of course, been they who opened the door and then stood in the doorway as the dog pushed past them and ran in.

"Was she always like that?" Hal demanded. He didn't have to specify who "she" meant. "She didn't used to be like that, did she?"

"No," I said, "she wasn't always like that." My mother's bossiness had arrived only in the last ten years, after my father's death, and I still hadn't figured out where it came from.

"Well, I wish she'd stay away, or go bother somebody else."

As I wished the same thing and felt disloyal for wishing it, I didn't say anything. Hal picked up the TV remote control, pushed the "on" button without noticing what channel it was set for, looked guiltily at me, and said, "Oh, shit."

I had known for weeks he had managed to figure out a way to remove the device the cable people put on to block MTV out of our house. I had decided to ignore the situation; if he wasn't watching MTV here he'd be watching it somewhere else, and he's quite a few years older and hopefully a little more responsible and a little less easily influenced than he was when I had it blocked off.

Harry, working on a term paper in the same room, did not appear to hear the racket. I sometimes think he could continue to work in single-minded concentration on his computer, or his ham radio, in the middle of a simultaneous earthquake and air raid. But I was not prepared to have a combination of heavy metal and a chain saw murder blasted into my living room while I was home. I took the remote out of Hal's hand, turned the TV back off, and said, "It is unfortunate your grandmother had you wash windows, but the fact remains that, as I told you this morning at breakfast, the lawn has to be mowed, and I certainly won't be up to listening to you mow it later this week."

How many times have I—how many times has any mother—listened to that resounding chorus of, "Aw, Mom!"

· · · · ·

24

I put the television remote into my purse. "You get this back," I said, "when the lawn is mowed."

I don't know how all remote control devices work. I do know how ours works. The television is turned on with the normal knobs. Then it is in some way that I do not pretend to understand, though I'm sure it's as simple to Hal as it is to Harry, hooked up to the cable box. Then it is turned off and on with the remote. This means that although in an emergency it could be turned off by unplugging it, and the channels can be changed by pushing buttons on top of the cable box, there is absolutely no way it can be turned on without the remote. I had taken advantage of that situation before.

Hal stomped out the door, muttering under his breath to Lori, whose soothing tone was audible but whose words were too soft for me to hear. In a minute I heard the lawn mower start up.

We do not have much yard, and much of what we have grows no grass because it is too heavily shaded by the mesquite tree. It took approximately twenty minutes for Hal to mow it all. Harry banged things the whole twenty minutes.

Hal came back in, followed as usual by Lori. Lori's father died several years ago; she lost her mother last year under bizarre circumstances, and she now officially lived with an aunt who I suspected didn't like her much. Actually, except for sleeping, she lived with us. She was still feeling horribly insecure. She has better sense than to hug Hal all the time, and she's still a little too shy to cling to me, so she spends a lot of time holding the baby. Now, with the baby gone, she was looking lost. When one of the cats wandered in—unfortunately, it was Margaret Scratcher, who is rather purr deficient—she grabbed the cat.

Harry went on slamming reference books, rattling papers, and pounding the keys of a four-thousand-dollar computer with unnecessary violence.

The hell with it, I thought, and waded through the not-yet-dry bedroom carpet to the bathroom, to soak in a hot bath.

· · · · ·

On Thursday morning, gambling that Rafe Permut had not been fully informed of what Captain Millner considers the worst of my habits, I called in and said that I needed several more hours of comp time. As I had hoped, Rafe told me to take it and get in when I could.

Collecting the portable radio I had brought home with me in the hopes of that result, I headed for the Miller household. They might not be there, of course; they might be at the funeral home. But an autopsy is mandatory in this sort of case, and I was gambling that the body had not been released yet.

Apparently I was right. Seth Miller, whom I had seen briefly but had not officially met before, answered the door and somewhat reluctantly, but evidently assuming (as I had meant him to assume) that a police visit now was routine, let me in and then sat back down at one end of the couch. Ellen Miller, whom I had first met standing against the wall with her hand over her mouth while her daughter jumped out the window, was now sitting at the far end of the couch with her hand over her mouth. The child who'd been wearing pink—a girl I'd guess to be about ten years old, with the same blue eyes and blond hair I'd noticed on Dusty—was once more standing in the hall, looking into the living room as if she wanted to know what was going on but didn't want to be within touching distance of either of her parents.

I seated myself, uninvited, in an empty armchair and said, "I'm sorry to have to disturb you at a time like this, but there are some questions I really must ask."

Mrs. Miller sniffled. Mr. Miller didn't say anything. And once again, the impression I had felt yesterday—that there was something badly wrong here that nobody was telling—rose in me. For a moment I wondered where that feeling came from, but a second glance let me know: in a crisis, family members usually pull together. But here no one wanted to be near anyone.

"Tell me about your daughter," I said.

· · · · ·

"Why?" Seth Miller asked baldly.

"We need to know—"

"Why?" he asked again, sounding more irritated and even stuffy than grief-stricken. "She's dead. Nothing you ask is going to bring her back."

"Seth—" Mrs. Miller began timidly.

"She was always a troublemaker," he went on. "Both of our older daughters. Acted like little angels out in public, but at home it was another matter. No respect for our authority, no gratitude. Neither one of them ever cared anything about all that we gave them, all that—"

"Seth," Mrs. Miller said, a little more loudly.

"Now, Doreen's not going to be like that, are you, honey?" He walked over to the child and put his hand on her arm. She pulled away from him and crossed the room, now standing in the doorway to what had been Dusty's room.

That was odd, I thought, as the condo's arrangement finally registered on my conscious mind. One bedroom by itself, off the big front room; the other bedrooms, however many there were, down the hall somewhere. When one bedroom is such a discreet distance from the others like that, it's always meant to be the master bedroom.

So why had the adult Millers taken one (or two, as the case may be) of the other rooms and left the solitary bedroom to their oldest daughter?

I had a hunch I could answer that question. Of course, my hunches aren't always right. But if this one was right, it was more for the sake of the living child than her dead sister that I was pushing this case.

I opened my mouth to start asking questions, and Seth Miller stood up. "I'm not going to talk to you," he declared. "You can't require me to, and I see no reason for it." He glanced at his wife. "If you want to, go ahead." It seemed to me there was something of warning in that glance, but perhaps I was seeing something that

. . . . .

wasn't there; perhaps I was seeing ghosts, as he stalked out of the room and down a hall, opened a door and stepped through it, and closed it with a vicious little click that was somehow more aggressive than a slam would have been.

"I'm sorry," Mrs. Miller said. "He . . . he's very upset. And he doesn't take things well."

"I can understand that," I said. "And as I said, I'm really sorry to have to ask questions now. But . . ."

There's no use recounting the rest of the conversation. Dusty—whose real name was Dorothy Marie—was sixteen. She was an honor student at Burroughs Hall, an expensive nonreligious private high school, where she was on the drill team and a member of the National Honor Society. Her parents had decided to put her into Burroughs after her older sister had been damaged emotionally by the public school system in the suburb where they used to live. All her friends loved her. All her family loved her. Her father didn't really mean it when he talked about her that way, he was just upset, surely I understood that. She dated, but she wasn't going steady with anybody. She attended St. Mark's Episcopal Church. She didn't do drugs. She didn't smoke. She didn't drink. The only reason she hadn't sprouted angel wings was because they wouldn't fit into her Neiman Marcus clothes (well, a few of them were Dillard's, but that was slumming it).

There was no reason for her to commit suicide. It had to be a mistake of some kind . . .

I won't say I didn't believe a word of it. I was sure she had attended Burroughs, where she had been on the drill team and in the National Honor Society, because that would be too easily checked for them to lie about it. I was reasonably certain she had attended St. Mark's Episcopal Church. But beyond that—well, maybe some of it was true. Maybe all of it was true.

But if it was all true, then something else was going on. Because a person whose life is going perfectly doesn't usually commit suicide, and even Dusty's mother was saying *mistake,* not *accident.*

· · · · ·

I got names and addresses of friends, most of whom were female, most of whom attended Burroughs Hall or St. Mark's or both.

The entire time I was there, Doreen said exactly one thing. She said, "My sisters are not bad. And it wasn't Dusty's fault . . ." She started crying again then, and stopped when Mr. Miller returned to the living room and handed her a Kleenex box and looked at her. Hard.

I asked to talk with her alone, but Mr. Miller refused, and he had the right to refuse. So I left, glad I had got the names of Dusty's friends before he returned to the living room.

Then I drove over to Burroughs Hall, where the principal—one Mary Margaret McDowell—located Tammy Wilson and Elaine Paden for me. Tammy had dark brown hair, shoulder length, in a curly perm. Elaine had dark blond hair, shoulder length, in a curly perm. Both had on exactly the right amount of makeup to make them appear to have perfect complexions, bright eyes, and no makeup at all. Both looked about sixteen, well fed, well dressed, well groomed, and both looked at me with that limpid expression of teenagers who have already made up their minds that they are going to tell this nosy adult absolutely nothing. When I ventured the first question, Tammy burst into tears, and Mrs. McDowell, who was already pretty uneasy about the whole situation, said, "Mrs. Ralston, I'm beginning to feel I shouldn't let you talk with the girls without their parents present."

She was probably right. "I don't want them to tell me anything they don't want to tell me," I said, "but if either of them has the least idea of anything that might have been troubling Dusty—"

"*Nothing* was troubling Dusty!" Elaine burst out. "That's why it doesn't make sense. It has to be some kind of mistake."

But her eyes were guarded; despite the overt display of emotion, I could tell she was choosing her words carefully.

Mrs. Miller had said that, too. *Some kind of mistake.* "What kind of mistake could it have been?" I asked. "Are you saying that it wasn't really Dusty?"

· · · · ·

29

"Of course it was Dusty," Tammy said. Her eyes, too, were guarded, her words carefully chosen. And she was looking to Elaine for guidance as she continued: "But . . . she must have fallen. She wouldn't really have . . . have . . . jumped."

And both of them stuck on that. It was a mistake. It was an accident. Nothing was wrong with Dusty, both girls insisted before returning to their classrooms.

They were lying. I knew they were lying. Something was wrong and at least one of them—Elaine—knew what it was. Tammy might not know, herself, but she knew Elaine knew. But neither of them was going to tell me.

I asked then whether I could talk with one of her teachers, one who knew her well. Mrs. McDowell sighed. "I probably knew her as well as anyone," she said. "I was just promoted to principal this year; prior to that I was a counselor. And . . . I'll have to agree with Elaine and Tammy. It doesn't make sense."

"You don't know of anything at all? She couldn't have been keeping something from you?"

"Oh, of course she was keeping something from me," Mrs. McDowell said. "Adolescents always do. But . . . I wouldn't have thought there was anything serious."

That was all I could get out of anybody. I left the school and started my car, thinking as hard as I could. If she was pregnant the autopsy would tell me—but she hadn't been; she had a bathroom of her own attached to her bedroom, and the trash can had six used sanitary pads in it I'd found while searching, without success, for a hint of drugs, probably the most common cause of teenage suicide. (Come to think of it, the sanitary pads could have been there because she had just had an abortion, something that certainly has in the past led to suicidal depressions in young girls. But I hadn't the least reason to suspect that, and the autopsy would tell me for sure.)

If she'd had a boyfriend, nobody would admit it. I could go on

· · · · ·

trying to find him. But as long as everyone insisted she didn't have one, it was hard to know where to look.

Maybe Captain Millner was right. Maybe I was interfering where I had no business. If I just hadn't had that feeling . . .

I wanted to talk again with the first officers on the scene, the one who had called for a woman, and the one who had been in the apartment trying to get the bedroom door open when I got there. What were their names? Andersen and Woodall? I didn't know either of them.

But they'd be on day watch; probably I could get them called in one at a time for me to talk with.

But it seemed I would have to wait. Because when I got into the police department to go officially on duty, hoping to begin by calling up the report on my computer screen, I found a case waiting for me.

"Her name's Ruth Bonando," Rafe said to me privately. "She sounds a little bit screwy to me. Says she has to talk with a woman officer. I couldn't get out of her what was wrong. See what you can do. It may be a mare's nest, but you never know."

That was perfectly true. People turn up at police stations with major problems, minor problems, and no real problems at all; I remembered one time when, in a one-hour period, all three members of a love triangle showed up, each insisting the other two were conspiring to murder him or her.

But that was a long time ago and no longer my problem, if it had ever been. I headed for the interview room where Ruth Bonando sat. She looked up sharply as I entered, so I got a good look at her. A little younger than me, I thought—about midthirties. Dark hair, dark eyes, fair complexion; a startled, secretive, and somehow wild, I thought, look on her face.

"I'm Detective Ralston," I said, deciding after that first glance at her face to substitute that for the "Deb Ralston" I usually use when introducing myself. "What can I do for you, Ms. Bonando?"

. . . . .

"Mrs.," she said. "I don't like that 'Ms.' very much. It seems to detract . . ."

She came to a sudden halt. "A lot of people feel that way," I agreed, wondering what it seemed to detract from. "But other people are offended when you use anything else. So it's hard to know what to say. I'm sure you've noticed that."

She said nothing at all. That was discouraging. I tried again. "What can I do for you?"

"I've got this problem," she said, and halted again.

"What kind of problem?"

"It's these people."

"Uh-huh." I was beginning to wonder whether she was a customer for Susan Braun. She certainly wasn't making sense to me.

But then, all in a rush, she said, "They're neighbors. The Washingtons. David and Laura Washington. And . . . they've *approached* my daughter."

"Approached her how?" I asked.

She fluttered her hands vaguely. "Oh, you know. Just . . . approached her."

"Well, what did they want her to do?"

"You know."

"I'm afraid I don't know," I said politely. " 'Approached' can have a lot of meanings."

"Aren't you going to do anything?" Her voice began to rise.

"Mrs. Bonando, I can't do anything until I know what's going on."

"I *told* you what's going on! They *approached* her!" Her voice continued to rise, became more shrill.

"How old is your daughter?"

"Sixteen. Her name is Janine. And they keep, you know, *approaching* her." She twisted her wedding ring around and around on her finger.

"Tell me about the Washingtons," I suggested. Rafe might be right; this might be a mare's nest. But on the other hand it might

· · · · ·

be something that did need to be checked out. The Washingtons, whoever the Washingtons might be, might have "approached" Janine to star in blue movies, or join a prostitution ring, or baby-sit their children.

"They're sort of neighbors," Mrs. Bonando said, abruptly abandoning her wedding ring and beginning to fiddle with her necklace. "They live a couple of streets over from us, and they go to our church."

"What church is that?"

"Catholic. St. Barbara's."

"Okay, when—and where—and how—do the Washingtons approach your daughter?"

"At church. You know, in the foyer. And when she's walking home from school. It's mostly him. He says, like, suggestive things."

"What kind of suggestive things?"

"Just . . . suggestive things. And they're black. I don't think black men ought to be saying suggestive things to white girls, do you?"

"I don't think any men ought to be saying suggestive things to any girls," I replied. "Race has nothing to do with it. But I also think I had better go talk with your daughter. Is she at home now?"

"She goes to school, but—"

"I'm sure she does," I agreed, "but I thought if she was very upset she might have stayed out of school—"

"Oh, well, yes. Actually, I told her to stay home, that way she'd be safe—"

"But you didn't bring her with you."

"I don't think a police station is at all an appropriate place for a young girl, do you? And I didn't call the regular police because, you know, I didn't want her to have to try to explain to a man . . ."

The tone of her voice indicated that men were strange, foreign, definitely frightening beings. But then, thinking of how Roger or Wayne might respond to this kind of nonreport, I had to at least

· · · · ·

partially agree with her. "I see your point, of course. If you'll give me your address, I'll follow you back home and have a little talk with your daughter."

After a little more dithering, she said, "Well, I had been going to stop and pick up a little more groceries on the way home—"

"Would either of the Washingtons be home now, do you think?" I interrupted.

"I think . . . they both might. They're retired, they're an older couple."

We finally agreed that I would go talk with the Washingtons and then go talk with Janine; presumably, since the groceries Mrs. Bonando had to pick up consisted of one gallon of milk, she would be home by then.

A few years ago there was a very funny commercial on TV for some kind of laxative, where the wife keeps waving around the bottle of laxative while the husband is just about dying of embarrassment, saying things like, "But we don't even know these people!" I normally hate commercials, but that one I liked because the people in it were so real.

The Washingtons reminded me of that commercial—not that they were carrying around bottles of laxatives, of course. But they seemed simple, down to earth, with real human dignity. And they were both extremely upset by Mrs. Bonando's accusations.

Unfortunately, that didn't necessarily mean nothing was going on. A lot of sex offenders seem, in any other circumstances, to be simple, down to earth, dignified people, and a lot of them—most of them—are extremely upset when they're caught.

"I don't even know who Janine Bonando is," Mr. Washington said. "I mean, there are a lot of girls go to mass. Not so many as you'd wish, nowadays, but still quite a few. I know them by sight, not by name. And young girls, they feel so insecure, you know. And so I say, like, 'That's a mighty pretty dress you have on today.' Or, 'That new haircut looks right smart.' And walking home? The

· · · · ·

34

high school's just a couple of blocks over. If I happen to be on my front porch, or out doing yard work, and somebody comes by I know, of course I say 'Good afternoon' or something like that. But approach? I don't even know what she means, approach."

"You ask me, that woman's crazy," Mrs. Washington added indignantly. "My David, he wouldn't do anything. We *love* kids. Now that we're both retired, we've applied to take in foster kids. They're doing a home study right now."

All of that might very well be true. If I were to judge only by my first impression of the Washingtons, I would guess it was true. But a lot of child molesters love kids. Unfortunately, a lot of child molesters apply for, and even get, foster children. And a lot of child molesters are very convincing when they begin to deny everything, and a lot of wives never believe a word of it. The Washingtons seemed very upset, but Mrs. Bonando also was very upset. And I hadn't seen Janine yet.

I stood up. "Thank you for talking with me," I said. "I'm going over to talk with Janine now, and I'll let you know if I see anything further to ask you."

"You ask anything you want to," Mrs. Washington said, "'cause we've got nothing to hide."

Like her mother, Janine had dark hair, dark eyes, very fair skin, a secretive face. They could have been Celtic or Sicilian or a mixture of both; I couldn't begin to guess. "Your mother tells me the Washingtons approached you," I said. "What kind of things did they say?"

She tossed her hair, sending straight fine black hair flying. "It wasn't so much what they said," she answered. "It was . . ." She looked at her mother for guidance.

"It was the way they said it," Mrs. Bonando said quickly.

"I want to hear what Janine has to say now," I said.

"It's like Mom said," Janine said, still looking at her mother. "Like . . . he'd tell me I had a pretty dress, and then he'd keep on,

· · · · ·

35

like, looking at me and looking at me. Or, like, I'd be walking home from school and he'd be out pruning his roses or something and he'd *look* at me."

"Did he ever say anything?"

"I told you! He'd say, like, I had a pretty dress, or my hair looked nice. It wasn't what he said, it was the way he *looked* at me."

"Did he ever touch you?"

"No!" Janine cried. "You think I'd let a nigger touch me?"

Oh, dear, I thought. *Here's a tempest in a teapot, and a racist tempest at that.* But aloud I said, "Janine, could I have a picture of you? Your most recent school picture, maybe?"

"Why do you want that?"

"It might help me make sure you don't get approached again."

She looked at her mother again, and then went to get a picture. I drove back over to the Washingtons' and got out of the car, taking the picture with me. "Do you know this girl at all?" I asked, after explaining briefly what the Bonandos had said.

Mrs. Washington looked at the picture, passed it to her husband. Then she said, "I know her by sight. Is that Janine Bonando?"

"Yes," I said. "Mr. Washington, do you know her?"

"By sight," he agreed. "She usually goes to mass the same time we do, and she walks by here on her way home from school. I'm always sorry for her; all the other girls walk with a passel of friends, and she's always by herself." He paused. "She says I look at her. I probably do look at her. She always looks so lonesome. And she always looks so unhappy—even at church. All the other girls get together in groups, they're out in the foyer laughing and talking and she's . . . standing by herself, twisting her hair around her fingers. So yes, I've spoken to her a few times. Trying to cheer her up. I . . . Y'know, it was the darndest thing. Yesterday it was, she walked by here, and stopped for a minute like she was maybe waiting for somebody who hadn't showed up. I was trimming the roses, cutting off the dead ones so's the new buds would show up better, and I offered her a rose. I mean, it wasn't like we were

· · · · ·

36

strangers. I see her at mass every Sunday. And darned if she didn't take off running."

"For your own sake," I said, "I would strongly suggest that you not try to cheer her up again."

"There's an outside possibility," I said to Rafe, "that there's really something going on. But I don't think so."

"It sounds to me as if you've got it settled," Rafe agreed.

And I was finally free to look for Andersen and/or Woodall, except that by now I had practically forgotten what I had wanted to ask them. But I knew I had better remember, because one sure thing was that I was not going to be up to asking anybody questions for the next few days.

Andersen came in first. I'd guess him to be in his midthirties. The fact that he was still at patrol officer rank might not say anything—I didn't know at what age he had entered the department, and furthermore this is a large department and not everybody can get promoted—but on the other hand it might say something. He was the one who'd been standing almost in the doorway, yelling into the radio, when I had arrived at the suicide yesterday, and he was on the defensive. Instead of sitting, he loomed over me, almost but not quite threateningly. "You don't think there was anything hinky, do you?" he demanded. "Because I'm telling you, there was *nobody* in that bedroom but the girl."

"I don't think there was anything hinky," I said, "but I want to know why she did it."

"What difference does it make?" he asked baldly. "She's dead."

"Andersen," I asked, "do you know how many teenagers a year commit suicide in this country?"

"No," he said.

"Neither do I, but if it's not the leading cause of death, it's pushing the leading cause of death. If we can find out why on a few of them we might be able to prevent a few more."

· · · · ·

37

"True," he said, and sat down. "Okay, what do you want to know?"

"Were you the first officer on the scene?"

"I guess me and Woodall arrived about the same time." There was something indefinable in his voice when he mentioned Woodall; it was evident there was no love lost there.

"And you went upstairs together?"

"No, I went up the elevator and Woodall went up the stairs. I mean, I don't usually take the elevator with something like that going on, usually I go up the stairs, but man, that was seventeen stories."

"Who got there first?" I asked.

"Woodall. But I was right behind him."

"What's the first thing you saw?"

"This broad screaming. She said . . . let's see, how did she put it? She said, 'Dusty's locked herself in the room and I think she's going to jump.' And I asked who Dusty was and she said it was her daughter, and Woodall, he went to the door and called, I forget what he said, and the girl, she said, 'I won't talk to any man.' And that's when I yelled for a woman."

"Then what happened?"

"Then I could hear the girl inside screaming, 'I'm gonna jump, I'm gonna jump!' And I told Woodall to get the door open, and the woman screamed, 'Don't open the door. If you try to she really will jump!' But I figured, you can't stop 'em from jumping if you can't get where you can grab 'em or at least talk to 'em not through the door, and I told Woodall to get the door open or *I* would. So Woodall, he was at the door talking to the girl, and he said, 'Dusty, nobody's going to hurt you. We've got a woman coming. All I want to do is talk to you.' And then I told him if he didn't get the door open or get out of the way I'd break the door down, and he said, 'Don't do that!' And that nail file doohickey was already there, like the woman had been trying to get the door open, so Woodall picked the nail file up and started to fiddle with the lock, and I said

· · · · ·

if he didn't have it open in one minute I was breaking the door down, and right after that you came in. If that jackass Woodall would have gotten out of the way so I could get the door open, we might have saved her."

It wouldn't have done any good for me to tell Andersen he was a fool, so I didn't. I just thanked him for coming in, sent him back out, and asked dispatch to get Woodall in to talk to me.

Woodall was there in a couple of minutes; it was shift change time, and he must have been on his way in already. Unlike Andersen, he didn't loom over me threateningly. He just sat down, with a look on his face as if he was expecting me to dislike him. I couldn't imagine why; he'd given me no reason to dislike him, but you can always read that expectation in somebody. I'd guess he was about twenty-six, twenty-seven, quiet where Andersen was boisterous.

"Tell me what happened yesterday with the suicide," I said.

He rubbed his hand over his mouth. "What happened. I got there about the same time Andersen did. He went up the elevator and I went up the stairs. When I got there the woman—Mrs. Miller—was pretty hysterical, and when we finally got out of her what was going on, Andersen started radioing for help. I went over to the door and was trying to talk to the girl. She didn't want to talk to me, she wanted to talk to a woman. So I asked Andersen to call for a woman. He was . . . he was sort of hysterical himself. He wanted the door open right then, and I was scared she'd jump if we rushed the door. I kept trying to tell him that, and he kept telling me to get out of the way if I was too much of a coward, so I started fiddling with the lock, trying to be quiet—the girl was in there crying, and I hoped if I stayed real quiet she wouldn't hear me—and then he yelled again that he was going to break the door down, and then . . . I heard her go. I heard her go. It was like I could hear her crying and then I heard this slithering sound and I heard her scream and like, you know, the scream is getting farther and farther away. I don't know why I kept working on the lock, except . . . it was something to do. You came in while the scream was . . . going away."

. . . . .

So now I knew what the final trigger had been. But I couldn't blame Andersen too much; it was possible—even probable, considering how distraught she was—that she'd have jumped anyway.

But the trigger isn't the cause.

The cause was what I wanted to know, and although I had a hunch what it was, I was no closer to proving it than I had been when it happened.

Woodall stood to leave. Then, turning with his hat in his hand, he asked, "Should I have let him break the door in?"

"What do you think?"

"I still think I was right. I think if he hadn't scared her, yelling that he was going to break the door down, she might . . . might not have jumped. But I'm not sure about that. I don't want to blame Andersen."

"Even if he's blaming you?"

Woodall's face reddened slightly. "I'm used to being blamed." He didn't clarify that, and I decided not to ask him to. It was one of those questions I could ask and get an answer to, but the answer might turn out to be something I didn't want to hear.

"Well, this time you're not to blame," I said. "You were right. Not that she wouldn't have jumped—none of us can ever know that—but that she might not have jumped. But there's nothing we can do about that now."

"No," Woodall said gravely, and went away.

Damn, I thought, and went home. Sitting around here would be stupid; it was past four, and Harry had to leave by five to get to school in time, which meant I had to go home and feed him. I'd be so glad when he was through with that silly school . . .

Then, conscientiously, I reminded myself that the school was intended to get him back into the work force, to the benefit of the entire family. It wasn't his fault it had seemed to control us all for the last two years, and he, too, would be relieved when it was over.

. . . . .

Three
· · · · · ·

THE DOCTOR WANTED me properly relaxed for surgery, so we started out with the normal pre-op ten milligrams of Valium at bedtime and nothing by mouth after midnight. If—as usually happens when you stay in the hospital overnight—they had been able to get me right into surgery at seven in the morning without me ever fully wakening, that would have been okay, but that's not the way outpatient surgery works.

To start with, I don't know what Valium does to other people, but it gives me strange dreams. I mean *very* strange dreams. Unfortunately, this time what it did was bring to the forefront of my subconscious an anxiety dream I had had several times in the past. In the dream, Hal is driving and I am in the backseat. Don't ask me why. I very rarely ride in a car that Hal is driving, and when I do I am in the front seat. Anyhow, I suddenly realize that Hal is no more than six years old, and quite incapable of driving a car. I am trying to get to the front seat to take over, but every time I start to climb over the seat the car starts to veer toward a cliff and I have to grab the steering wheel and steer from the backseat, and about that time I realize it's not just a car, it's an entire bus, and I'm having to stretch so far so I can reach the steering wheel from the backseat of the bus. Someday when I have that dream, I hope to make it into the driver's seat and actually get hold of the steering wheel and the pedals, but this hasn't happened yet. Instead, I woke up—as I usually do with this dream— panting, sweating, and very thirsty.

· · · · ·

It was 4 A.M., and I could not have anything to drink.

I went and brushed my teeth and rinsed my mouth, conscientiously not swallowing any water, and returned to bed. The Valium took over again, and it seemed only a couple of minutes later when Harry woke me at five-thirty, which I considered ridiculously early, since I didn't have to be at the hospital until seven, but the hospital is across town and traffic at this time of day is horrendous.

We had discussed at some length what I was going to wear this morning. I agreed with Harry that despite the normal rule that I had to have my pistol with me at all times even if I was off duty, I was not taking it with me today, and he had locked it in his gun chest. But I maintained that I was not going to sit in the outpatient surgery waiting room in a nightgown and bathrobe, and he maintained that if I wore my usual slacks I might have a very interesting time getting them back on to go home in.

We compromised. I wore my slacks and shirt *and* took along a nightgown and bathrobe to wear home.

So at 7 A.M., there I was sitting in a waiting room in my slacks and shirt, thirsty and hungry and still foggy from the Valium, trying unsuccessfully not to smell the coffee and hot chocolate and doughnuts that were in a little side room for the families of patients. Finally a nurse came and took me back to a dimly lit little cubicle about one-fourth the size of my bathroom and had me dress in a paper nightgown and paper shoes. She then went away again, taking away my clothes and leaving me on a gurney in a somewhat too cool room in a paper nightgown and paper shoes with no cover except a sheet and nothing at all to do or even to think about except how hungry and thirsty I was.

A woman about my mother's age came in, told me she was the anesthesiologist, and spent about three minutes telling me what kind of anesthetic I was going to have and asking if I had any questions, which I did not, and then she left again. Of course by that time I needed to go somewhere and pee, but I didn't know if I was allowed to get up and walk around in my paper shoes.

· · · · ·

42

About twenty minutes later another nurse came, told me yes, I could walk about in my paper shoes, and told me where a rest room was that did not involve going through the waiting room in a paper nightgown. That was fortunate, as I felt extremely vulnerable, so vulnerable in fact that I wrapped the sheet around me to go to the rest room. When I got back, trailing what felt like several yards of percale, I found she had brought me a long-overdue blanket. After tucking me back in (literally), she started an IV in the back of my right hand, and about twenty minutes after that I was actually taken to surgery. I say taken; *guided* would be more accurate. In my paper nightgown that opened down the back (with no sheet this time; they said I had to leave it in the cubicle) and paper shoes, I walked down the hall to the OR with the nurse scurrying beside me carrying the IV bag. That was interesting. I have never been allowed to do that before. Usually on checking into the hospital one is instantly declared an invalid and carried about on gurneys or in wheelchairs.

One very good thing about an IV tube is that while you have one in they do not have to give you other shots. They give the other shots to the IV tube, which feeds the medication into your arm. I remember telling Dr. Brandon that usually when I was in an operating room or delivery room I start babbling about autopsies, because I have seen so many and the resemblance between the standard operating room and the standard autopsy room is so striking. He reminded me I had already told him that and said don't worry about it, nobody ever pays any attention to what people say in the OR, and the next thing I knew, I was back in the little cubicle I had changed clothes in, feeling somewhat chilly and ill and somewhat less thirsty except that my mouth tasted like glue, with Becky and Vicky hovering over me looking as anxious as if I were dying instead of merely having foot surgery.

I finally managed to get one of them to tell me that it was about noon and I'd been back in my room a little over an hour. Shortly after that Dr. Brandon stuck his head in long enough to tell me that

. . . . .

the surgery had gone very well, though he'd had to disentangle a badly inflamed tendon from the heel spur. The surgery had taken twice as long as he'd planned, which was why I had had so much anesthetic. He promised to come back and explain more fully after he'd grabbed a bite, but for now I could have something to drink if I thought I could keep it down. Both daughters at once agreed that the Coke the nurse was willing to give me was unsuitable—which it was; at the best of times I throw up when I drink carbonated beverages with sugar in them, and I use caffeine so seldom now that when I do I feel like I'm bouncing off a wall—and began to wrangle over which of them was going to get me a caffeine-free Diet Coke. Wishing they had been this agreeable and eager to help when they were teenagers and I wanted dishes washed, I settled the matter by sending Becky, she being the less pregnant of the two, to get me a Diet Sprite—I didn't want a Coke, diet or otherwise—and sending Vicky to find out when I could get out of this paper gown, which was chilly as well as overly revealing, and have my own clothes back.

A nurse stuck her head into the little cubicle and told me not to rush things; if I tried to get dressed now I would probably get sick, and we wouldn't want that, would we?

I tried to sit up and at once had to agree that she was right. If I tried to get up and get dressed I would get sick, and we wouldn't want that, would we?

At least one of us wouldn't want it.

Dr. Brandon came in after that, to tell me that the chronic slightly sprained ankle I had been complaining about for the last year was not a sprained ankle; it was tendons kept constantly inflamed by the heel spurs digging into them. "I had to separate the tendons a little to get the bone fragments out," he said, "and you're going to be a lot more sore than I had expected. You *must* stay off that foot longer than I had originally said, or that inflammation is going to flare up again and get a lot worse."

· · · · ·

44

I finally got home about three o'clock, carrying a cute pink barf dish in my hand all the way in case I got sick in the car. It took Harry and Becky both to get me into the car, because I had discovered that on crutches I have a disturbing tendency to fall over backward. But with my left foot in a cast that kept it in a very distorted position, I wasn't going to get around any way except on crutches, unless I felt like crawling. Over my protests that I could do it myself, Harry helped me out of the car and into the house; he offered to carry me, but I doubted his ability to carry a hundred and twenty pounds plus the weight of the cast, especially considering that he was still limping badly from a helicopter crash three years ago, and we didn't need both of us in bed at the same time. Obviously I was going to have to learn to walk on crutches before I could go back to work, but I was pretty sure I wouldn't be doing that for the next day or two anyhow.

Fortunately there is a bathroom attached to Harry's and my bedroom, which meant I wouldn't have to navigate the entire house every two or three hours. It was pretty obvious that Harry and Hal were in charge of cooking, cleaning, laundry, and so forth for the duration.

Harry must have come home while I was in surgery, because I didn't know of any other time he could have accomplished everything he had done since we left this morning. He had thoughtfully pushed the bedside table on my side of the room over against the wall where I could still reach it from the bed; on it he'd put the telephone and telephone book; crackers, potato chips, and Cool Ranch Doritos; and some books he'd got out of the library for me (he had to have got Vicky, Becky, and Hal to help with the selection, as he certainly wouldn't have chosen so well himself: he'd brought home everything by Jean Auel, as well as an assortment of mysteries, romances, science fiction, and fantasy, which would certainly hold me somewhat longer than I would be in bed). In the space right beside the bed he'd put an ice chest, containing

• • • • •

ice, several flavors of soda pop, and assorted cheese, fruit, and other snack foods that I definitely wasn't in the mood for at the moment. The snack foods, I mean. The ice and soda sounded like heaven, except my foot was killing me. The doctor had warned me that bone surgery is extremely painful, and I had several different pain prescriptions with orders to take them when I needed them. The doctor had explained that (a) people who take pain medication only when they need it actually take less than people who take it on schedule, and (b) it takes much less medication to prevent pain than to stop it once it really gets going.

He'd added, however, that I was to take the ibuprofen every four hours whether I thought I needed it or not, because it was fighting inflammation as well as pain, and then take the other stuff for pain only if I thought I needed it. I'd better, he said thought-fully, eat pretty often, with that much ibuprofen, if I didn't want to get an ulcer.

I've had an ulcer once. I did not want an ulcer again. I was glad Harry had put plenty of food within my reach.

He'd even, I noticed with a mixture of relief and mild regret, removed my attempt at desktop horticulture. I had really tried on that one: in November, after all the tomato plants had frozen, I had planted a cherry tomato in a five-quart ice cream drum on my dresser, after punching holes in the bottom of the drum for drain-age, filling it with potting soil, and setting it on its own lid, now gravel-covered. I should have done it sooner, if I wanted it produc-ing through the winter, but I didn't think of it sooner. Anyhow, after it sprouted I put it under a fluorescent desk lamp and kept the light on eight hours a day, and I fed it tomato food when I happened to think of it. It grew. And grew. And grew. We had to figure out a way to plug a true-daylight fluorescent bulb into the ceiling fixture. I tied the plant with strips cut from plastic grocery bags to a couple of plant hooks left in the ceiling from a previous attempt to grow a philodendron in the bedroom.

· · · · ·

46

The tomato plant grew, and grew, and grew, and I had to water it every day.

It got to be huge: Harry called it the triffid or, affectionately, Trif.

And from November to March, Trif produced exactly eight cherry tomatoes.

Now Trif was gone, and it seemed my dresser—which at present I couldn't get at—was the size of the Gobi Desert.

But that was just as well, because nobody else would ever have remembered to water Trif, and I certainly wasn't up to it. I returned my attention to my bedside table.

The only remaining problem I could see was that my medicine wasn't here yet. I knew where it was, of course. Becky had returned home, where she had a baby-sitter looking after both hers and Vicky's children, and Vicky had gone to get the prescriptions filled and hadn't arrived here yet. I needed my medicine *now*. Whatever they had given me at the hospital had totally worn off, and I was not a happy camper. Harry rummaged through the bathroom shelves and finally found some Tylenol 3, the kind with codeine, left over from his back surgery. Since that was what one of my prescriptions was for, I felt safe in taking it with part of a can of ginger ale. Then I lay back down, my head spinning.

Gradually it began to seem that I was watching a movie or television show, and then it became more real, as if I were really there, except that I was in no way involved with what was happening. I was a silent, invisible spectator at a teenage Halloween party at a lakeside cabin. It looked cheerful and friendly except that there was a lot of drinking going on, but then I came to know—I don't know how—that these nice, clean-cut, healthy-looking teens—six girls, six boys—had picked this spot for what I would consider an unhealthy reason.

Five years earlier, in that same lakeside cabin, a fifteen-year-old girl had hanged herself because she was pregnant. She was found weeks later, because nobody had thought to look at the cabin when

. . . . .

the search for the missing girl began. The weather had been cool enough that the body had not decomposed completely, but . . .

The discussions among the teens contained delighted *frissons* of horror. I was somewhat less delighted. These children hadn't seen a body found several weeks late. I had.

The drinking went on, mainly among the boys, and some cuddling began. Just cuddling, no more. This wasn't a contemporary party, I suddenly realized. The girls were wearing the button-front white starched blouses, tight waists, full multicolored print cotton skirts with layers of crinoline petticoats, and flat pastel shoes of my early teens, and the boys had on the corduroy trousers, button-down plaid shirts, and white buck shoes of that pre-hippie era. The girls' hair was in pageboy or cut-and-set styles that pouffed or fluffed on top of their heads and curled neatly near their ears, and the boys' hair was in flattops or crew cuts, not today's skinhead look but the longer crew cuts of the fifties. And they were Nice Kids, you could tell by looking. Of course that didn't mean no teenage pregnancies—kids were human in the fifties and sixties just as they were any other time—but it did mean no group sex.

So it was just a little beer, a little cuddling and petting, until quite suddenly one of the boys, obviously drunker than the rest, jumped one of the girls with the intention of satisfying himself whether she was interested or not. There was a lot of screaming as the other girls, and several of the more sober boys, pulled the two apart, and all the girls, in their billowing skirts and delicate-looking flats, ran away in a group, under a full white moon, up a dry, dusty dirt road toward another cabin. No, they didn't have or need jackets; in this part of Texas Halloween is shirtsleeve weather ninety percent of the time.

Only then did I realize that nobody had any cars at the lake; their parents had taken them to the cabin on Halloween night and would return and get them the next morning. (Stupid of the parents, I thought, and then reminded myself that this was only a dream. Yes, it was that kind of a dream, what Susan once told me

· · · · ·

is called a lucid dream. I knew as I dreamed it that it was a dream.)

The girls went to another cabin nearby and found a way in—it might be that the other cabin belonged to the family of one of the other girls—and for a wonder the boys didn't follow them. The girls talked awhile, until the one who'd been jumped calmed down and stopped crying. Then they talked some more, sitting on the floor or moving around taking off their outer clothes, their crinolines, finally going to sleep at the other cabin in panties and the slim nylon half-slips that were always worn under the layers of starched petticoats. They pulled the elastic of the half-slips up above their breasts, so that they looked like short nightgowns. The boys argued a little, haranguing the culprit, made a few coarse jokes, and then finished the booze and went to sleep themselves. In the morning, assuming the boys were sober now, the girls decided to return to the truncated party, where they had planned to make pancakes for breakfast. They grumbled because their purses, with makeup and hairbrushes, were at the other cabin, but nobody was willing to go alone to get them.

I had counted the girls. There had been six of them. There were six of them all night long, and six of them as they decided to return to the other cabin. But now, as they trudged back down the dirt road with dust flying up where they stepped, there were seven, and the seventh's footsteps raised no dust.

The seventh girl had long dark blond hair trailing down her back. She was wearing a long white organdy dress, and she was as pale as the cloth. Her throat was swollen and blue, and five of the other girls ran away from her, but the sixth stayed to try to talk with her.

She could not talk because her throat was swollen and because she was dead; she had hanged herself at that cabin. Or had she? By improvised sign language she finally managed to make the girl who had stayed with her, who must have known her in life, understand that she had *not* hanged herself; her mother murdered her because of the embarrassment of her pregnancy, hoping that by the time the

. . . . .

49

body was found it would be too late for anybody to tell the girl had been pregnant.

For some reason then—still in my dream—I found myself thinking of a play I saw once during my one partial semester in college, *The House of Bernarda Alba,* that terrible last scene where the body of the youngest daughter twists on the rope, the long skirts clinging to her torso and clearly outlining the bulge of advanced pregnancy, while the harridan shakes her fists and shrieks, "The daughter of Bernarda Alba died a virgin!"

The scene shifted then to the cabin, where the boys—now sober, hung over, and very unhappy—were going through cartons of milk at a tremendous rate of speed. Somewhere one of them must have had a boom box on, because I could hear the filtered sound of heavy metal (which, when filtered, seems to consist entirely of drums and bass), but I couldn't see the boom box, and come to think of it, neither boom boxes nor heavy metal existed when I was that age. One of the boys began to yell at another for having the television turned too loud. That was funny; I didn't remember there being a television in the cabin . . . then I realized Harry was screaming at Hal. He'd got home from school and wherever it was he was going today after school, and had turned on MTV. I couldn't actually hear MTV that much, not until I was awake, but I could certainly hear Harry. "We are not going to have that noise when your mother is trying to sleep!" he was shouting.

Good thinking, Harry, I thought, *now what about your noise?*

Damn it, *why* did he have to wake me up? I was certain that the dream had something to do with Dusty Miller's suicide. But it couldn't be telling me what really happened, because I knew what really happened. No matter what had happened to the girl in my dream—*and where in the hell had that dream come from?*—Dusty Miller, like the daughter of Bernarda Alba, undoubtedly had taken her own life. Maybe the dream was telling me the reason?

But I would have to wait awhile before calling anybody at the medical examiner's office. I had something else to attend to first,

. . . . .

and it might get very interesting, because there was no way I was going to yell at Harry to come take me to the bathroom.

It was not that I didn't need help; clearly I did. And it was not that Harry would be unwilling; he would be delighted to help me. No, the problem was more fundamental: Harry was still limping badly from the aftermath of a serious helicopter crash, and the limp had him off balance. I was afraid that if I tried to lean on him, both of us would wind up in a heap on the floor, and most likely he would very shortly thereafter land back in the hospital. As that would do neither of us any good, I had to pretend not to need—or at least not to want—any help.

The problem was that if he saw me in difficulties he would feel churlish at not helping me, and I would seem grouchy at not wanting him to help me. So—and this would be much more difficult—I had to pretend cheerfully not to need the help I clearly did need.

I wasn't sure I could work that out.

We had already established that I couldn't balance on crutches without somebody in front of me and somebody else behind me to catch me when I fell over, usually backward. I definitely couldn't walk. That left only one way to get to the bathroom: obviously, I was going to crawl.

It is, I soon discovered, impossible to crawl in a nightgown that goes below the knees. Well, I didn't have to go through the living room to get to the bathroom, and my bedroom door was firmly shut. Nobody was going to open it, because I was theoretically asleep and not to be disturbed. I took the nightgown off in the middle of the bedroom floor and crawled on into the bathroom.

The bedroom floor is carpeted. So is the bathroom floor. How in the world do babies do it? My knees were already sore by the time I crawled back to bed, collecting my nightgown on the way and putting it back on when I got back to bed.

Then, on second thought, I crawled to my dresser, which fortunately was quite near the bed, and dug out my Tienenman Square

. . . . .

goddess of liberty T-shirt, a pair of white cotton panties, and a pair of yellow knit shorts I hardly ever wear because I decided they were ugly about three days after I bought them. That was going to be my sleepwear for the duration, even if it was difficult to get the shorts over the cast. I managed to get them on anyway, though, tossing the nightgown over onto Harry's side of the bed to be put in the hamper later because I absolutely was not going to crawl back into the bathroom again at this time. Now I was halfway decently clad; I could crawl with a small—*very* small—degree of dignity no matter who happened to be in the room.

By that time I was already tired, thirsty, and sweating and beginning to get chilled from the sweating. *This is idiotic,* I thought, and covered up with a blanket and drank some more ginger ale, noticing as I reached for the ginger ale that several prescription bottles were neatly arrayed beside the telephone. This, presumably, meant that Vicky had come and gone.

Finally, deciding I wasn't likely to get any less tired at any time today, I stretched precariously over to the telephone and called the Medical Examiner's office. That was a number I didn't have to look up. But the phone rang unanswered.

Startled, I looked at the clock. Yes, it was after five. *Well* after five. And I didn't know Andrew Habib's home number. Of course, I had it in my Day Runner, but my Day Runner was in my purse, which was in the living room, and I was darned if I was going to ask Harry to bring it to me because he would—perfectly reasonably—yell at me for trying to work.

I also didn't know for sure that Andrew Habib had done the autopsy. The fact that he was my favorite pathologist didn't always ensure that he was the pathologist I got.

For that matter, I didn't even know for sure that they'd done an autopsy. Theoretically, the law mandates one in the case of any sudden or violent death, but sometimes when there is no real question about the cause of death, and no reason such as a lot of insurance to raise questions, the law is ignored.

· · · · ·

I called dispatch and asked whoever I talked to—I didn't recognize the voice and didn't ask—to find out who had done the autopsy, and have that person call me. I was gambling that I could reach the phone before Harry or Hal did.

Of course, I did not win that bet. Seconds after Harry said, "She's asleep," I said, "No I'm not."

"Well, you're supposed to be," he said accusingly.

"She asked me to call," Habib said patiently. He'd been the third corner of discussions—or quarrels, as he preferred to call them—between Harry and me before.

"Yeah, I just wanted to ask you if you did a postmortem examination on the Miller girl," I said, carefully avoiding the term "autopsy," which Habib insists—incorrectly—means surgery on oneself.

"I did indeed, about nine o'clock this morning. I wondered where you were and called, and Millner told me you were in surgery."

Very often I do go and watch the autopsies when it's my case, even though Identification considers that their prerogative and some of the Ident officers get mad at me for poaching. When that happens, I always point out to them that I used to be in Ident myself. This time, however, there would have been no official reason for me to do so even if I had still been in Ident, because officially the case was closed.

"I was in surgery," I agreed.

"Then what the hell are you doing calling me at"—a pause, probably while he glanced at his watch—"six-forty-five in the evening?"

"I wondered the same thing," said Harry, who had not got off the phone.

"It was something I dreamed," I said, "that made me wonder about something."

"Anesthetics can make you have some funny dreams," Habib said blandly.

. . . . .

"Right. When's last time you used any?"

"Don't need any. All my patients for the last twelve or so years have been dead. But I've had some myself a time or two lately."

That was true. He'd been getting impacted wisdom teeth out.

"Okay, what did you want to know?" he added.

"Was she pregnant? Or maybe just had an abortion?"

"Nope. *Virgo intacta.* But . . ." He paused.

"But what?"

"There was some funny bruising around her clitoral and perineal area."

"Funny how?" I asked. "Like she'd been masturbating?"

"Not likely," he answered. "Bruised enough that whatever happened hurt. And she had a severe case of yeast infection. Not that that means anything. That's one of the things you really can catch from a toilet seat occasionally. There weren't any common STDs. I checked, after seeing the bruising. And I'd have checked for AIDS anyway, the way blood splashed around and got on so many people."

"Could she have been, say, riding a boy's bike and crashed on it?" I asked, trying to think of anything that would cause obvious pelvic bruising and trying not to think of my sister, Rhonda, five years younger than I and dying.

"No," Habib said. "The locations were a little too . . . specific, if you know what I mean. I'll get you a formal report in a couple of days. You want me to mail it to your house?"

"I'll be back at work by then," I said, ignoring Harry's audible growl and the click as he hung up, leaving Habib and me on the phone.

"Okay, I'll mail it to the office," Habib said. "Oh, yeah, just in case you wanted to know, she died of a skull fracture. She knew she was falling, but she didn't feel anything after she landed."

That was good news, I supposed. Remembering how that body had looked, I wouldn't want her to have felt anything after she landed.

. . . . .

54

By the time I was off the phone, Harry was into the bedroom looking exasperated. But he managed to control himself; instead of biting my head off, he asked, "Do you want some supper?"

"What is there?" I asked, visions of cold pizza and cold hamburgers not exactly dancing through my head. Neither Harry nor Hal will cook anything except on the grill, and I was pretty sure neither of them had been at the grill this afternoon.

"Lasagna," Harry said surprisingly. "Somebody from your church brought it over." He calls it my church because I go pretty often, although Hal is the only one in the family who's actually a member. "She said it was cooked and just needed to be heated, but Hal and I tried it and actually it's pretty good cold. I think it's got about four kinds of cheese in it, and all kinds of spices and stuff. You want me to heat you some?"

"I'll try it cold, too," I said.

"But if you don't like it, tell me and I'll heat it."

"Fine," I said, glad that we'd managed to come up with something he could do to help.

The lasagna was good cold. So was the crisp, tart salad with homemade dressing that went with it, and the green beans and new potatoes that tasted home-canned (and anybody who doesn't know the difference between store-bought canned green beans and home-canned green beans doesn't know what green beans are supposed to taste like).

But before I was through eating even the few morsels I could manage (it's amazing how weak such a small amount of surgery can leave a person), my daughter Becky called me. And she was crying.

This alarmed me. Becky is not much of a cryer.

When I was finally able to make out what she was saying, I realized she was asking me about Dusty Miller. "Did you know her?" I asked in surprise.

"A little," Becky said. "Don't you remember my friend Sandy, from high school?"

Sandy I remembered, not favorably. Most high school kids drink

. . . . .

every now and then, if only as a declaration of independence. Sandy drank heavily. Most high school kids wear makeup. Sandy wore it an inch thick. Most high school kids swear occasionally. Sandy would shock a convention of Navy fliers. She also wore clothes at least a size too tight and ten inches too short, smoked (both tobacco, which I wouldn't have minded too much by itself, and marijuana—not at my house, of course, but I had often smelled it on her clothes when she came in), and I was pretty sure she used other drugs as well. I had been, to be perfectly honest, rather relieved when Sandy dropped out of school in the eleventh grade, and after that I never saw her again. "I remember Sandy," I said.

"You never did like her . . . but Mom, she had a shitty situation and she really needed friends. I was the only nice girl who'd be nice to her."

"I'm sure she must have needed friends," I agreed, feeling a little guilty that I had been unwilling—or unable—to befriend her myself and again, for some reason, finding myself thrusting thoughts of Rhonda into the bottom of my mind.

"Dusty Miller was her little sister. You know, that . . . that suicide yesterday? Sandy said you were on it. She said she saw you on television, talking to somebody near the body."

And that, I would have to admit, was a surprise—not that Sandy saw me on television (I seem to wind up on television more often than I wish I did), but that Sandy and Dusty were sisters. I would have taken Sandy for—to use sociological terms I may not understand as well as I think I do—no more than upper lower class, if that; Dusty's family was at least upper middle class, possibly even lower upper class. "Are you sure?" I asked. "I mean, where they live isn't in our school district—"

"They moved," Becky said. "After Sandy . . ." She stopped. "Mom, Sandy wants to talk to you. Now, if possible."

"Now isn't a very good time," I said, trying to sound even more feeble than I felt. "How about tomorrow?"

. . . . .

"She can't tomorrow," Becky said, her tone somewhat evasive. "She has to work."

Now, what was Becky sounding evasive about, I wondered. If Sandy had to work tomorrow she had to work tomorrow, though come to think of it, it was rather odd that she'd be working the day of her sister's funeral. "What does she want to talk to me about?" I asked resignedly.

"She isn't sure it was suicide."

"I'm sure," I said, and began explaining to her why I was sure.

Becky wasn't listening, she was still talking to me. "Mom, I wish you had mentioned it to me. I didn't know what to say to her. I didn't even know you were on the case."

"There was no particular reason for you to know," I replied. "I didn't know you knew the girl, and it's not as if you don't have enough of your own to worry about—"

"Mom, she really needs to talk to you," Becky said again, and naturally I caved in.

Harry was in the bedroom well before I hung up the phone, listening to my end of the conversation, and now he sat down on the edge of the bed and looked at me accusingly. "Deb," he said, "why do you go on trying to work on this? I mean, I can understand why you feel bad about it, but whatever the reason, it doesn't *matter* now."

"Captain Millner said something like that," I replied, "and I didn't like hearing it from him either. How can anybody say it doesn't matter?" I pushed the blanket down and immediately pulled it back up; with it I was too hot, but without it the sweat from the overheating (and probably fever, and did I even have a thermometer in the house, and if I did could Harry find it?) chilled me.

Harry shook his head. "Maybe we mean different things when we say 'matter.' I don't mean it's not important. I don't mean you shouldn't care. Hell, Deb, I've known you over forty years."

That was perfectly true. Vacation Bible School, before I started to school. The preacher's cat brought in a purple martin, and our

· · · · ·

teacher rescued it and then found out it had a broken wing. She asked us all to go out when we got home and catch butterflies and moths for it to eat. I dutifully went out after sunset and caught several moths, which I took to Bible School the next day in a mayonnaise jar. Harry brought butterflies. A *lot* of butterflies. All belonging to his older brother, and all neatly and horribly skewered to the back of cardboard shirt boxes. I took one look and, to Harry's complete bewilderment, began to howl.

My teacher, trying to comfort me, assured me the butterflies were dead before they were put on the pins. That comforted me not at all. For me, butterflies shouldn't be dead.

I must have been eight before I forgave Harry for those butterflies. It wasn't until after we were married that I found out it took him a whole lot longer to forgive himself for making me cry like that.

"You can't not care about something like that," he went on, "not and still be you. I just mean . . . suppose you spend six months finding out what happened to cause her to jump. Then what? What has knowing changed? Nothing at all; she's still dead and whatever triggered it still happened and whatever caused it still happened. And right now, you need your strength for getting well."

"I know," I said. "But I keep thinking, if I can find out what happened, what caused it, maybe I can do something to prevent something else from happening." A mental picture of Doreen Miller flashed through my head and was gone as quickly.

He shook his head. "Get some rest," he said. "When those kids get here they're going to talk you to death." He took my supper tray and went away.

And then I thought, *Becky and Olead have an unlisted telephone number. So how did Sandy find Becky? They must have stayed in touch all along, and I didn't know.*

Well, why should I know? I hadn't been exactly reasonable about Becky's friendship with Sandy.

. . . . .

Four

· · · · ·

HARRY USHERED THE girls in. That was totally unnecessary—Becky certainly knew the way—but I supposed he wanted to make clear his displeasure that I was being disturbed. Through the open door I could see Lori bustling around spiffing up the living room, carrying dirty dishes toward the kitchen. She ought to be at home by now, I thought, and wondered vaguely what time it was. I had lost all track of time, and was surprised when I glanced at the clock to realize it was only eight-thirty.

It was a little surprise to see Sandy again after so many years. She had changed, and visually at least she had changed for the better. Her clothing was neater and fitted her better; she had—perhaps for my benefit, perhaps by preference—abandoned the too-short, too-tight skirts and was wearing a loosely fitted and beautifully tailored pair of tan slacks and a buttoned cotton blouse. The simplicity of the ensemble suggested it had cost about what I would pay for my entire summer wardrobe, and her sandals looked like Italian leather. Her hair was reasonably neat, given the current preference for cocker spaniel curls, and her makeup was less and in better taste than I had ever seen it before. "Hi, Sandy," I said.

"Hello, Mrs. Ralston," she answered. That, too, I had forgotten. She was about the only one of my children's friends who never learned to call me Deb.

She eyed me for a moment, somewhat warily it appeared (and that, too, was a change; in the past she would eye an adult for a long

· · · · ·

time but defiantly, not warily), and then looked around for a place to sit.

Becky plopped down beside me on Harry's side of the bed and motioned Sandy to a chair that frequently—when my mother hadn't been around—was full of clothes I needed to sort (I get around to washing the clothes far more often than I get around to sorting the finished laundry). Then she asked, "Mom, how are you feeling?"

"You don't want to know," I replied. Then I looked again at Sandy. "I'm sorry I didn't realize Dusty was your sister."

She shrugged. "Why should you know? I just appreciate your letting me come over. There's probably not anything you can do, but . . . Becky said you were sure it was suicide. How can you be sure?"

I told her, and she nodded. "Then I guess it was. The old bastard didn't do it. I thought he might have."

"What old bastard is that?" I asked.

"The old man. My *father*." She forced a harsh laugh. "You don't get it, do you? I suppose your father treated everybody nice."

The question and comment caught me off balance, and for a moment I saw my father clearly, as he really had been, not as my mind had idealized him in the years since his death—the years during which I had, almost, managed to convince myself that my childhood and adolescence had really been as normal as they had looked from the outside. Not that I had really ever forgotten anything; often I wished I could. In this flash of memory his face was distorted and livid with rage; he had a doubled belt in his right hand and was patting it threateningly into his left palm. I choked before I was able to say, "Well, no, not exactly."

"Wasn't he usually pretty nice?" Becky said. "I thought you said he was."

"He wasn't." To me, my voice sounded flat, and I wondered if Becky had noticed. No, my childhood wasn't nearly as idyllic as I had represented to my children that it was, and my adolescence was

. . . . .

60

a whole lot worse. But even as a child I could see that compared to some of my friends I *did* have a normal life, at least on the surface. My father was a milkman, my mother was a housewife; my father acted reasonably normal when my friends were around, and what happened when they weren't around I didn't see a need to discuss with them. Some of my friends—especially my friend Fara, who lived with her grandmother, whose mother was a movie star and whose father was dead—envied me.

"Well, at least I bet he didn't treat you like my old man treated me."

I didn't answer that; instead, I said, "Sandy, I don't want to be rude, but I had surgery this morning and I don't exactly feel great. So if you'll tell me what you came here for . . ."

"It's hard to know where to start," Sandy answered. "I . . . Honestly, when I heard about Dusty . . . I heard it from the radio news, you know."

"Why in the world . . . You mean they didn't tell you?"

"Uh-uh." She shook her head emphatically. "I'm not part of the family anymore. I'm the black sheep, baah, baah, baah."

I must have looked totally baffled, because she laughed, then, harshly, a sound that didn't mean to be a laugh at all. "See, Mrs. Ralston, I'm the one that took up the work they trained me for." She stopped, eyeing me again, this time quizzically. "You still don't understand, do you?"

"I don't know what you're talking about."

"Well, let me tell you about a hunting trip my daddy took me on." She glanced at Becky. "I haven't told you all of this, have I?"

"You've never told me about a hunting trip," Becky answered.

"Well . . . I started to say take a hike, but you might as well hear it, too. See, Mrs. Ralston, when I was twelve I was pretty well physically mature. And even before that my nice, dear, sweet daddy, he'd come into the bathroom when I was taking a shower and when I'd yell and grab for the towel he'd say, 'You don't have anything I haven't seen before.' And he'd come and visit my bed,

. . . . .

61

and, you know, just check to be sure my breasts were developing right, you know. And then he wanted to be sure I'd know how to please my husband. And he wanted to be sure I'd be all ready for my husband when I got married, so my husband wouldn't have to teach me what life was all about."

"Are you saying he raped you?"

"Oh, nothing so crass as that," Sandy said. "Virginity is worth something, if you find the right buyer. My daddy always knew what things were worth—in money. And in social standing, for that matter. I think the idea was that I was going to marry some nice old-money lawyer or doctor or somebody like that, somebody who could get my daddy into the right country club, one he couldn't buy his way into. So this . . . well, it actually started when I was eleven, when my breasts were first starting to develop. Before that I wasn't anything to him but a punching bag. You know, you lose your duck call, you don't ask where you might have lost it, you grab the closest kid and whale the daylights out of her for taking it to play with, and then if you find it later in the pocket of your hunting jacket you don't apologize, you just go around quacking half the night, and never mind if your kid has a math test tomorrow that you're going to beat her for not making an A on. The kitchen isn't clean and everybody is in bed, you don't finish cleaning it yourself or wait for somebody to get to it tomorrow, you wake up the whole household yelling and swearing and whale the daylights out of the kids. Or if a record gets broken or a letter gets lost, never mind who broke it or lost it, you blame the closest kid and whale the daylights out of her. Or if you're trying to sleep and it's noon and the kids are making some noise, you don't close the door and turn on the fan and you don't ask the kids to quiet down, you just grab the belt and light into the kids. Or if you haven't got enough money to pay your bills, you don't decide maybe you can't afford to smoke two cartons of cigarettes a day, you tell the kids to stop drinking so much milk and stop leaving the lights on and then you whale them to make sure they remember.

. . . . .

62

From the time I was able to walk until the time I was about twelve I hardly ever remember sitting down without a bruised butt. But then, when I was eleven, that was when he started, like, checking to be sure my breasts were developing right, and when I was twelve, well, about that time he mostly stopped beating me because he could use me to get rid of his frustrations other ways. See what I mean?''

I did see. I wished I didn't. But I wasn't surprised, not after what I'd seen at the Miller household.

"So anyhow," she went on, "he kept me for himself till I was about sixteen. I guess he meant to go on keeping me for himself, at least till I met just the right young doctor or lawyer. Because he was, like, you know, in the way he talked he was *totally* puritanical, like he was always warning me to be careful of the guys, they only wanted one thing. See, *he* was different, *he* just wanted to make sure I was sexually well adjusted because he didn't want me to be like my mother because she was frigid—which she wasn't, by the way; they didn't know I heard anything, but my bedroom was next to theirs and I've got ears, and she *wasn't* frigid—but he was always warning me about the guys. And he wouldn't let me wear makeup, he'd even search my purse to see if I was hiding any, so I had to keep it in my locker at school or let my friends keep it for me and put it on when I got to school, and then I when I got home I had to wash it off real quick before he got home to catch me wearing it. He did catch me, a time or two, and he'd whale the daylights out of me even if he did want me to, you know, *do it* an hour or two later. He yelled a lot about my clothes, too, but Mom was the one who took me shopping. She didn't like the clothes either, but she wasn't as stubborn as I was, so she convinced him that was how all the girls dressed." She grinned. "It wasn't, was it?"

"No, it wasn't," I agreed.

"I know. I looked like a slut. Well, he made me a slut, and I figured I might as well dress like one. But he didn't like it. That was part of why I did it, of course—because he didn't like it—and

. . . . .

63

that was one thing I could manage to get away with that he didn't like. And he didn't want any other guy near me. If I wanted to go out on a date he'd cross-examine the guy, you know, like where are you going, what are you going to do when you get there, who are you going to be with, have her home by ten o'clock or I'll go looking for her, that kind of thing." She half laughed. "Some of my friends said they really envied me, having a daddy that cared that much about my safety! If only they'd known."

I glanced at Becky, who was staring at Sandy with her mouth open. There were a lot of things I had, through the years, been mad at Harry about. But he'd never treated his daughters the way Sandy's father treated her, and I wasn't sure Becky was even aware that that type of problem existed. She'd told me Sandy's father was overbearing and overprotective, but I think that was all she knew when the girls were in school together.

"But when I was sixteen," Sandy went on, "he and some of his buddies were going on this deer hunting trip. I mean, it was a big deer hunting trip, one of those week-long things where they rented a great big cabin and in the daytime they were supposed to go out and hunt deer—actually I think it was elk—and in the evening they'd sit around and drink and play cards, and my daddy got this bright idea, it would be nice to have somebody around to, like, make the beds and cook. So he told me I was going along. Didn't ask me. Told me. He never—even when he'd go through a spell for a week or two when I was real little when he might remember for a little while that I was a kid—he never asked me whether I wanted to do anything. He was the boss. He gave the orders."

"Okay," I said, remembering my father also warning me what the guys were like, my father also giving the orders.

"And then . . . well, I knew what that hunting trip would be like. Because at home, he had to, you know, sneak around when Mom wouldn't catch him, like when she was gone to play bridge or something like that, or when she was taking a bath or off visiting

. . . . .

64

her friends. But on the hunting trip, he wouldn't care *that* much what his buddies saw and what his buddies thought, because he wouldn't have picked them for his buddies if they didn't think the same way he did. That was what I thought to start with."

"But why didn't your mother do anything about it?" Becky interrupted.

"Like what?" Sandy answered. "She didn't even know what was going on. At least she acted like she didn't. I'm not sure, now. Because he held the purse strings. She didn't want me going on the hunting trip. I remember she said, 'But, Seth, do you think it's right, a young girl with all those drunken men?' "

"But she let you go anyway," Becky said.

"Yeah. She let me go anyway." Sandy took a deep breath and then went on. "But when I got there then I found out these weren't his buddies at all. These were . . . Let me back up. My dad . . . We didn't used to be as, well, rich as they are now. We . . . He worked for this company and he was like an engineer, you know, a geological engineer, that was what he originally was trained for, and he made a living, but never an extra good one. And then he went to work for another company selling parts for oil wells, and you know, you can do pretty well in sales if you're good at it, and I guess he was. And all of a sudden there was a lot of money and Mom was really enjoying it—she was buying new clothes and new furniture and she got a real nice car and so forth—and then the bottom started falling out of the market. I don't understand all this economic shit, but it was like all of a sudden we were buying all this foreign oil and the price kept going up and up and up and you'd think that would have made the domestic oil market improve a whole lot but I don't know what happened or why it happened but it just fell on its nose and all of a sudden nobody in Texas or Louisiana was drilling and so of course nobody in Texas was buying oil well parts. But he was used to the money and he didn't want to lose it, and he was courting the foreign market, and he'd bring over all these people from Scotland

· · · · ·

or South America or all these desert sheiks or whatever they were and he'd be entertaining them. And the guys from Scotland and the guys from South America, you know, they didn't expect a whole lot, dinner and a few drinks was enough, but the Arab guys, they didn't most of them drink but they wanted these big, big hunting expeditions. And that was what this hunting trip was, a lot of Arab guys. Well, I say a lot, there were six of them really, and my dad and one other guy from his company, and this cabin my dad had rented, they called it a cabin but it had about ten bedrooms and it was like, you know, on a private game refuge, a deer ranch or an elk ranch or something like that, so you could hunt all year round."

She paused for breath, and I said, "Uh-huh."

"And I don't think the Arab guys knew he was my father. Because he wasn't treating me like his daughter, you know. I mean, I was making eight beds a day—I didn't bother to make mine—and doing laundry—they'd get real dirty out chasing those poor Bambis—and cooking meals for everybody—and most of the time I didn't even sit down at the table with them, not that I wanted to—and washing all the dishes and everything. Turned out he didn't want the other guys to know what was going on, so he'd, like, sneak into my bedroom when he thought everybody was asleep. And he was drinking a lot because he always did on any kind of hunting and fishing trip, it was an occasion for partying, you know, like he was some kind of high school kid whose mommy was looking the other way. But the Arab guys, they weren't drinking, and you could tell they despised him. At least I could tell. I don't guess he could, any more than he could tell they knew he was sneaking into my room, because he was staying, you know, skunked, and sometimes he couldn't get it up even *with* my help, and then it was like, you know, it was my fault and he'd belt me around some. And then one day . . . it was early in the morning, and he and the other guy from his company and most of the Arab guys were out chasing these poor defenseless grain-fed deer and feeling like big macho men doing it, and one of the Arab guys had

. . . . .

66

said he was going to sleep in, and after everybody left he came to my room—I did at least have a room of my own, I told you that, and I wished it would have had a lock on the door, well, actually it did, I guess it had to because they'd have different guys on these trips and sometimes they wouldn't even know each other, so it had a deadlock on every bedroom door, but it locked with a key on both sides, I mean, you couldn't just throw a bolt or something, and my daddy kept the key to my room so I couldn't lock him out—and he, this Arab guy I mean, said, 'Are you a private hunting ground?' And then I thought, boy, wouldn't that be a kick in the teeth for my old man, and so I said, no, and the Arab guy . . .''

She paused, took a deep breath. "He was real surprised to find out I was a virgin. He said something real poetic, like he did not know the pearl had not been pierced, and then he called me a *houri* and he was real nice to me. And he laughed, and laughed, and laughed, you know, not mean but real pleased with himself, like he'd won grand prize in a hog-killing contest, and then, man, I was so surprised I didn't know what to do, he gave me a *thousand dollars!* I mean just like that, he pulled this big roll of money out and he started peeling off hundreds and giving them to me. I'd never had more than twenty dollars at one time before in my life. And right then I realized I didn't have to stay home and get slammed around by the old man until I was old enough to go to college or get married or something to get out of the house. I could leave right then. So I did. Right after I got back from the hunting trip. I got this guy I knew to come over one time when everybody was gone and I packed up all my stuff and left. The thousand dollars, it was enough to get me this little furnished efficiency apartment and pay the deposit on a phone and everything. And . . . I was right. You go where the money is. And they don't—most of them don't—want you to look like a tart. They want you to look like a college kid. I always wondered if some of them were screwing their daughters, too. Or if they wanted to and weren't and that's why they wanted somebody their daughters' age. Except the young

.   .   .   .   .

67

ones, I don't know what they want, some nice-looking girl their wives' age that they don't have to put on a pedestal I guess, but I'll bet I meet more of those doctors and lawyers than I ever would have if I'd done what my daddy wanted me to. And that's what I've been doing ever since."

"Do you like it?" I asked.

She laughed harshly again. That couldn't be the only laugh she had; I could imagine the musical tinkle of laughter that must greet her customers' humor; but that might be her only real laugh. "I must like it, mustn't I? Because I'm doing it. But it's a living, that's all. And don't give me a lot of guff about how I'm a smart girl and I could be doing whatever I want to. I'm doing what I want to."

"And what is that?" I asked.

"I'm making a lot of money. And I'm saving a lot of money. And I'm going to get my baby sister out of that bastard's hands before another year is out. I don't know when and I don't know how I'm going to talk her into it, but I'm going to do it, and then I'm going to disappear with her. I tried to get Dusty to go with me but she wouldn't, she was scared, she said if she left and Daddy found her he'd kill her. And . . ."

She paused for a moment and then went on. "She used to tell me nothing was happening. She knew I knew she was lying, but . . . I don't know if all abused kids are like this, but it was like . . . like she'd learned not to trust her own perceptions. Like, your butt is bruised from your waist to your knees and your daddy is coming into your room every night so you can jack him off or suck him off, and you sit around looking blue and your mom says, 'What are you looking so gloomy about, these are the best years of your life,' and you think, *Gee, if these are the best years of my life I sure don't have much to look forward to.* Or your dad says, 'You kids are spoiled rotten, you've got everything going your way,' and you think, *Well, gee, I guess I just be an ungrateful kid.* And they tell you, 'We are a happy family,' and you think, *Well, we must really be a happy family and I just can't see it.* They make you not trust yourself,

. . . . .

they make you think their version is right and yours is wrong even though every sense you've got is telling you your version is right. So . . . when I heard on the car radio, driving to work at this motel . . . I thought he'd killed her. I really did. I thought she'd tried to get away and he'd killed her, or I thought he'd gone farther with her than he had with me and got her pregnant and killed her so she wouldn't tell. Are you certain—"

"I'm certain nobody killed her," I said. "I told you already there were two police officers in the condo when she jumped. She had her bedroom door locked, and one of them was trying to get it open. And she definitely wasn't pregnant."

"I guess they had to, like, cut her open and see," Sandy said.

"That's right." I changed the subject then, or tried to. "If you really want to get Doreen away from your dad, would you be willing to talk to the social workers, or if necessary to testify in court, about what he did to you?"

She leaned back in the chair, her laughter more real-sounding than the previous laughter I had heard from her. "Oh, man!" she said. "That is a joke. That is a real joke." She sat up straight again. "Who's going to believe me? You ever seen my rap sheet?"

"No," I said, "why would I?"

"I suppose not. Well, trust me. I've got one. And if I went into court to try to testify that he molested me, who do you think would believe me? And if you think you could get Doreen or Mom to testify, think again. I told you Mom likes the long green; that's true; but on top of that she's scared of him. And so is Doreen. For good reason. No, I've got my own way of taking care of Doreen."

"Sandy, that's kidnapping," I said, "and if you're caught—"

"I won't be," she said. "I've made a lot of preparations. When I disappear I'll disappear good. So . . . I can tell even you, knowing you're a cop. Because you won't find me. Nobody will."

"Do you think Dusty committed suicide because he was molesting her?" I asked.

. . . . .

69

She shook her head. "I don't see why she would now if she didn't before. She's . . . She was sixteen. And he started on me when I was eleven. I don't guess he started on her till after I left, but even then it was five years ago. So why now? Why would it be any worse now than it was five years ago? Unless . . . unless Mom really *did* convince her these were the best years of her life. Because I'll tell you, if being my daddy's teenage daughter is the best years of your life, you're a heck of a lot better off dead. You think I've got a lousy job now? Well, let me tell you something. I can tell them *no* now, and I never could tell him no. And at least I'm getting paid for it."

I couldn't answer that. And there was another question I couldn't answer.

"Sandy," I said, "I still don't know why you came. I understand what you've told me, of course. And I'm not going to tell you what you're doing is dangerous, because you already know it's dangerous. But knowing what happened can't bring Dusty back, and it can't even protect Doreen if you aren't willing to talk to anybody other than me. Trust me, they *will* believe you. Especially the social workers. They've heard—"

"I wish I could trust you," she interrupted. "I wish I could trust anybody."

"What it boils down to is, you've asked me to help you and Doreen, but you won't let me provide the help you've asked for."

After a long silence, she said, "I guess that's the size of it. Dumb, huh?"

"No," I said, "not dumb. And I'll go on investigating. But if you won't help me help Doreen, then why—"

"I don't know," she said. "I don't know. I just . . . I guess I wanted you to tell me that my sister wasn't murdered. And now that you've told me, I still don't believe it. Maybe what I really wanted was for you to tell me that my sister *was* murdered. Oh, I know now that she went out the window by herself. I don't doubt that. But why? How did the old man rig it, how did the old man

. . . . .

push her into it? Because what I said, I don't really believe it, that she thought it never would get better. She and I used to laugh about that. I told her it *does* get better, a whole lot better. Anything's better than living through that. I told her if she wouldn't come with me just stick it out, she was a high school junior, one more year and she could get away. So why did she do it? And how did he make it happen? That's what I want to know. Because whether he meant to or not, he made it happen. And I thought, maybe, if I told you . . ." She took a deep breath. "Mrs. Ralston, I can't testify in court because it wouldn't do any good. But if you could get some friends of Dusty to tell . . . because she must have told somebody . . ."

"How did you know she must have told somebody?" I asked. "Who did you tell?"

She grinned, casually waved one manicured hand with a thin gold bracelet on the wrist. "Touché. I told you. Tonight. But I do think she would have told somebody. Could she have left a note?"

"If she did I don't know who she left it with," I said. "She didn't leave one in her room. I know that. I searched thoroughly. And people who leave suicide notes don't hide them; they mean them to be found. Look, I'm sorry, I realize this must be very difficult for you, but my foot is killing me and I have to take some more medicine."

Becky sprang up, instantly solicitous. "Mom, I'm sorry, I should have thought. Can I get you anything?"

"I have everything I need," I answered. Mainly, by now, I wanted them to leave so I could crawl to the bathroom without having to worry about who saw me crawling, and then return and take my medicine.

Sandy glanced at Becky, stood up also, looked back at me, and said, "Thank you for listening to me."

"I don't know what I can do," I told her, "but I'll see what I can find out. If there is a way of getting Doreen away safely

. . . . .

71

without risking your freedom and having Doreen wind up right back in the same place—"

"Nobody will find me," Sandy said, smiling slightly. "But if you can get her away, I'd appreciate it."

She went out the front door, and moments later I heard Hal asking her, "Do you know how to sing?"

"Yes, I know how to sing," she said, sounding coolly amused.

"Then I want to talk to you—"

"I don't have time now," she said, "but I'll give you my phone number."

Great, I thought. *Just what I want. My son getting a prostitute's phone number.* But of course he didn't know her occupation, I reminded myself conscientiously, and then forgot the question entirely when I inadvertently moved my foot and very much wished I had not done so. On second thought, I would take my medicine and *then* crawl to the bathroom, so that the medicine might, if I was lucky, begin to take effect by the time I got back.

Which it did. But as I began to fall asleep I began to remember . . . a fishing trip, my dad going fishing . . . at Caddo Lake . . . with some other guys . . . and he wanted somebody to go along and cook for them . . . and I had to . . .

I was almost asleep when I was awakened again by, surprise, surprise, another argument between Harry and Hal. This time Hal was the loudest: "But Dad, I've got to practice!"

"You're not going to start that kind of racket when your mother—"

"But we open next week at—"

Between them I could occasionally make out the tone of Lori's voice, but not the words. I did not, however, need the words to know what was going on. Hal and several of his friends had recently decided to form a rock group, centered around the drum set that, in what must have been a moment of complete madness, I had bought Hal when he was in junior high and that had resided, generally untouched, in the garage ever since, along with his also

. . . . .

unused weight bench. They had named the group Hey Fever and had even managed, somehow, to get a date to play at a prom for a very small school. Lori was the group's lead (for which read only) singer; this presented a major problem, as her voice had recently become even softer than it used to be, and no matter how amplified it was, it was virtually inaudible over Hal's drums, Sammy's electric guitar, what's-his-name's electric bass, Billy Cawdor I think, and Joan Harper's keyboard, which was included because Joan and Sammy were dating. I considered the whole thing at best a cacophony—Hal apparently had selected his group not on the basis of talent but on the basis of who owned an instrument—but then I consider virtually everything that comes over MTV to be a cacophony, so who am I to judge?

"You might as well let them practice," I called resignedly. "I'm awake now."

Actually, it turned out, Lori was the only one practicing; she was singing against an instrumental tape the rest of the group had made, and I considered pointing out to Hal that turning the volume down to make Lori more audible wasn't a good idea, as the sound wouldn't be turned down when the instruments were actually present. But I decided against it. I would much rather hear Lori than a drum, guitar, bass, and keyboard.

I definitely did not have the energy to read. Furthermore, I did not, as paradoxical as it may sound, have the energy to go back to sleep. I finally got the crutches and made my slow and awkward way into the living room—Harry offered to help, but I declined, for reasons already mentioned—and lay down on the couch, picked up the remote, and began channel surfing.

One channel was rerunning that Oprah Winfrey special on child abuse. It was a terrific show, and she ought to get a special Emmy for it (I could not, at this moment, remember whether she had or hadn't actually done so), but I didn't have the emotional energy to watch it again, so I went on channel surfing, finally settling down to watch a PBS show on winged predators.

· · · · ·

73

Despite the noise from the garage and the sound of the television show, I managed to doze off again, and when Harry woke me much later to see whether I was ready to go to bed, I said earnestly, "Large vipers must be swallowed with great care."

Pardonably, he said, *"Wha-a-t?"* and put his hand on my forehead.

"It was on TV," I said. "I don't have fever. Well, actually I do, but that's not why. I was watching it on TV. A baby eagle was eating a great big snake headfirst, and the announcer said, 'Large vipers must be swallowed with great care.'"

"I'll remember that," Harry said, "if I ever happen to decide to swallow a viper. What's a viper, besides a snake?"

"A poisonous snake," I explained. "You know, like pit viper. You ought to know that, as much as you camp out, at least as much as you used to camp out. I think that one was a rattlesnake. It looked like a diamondback, and it was wriggling like mad. I mean, it was half-swallowed, but the half that was still hanging out tied itself in a knot and the little eaglet was looking very bewildered and the mama eagle came and helped untie it."

"I see," Harry said, sounding very bewildered himself.

"I mean, what would you do if your spaghetti tied itself in knots and you didn't have any way to cut it? So the mama came and untied it. But anyway, they said the baby eagle lives on snakes until it's big enough to catch its own prey, and the mama and daddy eagle bring it the snakes. And you have to eat it headfirst because that way it has a lot less time to bite you."

"Unless it bites your tongue."

"I don't know if birds have tongues."

"They do," Harry said. "I've seen eagles with their mouths open and they have tongues."

"Then maybe they swallow the viper so fast the viper doesn't have time to get its mouth open."

"How did we get onto this discussion anyway?"

"I don't know," I said.

. . . . .

So he helped me to bed, as much as I dared let him help, and told me he'd sleep on the couch, because I didn't need him thrashing around all night. I dreamed about trying to swallow a viper. For some reason the viper was all tangled up in my mind with the time I went on the fishing trip with Daddy and the viper was spitting poison in my mouth and I kept gagging and gagging and the viper wanted me to finish swallowing it.

My mood was not improved at all when I was awakened by Rags running in at 2 A.M., through that cat door I wish heartily that Harry and I had never thought of. She was carrying a garter snake, which she at once let loose in the bedroom and began that soft, rhythmic "mrower, mrower, mrower" by which she means "Please get up at once and help me play with my prey."

I called to Harry, who came in, grabbed the snake jar—she has brought in so many snakes lately that we keep a snake jar in the bedroom—and nudged the snake into the jar and put the perforated lid on top. He would take the snake out tomorrow and release it a few miles away so that Rags couldn't find that particular one again. Rags went around for a while saying "mrower, mrower, mrower" in a very disappointed tone of voice, while I took another pain pill, crawled to the bedroom, and went back to bed. Then she lay down with her head on my hand, that being one of her favorite positions lately, and began to purr, which I suppose meant she had forgiven me for stealing her snake.

I went back to sleep again and, unfortunately, fell right back into another variant of the same dream. I was still on the fishing and camping trip, and my daddy was there, but he wasn't protecting me from the snake. This time I was still trying to swallow the snake, only I didn't want to, and it was spitting poison down my throat and the poison was bitter and Oprah Winfrey came and tried to help me fight the snake off, only then the snake began to bite us both.

· · · · ·

75

Five
. . . . .

BY TEN O'CLOCK Saturday morning I felt about ready to go out of my mind. The day had begun well enough, with Lori and Hal bringing me breakfast in bed (which was fortunate, as I was pretty sure I was not up to getting up for it), but things rapidly went downhill from there. To start with, the cat—Rags, not Margaret Scratcher—had hysterics. She leaped up on my dresser, where she liked to pounce on the tomato plant (which come to think of it might explain why I had few tomatoes), and then realized the plant was gone. Obviously it had never occurred to her before that a plant could go anywhere. She howled. She yowled. She jumped from the dresser to the bed to the dresser to the bed to the dresser and then sat and howled some more. Then she finally quit howling and just sat, staring at where the plant used to be, her eyes the size of quarters. Finally, in desperation, I asked Harry if he could return at least part of Trif to the dresser so the cat would settle down. "I got rid of it," he said. "Maybe if I take the cat outside and show her another tomato plant . . ."

A fat lot of good that did. Rags did not want another tomato plant, and the cats have a cat door. She came right back in and resumed her vigil, apparently hoping that if she stared long enough Trif would return.

On top of a hysterical cat I had a smothering teenager. Lori hovered. She tried to mother me. At my age—well past forty—I detest being mothered by anybody, and especially by a teenager.

. . . . .

Hal alternated between turning the television on, remembering I was not up to listening to MTV, and turning it back off again, so that I never knew when I would be jarred out of my half drowse by drums and shrieks, only to have the sound stop by the time I was a third of the way awake.

On second thought, maybe Lori wasn't trying to mother me. Maybe she was trying to daughter me. I will be very surprised if she does not one day become my daughter-in-law, and her consideration was touching, but after all, I had only had foot surgery. I was neither ninety years old nor in a totally advanced state of decrepitude.

Eventually Harry managed to tear himself away from his computer long enough to realize what was going on. "You're driving your mother nuts," he told Hal. "You and Lori find something else to do."

"Like what?" Hal inquired.

"I don't care. Go to the zoo. Go to Six Flags."

"It isn't open yet."

"The zoo is. Hell, I don't care, go catch mice. Just go *somewhere* and leave your mother alone for a few hours."

"Can I take the car?" Hal asked, elaborately casually.

"You know damn well you can't take the car," Harry retorted. "Take the truck. If I need to go anywhere, *I'll* take the car."

After they left, he came in and asked me if I needed anything. "No," I said, "but thanks for asking."

"You sure?" he asked. "Because I'm going to take off for a few hours, too. I've got some library research to finish up, and I know you need some peace and quiet. You want me to take the phone off the hook?"

"No, leave it in case I decide to call somebody."

"Then if you decide to go to sleep, you take it off the hook."

"I'll just turn the bell off," I said. "The phone company doesn't like people to leave the phones off the hook. It does something nasty to the system."

. . . . .

77

"Only if about a fourth of the phones in the system are off the hook at once. Deb, promise me you'll get some rest?"

"I can scarcely do anything else," I pointed out.

He hesitated, dithering. "I don't know if I ought to lock the door," he said. "If somebody comes to the door who you want to come in, they can't if it's locked, unless you go to the door. But if somebody you don't want comes to the door—"

"Bring Pat around to the front yard," I said. "He'll take care of the matter."

"The mail hasn't come yet."

That could present a problem, I thought. Pat formerly had no particular interest in the mail carrier, other than announcing his presence, until one day a substitute mail carrier mistook the announcements for threats and pepper-sprayed him. Since then Pat tries to eat not only the mail carrier but anybody else in uniform, and we have been warned that the mail will not be delivered if Pat is visible in the yard.

Then I had the solution. "Bring Pat inside," I said. "Oh, and you might drain the ice chest. It's sloshing."

Harry took the ice chest outside, drained out the water through the plug so as not to disturb the soda pop, put in another sack of crushed ice from the freezer, and replaced the cold cut tray before going to get the dog. At the back door he hesitated, looking back toward me, just visible through the door from the bedroom to the living room. "What if he wants to go out?"

"He can wait. Or I can get to the back door."

Harry's expression said he still didn't think that was a good idea, but he opened the door and called, "Pat!"

I would like to have seen the expression on the dog's face, considering that he is normally not even allowed in, much less invited in. Anyhow, seconds later I heard the click of the dog's nails on the hard vinyl tile we had bought several years ago to replace the ratty brown carpet that had been in the house when we bought it. (It hadn't been ratty then, of course.)

· · · · ·

78

I heard the click of the dog's nails for quite a while. Clearly the dog was looking for the baby. The baby was not around.

"You want me to bring you anything?" Harry asked before departing.

"Yeah," I said. "Bring me a hanging plant. Maybe that'll make the cat feel better."

"Any special kind?"

"A spider plant," I said. "A big one. They're not very messy, and I understand they help to purify the air."

Harry departed, leaving behind a search dog.

The dog looked a lot of places. Most of them he looked more than once, before he finally came in, looked anxiously at me, and whined. "I know," I told him. "I didn't accidentally misplace Cameron. He's gone visiting. We'll bring him home later."

Clearly disbelieving me—*people always lie to dogs*—Pat went on looking for several more minutes before he apparently gave up. Then he sniffed interestedly at the ice chest (which contained, among other things, ham), and then finally curled up on the floor beside my bed about six inches away from Rags, who had temporarily abandoned her vigil to enjoy the chance to nap with me. Rags sat up indignantly, spat, and then settled back down; like our old cat, she has long since figured out that Pat is a canine pushover.

Unlike the rest of the house, our bedroom floor is still carpeted. Clearly, Pat was enjoying the chance to sleep on carpet. He stretched out, moving his legs as if he were chasing rabbits (or cats) in his sleep, and then relaxed as if settling in for a long night. He smelled doggy, and he snored. Maybe this wasn't such a good idea after all.

I had taken enough painkiller that I wasn't up to reading or watching television or even sitting upright on the bed to play solitaire. But I felt that I'd slept enough for six months in the last day and a half, and I didn't particularly want to go to sleep again. I lay on my back and stared at the ceiling for a while, and then I called my new office. Rafe answered. "What's going on?" I asked.

. . . . .

"What's going on," he repeated. "Nothing new on that Bonando thing, so apparently you did shut them up adequately. A date rape, probably legit but we're not going to be able to prove it."

"How come?"

"Victim took a shower and douche before reporting it. But I don't know, we might not could have proved it anyway. We could have proved intercourse, but not that it was unwanted. She's hysterical, but he didn't do anything that left a mark. And the bastard is strutting around like a bull elk—he's done it before, I'll lay odds, and gotten away with it before, and he'll keep doing it until somebody successfully blows the whistle. And damn it, if we could ever get it past the DA I figure we could get it past the grand jury and a trial jury easy enough. She's smaller than you are—I figure, about five feet, eighty-two pounds—and he's this big bruiser, six feet two, shoulders like if he was playing football he wouldn't need shoulder pads. Blond. Good-looking in a caveman way."

"Predator," I said thoughtfully.

"What?" Rafe said, and then half snorted. "Yeah. Predator. Hunting the vulnerable prey. And God knows this one looks vulnerable. I don't know, maybe I will try to get it past the DA."

"Anything else?"

"Uh-uh," he said. "At least nothing new. Nothing to go on."

Which meant the Super Glue rapist and the TCU rapist were still out somewhere, waiting to hit again, I thought as I returned the telephone to the shelf where it belonged. Or else it meant the Super Glue rapist and the TCU rapist had hit again and the victim was too afraid—or too ashamed—or too intimidated—to make a report. That happens more often than any of us like to think about.

I still didn't have anything to do. The house is rarely this quiet. I reached for one of the books the family had left conveniently within my reach, read about three pages, and then realized I couldn't remember what I had read, which made further reading

. . . . .

pointless. The house was so quiet I could hear the refrigerator running.

Saturday, at least on those Saturdays I don't wind up working, is usually my run-errands day. Sunday is church and family visit day. I normally have no do-nothing day. Having one confused me.

I reached for the phone to try to call my mother, and it rang again. "Hello?" I said.

"Update," Permut said, in an excited voice. "I thought you'd like to hear this one before I go out on it. The TCU rapist tried it in broad daylight, in some bushes behind a women's dorm. The woman had a can of pepper spray."

I sat right up in bed. Pepper spray—which is produced from the hottest of cayenne peppers—is made by any one of several manufacturers, though the one I'm most familiar with is called Body-Guard. Unlike Mace and tear gas, it is—so far as I know—legal for civilian possession in all fifty states. Unlike Mace or tear gas, it's never been known to produce permanent damage to anybody, no matter how susceptible. Unlike Mace or tear gas, it will subdue even the most out-of-control psychopath or spaced-out drug user, as well as savage animals, many of which are not affected by other chemicals. Sprayed from a distance of as much as five feet away or as close as contact, it will affect the eyes and the entire respiratory tract, and will put a person out of action immediately and keep the person out of action, clawing at his eyes and trying to remember how to breathe, for up to twenty minutes. "So you got him?" I asked.

"No, dammit. She hit him in the face and then ran back into the dorm, leaving him lying on the ground clawing at his eyes and cursing. But when she called 911 she didn't mention she'd gassed him—just said a man had tried to jump her in the parking lot, and when dispatch asked for a description she was so rattled she described clothing and so forth without mentioning she'd left him lying in that parking lot. So uniform cars cruised the area looking for him before contacting her. And by that time, he was gone."

· · · · ·

"How long was that from the time the woman called?"

"Fifteen minutes max," Rafe said.

"Give her another two or three minutes to get to the phone—"

"And that's stretching it," Rafe agreed. "I expect she was to the phone within two minutes at the very most."

"He couldn't have gotten very far under his own steam yet."

"That's how I read it," Rafe said. "Means somebody's running with him."

"Frat rats, you think?" I asked doubtfully. Fraternity kids at times think up very unfortunate things to do as stunts, but this would be pushing it for any fraternity and especially one attached to a religious school.

"No telling," Rafe said. "But I've told dispatch to notify all emergency rooms. With luck he'll turn up in one. Gotta go now— she might have seen more than the patrol officers got out of her."

With luck, I thought, lying back against the pillows already sweating and tired from sitting up so short a time. Luck is always what it seems to come down to in police work. You do all the routine stuff, you talk to all the witnesses and see what leads they can give you and what ideas for more people to talk with and then you go talk with them, you go for the fingerprints and the tire tracks and the DNA and you name it, but so often it seems ultimately to come down to luck: either you have it or you don't, and if you do, somebody says the right thing that points you in the right direction, and if you don't, you spend all that time spinning your wheels while the criminal strikes again and again until finally you *do* have the luck.

If that silly girl—only she wasn't so silly, was she, if she had the pepper spray with her going out the back door of the dorm into the parking lot—had just told the 911 operator that she had the man lying in the parking lot cursing with a face full of red glop . . .

But even that might not have been fast enough. If, as Rafe and I both surmised, he had at least one running mate, then he might

· · · · ·

have been bundled into a car and driven away before the victim finished punching numbers into the telephone. *Damn,* I thought.

And then I sat up again, reached for the phone, and called my mother.

Rhonda answered.

I wouldn't have bet on recognizing her voice. It had been more than ten years since I had talked with her last. But I did recognize it. "Hello," I said, "let me talk with Mom."

"I'll get her."

And when Mom came on the phone, I said, "Please bring Cameron home."

"Debra," Mom said in that super-rational voice that always makes me want to bite, "he's perfectly safe. You can't catch AIDS from the toilet seat or—"

"Who said anything about AIDS and toilet seats?" I interrupted. "I know how AIDS is and isn't transmitted. I see a lot of people with AIDS. I'm not worrying about Cameron catching AIDS; I'm worrying about his safety around that girl. Rhonda is a ding-a-ling. Don't you remember when Vicky was that age and Rhonda was carrying her around in a pillowcase to tease her and the pillowcase was too old to hold a three-year-old and it ripped and Vicky fell out on her head and wound up with six stitches? Don't you remember Rhonda and that boyfriend of hers, the one with the convertible, driving around with Vicky sitting up on top of the backseat, so that if they had hit a bump and turned too fast she'd have been thrown right out of the car, and them both thinking it was funny to have her sitting there? I don't want another one of my children—"

"You wouldn't recognize her," Mom said. "You wouldn't know her, Debra. She hasn't . . . There's no fun left in her."

"Bring Cameron home anyway," I said.

"All right," Mom said, "but I'm bringing Rhonda, too." And she hung up before I had time to argue.

Oh shit, I thought, lying back down. I could just hear Harry's

· · · · ·

response if he returned home to find Rhonda there, or if he came home before Mom got here and Rhonda walked in the front door. But clearly there was nothing I could do about it.

I opened a ginger ale. I hadn't had a pain pill in about five hours, and my foot was throbbing. Maybe if I went back to sleep before they got here . . .

I did. But I still woke up when they came in. Who wouldn't, with a three-year-old tornado screaming "Mommy!" and the dog standing up and wagging his hindquarters, which is what dogs wag when they have no tail.

Mom was behind Cameron, and Rhonda was behind Mom.

I wouldn't have recognized her. She was younger than I was, and when I'd seen her last her hair had been a gorgeous black mane down her neck and her eyes were so deep a blue they were almost violet. She'd been wearing a purple knit tube top, sleeveless and waistless, skin-tight black leather slacks, and purple spike-heel sandals. Prostitution, I had thought then, rather spitefully, must pay pretty well.

Now, if you put Mom, Rhonda, and me together in a line and asked somebody to pick the oldest, almost anybody would have picked Rhonda. Her body, once slender, was scrawny now. She'd had teeth pulled without bridgework to replace them, and her jaws were sunken. Her eyes now were just blue, and her now-sparse hair was visibly dyed black, so visibly that three-quarters of an inch of gray root was visible at the base of her scalp. A faded red sweater topped faded blue jeans—not fashionably faded, just old, and too loose on her besides—and she had rubber thong sandals on dirty clawlike feet. In view of Mom's soap-and-hot-water fetish, that had to be ground-in dirt that wouldn't wash off fast.

Nothing there to be jealous of, I thought, and instantly was horrified. When was I ever jealous of Rhonda? But of course I had been jealous of Rhonda. She was prettier than I was. She knew how to flirt—she'd contradict the boys and argue with them and giggle,

· · · · ·

and they'd flock around her like bees around flowers, and I tried to treat the boys decently and they all treated me as a sister—*all except Harry,* I reminded myself, *all except Harry.*

She convinced Mom she was too frail to do housework half the time, so I wound up doing her share and mine, too, though on the days she decided not to be too frail she would appear to waft gently through the living room leaving behind a trail of order instead of her usual trail of disorder, so that the room looked better in fifteen minutes than it did if I slaved on it for two hours.

She—

But that was over twenty years ago. And now I had a good husband, a good family, children and grandchildren and cats and a dog and a good job and friends, and was living in a house that, despite its inconveniences, at least was mine, and Rhonda was standing in front of me looking like she hadn't any business trying to stand, and most likely she didn't own much more than what she had on.

I glanced over at Cameron, who was now trying to strangle a delighted-looking dog, and recalled that Rhonda had been pregnant six times that I knew of. She gave her first and second babies up for adoption. Her second had become my second, Becky. That was after Rhonda had announced the intention of dating, for six months each, at least one member of every Native American tribe she could find, and although the father, a Comanche, agreed the baby was probably his, he said he certainly didn't want it, and although Rhonda might in one part of her mind have wanted the baby, she knew she couldn't care for a child. First she acted like a crazy thing and put the baby in a dumpster behind the apartment complex where she had been abandoned herself when her boyfriend walked out, where fortunately the baby was found before the garbage was collected. I'd already called Dallas—along with several hundred other people, they told me—asking to adopt the abandoned child before Rhonda called the police department,

· · · · ·

crying, to 'fess up; then, with Rhonda agreeing to relinquish the baby only if it was to me, there was no trouble at all with my getting her.

Rhonda had said to start with that she was going to stay in close touch. She didn't, much to our relief; I knew I wouldn't have had the heart to refuse her if she asked to visit, but I hadn't relished the thought of Rhonda, drunk or high, crying or having hysterics, hanging around my house. All the same, I'd really been surprised when she never came back after the first visit, when Becky was four months old. The result had been that although Becky knew that Rhonda was her birth mother, she never really seemed to think of the matter at all.

Rhonda's third baby, which she wanted to keep (being temporarily—very temporarily, as it turned out—married), was born with spina bifida and died two days later. She miscarried the fourth, in the state mental hospital where she'd gone for drug treatment when she was six weeks pregnant. The fifth was severely mentally retarded, but her husband-of-the-hour had kept it. The sixth was born dead. Effectively, I had everything, including what had been Rhonda's child and what would have been Rhonda's grandchildren, and Rhonda had nothing. I was ashamed of myself for being so petty as to even think of the past.

"Sit down," I invited. "I'm sorry there's only one chair; one of you can sit on the bed."

After a glance at Mom, Rhonda sat in the chair. "Someone left the front door unlocked," Mom announced.

"I asked Harry to," I answered.

"And absolutely anybody could have just walked right in—"

"With Pat around?" I inquired drily.

That shut up even Mom, at least temporarily. "Have you had lunch?" she demanded next, looming over me.

"No, but—"

"Why in the world not? It's the middle of the afternoon!"

"It's only one o'clock," I replied. "And I had a late breakfast—"

. . . . .

"What difference does that make? You need lots of protein."

Before I could tell her I had ham in the ice chest she had headed for the kitchen to check the refrigerator, which she had last checked two days earlier. "There's nothing in here," she called, her voice slightly muffled. "What have those men been doing?" *Those men,* I assumed, were Harry and Hal.

"Eating, most likely," I muttered.

"What's that?"

"I don't know what they've been doing," I yelled. "I've been in bed."

"Well, I'm going to get you some groceries. Cameron, come with Gammie."

"Stay with Pat," Cameron replied. So much for filial loyalty. Never mind staying with Mommy, he wanted to stay with the dog. Oh, well, I don't kiss him half as much as the dog does. Or half as sloppily. After one glance, I averted my eyes.

"Gammie'll get ice cream," Mom said, in a wheedling tone she'd certainly never used on me.

So much for loyalty, period. I heard Pat's head thump to the floor as Cameron dropped him. Then Pat scrambled to his feet and tried to follow Cameron, catching up in the front bathroom, where Cameron was having his hands and face washed, but succeeded only in being escorted out the door and then abandoned in the front yard.

That, I am sure, did not make his day. Because he is not allowed in the front yard until after the mail comes, and because we got tired of locking him in the garage all day, we now have the front and backyards separated by an elaborate system of fences and gates that allow humans and cats to get through but not dogs, unless they are accompanied by humans. At night, when we want him to have access to the front yard, we chain the gates open, but they are routinely closed by the first person up in the morning and, I was quite sure, had not yet been reopened today.

· · · · ·

This meant that Pat was in the front yard, but his food and water dishes were in the back.

He'd enjoy the novelty of being in the front yard in the daytime for a while before he'd start to howl.

I glanced over at Rhonda, and to my surprise she was laughing silently. "Did you ever wonder," she said, "what the lead pin feels like when you bowl a strike?"

"No, I never really wondered that."

"With Mom around you don't need to wonder. Debra, when did she get that bad? She never was like that when we were kids."

"I don't know, and by the way, nobody but Mom has called me Debra in the last twenty years."

"What do you go by?"

"Deb."

"Sorry. I knew you always did prefer to be called Deb, but I thought you might've got more formal as you got older. I still go by Rhonda. In case you wondered."

"I assumed you did."

That conversation disposed of, and our present names agreed on, we had nothing further to say to each other. Rhonda sat and looked at me. I lay on the bed and did not look at Rhonda, except out of the corner of my eye, lest I be thought to be staring.

After a while Rhonda looked at Rags, who had resumed her vigil by where Trif used to be. "What's the matter with that cat?"

"Harry stole her tree."

"You had a tree on your dresser?"

"A tomato plant. But the cat thought it was a tree. And trees don't get up and walk away. So now the tree is gone and the cat thinks she's gone crazy."

"You don't like me much, do you?" Rhonda asked.

"I don't dislike you."

"But you wouldn't give me a key to your house, would you?"

"I don't give anybody a key to my house."

"But I'm your sister."

· · · · ·

"Mom doesn't have a key to my house. Why should you?"

"But I'll bet that woman that comes in to clean your house has a key."

"I don't have anybody to clean my house," I retorted.

"Well, you used to."

"When Becky and Vicky were little I had a woman who came in between the time they got home from school and the time Harry or I got home from work," I agreed, "and yes, she had a key."

"So you'll give a Mexican a key and you won't give a key to your own sister."

"Carlota," I said pointedly, "never stole my husband's guns and my jewelry."

"Ah, Deb," Rhonda said, "that wasn't me."

"The hell it wasn't!"

"Jacky said he'd beat me up if I didn't—"

"I'd just as soon not hear it," I said. "I already heard it too many times. Your pimp said he'd beat you up if you didn't give him enough money and you couldn't get enough men so you stole Harry's guns and my jewelry. Such as it was."

"Twenty dollars in a pawnshop," Rhonda said sadly. "For *all* of it. The jewelry, I mean. The guns were better."

"Even if the jewelry wasn't very good, it was *mine,*" I retorted, "including that Mexican silver ring Harry bought me on our honeymoon, which I never got back."

"That stone in it wasn't a real sapphire."

"I am quite aware of that. That didn't make it yours."

She sat for a while and then said, "All right, it was crummy of me and I knew it when I did it. And that wasn't even why. Jacky wasn't going to beat me up. I had enough men. There was a convention in town; I had all the men I wanted. I was just mad at you. You had a husband and I had a pimp. You had a house and I had a scuzzy motel room. You had children and I had the air. You even had *my* child."

"You threw her away."

· · · · ·

89

"I know it. And I didn't want her. I really didn't. But I guess right then I just didn't want you to have her either."

"Why?"

" 'Cause when we were kids you got everything."

"Yeah. I got everything. I got to baby-sit all the rest of you. And wash the dishes and clean the house and wash the clothes and hang them on the line and bring them in and iron them. And I got to do my work and yours, too, because you were too busy being cute, and half the time I got to do Mom's on top of that because she was in bed having a sinus headache. When *I* have a sinus headache I go to work all the same. I remember the time I fainted into the clothes basket hanging clothes on the line when I was too sick to stand up and you were out with a boyfriend and Mom was in bed with a sinus headache and an illegal Darvocet Dad talked a druggist into giving him for her. And besides that I got to sit home every Friday night and bite my fingernails while you were already dating. So don't tell me I got everything. Come off it, Rhonda, okay?"

Rhonda burst out laughing. "We sound like a couple of ten-year-olds, don't we? Deb, I really am sorry. I was on cocaine and I was higher than a kite or I never would have done it. Stole your stuff, I mean. And I did try to get the ring back, but the guy had already sold it. And really I'm glad you kept Becky. At least I knew she was all right. That was why I didn't stay in touch—you didn't need me around."

"But I wouldn't have minded—" I began, not quite truthfully.

"You told me when you took her that I could come over and see her whenever I wanted to. But you would have minded, whatever you said. Anyway, when I saw her I felt so guilty. When I think that if that man hadn't heard her crying she'd have been squashed up in that trash compactor on the trucks . . . Deb, I'm glad you got her. And I was sorry I was such a shit. I didn't want to come over and confuse her."

"I'm sorry we didn't get along better," I answered. "Maybe if

. . . . .

we'd been better friends when we were kids we could have helped each other more."

"Yeah. Maybe." She lapsed back into silence.

"How are you feeling?" I asked finally.

"Not too bad, so far, most of the time anyway." After a moment or two or three, she added, "You know, I didn't even catch this the way you probably think I did."

"Oh?"

"I've been working in a restaurant, truck stop restaurant, the last seven years. I got too old for the business, Deb. You can't make decent money when you look like you been run over by a truck. And when I couldn't make 'em pay through the nose for it, it wasn't no more fun. Because gettin' paid, that was the only part of it I did like. Gettin' paid, and seein' the pantin' dickheads for the idiots they were. But I quit, as soon as I was expecting Toby, and I never did go back to it again. I stayed on welfare until about six months after Toby was born, and then I got the job in the restaurant. But then I got in a car wreck about five or six years ago, and I was hurt bad enough I had to have a blood transfusion. The doctor figured, later, that was when I got it."

"Well, I'm sorry you got it at all, however you got it." I wondered, vaguely, which one Toby was. I didn't think any of her boys had lived long enough to be named.

"Mom said you didn't want Cameron around me. I ain't gonna do nothing to Cameron."

Nothing except teach him to talk in ways that would get him in trouble in school, I thought, and wondered where on earth she had picked up that grammar. She didn't talk like that as a child. Oh, Texans have all kinds of ways of putting things that you don't hear newscasters using on television, like "might could," but we didn't say "ain't gonna" and "wasn't no" in the home we grew up in.

Maybe Mom was right. Maybe I did need to eat, because I realized that my mind was wandering even as I tried to carry on this

. . . . .

91

conversation, and without meaning to, I was listening absently to the sounds around me. Pat whined a little in the front yard. Our old cat Margaret Scratcher, probably up in the mesquite tree as she usually was, hissed at him. A car door slammed on the street outside. Probably in the neighbor's yard, I thought, and was sure of it when I heard footsteps outside where my bedroom window was, not more than six feet from the neighbor's kitchen window, with the fence chastely between us. A gate rattled.

I still hadn't said anything, and I realized it. "I didn't think you'd deliberately hurt him," I said. "It was just that you were so careless when Vicky was a baby."

"How long ago was Vicky a baby?" she answered. "I don't carry kids around in pillowcases no more. And do I look like having a boyfriend with a convertible? Even if I did, I use seat belts now. See, my last baby, Toby, I kept."

"I didn't know—"

"I know you didn't know. I didn't tell Mom, and don't you tell her neither. See, Toby's daddy, he was black, and I knew Mom would have forty-nine fits."

That was probably true. Mom hadn't complained to me about my Cherokee, Comanche, and Korean children, and had at least formally accepted them as her grandchildren, but I knew she'd had quite a lot to say to her friends, including the often-repeated explanation that of course I wasn't *really* their mother, I'd just adopted them. If Rhonda had shown up with Toby and tried to introduce him as Mom's grandchild, Mom would have gone into a rapid decline.

"And Toby's daddy, he paid me some child support, you know, and like I said, I got the job in the restaurant then, and I got me a car. Not a real *good* car—I paid two hundred dollars for it—but most of the time it ran. But Toby didn't like seat belts, and so I didn't make him wear 'em. And then the winter he was two we had an ice storm and I *had* to go to work, ice storm or no, and I was trying to take Toby to the baby-sitter and skidded real bad and

. . . . .

92

hit a telephone pole and the door popped open and Toby, he flew out on his head."

"That was the wreck you got the blood transfusion after?" I asked.

"Yeah. And it wasn't till a week later they told me Toby was dead."

"Rhonda, I'm so sorry."

She shrugged. "He's probably better off without me as a mom. I was a pretty lousy mom. I used to leave him alone at night, sometimes, when I wanted to go out and get a beer. And I yelled all the time, and I'd hit him when I was mad at somebody else, and that kind of thing. I really felt crummy about it after he was dead. You tell Becky she's better off—where *is* Becky?" She looked around as if expecting to see her.

"She's married, Rhonda," I said. "She's been married for years. She's got three children and is expecting another."

"Three? At her age? And one in the oven? She's as bad off as me!" Rhonda sounded scandalized.

"The oldest is adopted," I hastened to explain. "Originally her husband's half brother. And believe me, they can afford as many as they want. Her husband's pretty well off."

That was an understatement. But somehow I felt it might not be a good idea to let Rhonda know the daughter she'd thrown away was married to a very rich man.

"Well, I'm glad things went okay for her," Rhonda said, sounding uninterested. "They never did for me."

"And nothing you decided had anything to do with that," I said tartly.

She glared at me, half rising from the chair. "Deb, if what happened to me as a kid had happened to you—"

"Nothing happened to you that didn't happen to me," I retorted.

"The hell it didn't!" she yelled. "Don't you know what that son of a bitch we called *Daddy* did to me?"

"I didn't know," I said, "but I can sure guess. I'll bet nothing

. . . . .

93

started happening to you until after I got married. He started in on me when I was nine. I got married when I was nineteen. Ten years, Rhonda, ten years of it that I tried as hard as I could to put out of my mind—not that I ever really succeeded. That didn't mean I had to throw myself into the garbage can. And you didn't have to either. You decided to."

"Oh, shit." She sat down again. "He told me he'd done it to you, too, but I didn't believe him. He told me you didn't care so I shouldn't neither."

"The hell I didn't care," I said. "I did too care. And he knew it."

"Then why'd you let him do it?"

"Oh, come off it, Rhonda. What was I going to do about it? Report him to the police? I was the oldest kid in the family. There were Jim, and Andy, and you, and Mark, and Skipper. And Mom couldn't even drive back then, much less hold down a job. And her parents were dead and his parents couldn't possibly have supported all of us, even if they would have been willing, which they probably wouldn't have been in a case like that. Was I supposed to cause us all to start living in a teepee to get him off my back?"

"I never looked at it that way," Rhonda muttered. "But couldn't you have made him leave me alone?"

"I tried to," I said. "I told him you didn't have the emotional maturity I had. I told him you'd flip out. He told me he'd leave you alone."

"Well, he didn't."

"I'm sorry," I said. "I really am, Rhonda. And I did try. If you'd told me, I'd have found a way to let you come and live with us. Harry'd have allowed that, then."

"Well, I didn't know it."

"I asked you about ten hundred times to tell me if there was anything wrong. I told you you could come and live with us if there was."

"I didn't know you meant that."

. . . . .

94

"I did. But look," I added, "please don't talk about it around Harry, because I never told him and I don't want him to know about it."

She shrugged. "He won't be hearing it from me. I just . . . wanted to talk with you, that's all. Because if it hadn't been for that I'd of been okay."

"Rhonda," I said, "estimates differ, but the most likely figure is that some sort of sex crime happens to one woman in four in this country. Not all of them as bad as what we got, but some of them a hell of a lot worse. And you can't tell me one woman in four winds up making the decisions you made."

"But I was frail."

"You decided to be frail," I retorted. "Dammit, woman, you know more judo than I do, and I'm a cop!"

"I had to learn to protect myself! And don't tell me you haven't been careful to protect yourself."

That silenced me. I was fairly certain that Rhonda had put her finger on the initial reason I had decided to become a cop. Because as a cop I could carry a gun, as a cop I would learn to protect myself. Yes, and my children, too, if necessary.

In the silence, I could hear the car starting again outside. Whoever it was hadn't stayed long. Not that that was any concern of mine.

I looked back at Rhonda, to see that she was losing what color she had left. "I'm sorry, Deb," she said, "you got somewhere I can lie down? All of a sudden I—"

"Yeah, sure," I said. "Hal's got the front bedroom now. Or Cameron's got the middle bedroom—"

"I'll just use the couch, if that's okay."

I remembered Vicky lying back on the couch before Barry was born, saying, "Mom, you've got the most comfortable couch in the world," and now Barry was almost five. "Yeah, use the couch," I said.

As Rhonda departed, I reached over to the shelf where my pain

· · · · ·

95

pills were, and then pulled my hand back. I felt like I was due another one, but by the clock I didn't need one.

And obviously I didn't, because with Rhonda now sleeping on the couch, the dog outside, and the cat cuddled up against me purring, I slept again, to wake an indeterminate amount of time later and hear Mom saying, "I locked the dog in the backyard and put your lunch beside you. It's covered, so flies can't get on it, and it'll keep until you're ready for it. Rhonda and Cameron are in the car. I'm taking him home; you can't possibly take care of him. Debra, I've got to ask you . . . Rhonda's been telling me the most awful things about your dad. They're not true, are they?"

I sat up. In a loud, harsh voice I scarcely recognized as my own, I said, "Let the past be past." Rather more prosaically, I added, "Leave the front door open. I'll be all right. Pat's in the yard."

But after she left, silently, I sat up for a long time thinking—thinking, and feeling like a worm.

I remembered asking Sandy Miller, in this very room, not twenty-four hours ago, "Who did you tell?" as if she should have told somebody.

But who did I tell?

My sister. Today.

Nobody else at all, ever.

. . . . .

Six

. . . .

A BABY EAGLET SAT *in a nest made of twigs and sticks, lodged on an inaccessible cliff. Its fluffy down was insufficient for flight, so it was wholly dependent on whatever nourishment its parents carried to the nest. The father eagle landed and brought it a snake—not a small snake, just enough for an eaglet to swallow, but a full-grown snake—and the eaglet was frightened. It pecked timorously at the snake, looking furtively at the father eagle, and then it saw that unless it ate the snake it would have no other nourishment. So it tried to swallow the serpent, headfirst as eaglets must do, but it gagged as the snake spat poison.*

Then I saw that it was not an eaglet but my sister Rhonda, looking about fourteen, crouched naked in the eagle's nest. "Swallow it," the eagle ordered. "Swallow it, I say."

Oprah Winfrey was there and I was there, on opposite sides of the nest. I was the middle-aged woman I am now, and Oprah was her present sturdy, well-groomed self. Working together, we tried to wrestle away the snake that Rhonda was gagging on. But the father eagle pecked furiously at both of us, as the mother eagle sat complacently with its head turned, pretending not to see. "Fight, Rhonda," I cried, and grabbed again to pull the snake out of my sister's mouth, but she seemed too terrified to fight.

But I could not fight, because I had a cast on my foot that made me as helpless as I had been at fourteen, and the father eagle was far stronger than I. He was advancing threateningly on me, bringing me a snake to eat, and I was no longer a middle-aged woman who knew karate, a cop who had a pistol and a shotgun and knew how to use them, but a frightened

. . . . .

twelve-year-old—was I this small when I was twelve, I don't remember being this small—and I cowered back in the nest beside my sister because I didn't want to eat the snake and I didn't know how to escape and I began to scream but I could scream only soundlessly because if I screamed aloud something awful would happen, and then I knew if I ate this snake and didn't keep gagging as I was gagging now I would not have to eat other snakes and I would grow up and get away from the isolated nest on the barren crag and then I would be safe, and I tried to tell Rhonda we'll get away, we'll get away, but Rhonda couldn't hear me and then suddenly Rhonda gulped down the snake, and swallowed another, and another, as the father eagle shrieked with rage and the mother eagle cowered against the side of the cliff.

And then I was older, I was twenty-one and Rhonda was sixteen and she was failing in school and I asked her if she wanted to come live with Harry and me, but she couldn't answer because her mouth was full of snakes and I could see their tails wriggling outside her mouth as she tried to swallow two snakes, four snakes, seven snakes all at once and Rhonda kept on gulping and more and more snakes ran to be eaten, until the world was full of snakes that Rhonda had swallowed and her skin grew great purple blotches from the poison the snakes spat in her mouth, and Oprah Winfrey and I retreated from the onslaught of snakes, both of us panting and gasping from the poison the snakes had spewed on us, the skin of our hands raw and bleeding where the snakes had bitten us, and Oprah said, "We've lost this child, but we will save others."

"But my sister," I cried, "do we have to lose my sister?"

"She's gone already," Oprah said. "It's time now for us to see to the ones we can save."

"I won't give up on my sister," I cried, and tried to run back through the wilderness crawling with snakes to reach Rhonda, but now Harry, and my children and my grandchildren, and even Captain Millner and Sgt. Rafe Permut had joined Oprah to pull me back away from the hissing, spitting serpents.

"She's lost," they told me, "leave her now and save those whom you still can save."

. . . . .

When I turned to look back I saw that Rhonda was virtually invisible, buried under a mass of serpents, which she eagerly ate one after another, while the father eagle and the mother eagle flew about pecking futilely on first one snake and then another. "I only told you to eat one," the father eagle cried. "I didn't mean for you to eat them all."

I didn't mean . . . I didn't mean . . . I didn't mean . . .

And under the mass of snakes Rhonda's skin was purple and her hair was falling out.

"Deb, Deb, what's wrong?"

I sat up before I knew I was awake, to find myself looking straight at Matilda Greenwood in buckskin and beads, her hair braided and down over her shoulder, with thin leather binding wrapped around the lower two inches of the braids and one small eagle feather plaited into the right braid, like a mythical Indian princess. I put my hands in front of my face, trying to shut out the memory of the thousands of writhing serpents, and Matilda said, "Bad dream?"

I nodded, still with my hands in front of my face, feeling myself dripping with sweat.

"I was about to knock on the door when I heard you scream, and the door was unlocked so I just came on in." She walked closer to my bedside and picked up my prescriptions, turning the bottle so she could read the labels. "Yeah, some of this stuff will give you lollapaloozas."

"It's not just the medicine," I said.

"You want to talk about it?"

"I've got to go to the bathroom first."

I absolutely refuse to crawl in front of my husband or my mother, and of course I use the crutches to go to the living room in front of everybody, but I didn't feel the least bit embarrassed to crawl to the bathroom in front of Matilda, who said nothing but, "That's one way to do it."

After flushing, I managed to pull myself upright in front of the long counter. I washed my face and, for good measure, my arms

. . . . .

and underarms and even ran a washcloth over my hair several times, rinsing it repeatedly and feeling thankful that I had remembered to get my hair cut last week. Then I grabbed a paper cup and drank about a gallon of water—well, actually probably about a quart, but it felt like a gallon—and then crawled back to bed.

The sheets were soaked. I must have been sweating even more heavily than I had realized. "You want to tell me where the clean sheets are?" Matilda asked, spotting my problem.

"In the top of my closet. The front one in the corner of the bathroom. I mean the one in the front corner of the bathroom." Our bathroom—Harry's and mine, not the kids'—is laid out in a peculiar manner. It is a wide rectangle, not quite a square. The door from the bedroom to the bathroom is in the front corner of one long side. Going on down that long side is a counter with two sinks and a lot of storage space, followed by a partial wall about a third of the width of the room with the toilet on the other side of it, crammed into a corner with a little window set in the wall midway between the toilet and the door to Harry's closet, a walk-in square fitting into the opposite long side. It's followed by the bathtub, which in turn is followed by my closet, another walk-in square exactly the size of Harry's closet, only facing the bedroom door instead of the toilet. The bathroom floor is carpeted except for a neat half oval directly beside the bathtub, which is some kind of superlinoleum. There's a towel rack on the short wall beside my closet for bath towels and a small towel rack below the one window for hand towels. Above the counter the half wall facing the bathtub is entirely mirrored, a fact that resulted in my losing about thirty pounds very quickly as soon as we moved into that house.

Matilda went and got the sheets. "Can you manage," she asked, "or would you like help?"

"I can manage," I said, which was probably very stupid. In fact, it was definitely very stupid, and I almost immediately changed my mind. If you have ever tried to change the sheets in a bed that you are occupying, with one foot in a cast and so sore that every nerve

· · · · ·

yells bloody murder every time you either move or touch the entire leg, you will never want to do it again.

After remaking the bed with me in it, far more deftly than I have ever accomplished such a task when one of my children was sick, Matilda asked, "Where's the washer? If you go on sweating like that you'll need these again before you know it."

I told her, and she went casually—a friend, not a mother—to stick the sheets into the washer and then return to park herself in the chair Rhonda had used earlier.

It wasn't until then that I really noticed her outfit. "You look gorgeous," I said. "You must have a sitting tonight."

"Uh-uh," she said, and stretched her hands over her head. "There was an intertribal powwow today in Grand Prairie. I'll be going back over there after a while, but I wanted to come see you."

"Oh, gosh," I said disgustedly, "I've missed the powwow then."

There is, in Grand Prairie—which is neither grand nor a prairie (though it is located on that vast expanse of limestone, covered by the thick fertile black muck that limestone decays into, called by Texans the Blackland Prairies), but rather a bedroom community near Arlington, about midway between Dallas and Fort Worth—a flea market that bills itself as the world's largest. That may or may not be true; what is true is that I have made numerous interesting finds there—most of them interesting for personal reasons, a few for official reasons—and that the large amphitheater there at various times houses rodeos, auctions, and the intertribal powwow, which is held annually at various times during the year. It's a really important powwow, attracting dancers, drums (a term that refers not only to the instrument but also to the group of musicians who play and sing), artists, artisans, and traders throughout the North American continent.

Although I am not Native American, my two daughters are three-quarters Cherokee and half Comanche respectively, so I try to go to the powwow every time it's held, and when they were smaller I always took them. At one powwow I purchased a glorious

· · · · ·

etching by Archie Black Owl, which my husband would probably kill me if he knew I paid two hundred and thirty-five dollars for, and I always check out the artists, artisans, and traders and watch the dancing, which is terrific. Matilda, who is Comanche, dances very well. My daughter Becky, who is half Comanche, admires her greatly and wants to learn, if she can ever stop being pregnant long enough, which at times I wonder about.

"I didn't tell you when it was," Matilda said. "I knew you couldn't go, so why make you feel guilty? And what in the world is the matter with that cat? Is she seeing ghosts?"

Remaking the bed had dislodged Rags, and after a quick nibble, sip, and visit to the cat box, Rags had returned to the dresser and was now staring intently at nothing at all. "If she's seeing ghosts they're the ghosts of a tomato plant," I explained, and Matilda laughed delightedly.

"Too bad you can't explain," she said, and I fervently agreed.

We drifted on into a conversation about anything and nothing; she didn't ask again about my dreams and I didn't explain. Then the phone rang, and I leaned awkwardly to answer it. It was Captain Millner.

"I debated whether to call you or not," he said. "I figured if you hear it first from the news you'll call me breathing fire, so I better call you, but I'm giving you a direct order, you are not to try to do *one thing* about it. The department is on it and we'll handle it."

"All right," I said meekly.

"I don't trust that tone of voice," he said.

"Use your own judgment," I answered. "But right now it's all I can do to get from the bed to the bathroom. What's the problem?"

"Doreen Miller is missing."

He had my full attention.

"The funeral was pretty early this morning," he said, "and after the funeral the family went home and stayed home. I guess everybody was sitting around being formal, you know how nobody ever

. . . . .

knows what to do after a funeral. After a while Doreen asked to go to a friend's place because she said the visit might make her feel better. Her father had gone out to check on pending business mail at his office, and her mother consented but told her to be back home in two hours. She didn't show up, and when her father got home and started throwing a fit and demanding to know where Doreen was, her mother called the friend."

"And?" I said.

"And Doreen had never gone there. Furthermore, she hadn't been expected there. So then Mrs. Miller called all Doreen's other friends and none of them had seen her."

"Any clothes missing?"

"Her mother checked her closet and says no. Now, listen, Deb, we don't have any reason at all to suspect a snatch. She went missing voluntarily, even if she didn't take any clothes with her. Her mother's sure of that—says Doreen had saved about fifty dollars out of her allowance, planning to buy some clothes her daddy didn't approve of, and that money's gone, along with her cosmetics and several of her favorite audio discs. That says she left on her own, taking with her as much as she felt she could walk past her mother unnoticed. We'll find her."

"I'm sure you will," I said.

"Take care of yourself," he said. "I'll talk to you later."

"Uh-huh." I hung up and lay back.

"Trouble?" Matilda asked.

"I think so." And before I knew it, I found myself telling her everything Sandy had told me. "I don't know why she'd do it now, right after telling me," I finished, "but I'm sure she did."

"Are you?" Matilda said. "I'm not. Have you thought of calling her and asking?"

"I don't have her phone number."

"You told me Hal does."

"But Hal's not at home."

"True," Matilda agreed, "but I'll bet he didn't take Sandy

· · · · ·

Miller's phone number with him when he went to take his girl-friend to the zoo or wherever they went."

That was a point I hadn't thought of, and I told Matilda where Hal's room was. Beyond the location of the room, I hadn't the least idea where the phone number might be.

She was back within about one minute, which is record time for anybody looking for anything in Hal's room. "On his dresser," she announced, looking rather pleased, and handed it to me.

I don't know whether I expected Sandy to answer. She didn't, but her answering machine did, with a coy-voiced, but reasonably dignified, message. "This is Sandy, and I can't get to the phone right now. But if you'll leave your name and number I'll call you right back. If you don't want to leave your name and number, try me again soon. Bye now."

"Sandy, this is Deb Ralston. It's Saturday at about"—I glanced at the clock—"four in the afternoon. Please call me as soon as you get the chance. This is urgent." I gave her my phone number in case she'd forgotten it, although it hadn't changed since the days when she called Becky two or three times a day, and then hung up.

"She's not there, but that doesn't mean anything," I told Matilda earnestly. "I mean, if she was there she could be by herself or she could have Doreen with her. And since she's not there, or at least not answering the phone, she can still be by herself or have Doreen with her."

"True," Matilda said, and stretched all over like a cat, looking critically at the beading on the toe of one moccasin and then glancing at her watch. "I've got to get on back. I would offer to ask the spirits about Doreen," she added, "but I'll bet you don't want me to."

That is the one bone of contention between Matilda and me. Matilda insists she is a medium, or channeler, or something like that. I do not believe in mediums, channelers, or anything like that. Matilda has invited me to watch a session, which she does not call a séance. I do not want to watch a session, whether it is called a

. . . . .

séance or not. I do not want to see a friend doing something I consider to be idiotic.

"At least you get the names right," I offered.

Matilda grinned at that; she and I had recently had a discussion about so-called mediums with so-called Indian guides who had named their Indian guides names that no Native American tribe either Matilda or I knew anything about had ever used.

"Okay," she said, "but if I hear anything I'll tell you anyway."

"I'd be grateful for any possibilities," I agreed.

"No matter what the source?"

"No matter what the source."

She departed, leaving the door unlocked. I heard her talking briefly to Pat outside, and it occurred to me to wonder why he wasn't howling by now, if he couldn't get into the backyard, where his food and water were. "Matilda," I called, hoping she could hear me.

"Yup?"

"Will you open the gate to let Pat into the backyard?"

"Gate's open," she called back. "I'm off."

That was a little bit of a mystery—who had opened the gate, and why? But of course Harry might not have closed it this morning, considering that he was putting Pat inside the house with me. No, that couldn't be right, because he'd had to close the gates early this morning in case the mail came early.

Oh, well. Not my problem. And by now I really *was* due another pain pill. I took it and then investigated the covered plate my mother had left for me.

Roast beef sandwich, with mustard and pickles. Homemade pickles. She must have brought them with her; I haven't made any in the last couple of years because I've been too busy coping with Cameron. Potato salad, also homemade. She must have brought that with her also. I was surprised, but also grateful, that the cat hadn't discovered the roast beef.

I ate fast, before the pain pills had time to take effect and dull my

· · · · ·

105

appetite as well as my pain. I was through and just about to doze off when the phone rang.

"This is Sandy Miller." She sounded cool and collected.

"Do you know where Doreen is?" I demanded at once.

"Doreen? I suppose she's at home, why?"

She was just a little too cool and collected. "I think you know why," I told her.

"What are you talking about?" She was a little sharper now, but there was no fear, no worry, in her voice at all.

I supposed I'd have to play along. "My captain called me," I said. "Doreen left today to go to a friend's house. She never got there. She wasn't expected there. She also never got home. Sandy, if you know where she is—"

"If I knew where she was," Sandy said, still coolly, "I certainly wouldn't tell you, because you'd tell your bosses and they'd go get her and send her back home. So little Doreen got smart and got out . . . Well, I'm proud of her for doing it. But I don't have her."

"Sandy," I said, slightly ashamed of the desperation I could hear in my voice, "even if I don't mention you to Captain Millner—and I won't, because he told me to stay out of the situation—somebody is going to, and somebody will be over to your apartment with a search warrant."

"I don't have her," Sandy said again. "They can search all they want to. They won't find her here. They won't find her, or her clothes, or her purse, or even her fingerprints, not in my apartment and not in my car. I don't have her. I haven't seen her in months."

"But I think you know where she is."

"If I do," Sandy said again, "I wouldn't tell you. But I will tell you this. Don't worry about her." She hung up.

It would be easier for me not to worry about Doreen, I thought as I lay back again, if I had some vague idea where she was.

But by now the pain pill was taking hold, and my mind was getting a little fuzzy again.

. . . . .

I had no idea what time it was. Harry was obviously in the living room, as CNN was on and Hal never watches news. I wondered why he hadn't come in to speak to me, but then I realized, of course, he still thought I was asleep. "Harry," I called.

He didn't hear me, and I was sick of the bed anyway. But I wasn't going to crawl into the living room. I got up, found the crutches, which I was going to have to learn to use if I expected to get back to work anytime in the next month, and made my extremely awkward and wobbly way into the living room. "Harry?" I said.

He turned and looked at me. He looked tired, worried.

"Are you okay?" I asked.

"I ought to be asking you that."

"I'm supposed to feel crummy right now. But there's no reason you—"

"I'm okay." He glanced back, once, at the television screen and then turned it off with the remote. "Hal called a while ago."

"I must have been sleeping soundly. I never heard the phone."

"You were totally out of it. I went in and hung your spider plant and you never even stirred. Anyway, Hal and Lori are over at the bishop's house for supper. They'll be home later. You want anything?"

"No," I said honestly, "but I guess I need to eat whether I want to or not."

"I'll see what I can come up with."

He headed for the kitchen and I stared after him. He was upset about something, worried about something, and it was pretty obvious he wasn't going to tell me what. But whatever it was, it made him seem older than he was. The gray at his temples that normally went unnoticed seemed to stand out, and his face was drawn and somehow gaunt even though there couldn't possibly have been any change in his weight since morning.

· · · · ·

★ ★ ★

No, of course I didn't go to church. Although I've got to the point that I go whenever I get the chance, I'm still not a member. Nobody—not even Hal—nags me about that. I think Hal would, but somebody must have told him not to.

All the same, all three members of the bishopric came to visit me Sunday afternoon. I should explain that the Mormon church doesn't have a pastor; a member of the congregation—which is called the ward—is called to serve as bishop for however long they want him to serve (I'm told the usual period is about five years). He doesn't preach every Sunday, and he doesn't spend all his time doing church things. He keeps his regular job, and two counselors, both of whom keep their regular jobs also, assist him. On Sunday morning there are usually two or three speakers selected from the congregation (in advance, so they will have time to think of something to say).

Every family in the church has home teachers—a pair of men—assigned to it, and if there is a woman church member in the family they also have visiting teachers—a pair of women—assigned. Although I am not a member, I get visiting teachers all the same, and actually I think it's pretty nice to have somebody who will come and visit me when I'm feeling cruddy and not want to do anything but be helpful. I am told that effectively this has all the women in the church going around teaching the same lesson to one another. But the real purpose of the home teachers and visiting teachers isn't teaching; it's to spread among everyone the work of pastoral care that in a regular church is done by one or two people. If somebody is mildly ill, their home teachers will come and visit.

If a woman is too ill to cook and has no adolescent daughter at home who is likely to be up to doing the cooking, her visiting teachers will tell the Relief Society—that's the women's organization—and somebody in the Relief Society will arrange to have dinners brought in until the woman is on her feet again. Harry and I discovered that about fifteen minutes after he ordered pizza

. . . . .

Saturday night, when somebody came in to bring us a delicious chicken casserole, full of chunks of white meat and noodles and shredded carrots. Harry ate the pizza anyway, but I gobbled the casserole. They promised to bring in dinner for at least the next week, and longer if we needed it, and asked me to promise to call if I needed any other help.

I expected that was the only call we would get, as our home teachers—at Hal's request—had come and given me a blessing before the surgery. But apparently if somebody has had surgery, the whole bishopric comes to visit.

And there the whole bishopric was, at three o'clock on Sunday afternoon, with Harry in the living room in paint-stained khaki pants and a T-shirt and me in bed in yellow polyester shorts and my old Tienenman Square T-shirt.

It could have been worse. I could have been in bed in panties and bra. Of course in that case they would have waited in the living room with Harry, who wasn't any too pleased about the invasion but didn't dare say so lest he wind up having to cook, until I had time to dress.

They didn't stay long. I was rather glad, because I was feeling sort of like a wrung-out dishrag and besides that I was embarrassed at the bishop—who happens to be a fellow police officer—and his two counselors, one of them a Frito-Lay delivery man and one of them an accountant, catching me in bed, though of course my being in bed was exactly why they had come. Lying down when other people are standing up always seems to put one so much at a disadvantage.

"What's wrong with that cat?" the bishop asked, as he stood to leave.

Rags was now sitting on my dresser staring fixedly at the spider plant.

"She's trying to figure out how a tomato plant on the dresser turned into a spider plant hanging from the ceiling," I said. "I think the poor animal is having a nervous breakdown. I thought the

· · · · ·

spider plant would help, but it seems to be making matters worse."

"She'll cheer up. Now, you call us if you need anything, and I mean it."

"I will," I said. "But Harry's pretty competent."

Harry grinned weakly and shook hands with all three men, solemnly, one at a time. After they left, he sat back down to watch whatever it was he was watching on television and I tried to settle down with *Clan of the Cave Bear* and ignore the discordances coming from the garage, where Hal and Lori were practicing so loudly they hadn't even known the bishopric came to visit.

The phone rang just as I was finishing the chicken and noodle casserole and kind of hoping we wouldn't get chicken again tomorrow night. I let Harry answer it, for all the good that did. He called, "For you. It's Jim." And then he closed the door so that he could hear the television better, because for some reason discussions between Jim and me tend to get a little noisy.

Jim is my brother. He is two years younger than I am, and he is a lawyer down in Houston. Unlike my other brothers, who most of the time are pretty decent, most of the time he is kind of a horse's rear end. He certainly was one tonight. "What have you been doing to upset Mom?" he demanded as soon as I said hi.

"I haven't been doing anything to upset Mom," I retorted, "and I haven't the slightest idea what you're talking about."

"I called her while ago and she was boo-hooing all over the place, saying you and Rhonda were telling her all kinds of awful stuff about Dad."

"I didn't tell her anything about Dad," I said. "She asked me, but I didn't tell her."

"Well, she's got it in her head that you and Rhonda are saying Dad molested you."

"Rhonda said it. I didn't. Probably I should have, because it's perfectly true."

"Bullshit!" he yelled. "Dad wouldn't have dreamed of doing

• • • • •

110

anything like that. What the hell kind of bandwagon are you jumping on now? The latest fad? Oprah Winfrey says she was molested, so Roseanne Barr—"

"Roseanne Arnold," I interrupted.

"Roseanne Barr says she was molested, so now you—"

"I don't know for sure whether Oprah Winfrey and Roseanne Arnold were molested," I said, "because I didn't work the cases. However, I have no reason to doubt that they are telling the truth. And I damn well know for sure that *I* was molested."

"Ever since you got on that feminist bandwagon—"

"Just what bandwagon is that?" I demanded. "I don't even think I know what a feminist is."

"If you damn women would just stay home like you ought to and take care of your children—"

"I take care of my children, at least the ones who are still of an age to need to be taken care of. Look, don't blame me if the economy has gotten so screwed up it takes two incomes—"

"*My* family doesn't need two incomes—"

"Well, whoop-de-doo. Getting criminals off pays pretty well, doesn't it?" I said spitefully.

"You damn cops are all alike—"

"Aren't we a long way off the original discussion?" I asked. "You called to accuse me of upsetting Mom. Well, if I upset her maybe it was past time for her to be upset, because she might not have known what was going on, but if she didn't, it was because she chose not to. If she'd even made the ghost of an effort to protect Rhonda and me—"

"You're so damn busy meeting your own agenda you can't even think about the family, can you?" Jim yelled.

"What family?" I yelled back. "I have a husband and four children. They're my family."

"I'm talking about your family of origin. That should matter, too!"

. . . . .

"Right, if it matters to you so much why did you move down there to Houston?"

"Because that's where my job—"

"Right," I said more softly. "That's where your work was. You're setting your own family's agenda, you and Marilyn. At least I hope Marilyn has some say in deciding what goes on. Well, guess what, Harry and I decide how our family is supposed to work. That's my family, my husband and my children and my grandchildren. My job is none of your business. As for the past, I'm telling you that Dad molested me until about six weeks before I married Harry, and after that he started in on Rhonda. I sort of halfway got over it, at least enough to function normally. Rhonda didn't. And if you'll check you'll find that just about one hundred percent of the people in Rhonda's profession started out being molested by somebody in their own family."

"Just because she was too lazy to go out and get a real job—"

"Sure, every woman walking the street for five bucks a lay and risking murder or AIDS every time she does it is lazy. You ever stop to think maybe she's desperate? Maybe she's too ignorant to find anything else. Maybe she feels so shitty about herself, because every man she's ever known in her life including her father and brothers treat her like a piece of meat, that she thinks she's not fit to do anything else. If you bastards that patronize prostitutes—"

"Don't include me in that—"

"*Bullshit!*" I yelled, goaded a little too far. "Don't tell me you don't. I was at Astroworld one time with you and Marilyn and a bunch of kids, yours and ours both, and a buddy of yours ran into you and you and he got to talking and you took off with him to go to this real nice 'house' he knew about, leaving Marilyn there with two children and her about eight months pregnant."

I paused to get my breath, with the memory vivid in front of me: the children asking who lived there, and the men snickering and saying "Just a lady."

. . . . .

The children, as children will, saying they wanted to go, too, and Marilyn angrily answering, "She isn't a nice lady."

My brother had finally refound his voice. "I told Marilyn I was just going with him, I wasn't going to do anything—"

"And I really truly believe that, especially when you came back looking like the cat that swallowed the cream. Marilyn cried for three hours. If I had been her I'd have shot you. I wonder, why are you defending Dad so much? Maybe I ought to talk to *your* daughters."

"You bitch, if you get near my kids I'll take a shotgun to you!"

He slammed the phone down, and I resolved to call my nieces the first time I knew he was in court out of town and wouldn't be there to keep the phone away from them.

I'd never before suspected him of molesting them; it would never have occurred to me before to wonder. But his reaction to Mom's phone call, his attitude during this conversation, really had me wondering.

I didn't want to believe any such thing . . . but my mother didn't want to believe any such thing about my father, either.

Unfortunately, if I did ask, I'd get the same answer whether anything was going on or not. My nieces would deny it, just as I would have denied anything was happening when I was their age.

·　·　·　·　·

$\mathscr{S}\varepsilon\upsilon\varepsilon n$

. . . . . .

THE HELL YOU'RE going to work!" Harry shouted.

I was astonished by his anger: I'd thought I was being perfectly reasonable. But by now I was angry myself, having explained—twice—what I was trying to do. "I'd rather go to work than sit here and be bored to death," I retorted, "and if you won't take me, I'll call somebody from the department to come get me. Look, it's not as if I were trying to be there all day. I know I can't do that yet. But you're going to the library as soon as it opens to sit up there and do research on your paper, and you can drop me by the department . . ."

Never mind the rest of the discussion. Suffice it to say that Harry parked in a loading zone in front of the police station to help me and my crutches get up the stairs before he drove off, in a considerable huff, to the library parking lot.

Captain Millner wasn't much better. He spotted me as soon as I got off the elevator and inquired, with a certain relish in his tone, "Just what do you think you're doing here?"

"I work here," I said.

"Ri-i-ight," he said. "Well, go home when you feel like it, which from the looks of you I would say would be soon."

Of course, I was a little pale and sweaty. What would you expect, when I had just navigated the sidewalk, the stairs, and an expanse of lobby on these dumb crutches before ever reaching the elevator? But simple logic would point out that it would take more

. . . . .

effort now for me to leave than for me to stay here. I said that, and Captain Millner snorted. "You're the hardest-headed broad I know," he said. "All right, have it your own way, but don't say I told you to."

"I wouldn't dream of it. By the way, have you heard anything about Doreen Miller?"

"She's still missing. Deb, stay out of it, will you? I know how you feel about the case. That's why I'm asking you to stay out of it. She went missing on her own, and I'm about a hundred percent certain she's okay. Now will you get your ass home?"

"No, I will not," I answered. "Anyway, I can't. Harry drove me here, and he already left." Captain Millner shrugged and headed for the men's room, and I made my way on toward my office.

Rafe Permut does not know me as well as Captain Millner does; therefore he was less rude. He did, however, raise both eyebrows and ask, "Are you sure you know what you're doing?"

"I'm sure," I said.

"Well, if you start to fall out, go find a place to lie down."

"I'm not going to fall out," I said. "If I just knew how to use these stinking crutches better . . ." Then I spotted something. "I wonder—will you push that library stool over here?"

A library stool—which we normally use for getting down things stored in places the shorter ones of us can't reach—has rollers on the bottom so that it can roll in any direction you want it to roll. And the top of a library stool is almost exactly the height of the bottom of my knee. What I was thinking was, if I bent my leg at the knee and rested the knee on the library stool, I could get around that way, rolling my nonfunctional leg, instead of having to wobble around on crutches.

It worked marvelously well, and to be honest, wearing my normal clothes—well, sort of normal, I had found out I could not get my slacks on over my cast, and so I was wearing a pleated skirt I normally wear only to church—and sitting up instead of lying down in shorts and T-shirt was terrific, even if I had been reduced

. . . . .

to carrying my pistol in my bag. A shoulder holster does not work with crutches. It felt like more than three days since I had been away; three days spent under anesthesia, or in bed with pain pills, or coping with Mom and Rhonda, are much longer than three days spent running errands and doing things with my family. I sailed on through the pile in my in-basket, which is no smaller in the Sex Crimes Unit than it is in the Major Case Squad (why "unit" for one and "squad" for the other, I wondered but did not ask), and then headed for the rest room. I glided past Captain Millner, who was in the hall on the way to court, and he yelled after me, "Hey, Deb, has anyone ever told you that you look just like Captain Ahab on a roller skate?"

Of course, I ignored him. Wouldn't you? However, I had begun to notice that my knee was getting sore. The corrugated top of a library stool was made for shod feet, not bare knees. While I was in the rest room I folded a handful of paper towels and put them on the stool for my knee to rest on.

About noon, Rafe stood up and walked over to my desk, where I was studying all the reports of all the Super Glue rapes looking for patterns. "Deb, I'm still not sure you ought to be here," he said. "Are you really up to working? If you're not, tell me so now, and I'll find another female from somewhere."

"Like who?" I asked.

"Margie Herrera, from Juvenile. I'm kind of thinking of trying to get her in our next opening, so it would make sense for her to fill in while you're under the weather—"

Now, why couldn't he and Captain Millner have decided that without picking me for this slot? But I knew why, because I know the size Juvenile is and the caseload they have. "Leaving a big hole in Juvenile, and they're understaffed anyway."

He shrugged. "So are we all. How about it?"

"I can understand your concern," I said, "and if I decide I can't work I'll let you know. But right now—"

. . . . .

"Okay," he said. "I'm going to lunch. Bring you back anything?"

"A hamburger and a vanilla shake," I said, and went back to the reports for about three minutes before the telephone rang. "Deb?" said the switchboard operator. "I wasn't sure you'd be in. You've got a call. Hold on. Go ahead, ma'am."

"Mrs. Ralston?" said the next voice.

"I'm here." The voice was vaguely familiar, but I didn't tie a face to it.

"I'm Laura Washington. I don't know if you remember me—"

"Of course I do." I sat up straighter, reaching for a pen and scratch paper. "What can I do for you?"

"I'm . . . Remember I told you I'm a retired schoolteacher? Well, I came in today to substitute—there's a citywide meeting going on and about half the teachers are gone to it, and they used a lot of substitutes today—and I think you better come out here."

"I've had surgery on my foot," I said, "and—"

"Mrs. Ralston, I hate to ask you, but I really think you better come out here anyway."

She sounded extremely distraught, and from what I'd seen of Laura Washington, I wouldn't pick her as the sort of person who would get very distraught. "What's the problem?" I asked. "Should I send a uniform car to hold the fort till I get there?"

"No, it's . . . nothing's going to happen right now. But I've called a social worker. And the child's mother. And . . . maybe you'd better bring a juvenile officer, too. It's . . . I don't want to talk about it on the phone. I'm in the office. But . . . maybe somebody else could handle it, I don't know, but from what I've seen of you, I'd rather it was you. So . . ."

So I got the name and address of the school, and then I called Margie Herrera. She could drive, and she could help me get to the car.

By the time I entered the principal's office, the social worker was

. . . . .

there, too, sitting in a turquoise plastic chair in front of the waist-high swinging door that bisected the counter. She was one Gayle Constantine, whom I had met before and wasn't absolutely overwhelmingly fond of. She was about five feet seven, slender, with wispy blond hair (deliberately wispy, not accidentally wispy, which meant very frequent very expensive haircuts), and she always dressed in dark suits, white blouses, and gold neck chains as if she were an attorney. To my mind at least she sometimes seemed to veer between having an aggravated sense of her own importance and being totally unable to decide what to do with a situation. "What happened to you?" she demanded as soon as she saw me.

"Surgery," I answered, looking past her.

Beside her was a thin nervous-looking dark-haired woman, about my size, maybe thirty years old, with eyes so dark they were almost black, rather fair skin, and attractive and slightly flamboyant makeup and clothing, who leaped to her feet the moment I introduced myself and Margie to the secretary. "Can you tell me what is going on?" she demanded. "I'm Gloria Reddich, and my daughter Diane goes to this school, and somebody from the school called me at work and told me I had to come in here, and then when I got here nobody would tell me anything except that she's not hurt—"

"I'm afraid we don't know anything yet either," I answered. "Maybe you . . ." I looked at the secretary, who shook her head.

"Then who does know something?" the woman demanded, not unreasonably.

"I'll call Mrs. Washington," the secretary said hastily, and reached for the switch to the intercom.

When Mrs. Washington arrived, she was not alone. With her was a tall, pale, thin, man I'd have guessed to be around twenty-three. He was blushing in that unattractive mottled way that some extremely fair people blush. "This is Mr. Daniels," she said. "Mr. Daniels, this is Mrs. Ralston, the policewoman I told you about." She left the rest of the introducing to me.

· · · · ·

The whole group—Margie Herrera and me, Mrs. Washington and Mr. Daniels, Gayle Constantine and Gloria Reddich—were in the teachers' lounge, and it was clear that Mrs. Washington, at least for now, was in control of the meeting. She had, I would judge from her manner, been in control of meetings before this one. She looked around at all of us and said, "We're going to discuss Diane Reddich."

"What about Diane?" Mrs. Reddich said quickly. "Nobody's telling me anything. Where is Diane? What's—"

"Diane is in the classroom," Mrs. Washington said, "and I've left an aide to keep things under control." To the rest of us, she went on, "Diane is six years old; she's in the first grade. Her class has a substitute teacher today. Her usual teacher is a woman, Mrs. White, but the substitute is a man, Elbert Daniels."

Here everybody looked at Elbert Daniels, who did not appear happy to be looked at. "You're making too much of this," he burst out. "I only said that—"

"I know what you said," Mrs. Washington answered him. To the rest of us, she said, "Mr. Daniels came in during break this morning to talk with me. Before I retired last spring, I was the assistant principal here, and Mr. Daniels substituted some while I was here. He knows me. And both the principal and assistant principal are gone, so that made me the only person he had to talk with, even though I'm here today only as a substitute teacher myself. He told me that he was extremely concerned about Diane Reddich, because she kept rubbing up against him in what he described as an 'unmistakably sexual' way."

"What exactly was she doing, Mr. Daniels?" I asked softly, as Mr. Daniels blushed again.

He was silent for a moment. Then, obviously unwillingly, he said, "She kept like leaning against me and pulling up her skirt and grabbing my hand and pulling it toward her crotch. I told her that

. . . . .

wasn't nice and she said . . . she said, 'Yes it is. My daddy told me so.' "

"After he told me that," Mrs. Washington continued, "I went to have a look at Diane myself, and I asked her about it. Diane told me 'That's what you're s'posed to do to daddies.' " She took a deep breath. "The obvious conclusion . . . is obvious."

"It's not obvious to me!" Mrs. Reddich burst out. "That's not . . . If you're trying to say Emil . . ."

Rolling over her protests like a juggernaut, Mrs. Washington continued. "Normally I would have gone to the principal, Mrs. Cohen, and told her of the suspected child abuse, but—"

"Why didn't you go to the counselor?" Margie interrupted.

"There's not one. Not all the schools have full-time counselors. This school has a counselor on Tuesday and Thursday only. I . . . don't think this matter should wait until Tuesday. That was when I telephoned you"—she glanced at Ms. Constantine and me—"and asked the secretary to call Mrs. Reddich."

"Nothing like that could possibly have happened," Mrs. Reddich said breathlessly. "You . . . you teachers . . . must have misunderstood. Besides . . . if it was happening . . . somebody would have noticed before, Mrs. White or some other teacher—"

"Mrs. White is female," Mrs. Washington said. "There are no male teachers in this school. There are two male janitors, but neither comes in close contact with the children. Mr. Daniels, had you substituted for Mrs. White before?"

"No," he got out, still looking stunned.

"I know you hadn't," Mrs. Washington said, "because I checked the records. Mrs. White has not been out this year before today. I checked further. Diane's kindergarten teacher was Miss Nichols. Miss Nichols did not miss work at all last year. Diane has never come in contact with an adult male in the school system before."

Still looking stunned, Mrs. Reddich said, "But that doesn't mean . . ." She came to a dead halt.

. . . . .

"Doesn't mean what?" Margie Herrera said. "If Diane hasn't been having sexual contact with her father, how did she get the ideas she clearly has?"

"I don't know!" Mrs. Reddich said. "All I can tell you is that Emil wouldn't do such a thing."

"Perhaps we'd better talk to Diane," I suggested, and glanced at Margie. This, I knew, could be a very ticklish situation. Normally we do not talk with children without their parents' consent, but in this case the child could be the victim of a parental crime. This meant that if we could not get consent—written consent—from at least one parent to talk freely with the girls, we'd have to get a court order.

Margie didn't say anything, and I reached a quick decision. "Gayle," I said, "Detective Herrera and I are going back to the police department. Will you please get Diane and follow us." Forestalling Mrs. Reddich, who had her mouth open to start yelling, I went on, "Mrs. Reddich, you may follow us into the police station, and you are welcome to call an attorney if you like. Mrs. Washington, Mr. Daniels, will you please come to the police station immediately after you get off work. We'll need written statements from both of you, but obviously you don't want to leave the children until school is out."

"You can't just take my child like that," Mrs. Reddich began.

"Would you care to make a small bet?" Margie said under her breath, just loudly enough that I could hear. Then, aloud, she said, "We aren't taking her into any kind of protective custody or foster care yet."

"Then what *are* you doing?" she interrupted, her voice loud and shocked.

"We are taking her to the police station," I said. "This is normal procedure when there is strong reason to believe a child has been the victim of a crime. Whether you will be able to take her home will be determined later. Mrs. Reddich, I'm sorry, I know this is a terrible shock for you, but if Diane is indeed being molested, then

. . . . .

121

getting her into a safe place, and under appropriate medical and psychological care, is critical."

I wound up giving her the address of the police station and agreeing to see to it that Margie drove slowly enough that she could easily follow us. I got only a glimpse of Diane Reddich as Gayle Constantine went out the front door with her; a small child, blond and thin, with curly hair, wearing a short skirt and white tights in place of the slacks that have become almost standard school clothing for girls.

I gestured Mrs. Reddich toward public parking, and then Margie and I pulled into the police parking garage. By the time everybody else—Ms. Constantine and Diane, and Mrs. Reddich—had gotten through the front office and reached the Detective Bureau, Margie and I were already there.

Margie ushered Ms. Constantine and Diane into the Sex Crimes office, and I—back on my Captain Ahab roller skate—went into the interview room to talk with Mrs. Reddich. She glanced, looking rather startled, at my rolling footstool. "Sorry," I said. "Foot surgery, and this thing is a lot easier to get around on than crutches."

"Oh, I'm sure," she said blankly, and went on staring at me.

"As I told you at the school, I'm Detective Deb Ralston," I said. "I'm sure you did some thinking in the car. Do you feel you understand what's going on?"

"How do you expect me to understand it?" she demanded. "The whole thing is perfectly ridiculous. I'm not going to lose my child, am I? I mean, this whole thing is perfectly ridiculous. That black woman said something about child abuse. Now, I ask you, does Diane look abused or neglected to you? She's as healthy as can be; she always gets proper nutrition and medical care, and we never leave her alone. We never even spank her. My husband and I don't approve of spanking children. I think they respond much better to firm but loving discipline, don't you?"

"I agree with you," I said, "but I'm afraid spanking or neglect

. . . . .

122

of basic essentials isn't the complaint. When Mrs. Washington mentioned abuse, she was using a rather more polite term to indicate her belief that the child is being sexually abused by her father."

"I gathered that," Mrs Reddich said, her face white with near-circles of flaming color just below the cheekbones. "And I'm telling you it's totally ridiculous. Emil wouldn't do any such thing."

"Maybe you're right," I said, not believing my words for a second. "If so, we should be able to clear the problem up quickly. We need your consent to have a long talk with Diane."

"I don't . . . Should I make such a decision without Emil here?"

"That's entirely up to you," I said. "I can tell you, however, that we are going to talk with her, with your consent or with a court order."

"Then it doesn't appear as if I have much choice, do I?" She sounded, now, more angry than frightened.

"Yes, you have the choice. You can allow us to talk with her now, and if the school has misunderstood something innocent then we can get the matter cleared up right now. And you can take the chance that we might not be able to get a court order. We think we can. Answer one question for me, if you will. Is Emil often alone with Diane?"

"Emil's a good man," she said, her tone defensive. "Why shouldn't he be alone with her? He's her father. But yes, we decided that rather than trust her to a baby-sitter we'd take turns. So I work in the daytime and he works at night. It actually works out quite well. I have to be at work by seven, and Diane isn't . . . well, till she started school she usually wasn't up until about ten. And Emil gets home about two-thirty A.M., and he's too tired to go to sleep until he's unwound a little, so he gets to bed about three A.M. and he wakes up about ten also. I'm back home by four-thirty, in time for him to get to work by five-thirty."

She paused for a moment, long enough for me to form a mental

. . . . .

picture. I'm told many men wake up horny. So a man wakes up horny about ten in the morning and there's only one female in the house—easy enough for a man with low inhibitions and no respect for females to satisfy himself wherever satisfaction was available. "Emil's a good man," she repeated. "He works hard, and he loves Diane so much . . . I don't know, you hear about these things, but I sometimes wonder if they really happen at all, or if the news people just blow everything all out of proportion—"

"Oh, it happens," I said. "It happens a lot more often than you ever hear about."

"Well, but you never actually *meet* people it's happened to," she said. "I mean, you hear about it on television, like that Roseanne Barr thing, but you know, her parents have said it didn't ever happen, and you watch Geraldo and Oprah Winfrey and you can hear just about anything, it's like walking into a supermarket and there are all those tabloid headlines, 'Face of Elvis Found on Mars!' and I really think these reports are like that. It always happens to somebody else a long way away, but nobody ever really meets people it happens to."

"Lady, you're looking at one," I said softly.

That focused her attention. "Not really," she said.

"Yes, really. My father was a milkman. On the surface he was as nice a guy as you'd ever want to meet. He had six children. He was the president of the board of elders at our church for years and years and years, and he was even a lay preacher for about six months, when our pastor was recovering from a heart attack and couldn't stand up in the pulpit for an hour every Sunday. I'm quite sure none of his friends would ever have believed a bad word against him. But all the same he molested my sister and me for years."

I could hear my voice shaking. This was the first time in my life I had ever actually said that to a stranger; Rhonda and I had discussed it, had agreed we both knew what happened, but even on Saturday, discussing it for the first time, neither of us had ever

. . . . .

actually said the words, and I wasn't sure I had even quite said it to my brother. There, now I had said the words.

She was staring at me as I went on. "My mother would never have believed it, so my sister and I didn't try to tell her. That's why it never stopped until we got away, because she never believed it and he never in his whole life was confronted with the truth."

"Well, I . . . of course, I'm sorry, but . . . but it's not as if things like that happen every day. He must—your father, I mean—he must have . . . have had a brain tumor or something."

"No brain tumor," I said. "Just the not completely uncommon belief that all the females in his family were his private property, to be used however he saw fit. And that's the whole point, Mrs. Reddich. Certainly not every man feels that way; probably very few do. But the fact remains that a certain percentage of the men in this and probably any other country do molest any female they can get their hands on, as long as they think they can get away with it. Things like that *do* happen every day. They've just been swept under the rug. And now that they're out from under the rug, nobody wants to look at them, because things that get hidden under the rug are dirty and slimy. But as long as we refuse to look at them, that's how long they are going to go on happening. We'd like to believe that men would stop abusing their daughters and stepdaughters and nieces and cousins because it's a terrible thing to do and the girls deserve better treatment, but it's pretty obvious that they won't. That means they're going to have to be made to stop the abuse by the fear that someday it will blow up in their faces and all their friends and neighbors will know about it. And unfortunately, that can't be done without embarrassing their families."

"Ms. . . . Ralston, is it?" I nodded, and she leaned forward, arms on the table. "I'm sure from what you say that things like that must really happen in some families. But not in *my* family. Given your situation, I know this is hard for you to believe, but I'm telling you the truth. *Emil wouldn't do anything like that.*"

Get your head out of the sand, lady, I thought but did not say.

. . . . .

"Emil *loves* his child," she said, looking defiantly at me, and I wondered whether it was me or herself she was saying it to.

"My father loved his children," I replied. "I remember that at Christmas dinner, the year after I got married, he broke down crying while saying the blessing because he had just realized that was probably the last time he'd have all of his children home for Christmas. Most child molesters love their children, Mrs. Reddich. They just don't love them the right way."

She took a deep breath. "I've heard about social workers talking with children, and asking leading questions, and getting them to say all kinds of things that aren't true—"

"I can't tell you for sure that never happens," I said. "But I can tell you I've never known it to happen. Children have an immense need to protect their families. When you hear of a child trying to divorce his family, just about one hundred percent of the time it's a child who has been in foster care so much that effectively he's already been divorced emotionally from his family. A child is far more likely to lie to protect his family than to lie to get someone into trouble that severe. Furthermore, unless their television watching is a lot more—complicated, let's say—than most children's television watching, a child the age of Diane is incapable of making up a coherent story about sexual abuse."

"Are they going to take my child away from me?"

"I don't know," I said. "I hope not. Unless it's essential for the protection of the children, the social agencies prefer not to take the children out of the home."

"I think I'd better not sign anything until Emil gets here," Mrs. Reddich said decisively.

"Do you know if Emil is on the way?"

"I didn't call him. If that woman didn't—"

"Let me check."

I went back out to the squad room, where Rafe and Ms. Constantine were talking, and reported. "She won't sign anything without Emil here."

．　．　．　．　．

126

"Emil is the husband?" Rafe asked.

"Yes. Has the husband been called?"

Rafe and Ms. Constantine looked at each other. "Not by me," Ms. Constantine said.

"Then I'll go see if she can call him and get him down here."

I grabbed a telephone we keep in the bottom drawer of a filing cabinet and went back into the small cubicle, to find Mrs. Reddich sitting in almost the exact same position I had left her, staring blankly at nothing the way my cat had stared at the spot from which the tomato plant had been removed. "Mrs. Reddich?" I said.

She jumped slightly and looked at me.

"Nobody has called your husband. If you'll just plug this in—I can't reach the baseboard. Would you like me to leave while you talk with him?"

"Yes. Thank you. . . . Let me speak to Emil. This is Gloria," I heard her saying as I exited.

"Roger, you'd better go get some court orders," Rafe said to Roger Hales. "What do we want, permission to speak with her and—?"

"We better get an order for a medical examination," Ms. Constantine continued. "I don't really want to, but we might need to take her into protective custody."

"I'd feel a lot better if we do that," Rafe returned. "I know you don't want to, but if the child's safety is at stake . . ."

"Anybody got her full name and date of birth?" Roger asked.

It developed that nobody had. "Well, surely we can at least ask her name and age," Roger said, and headed into the small room where the child was still holed up with the uniform policewoman. He emerged moments later, a slightly dazed look on his face, and said, "I'm going to legal."

It took about fifteen minutes for Emil Reddich to storm into the police station. I was not, of course, downstairs to greet him; none

. . . . .

of us were, and a uniform officer ushered him up to our floor. "What the hell is going on here?" he yelled before he was quite off the elevator.

"You're Emil Reddich?" Rafe asked, looking at him. I believe I have mentioned that Rafe is a rather small-boned man, about five-eight. In terms of size, Emil could have been his twin. But Rafe has command presence, and Reddich, despite his bellowing and ranting, had something inconsequential about him. In a crowd, nobody would ever notice Emil Reddich; even if he was alone in a room, he might somehow be overlooked.

"Hell, yes, I'm Emil Reddich, who the hell else would I be?"

"Now, I can't answer that," Rafe said. "We get a lot of people in here. As to what is going on, would you like us to stand here in the hall and discuss it in everybody's hearing, or shall we find a private place to talk?"

"If you've got my kid down here, I want to see her right *now*."

"That's out of the question," I heard myself saying.

He looked at me contemptuously. "Who the hell are you? I don't need to talk to secretaries."

"I'm not a secretary. I'm a police detective assigned to the Sex Crimes Unit, and I'm telling you that you are not going to see that child right now. She is perfectly safe, but you aren't getting near her."

"Who says I'm not?"

A door opened, and Gloria Reddich, now visibly crying, dashed out of the door of the room she had been placed in. "Oh, Emil, they're saying the most awful things—"

"Why did you let them bring you down here?" he yelled. "You haven't got the brains God gave a—"

"I didn't let them," she wept. "I had to come. They were bringing Diane and they said I could come if I wanted to—"

"Then why did you let them get their hands on Diane?"

I glanced at Rafe, and his eyes agreed with me. We were going

· · · · ·

to let them stand in the hall and argue if that was what they wanted to do, and we were going to listen while they did it.

Unfortunately for that plan, Reddich figured out what we were doing, and as Gloria Reddich said, "They called me down to the school and they already had this *woman* there and she——" he waved his hand.

"Shut up," he told her. "These guys are listening to everything we say." He looked back at Rafe. "Who's going to tell me what's going on?"

"Oh, I think Detective Ralston will do that," Rafe said blandly.

Although some individual officers are racist, with some unfortunate exceptions police departments in general, despite the accusations you hear on television, don't like racism. Or, at least they don't like racism addressed to police officers. Most police officers—with a few more exceptions than the exceptions to racism—also don't like sexism, at least not when it is addressed to fellow officers. That is, even though they themselves might not like the idea of policewomen, they will back a policewoman up publicly just as they would any other officer. I remember when I was in burglary, before being transferred to the Major Case Squad, when a warehouse was hit. The owner was known to be one of the biggest bigots in Tarrant County—he figured that blacks belong in the cotton fields and women belong in the kitchen—and I will never to my dying day really believe that it was pure accident that Will Brown—black, six foot four—and I were assigned to work the case.

The warehouse owner took one look at us, looking like a combination of Salt and Pepper (if you remember that Sammy Davis movie) and Mutt and Jeff, and refused to let us in. So of course we went on to another call, and another, and another after that before returning to the police station, where our sergeant was on the phone. He glanced at us, grinning, and then said into the telephone, "I'm sorry, sir, but we sent you two detectives and you

. . . . .

didn't want them. If you want detectives you get them or no-body."

He had to have a police report in order to file his insurance, and he wasn't going to get a police report without somebody making an investigation, so back Will and I went. I've wondered ever since whether his attitude was in any way mollified by the fact that Will and I caught his burglars and had his property back to him by noon the next day.

Rafe was playing the same game our sergeant that day had played. Emil Reddich didn't want to talk with a woman; ergo, a woman he was going to talk with. And that was that.

Normally I enjoy such a game as much as anybody. Today I wasn't entirely certain I was up to it.

But all the same I opened the door of the room Mrs. Reddich had come out of and said, "In here, please, Mr. Reddich."

Gloria tried to follow, and Rafe said, "No. You stay out here."

Emil Reddich didn't want to talk with me. He didn't want to be here. He didn't want his wife here. He especially didn't want his daughter here. And he was prepared to take it out on me.

So I started out briskly. "Mr. Reddich, if you want even the ghost of a chance to keep your daughter, and to stay out of prison, I suggest that you keep your temper to yourself. I will be glad to have a talk with you, but I do not feel like listening to you shout. Now, at the outset, I'm going to tell you that there is reason to believe a crime has been committed and there is reason to believe that you have committed it."

"That's a damn lie—"

"It's not a damn lie that we have reason to believe it. So listen to me for a moment. You have the right to remain silent . . ."

I went on through the Miranda litany and then asked, "Do you wish to give up these rights?"

"You're damn right I do! I don't have anything to hide!"

Not quite by coincidence, just about that time the door opened and Rafe sauntered in. "You have a use for me?" he asked.

. . . . .

"Mr. Reddich is willing to sign a rights waiver," I said. "You want to witness it?"

Those mandatory things over with, Rafe exited to another room, where—I knew but Emil didn't—Rafe would be watching the proceedings in here through a two-way mirror. On this side of the room all that was visible was a mirror. On the other side, when the lights were on, there was a mirror there, too. But when the lights were out in that room, you could see into this room almost as well as through plain window glass.

"Now I'll tell you what's going on," I said. "A suggestion has been made that you have been sexually molesting your daughter Diane—"

"That's a damn lie!"

"You sound like a broken record. Do you want to know what's going on, or not?"

"Who made the suggestion?"

"Diane," I said softly.

"That's a . . . I mean, I don't believe it. She wouldn't say things like that. Who did she say—supposedly say—it to? And who called you in?"

"She talked to her teacher. In the absence of the principal and vice principal, the teacher talked with the woman who was vice principal last year. She in turn called a social worker and me. The social worker, a juvenile officer, and I went to the scene, spoke briefly with the teachers and your wife, and decided the situation merited police intervention."

"I'm going to sue those damn interfering biddies for everything they've got or ever hope to have . . . All right, all right, I'm not shouting. Somebody said I was molesting Diane. What the hell kind of a thing is that to say? Do I look to you like a child molester?"

"Yes, Mr. Reddich, you do," I answered.

He stared at me.

"The thing is, Mr. Reddich, child molesters don't come exclu-

. . . . .

sively in any one color, or size, or shape, or financial or ethnic or religious background, or even—necessarily—sex. But there's one thing they do all have in common. They despise their victims. If—like most child molesters—they're men molesting girls, and that is far and away the most common form of child molestation, then they despise women. Heterosexual women child molesters despise men. Homosexual child molesters—and there are relatively few of those—despise their own sex, whether they're male or female. Well, every word you've said, every bit of your body language since you came in the door, has been shouting it loud and clear. You despise women. You scapegoat women. Never mind what happened and who called the police, your first assumption when you walked in was that your wife had done something stupid. You decided I was a secretary, and you despise secretaries, although I'll bet in your business—whatever business you're in— you couldn't get by without a secretary if you had to. So yes, Mr. Reddich, you do look like a child molester."

"I thought everybody was innocent until proven guilty. What went with that?"

"Nothing went with that. It's still around, and it's a legal presumption. You'll take it with you into whatever court of law you go into. This case will be thoroughly worked, and nothing will happen to you until and unless we have a case to take into court, and the court won't convict you unless the evidence is strong enough to preclude any reasonable doubt. But you asked me if you looked to me like a child molester, and I've answered you. Now, shall we get back to the matter at hand?"

"What is there to get back to? Some schoolteacher decided I'd been feeling up my kid and called the cops and now you're going to ruin my life."

"What about the life of your daughter?"

"I haven't done anything to my daughter! Now, I'm asking again, what the hell is going on?"

"Will you try keeping your mouth shut and letting me answer?"

. . . . .

132

It should, I thought, have been pretty evident by now what was going on, but if he wanted to play ignorant I'd oblige him. "Here is what is going on. A suggestion has been made that your daughter has been sexually molested. A suggestion—not a formal accusation, at this point—has been made that you are the perpetrator. A detective has gone now to get a court order for a medical examination of the child. If that examination shows that molestation has occurred, we'll proceed from there. However, in most cases there is no physical evidence for molestation." I paused; he had visibly blanched. "You have a question?"

"Yeah, uh, a long time ago, back when Diane was about two, she had this, uh, weird infection, she got like a Tinkertoy up her twat. Will your doctor be able to tell the difference?"

I'll bet she got a Tinkertoy up her twat, I thought. "Most likely," I said, "the doctor could determine whether it was something that small or something much larger. But I can't say for sure."

"Okay, well, say the doctor can tell the difference, what then?" He was wriggling in his chair.

"As I said, often there is no physical evidence for molestation. Therefore we are also applying for a court order that will allow us to talk with Diane."

"Yeah, well, she'll say everything's okay. She's a good kid, Diane is."

"I'm glad to hear it," I said. "However, if the results of that conversation give us reason to believe that molestation has occurred, we will proceed from there."

"Proceed how? I just want to take my wife and kid and get out of here."

"That is exactly what you will not be permitted to do. There are two possibilities at this stage: either Diane will be removed from your home and placed in a foster home until this case is resolved, or you will agree to move out and stay away until this case is resolved." I didn't have to say which I preferred. I wasn't getting my preference; Gayle had made that clear.

. . . . .

133

He stared at me, his eyes wild. "I can't . . . Get my wife in here."

The conversation went on from there, with Gloria alternately in and out of the room depending on what he wanted to say. At one point he said, "Look, I'm not saying I did anything. Let's . . . Hypothetically, okay?"

"Okay," I said.

"So there's this guy, not me, just this guy."

"Okay."

"And he works nights, and he wakes up about ten o'clock in the morning, only he's not all the way awake, he's just a little bit awake, and he rolls over, and he's horny, and there's this nice warm body in bed with him, now, how is he supposed to remember who it is, if he's half asleep? Or practically all the way asleep?"

"Most people," I answered, "would realize about the time the kid started screaming, even if they really were asleep."

"Yeah, but, suppose he didn't? I mean, that doesn't make him a criminal, does it?"

"Now, what do you expect me to say to that?" I demanded. "Do you expect me to give you permission to rape your daughter, provided you're half asleep at the time?"

"I didn't rape my daughter!" he yelled. "I love my kid . . . I take good care of her . . . I didn't . . ."

Finally, with Rafe sitting in and Emil Reddich doing a lot of yelling and Gloria Reddich doing a lot of crying, everybody agreed that Reddich would leave the police station immediately, go home and pack his belongings, and go live with his mother, having no contact at all with his daughter until the case was resolved one way or another.

And I did not believe for one second that he would really stay away, but Gayle had decided to do it that way, Rafe for the moment had agreed, and my arguments didn't seem to carry enough clout to change anything.

Mrs. Reddich wanted to stay at the police station. She wanted to see her daughter.

. . . . .

We left her in the interview room while we went into the squad room to talk about the whole thing behind closed doors. Roger Hales came back then, with the court orders, and said, "This whole thing is a farce."

"What do you mean by that?" I asked.

"That poor bastard didn't stand a chance with that little harpy. Listen, when I went in their to ask her name and birthdate, she tried to seduce *me*! And she'd never even seen me before."

"Tried to seduce you how?" Rafe asked.

"Smiling at me like a forty-year-old hooker. Rubbing up against me. And then she even tried to grab my crotch! After that she asked me if she could go home."

"Roger," I said, "do you honestly think a seven-year-old could think something like that up by herself? Don't you have sense enough to realize that for her to do something like that, she had to have *learned* it from somebody?"

"What the hell is that supposed to mean?" he asked.

"You can teach anybody anything, if you catch them young enough," I said patiently. "This is a strange place. Diane doesn't like it here. She wants to go home. Her father evidently has been to some pains to convince her that men make the rules. You're a man, that means you are the one who can let her go home. If Daddy also convinced her that to get the goodies you perform sexually, what is she going to do? Perform sexually, so she can get the goody, namely the trip back home. Learned behavior, Roger."

"Bullshit," Roger said. "You're trying to lay a guilt trip on every man alive. Well, it's not going to work."

"I'm not trying to lay a guilt trip on anybody," I said. "I'm trying to tell you that girl isn't acting like a normal child. You said she smiled at you like a forty-year-old hooker. Well, a young hooker might still think she can get somewhere. A forty-year-old hooker has already figured out she's dead meat. What do all forty-year-old hookers have in common? Despair, Roger. Despair. And that's what a girl child who's figured out she's nothing to her father

· · · · ·

135

but a piece of meat has. Despair. She's not physically dead, and she's not brain dead, but she's soul dead already. And she's too young for that."

Roger all but sneered at me. "Melodramatic today, aren't we? You must be on the rag," he said, and crossed over to his desk. "Who's going to do what with these stupid court orders?"

"Give them to me," Rafe said. "Roger, listen to what Deb said, because she's telling you the truth. You're full of water on this one. Right now, maybe you'd better go out and talk with that TCU housemother again. When you get back, I want a written report on what you just told me—*without* your commentary. It's part of the evidence."

After Roger had departed, Rafe sat down on the corner of my desk and said, "He's been acting sort of halfway flaked out ever since his divorce."

"I could tell something had flipped him out," I agreed, "but Rafe, with that attitude he ought not to be allowed anywhere near a sex crime victim."

"He's okay where there's visible harm," Rafe said, "like on the TCU rapist and the Super Glue rapist. But something like this, you're right. I've talked with him a couple of times about it, and I'm going to try again later today, after he makes that report. If he doesn't shape up pretty quickly, yes, he's shipping out. Voluntarily or involuntarily."

Eight
. . . . . .

I HAVE TRIED. Talking that evening with Harry, talking since then with friends, even talking on the witness stand, I tried very hard to find the right words to describe what I saw when I went into the interview room where the silent little girl and the silent uniformed policewoman were sitting together. But some things are just too strong for any words at all to fit.

Gayle Constantine was at my desk, using my telephone to call around to find a pediatrician who had some forensic background and could see Diane at once, and since we had the court order permitting us to talk with her I decided to get the ball rolling just a little.

Diane was sitting very quietly. She was pretty, with curly blond hair and large brown eyes, but her features, though she seemed of normal intelligence, were frighteningly listless. A compliant child, I guessed, one who would be no trouble to anybody. She wouldn't cause problems; she wouldn't disobey. The most resistance she would make would be quiet crying in a corner. She wouldn't jump out a window, the way Dusty had done. She wouldn't act out, as my sister had done, or resolve to win in life, as I had done. She would—if she managed to grow up—go through life as a quiet, conforming automaton.

She glanced up briefly as I came in, and then looked back down at her hands, clasped before her on the table in unnatural stillness.

I nodded to the uniformed officer, and she left quietly, shutting

. . . . .

the door behind her. I sat down. "Hi," I said, "I'm Deb Ralston. I've been talking to your mom and dad."

She nodded, and didn't ask what they said or what I asked. "Why is that thing under your leg?" she asked instead, not sounding really curious but more like someone making conversation in the operating room. When she spoke, I could see the gap left by the missing front tooth. That would have told me her approximate age even if I didn't know.

I hastened to answer her. "I had surgery on my foot, and now I can't walk very well. I keep falling off the crutches."

"Oh. Are you a cop?"

"Yes—"

"I didn't do anything bad. Can I go home?"

"Nobody thinks you did anything bad," I assured her, "but we think somebody might have done something bad to you."

"Oh," she said. "That's what that other lady said. Uh-uh. Nobody did anything bad to me."

The door opened behind me and I glanced around, annoyed at the interruption, to see Rafe coming in. And then I looked back again at Diane.

That's what I have no words for. Her face, fixed on Rafe, had paled slightly, and the forced gaiety of her smile differed from a real smile the way the flush on the face of a person who died of carbon monoxide poisoning differs from the radiant blush of a new bride, the way the rictus on the mouth of a prussic acid victim differs from the joyous grin of a child seeing Mickey Mouse for the first time. It was the ghastly smile of the child star of a porno snuff film who's just realized what's going on and still hopes if she's pretty enough, and sweet enough, and charming enough, she can buy her life. As I watched her sidle toward Rafe I knew exactly what Roger had meant when he said she smiled like a forty-year-old whore. He'd forgotten to tell me the forty-year-old whore was dying of TB and didn't have the money to pay for a cardboard box to sleep in to get out of the snow.

.   .   .   .   .

The stunned look on Rafe's face told me he'd seen the same thing I'd seen. And he'd been watching through the one-way glass as I talked with her; he knew now, as well as I did, that she was a halfway normal, if slightly listless, child around women. It was only around men that she turned into Lilith, into a succubus, into a hideous parody not only of a child but of a human being.

"Gayle's ready," he said to me, and got out of the room fast, before Diane could reach him.

"Ms. Constantine is going to take you to a doctor," I told her.

"Will the doctor give me a shot?" It was the first ghost of normal childlike reaction I had seen from her.

"I don't think so." I did not judge it appropriate to explain right then that the doctor would give her a pelvic examination; I hoped she would be suitably sedated, if not totally anesthetized, for it, and there was no use frightening her now any more than she already was frightened.

After Diane left with Gayle Constantine to go to the doctor, I took the time to go to the vending machine and get some cheese and crackers and a carton of chocolate milk. It was not that I was hungry. The pain medicine seems to suppress hunger. I was aware, however, that it was now after one o'clock, I had not eaten since nine, and I was going to run out of energy a lot faster if I didn't eat.

Who was I trying to kid? I was already out of energy and wondering when Harry was going to get through at the library and come back and get me. But I was also aware that if he did show up right now to take me home I would undoubtedly refuse to go, on the grounds that I needed to stick around until we finished what-ever we were going to do today on the Reddich case. Sometimes I don't understand me at all.

But my foot, despite the eleven o'clock medication, still felt hot and throbbing. I didn't dare take anything else right now, not if I wanted to stay awake. I was beginning to have the feeling that maybe, just maybe, Harry and Captain Millner and Rafe Permut

．　．　．　．　．

had been right—maybe I shouldn't have tried to come to work today.

Actually there was no "maybe" to it. In one part of my mind, the part I tend not to listen to, I knew before I left the house that I had no business doing it.

But I hate feeling helpless; I hate being confined to bed. It makes me feel like a kid, and frankly, I didn't enjoy being a kid. I suppose I wasn't as miserable a kid as Dusty had been, as Diane seemed to be, but my childhood was rotten enough.

Once again I found myself wondering what had made the difference for me—was it just my grandparents?—and I had a briefly vivid flash of memory. I was five; my brother Jim was three, and we'd been to the birthday party of my twelve-year-old cousin who for some reason still incomprehensible to me had decided to have a bingo birthday party. I won nothing; my brother—with my father watching his numbers—won a small red comb. I cried all the way home. My father yelled, "I'll buy you a comb, dammit, now stop bawling!"

From the backseat, where my head was buried against the door, I yelled back, "I don't want a comb, I want to *win*!"

In some ways I suppose that one sentence sums up my entire attitude toward life. Never mind what I win; I want to win, and I'll fight however I have to. Had Dusty given up? I didn't need to ask whether Diane had given up; I had seen bitterly exhausted resignation all over her six-year-old face.

But perhaps they had picked the safest way after all. It's unsafe to want anything you can't ever have. Even if you starve to death, whether it's for want of food or want of love or simple want of normality, you can avoid adding ulcers to starvation if you give up instead of going on wanting. Perhaps I had lost something by fighting all my life.

Perhaps. But there was no doubt at all that Dusty had lost her very life, that Diane had lost everything that makes life worthwhile, because both of them had decided, somewhere in the depths of

. . . . .

their beings, that life never will get any better than it is right now.

My will to win had brought me a long way. But undeniably, sometimes it gets me in trouble, as it had today.

But despite my feelings, either emotional or physical, the cold fact was I was stuck here until Harry got through at the library and came back to get me, because if I got somebody else to take me home and then he came looking for me, fur would fly when we both got home. And unless Gayle Constantine and Diane Reddich were back from the hospital or doctor's office or wherever it was that they had gone and we got something resolved, I would be stuck a little longer than that, considering that Rafe had asked me not to get started on this one unless I could stick with it at least as long as necessary today.

So I took the cheese and crackers and milk back up to my desk—yes, I was still using my Captain Ahab roller skate, even on the elevator, which made me a bit giddy because whenever the elevator stopped or started I was afraid the library stool was going to take off flying—and sat down to eat, and then I dictated into a tape recorder my share of the reports on what we had done so far on the Reddich case, and then I went and hassled the Major Case Squad to see what was being done about Doreen Miller.

I felt highly ambivalent on that one. On the one hand, I wanted to know that she was all right. But on the other hand, based on what Sandy had told me, I wanted Doreen out of that home — which meant that I was not at all sure that I would have told Captain Millner where Doreen was, assuming that I had happened to know, if I was sure she was safe.

A little after two-fifteen Gayle Constantine and the uniformed policewoman who had left with her returned with Diane. Another woman was with her, a woman tall and rather thin and ramrod straight whom I'd estimate to be about sixty-five. "This is Dr. Florence Pederson," Ms. Constantine said. "She's a consulting pediatrician for the Department of Family and Children's Services."

· · · · ·

"I'm retired from regular practice," Dr. Pederson added. "This consulting work is all I do now, along with some writing." Her voice was slightly gruff, and her short-cut iron gray hair was thick and healthy looking.

Well, I thought, that explained why Diane was able to get in so quickly.

"I'd like to talk privately with the officers on the case," Dr. Pederson said, with a rather annoyed glance at Gayle. Only after Gayle had departed, and Margie, Rafe, Roger (unfortunately in my opinion, but Rafe thought hearing the doctor's comments might civilize him), Manuel (because he'd never worked a case quite like this before), and I were sitting with her in an interview room, did she add, "I wanted to place the child in the hospital at least overnight, but Ms. Constantine is hellbent for returning the child to her mother."

Rafe made some loud and profane exclamation, Margie said, "What?" and I sat up straight, although of course we all already knew it. It was just that we'd hoped the doctor could change Gayle's mind.

Dr. Pederson grimaced. "Ms. Constantine," she said, "is convinced that now that the mother knows what is going on she will protect the child. Statistics . . . indicate otherwise. As do the facts in this case. When Ms. Constantine told me the situation as it had developed thus far, I was horrified. When I examined the child I was even more horrified. Her vagina looked like the vagina of a woman in at least her thirties, a woman moreover who had had an active sex life."

"Not a Tinkertoy, then," I muttered.

"Not unless it had a two-inch diameter," she returned. "Is that what the father said?" When I nodded, she added, "He could have shown a little more imagination. Tinkertoy, indeed! I . . . before I began to talk with Ms. Reddich I suggested Diane should go into the conservatory, where my husband was working with his plants—he's a botanist, you know—because I wanted to take some

. . . . .

time for the sedative I gave her to begin to work. Before I left the house to come up here, he called me aside and told me Diane had made a . . . rather determined approach toward him. That is of course learned behavior; it cannot be natural to a child. Needless to say, I do not agree with Ms. Constantine's assessment of the situation."

She paused, and then went on miserably, "Ms. Constantine seems to believe that the mother failed to protect the child because she did not know the molestation was occurring. I can only reply that if she did not know it was because she chose not to know. Although by now all injuries are healed and scarred over, there had at an earlier date to be considerable pain, bleeding, infection. It is inconceivable that the mother was in total ignorance of the situation. If the mother failed to protect a three-year-old who was being repeatedly raped—and the assaults began at least by then, if not earlier—there is no earthly reason to suppose that she will protect a six-year-old.

"I . . ." She grimaced. "When I first entered forensic pediatrics, I once met a family doctor who had been called in by a mother whose child was bleeding from the vagina and crying. This doctor was convinced that the child had seduced the father. He said to me that obviously there was some innate diabolatry in the child which her parents simply failed, through ignorance or malice, to stamp out. I remember he said something like, 'It is difficult to believe, I am sure, that innocent-seeming newborns in their cradles have the evil of Satan in them, but the fact remains that scriptures make it clear that such is the case, and this evil remains in them unless they are cleansed of it, and rigorously trained in the right ways of conduct, with such punishment, however severe, as seems necessary.' He went on to say that Freudianism, though a false religion, is absolutely correct in this matter of innate evil, and the scriptures make that plain. I should add that I was supposed to be learning about family practice from this doctor. I couldn't believe I was hearing what I was hearing."

· · · · ·

"That doctor must have been out of his mind," Margie said.

"I certainly thought so," Dr. Pederson agreed.

I said, "But surely no reputable psychiatrist, even the most ardent Freudian, believes that crap anymore."

"Some of them still do," Dr. Pederson said. "Some Freudians, and some people who consider themselves Christians. If they're Freudians they talk about acting out an Electra complex; if they're religionists they say things like the heart of man is evil from his birth, which of course is scriptural, and then they explain that that, of course, means all humanity, not just women. Someone—some kind of holy roller—actually said that to me once. Interesting Freudian slip, I thought—she said *women* instead of the much more logical—given the construction of her sentence—*men.*"

I glanced at the others. Margie and Rafe had about the same expression I probably had; Roger seemed oddly pleased. "Can we get off this subject?" I asked. "The problem now is what to do about Diane."

"Is that the whole problem?" she asked. "That's the immediate problem. But people who believe children are innately evil, whether through the sins of Adam and Eve or through Oedipus and Electra complexes—and who go out of their way to prove the point—are the larger problem, perhaps even a more serious problem than the ones who actually do the molesting."

"Surely nobody believes anything like that now," Margie said, ignoring the fact that Dr. Pederson had spent the last five minutes explaining that people *do* believe such things.

"You think not?" she asked then. "I read something virtually identical to that—the scriptural viewpoint, I mean—in a home school manual I was examining when my daughter was thinking of home schooling her children, and the manual was published only a couple of years ago."

"Then that person and I must not have the same scriptures," I said, forgetting I'd said we needed to get off the topic.

"Oddly enough," she added, "the person who wrote the book

· · · · ·

obviously loves her children dearly—which makes me wonder if she really believes what she says she believes. Well. That's neither here nor there right now; as you said, the question now is, what to do about Diane? Because unfortunately, it's the social worker, not any of us, who decides whether the child is to be placed in a foster home or returned to her home. I wish there were more I could do right now, but I'm afraid my input is limited to medical facts. I'll get you a written report by tomorrow, and of course I'll be available for court. Are you through with me?" she asked then. "My husband is in poor health; I hate to leave him alone for long."

"Yes. Thank you for coming," Rafe said.

She left the interview room; the rest of us continued to sit there. Roger said, "Interesting she doesn't agree with that other doctor, the one that taught her."

"That other doctor was an idiot," I retorted, "and she made that plain."

"You always think you know more than the doctors, don't you?" Roger said.

"Roger, shut up, won't you?" Margie said, from which I surmised that she knew him about as well as I did and liked him about as much. "What's he talking about now, anyway?" she asked me.

"He's talking about the last time I was in this unit," I said, "and he was trying to lose weight and came in and said that his doctor told him he'd lose weight if he'd start drinking Sprite instead of Coke, because Sprite doesn't have sugar in it. I said, and I was entirely right by the way, that it wouldn't make a bit of difference unless he drank Diet Sprite, because the only thing regular Sprite lacks that regular Coke has is caffeine and food coloring, not sugar."

"I lost weight, didn't I?" Roger said, and glanced around as Henry Tuckman came in.

"Yes, but that was because you started spending time in the gym, not because you changed from one glob of sugar to another glob of sugar."

. . . . .

"You never give up," Roger said. "That brat tried to seduce her teacher. She tried to seduce me. She tried to seduce that doctor's husband. But you're still insisting she's injured innocence and her old man is a monster."

"Roger, you're a complete idiot," Margie said. "Haven't you got sense enough to realize—"

"The little cunt knows what she wants!" Roger yelled. "She's made that clear to every male she sees."

"Yeah, but, Roger," Manuel said hesitantly, in his slightly accented English, "little girls are *little*. I mean, they are little all over. I don't see how anybody could have intercourse with them without half killing them. That doctor said she'd have been bleeding and hurting, and I believe her. And Deb's right. If her vagina looked like the vagina of a thirty-year-old woman, then it had to start early. You talk about believing doctors—you heard the doctor saying it started at least by the time she was three—"

"All I've got to say," Henry said in that deep baritone voice he has, "is that if anybody tried it on my daughters I damn well *would* kill him."

"I'll bet your daughters don't go around trying to seduce anything in pants, either," Roger said. "Yours don't either, do they?"

He was looking at Wayne Harris, and Wayne replied, "No, but then I didn't teach them to."

"You're all taking the side of that little bitch," Roger said. "Isn't anybody going to say anything for her victim?"

At that point about four of us started yelling at once, on the subject of who was whose victim, and Rafe yelled, "Shut up!"

When the noise stopped, he said, "Roger, you're out of line. You can be as sympathetic as you want to for the father on your own time, but no matter what you personally think of the moral standards of the child—and I suggest you do a lot more reading about this, fast, because you're dead wrong—the fact remains that she's below the age of consent and the father has broken the law. Child molestation, rape, and incest are all illegal, and it appears to

. . . . .

me that he's done all three. Unfortunately, what I've got to think about now is not what he's done but what I can convince a jury that he's done."

That set us all off again, with Margie's and my voice leading the pack. "With her physical condition—" I was saying, and simultaneously Margie was yelling, "With what all he's done to her—"

"Her physical condition is appalling," Rafe readily agreed, "and all of us, with the possible exception of Roger, seem to agree as to who did it and probably why. We can certainly convince a jury she's been raped. But the question is, can we convince a jury her father did it? That's the problem, because it would have to ride on her testimony, and would anybody care to make a small bet she won't change her story?"

There was a little silence. None of us cared to bet on that. The degree of abuse a child will take from parents, while continuing either to protect the parents or to assume that the situation is normal and nothing can be done about it, can be mind-boggling.

"I'm going to talk to the DA about it as soon as I can get an appointment," Rafe added, "but I predict he's going to tell me not to take a warrant until we've had a lot more input from the child."

"I suppose she should be removed from the home," Ms. Constantine, who had come in moments earlier, said gloomily. "But I always hate to break up a family—"

"What family?" Rafe demanded. "You can get a court order readily enough. And in the meantime, don't tell me you can't remove her without a court order, because I know you can, and I also know as well as you do that the higher courts are beginning to react pretty strongly when children aren't protected in such situations. So I'd say that for your own safety, as well as the girl's, you need to get her out of the house."

"Let me think about it," she said. "Give me an hour." With that we had to be content for the moment.

We scattered, each to our own desks, Ms. Constantine to talk with Mrs. Reddich, who was crying quietly in one interview

· · · · ·

room, and me to my desk, preparatory to trying again to talk with Mr. Reddich. The uniformed policewoman came into the squad room and said, "That child never did get lunch. Any idea how much longer this is going to take?"

"None," Rafe said.

"Then I need to take her somewhere and feed her."

Rafe handed her ten dollars from the informant fund and said, "Feed her well." Then, to me, he said, "I may be stuck a while, so I'm going out and grab a bite, too. Deb, if you need to leave, do it; Margie can cover for you. Margie, you better hang around a little longer just in case."

He didn't say in case of what. That's one of those things that don't need to be said.

Ten minutes later, Margie and I were alone in the squad room. "I never did ask you what happened to your foot," Margie said.

"Heel spur surgery," I answered. "It's really pretty minor. It's just that feet . . . you know."

"I know," Margie said. "Sore feet can ruin your entire day." She took off one shoe and rubbed her stocking feet. "If men had to wear high heels they'd never have invented them. And I don't care what anybody says, no one's ever made high heels you can play baseball in."

"Or basketball. Or run track," I agreed.

"Whatever," Margie said.

There was a little silence, and then Margie commented, "I wish somebody would shoot Roger Hales. That's a crummy thing to say about your fellow officer, but I really do. Did I ever tell you what he did to me last year?"

"Uh-uh."

"Well, there was this girl. I'm not saying she was a shining example of virtue, because she wasn't. She was fourteen, and she was in long-term detention for burglary and auto theft. Anyway, she managed to get a weekend pass to go home for her mother's birthday, and when she got back to the detention facility the house mother called me—the girl had been my case two or three times, so the house mother knew I knew her—and said I needed to know that Arlene, that's her name, had come back very badly bruised, and the housemother—Jenna Rainwater, do you know her?"

"Uh-uh," I said. "I think I've heard of her, though. Isn't she that black woman that used to be in Traffic before she got a degree in corrections?"

"That's the one," Margie said. "So Jenna asked Arlene what happened, and Arlene said a guy beat her up and raped her. Jenna asked her why she didn't call the police, and Arlene said the police wouldn't believe her. So that's when Jenna called me. I went out there, and you wouldn't believe the bruises. I mean, somebody had beaten the tar out of her. Her face and shoulders and ribs were just purple—I think he'd kicked her as well as hit her—and on top of that there were hand-shaped bruises on her neck, so it was pretty obvious somebody had tried to strangle her. So I finally got out of her who did it, and it was Dack Gammon."

"Oh, shit," I said. "But it's unusual for him to resort to violence. He usually goes in for date rape, doesn't he?"

"Well, he's been violent before, but we never could get the victims to testify. And he got acquitted on one date rape. Anyhow, I went over to his place, which is only about half a block from Arlene's mother's place, and started prowling around, and I found five witnesses who told me that Saturday evening after she got home that Friday night they'd seen him dragging a naked girl around in his yard by her hair, hitting her in the face with his fist and kicking her. I asked why they hadn't called the police."

"They didn't want to get involved," I said.

"Got it in one. Anyway, I knew I couldn't prove rape, but I could certainly prove aggravated assault. By the time it was supposed to go to the grand jury I had the flu, so I went on and testified with a temperature of a hundred and four, and I got all my witnesses in, and then I went home and went to bed. The DA called me later to say they'd brought back a true bill. But then he

· · · · ·

called me again a couple of hours later. Seems Dack Gammon is one of Roger's snitches. And Roger went into the grand jury and took Dack to testify that the girl had stolen some jewelry from him and he was just trying to get it back."

"So all of us drag naked people around in the backyard, hitting them in the face with our fists, to get jewelry back," I commented.

"Exactly. He said she wouldn't tell where she'd hidden it. Like that makes assault legal. Anyhow, Roger managed to convince the grand jury that I was just spiteful. He pulled that 'all females stick together' shit. The DA said the grand jury was just about to reverse itself, and he asked me if I could come back in. Deb, I could not. I absolutely could not. My temperature was up to a hundred and five and my legs were like Jell-O and I couldn't even get to the car, much less drive back downtown. So the grand jury reversed itself and no-billed the case and Dack walked, and the next time I saw Roger he gave me that shit-eating grin he's got. It was all I could do not to knock his face in."

"I believe you," I said.

"And then he brought in a book about castrating females and gave it to Captain Millner and said he thought I ought to read it. Captain Millner told him to take the book back to the library, but he'd done it in the squad room so everybody knew about it. That's how I found out—about four different people told me."

"About that time I *would* have knocked his face in."

"No, you wouldn't," Margie said. "And neither did I. But I'll tell you now, I'll be happy to dance at his funeral. Deb, can you cover for me for about half an hour? I've got to get something to eat. Want me to bring you back anything?"

"Uh-uh," I said. "I ate a while ago. And I'm not really very hungry. You could bring me a caffeine-free Diet Coke. A big one with lots of ice. I think I've got a fever again. I'll probably have to stay home tomorrow."

"When was the surgery?"

"Friday."

· · · · ·

"You should have stayed home today."

I had no answer to that, so I didn't try to make one.

Alone in the squad room, I pulled out the notebook in which I was keeping information about Dusty, Sandy, and Doreen Miller and started making more telephone calls trying to locate Doreen. I was still on that when Captain Millner walked into the squad room, quietly enough that I didn't know he was there until I hung up from the latest unfruitful call and he said, "Deb, I told you not to do that."

"I know you did," I answered.

He sat down across from me. "If you think you're the only one concerned about the situation, think again," he said. "When a family has two children, and within a single week one commits suicide and the other vanishes, almost certainly a runaway—yes, I'm aware there's a serious problem. But you're not the only one capable of handling it. And worrying yourself into a tailspin isn't going to—"

"The family had three children," I interrupted.

"What?"

"The family had three children," I said. "The oldest ran away at the age the second killed herself. The family has disowned her. She now works as a prostitute."

"How do you know that?" he asked. "It wasn't in any of your reports."

"I know the girl. Alexandra. Sandy, they call her. She used to be a friend of Becky's—still is, I suppose. I talked with her Friday night. And before you ask, no, I didn't call her. She called me and asked if she could come over."

"What did she tell you?"

I hesitated. "I don't have her permission to tell you that. But think about it. Sandy runs away when she is sixteen, to . . . to take up her present profession. Dusty kills herself at sixteen. Then Doreen runs away at ten or eleven or whatever age she is now. Does that say anything to you?"

· · · · ·

"She's eleven. Just hit puberty a couple of months ago, according to her mother. And yes, I think that's relevant—which is why I asked her mother." He stood up. "Yes. Yes, I believe it does say something to me. But Deb—let us take care of it now. We'll do the best we can to protect Doreen. But don't assume it's all on your shoulders. There are plenty of people trying to find her. I don't want you to try. I have a very good reason for keeping you off the case, and that is the fact that you're too emotionally involved in it. Deb, you're sick. You shouldn't have been here at all today, and you know it as well as I do. You need to be home in bed. Don't even think about coming in tomorrow. And stay off this case, because if you try to stay on it you're going to demolish yourself emotionally, and I need you healthy. Got me?"

After a moment, I said, "I don't like it."

"I know you don't. I don't blame you. But I do expect you to follow my orders."

I didn't answer, and after a moment he said, "Stay out of trouble," and left.

Moments later, Gayle Constantine came out of the interview room we'd stashed Emil Reddich in. I was surprised; the last time I'd noticed her whereabouts she was entering the room Gloria Reddich was in, and I thought Emily Reddich had left already. She looked rather triumphant. "The father has already agreed to remain out of the household until the investigation is complete, and not to meet the daughter at all without supervision. In addition to that, I told him I'll get a court order to that effect, and he's agreed to abide by the terms of it even before I get the court order. So we'll at least be able to keep the mother and daughter together."

"And you know, and I know," Rafe said later, after I told him the decision that had been reached, "that that order isn't worth the paper it's written on unless the mother will call the police if he shows up. And she's not going to. Why don't you go on home, Deb? You look like hell."

"I think I will do that," I said, and grabbed the phone to call the

. . . . .

library and ask a librarian to find Harry and send him to fetch his sick wife home.

"What's this?" I asked, looking at what Harry had just handed me, immediately after opening the white envelope it had been in. Actually it was pretty obvious what it was: it was a thin catalog printed on pulp paper and listing just about all manner of grocery items known to woman. What I really wanted to know was, what was I supposed to do with it.

"There's a grocery store chain in town that's started delivering," Harry said. "They used to charge ten dollars an order to deliver and that felt like a little much, but they've lowered the cost to five dollars an order now, and that's more acceptable. And I got to thinking, you never have time to grocery shop and it always wears you out, with everything else you've got to do, and now you're *really* not up to it, so when I heard about this I ordered the catalog. I thought if you would go through it and underline everything you ever buy from a grocery store, the right brand and size and every-thing, then I could enter it all on the computer and then all you'd have to do is sit down at the computer—I'll load the program and call up the list and everything—and delete everything you *don't* want that time, and then I'll fax the order to the store and then they'll deliver it and I'll write a check, or you will, and think of all the time it will save."

Frankly, a lot of Harry's housekeeping ideas turn out to be idiotic. But I loved this one. Especially right now, when either hobbling through the grocery store or sending Harry or Hal with a very carefully written list which they would of course misunder-stand felt like equally lousy ideas. Of course, for now at least, they'd still have to put the groceries away, as I wasn't even up to that, but surely they could manage it.

After swallowing assorted medications, I tried to sit down in front of the television set with my foot propped up on the coffee table. That wasn't such a good idea: the coffee table is very hard,

. . . . .

and no matter how I rearranged myself, the sorest spot on my heel always seemed to be pressing against the portion of the cast that was pressing against the coffee table. With some help from Lori, who had shown up about that time without Hal, who was practicing for a track meet, I wound up arranging myself on the couch with the foot propped on several pillows and another pillow behind my head, so that I could see the TV while I rested.

After supper—fried chicken, this time, delivered by a church member I didn't even know, but it was accompanied by real mashed potatoes with cream gravy, fried okra, and green beans that must have been frozen because they tasted absolutely fresh—I sent Harry out to buy some more pillows, pillowcases, and a library stool. "I can see the need for pillows," he said, "since you're using every pillow in the house and still need more, but why a library stool? You've got a kitchen stool to reach high shelves—"

"You'll see," I said. "Be sure the one you get is about this high"—I gestured—"and has wheels so it can roll about in all directions."

"Okay," he said, in that resigned tone of voice that really means "I don't know what you think you're doing but we won't argue about it."

After he left, I propped myself up a little more and sent Lori to find a ruler, a red pen, and the lap desk, the grocery store catalog being a little too flimsy to use unsupported. Laying the grocery catalog on top of the lap desk, I began underlining things, occasionally writing in the margin items I buy that were not listed. "Lori," I said once, "would you go in the kitchen and find out the name of that stuff I put on the hamburgers?"

Leaving her English book facedown on the floor beside the hearth on which she was sitting, Lori headed for the kitchen, and returned moments later with a bottle of steak sauce. "Is this what you mean?" she asked.

"Yes, thanks," I said, and wrote the brand name in the margin, then handed the bottle back.

· · · · ·

As she began to return it to the kitchen, the telephone rang. Lori answered and then said, "It's for you. Somebody named Jim."

"Okay," I said, not exactly overwhelmed with joy at the thought of talking with my brother again, particularly in Lori's hearing. So I said, "Lori, I just remembered, I forgot to ask Harry to get some ice cream and I really want some. Would you mind walking over to Stop 'n Go? There's a five in my purse."

She got the money, the expression on her face saying I hadn't fooled her in the slightest, and went out the door before I maneuvered over to the chair and picked up the telephone. "Hello," I said.

"Deb, I just called to say I'm sorry," Jim said abruptly. "About what I said yesterday . . . Look, it just really upset me, that's all."

"Gee, what a coincidence," I answered. "It really upset me, too."

"The thing is . . ." I could hear him swallow. "The thing is, I *did* know it was going on. That Dad was molesting you. And I didn't know what to do about it. I could tell you were miserable all the time, but I just didn't know . . ."

That surprised me, though I suppose it shouldn't have. "Jim," I said, "I never *expected* you to do anything about it, and I'm sorry if you thought that was what I meant. There wasn't anything to do. I didn't know anything I could do then and I still don't know anything I could have done about it. All I want—and I didn't even ask this, but since you called me throwing a fit last night—all I want is for you to admit that it happened. That I'm not making it up."

"All right. It happened. And about my daughters—I'm not. Don't ever think that. I was a jackass that time at Astroworld, and I admit it, but not my daughters. I just didn't want you to tell them that their grandfather . . . Because they loved him, and he didn't do anything to them."

"I hope you're sure," I said. "I never would leave Vicky and Becky alone with him, and it always worried me when you left—"

. . . . .

"I'm sure. Really. And . . . look, if there's anything I can do to help you—"

"There's not," I said. "All I'm asking for is the truth."

"Dammit, I felt so helpless," he burst out. "I remember—Mom would want to see some movie, and he'd say they couldn't really afford for both of them to see it and besides that we kids shouldn't be left alone that long, so he'd take her and tell her he'd go back to get her, and as soon as he got home from taking her he'd park the rest of us in the living room to watch television and then he'd take you in his bedroom and lock the door, and dammit, I was two years younger than you, I was only eleven when it started—"

"You were seven when it started," I said. "You might have been eleven when you became aware of it, but you were seven when it started."

"I . . . Dammit," he said, "I knew there was something wrong, but to start with I didn't know what. And then we'd go swimming down in the stock pond and he'd always be playing with us in the water, only he'd hold onto you a lot longer and you always looked so unhappy."

"I was," I said. "But look, Jim, I know you couldn't do anything about it. The only one I'm mad at for not doing anything about it is Mom, because I know she could have."

"But if she didn't know it was going on—"

"If she didn't know, it was because she chose not to know," I retorted. "She could have known. If he could afford three dollars a day worth of tobacco he could darn well afford the extra dollar to take both of them to the movie instead of just her. And they sure didn't mind leaving me alone to watch the rest of you for hours when it was something he *did* want to do."

"I know all that. All I'm saying is—"

"That you couldn't do anything about it. You don't have to say it again, Jim. I believe you. I know you couldn't do anything about it. All I'm saying is that I want you to admit the truth, and you've done it."

· · · · ·

156

"Okay," Jim said, and then paused awkwardly. "Listen, there's something I really want *you* to know the truth about. That thing at Astroworld—I got my boss to explain to Marilyn right after it happened, but I never thought about telling you. That *was* my boss, not just a buddy, and he was skunk drunk."

"I noticed that," I said.

"Well, right then he was at the giddy stage, but he turns into a mean drunk real fast. I was afraid if I didn't go with him he'd land in jail before the afternoon was over. But I swear I didn't do anything myself. You think I want to risk bringing a case of clap or something worse home to Marilyn, you're crazy. And I just—it really upset me that you'd think I'd do it, especially with Marilyn eight months pregnant. That's why I yelled at you when you started talking about it yesterday. I should have explained then, but you know me."

Jim's only two years younger than I am, and I do indeed know him and his temper. Generally I can tell when he's lying. This time I was pretty sure he wasn't. "Okay," I said. "But you can see how it looked to me."

"Yeah," he said, and then asked, "Will you be all right?"

"Why shouldn't I be?" Then I realized how testy my voice sounded, and added, "Yes, Jim, I'm all right. Really."

"You sound funny."

"I sound funny because I had foot surgery Friday and tried to get up and go to work today and I ran my fever up and I feel lousy. That's all. But I need to go lie down now. So if you don't mind—"

"Okay," he said. "I'm sorry I sounded like a jerk yesterday. Talk to you later."

When Lori came back with the ice cream I was back on the couch, diligently underlining groceries. "Do you want some ice cream now?" she asked.

"I need to let my dinner settle a little more," I said. "And Lori, don't worry about the phone call. It was just my brother, and he and I had a fight yesterday and I didn't want you to be where you

· · · · ·

157

could hear it in case we started having a fight again today. But we didn't; he just called to apologize."

"That's okay," she said. "About wanting to talk in private, I mean. I'm glad your brother apologized. I got chocolate fudge ripple. I hope that's okay."

"It sounds wonderful," I said. "And I think I could use a little right now after all."

. . . . .

\mathcal{N} i n \varepsilon

THE EXAMINING CHAIR in a foot surgeon's office is like the examining chair in a dentist's office, minus the tray and all the little nasties the dentist keeps on the tray, except that it leans back somewhat farther. I was leaning way, way back with my foot propped up while Dr. Brandon was examining those portions of my foot that were visible under and above the cast.

"I told you," he said, after straightening up and washing his hands, "that you would need a lot more bed rest than I had originally thought, because you had a lot more tendon involvement than I had anticipated. And I had told you to start with that you'd need to stay in bed or on a couch or chair, with your foot elevated on two or three pillows, for at least a week. Doubling that week—and doubling it is the absolute minimum you can get by with—adds up to two weeks, and I told you that, too. So what did you expect, when you tried to go back to work after only three days? Actually, more like two and a half days, counting from the time the surgery was completed. What you have now is a severe case of tendinitis—that means an inflamed tendon. Deb, that heel spur was tangled with the tendon in about six different places. I practically had to dissect the tendon to get the calcium deposits out, and damaged tendons don't heal overnight. Neglected tendon damage doesn't heal at all, which means if you don't get the necessary rest now you can count on trouble from this for the rest of your life, and that's exactly what this surgery was designed to prevent. And on top of that, you're on the verge of setting up an infection along the line of the incision, because you're lowering your resistance so much by trying to do more than your body is ready to do. I've given your husband another prescription for penicillin, which he will go and fill for you *after* he's deposited you where you belong. Now take yourself home, and put yourself to bed, and *keep* yourself in bed, if you don't want to lose the next two months of work instead of just the next two weeks. If for any reason you find it absolutely essential to go to work, or to church, take a pillow with you and get an extra chair and keep your foot propped up on it. As for the library or shopping, send somebody else."

Harry, lounging against the wall, prudently kept his mouth shut, because the only thing he would have had to say would be along the lines of "I told you so," and he knows how much I adore hearing that phrase. But then, come to think of it, he hadn't seemed to have much to say to me for the last couple of days anyway, and he'd been growing steadily more morose. Of course, having me down was annoying him, but still . . .

Deciding, probably correctly, that it would do me no good whatsoever to tell the doctor I didn't want to go take six hundred milligrams of ibuprofen and however many milligrams it was of whatever that other stuff was because they made me dream about snakes, I said meekly, "Okay. Thanks for seeing me without an appointment."

"You're welcome," he said, "but for your sake I'd just as soon not see you back until your regular appointment. And I won't have to, if you'll do as you're told."

No, I was not using my Captain Ahab roller skate at the moment, but rather the crutches I used outside the house and the office. I made my laborious way back to the car, which Harry had pulled up in a "patients only" parking slot directly in front of the building, thrust the crutches into the backseat while I clung to the back of the front seat, maneuvered myself into the car with some

. . . . .

difficulty, and sat down and fastened my seat belt. Harry started the car without saying much of anything and turned to head back toward home.

On the way home I said, "Harry, if we could just stop at the grocery store for a minute . . ."

He didn't say anything. But he thought very, very loudly.

"On second thought, I'll make a list," I said hastily. "You can get it while you're out getting the prescription refilled."

"Good thinking," he said, the jolliness in his voice sounding quite forced. "You want me to bring you a hamburger and milk shake?"

Well, maybe he wasn't quite ready to kill me after all. The hamburger I could do without, but a milk shake sounded wonderful.

What I really wanted, though, was an avocado. Maybe two or three avocados. Or four or five. Nice soft extra-ripe avocados. Chopped up in salad, with lettuce and tomatoes and mayonnaise, or squished up with chopped tomatoes and salsa, to dip up with corn chips. I was absolutely drooling for avocados. In view of the fact that I want an avocado about three times a year, and avocados are loaded with vitamin A, maybe my body was talking to me. But if it wanted vitamin A, why couldn't it talk about carrots or apricots, which don't contain all the fat of avocados? Maybe my body wanted that special kind of fat avocados contain.

Or maybe I was just a little bit crazier than usual.

Caviar would be nice, too, on very crisp thin-sliced whole wheat toast . . . I want caviar about once in three years. I must have been a little bit crazy.

But once I got home, I unfortunately wasn't able to stay awake long enough to get either the milk shake or the avocados, and I didn't even ask for the caviar. *Why should I let Harry know I'm crazy today?* Anyway, I dozed off waiting for the milk shake, the avocados, and the penicillin, and of course, I dreamed about snakes.

· · · · ·

This time I was fourteen, not as small as I had been when I was twelve but still quite small enough that a heavy wind could knock me over. I'd forgotten how thin I was then, although I knew quite well what my weight on the scales had been because I'd stayed that weight for seven years. But my subconscious remembered. Five-two, a hundred and nine pounds, might not be thin for some body builds, but I have a very heavy bone structure, and for me a hundred and nine pounds was practically emaciated. I was walking barefoot through a barren landscape. I was on a bluff overlooking the sea—why the sea I do not know, as I have not even seen the ocean more than three or four times, and never from a bluff. I think I must have been in the Hawaiian Islands, or maybe on the Pacific Coast of the American mainland. I stood and watched the tide go out—and out—and out. Fathers sent their daughters out with baskets to collect the sea's treasures abandoned by the retreating water—the starfish, the sea anemones, the eels, the eels, the eels, and then the fathers walked together, slowly, stealthily, back up the beach, looking back over their shoulders to see to it the children were still collecting the eels as the fathers moved steadily to higher ground, to safety, because then I realized that this was not just a tide going out, this was something else, this was the retreat of the waters before the onrush of a tsunami, often but mistakenly called a tidal wave. I screamed for the children to drop the eels and come back to high ground where they would be safe, but they didn't hear me, and they went on collecting the eels and then the water came back with a terrible rush like a train, like a tornado, much higher than normal high tide, burying the children as if they had never been, and the water rose so high that it dashed against the bluff I was standing on and I was wet by the spray, and I backed away and turned and ran up, up, up, toward a single palm tree standing at the highest point, and still the water pursued me.

When finally the water went away, back down to its normal level, huge snakes crawled out of the mud. They were sluggish, to begin with, and the first one crawled toward me slowly and I

. . . . .

retreated, and then more and more snakes crawled toward me as if the mud itself were breeding snakes and all came to be six feet long and as thick as a large man's wrist and they began to move faster and faster and there were more and more of them, and then the whole landscape was filled with snakes and from all directions they pursued me.

Behind the single palm tree was a church—a generic church, I supposed, as I could see nothing that would let me know what kind of church it was. It was a small white building, a chapel only, with perhaps two small Sunday school rooms, and the entire building couldn't have held over sixty people. The exterior was white asbestos siding or clapboard, I couldn't tell which, and a steeple rose from the center of the roof. The steeple also was covered with asbestos siding or clapboard, except for the bell tower, which had no bell in it but was open on all four sides, with a weather vane of a pattern I couldn't make out on top instead of any kind of religious symbol.

Surely the snakes can't follow me into the church, I thought, and ran for the porch and the open door, but when I ran in I saw that the floor was like Indiana Jones's worst nightmare, solid with crawling, writhing snakes slithering atop one another, sliding across the pulpit, creeping over the piano (there was no organ), gliding under and over the pews, flowing as smoothly as water and as inexorably as an avalanche, and I saw that there was nowhere for me to go at all to escape them.

This time I had no help. My sister was not there; Oprah Winfrey was not in this dream. Only me and the snakes.

I woke sweating, my heart pounding, and sat up and reached for ginger ale and then for the phone to call Susan or Matilda or my mother or anybody, but then I decided against the phone and tried to calm myself and think.

Most dreams are just dreams, I suspect, but repeated dreams are likely to be saying something important, even if it is highly coded. So what was this dream saying to me?

. . . . .

The earlier dreams had made the meaning of the snakes abundantly clear, and it was the usual Freudian meaning of snakes, but what did this particular dream mean—not according to some general scheme of what dreams "ought" to mean, but in my particular dream code?

Oddly enough, in real life I have never been particularly frightened of snakes, as long as they are snakes to which I have been properly introduced so that I know they are nonpoisonous. I remember once at a rural crime scene when a deputy sheriff decided to chase me with a grass snake, and was very disappointed when I took it away from him and chewed him out for snake abuse. It was a beautiful animal, green on top and yellow beneath, with eyes like rubies cabochon cut, and I carried it around my neck until we finished the crime scene, releasing it only after that particular detective was gone so that he could not have caught it to abuse it again. So the terror of snakes in my dream had to be terror of symbolic snakes, not of real snakes. But then, I had already decided that.

I have never lived by the sea, but our house during my entire childhood was on a little hill overlooking the stock pond where a dairy farm owner's cattle went to drink, and it was shaded by one pine tree as the church in my dreams was shaded by one palm tree. When we swam in the stock pond my father would put his hands down my swimsuit, would take my hand and thrust it inside his swimsuit, while just a few feet away my brothers and my sister swam and played. Once some water moccasins moved into the stock pond and stayed there until my brothers killed them with machetes, and once a big water moccasin came and lay sunning itself along the windowsill right outside my bedroom and my father and brothers jeered at me for being afraid of it and refused to do anything about it; they said I was a sissy, although in fact I have never been a sissy. So there I had the water and the Freudian snakes and eels, and there was the source of my revulsion and fear, the fear

.   .   .   .   .

that the rest of my life would be filled with the same nasty furtiveness of my teen years. *The children gathered their fathers' eels until they were drowned, but the fathers watched unharmed. Not only unharmed but uncaring, as if they lacked the realization that the children could be harmed. And that is the theme song of the molesting father: I didn't hurt her none.*

The fathers have eaten sour grapes and the children's teeth are set on edge. The sins of the fathers are visited on the children. Not as a threat from God, not as a punishment sent by an abusive superfather somewhere in the stratosphere, but as an inevitable consequence humans bring on humans. Oh, they taught me the Bible when I was a child. Abused me on Saturday night and saw to it I read the Bible on Sunday afternoon. But I had to figure out the meanings for myself, because the meanings my father taught from the pulpit weren't the meanings at all.

Walking barefoot through a barren landscape was pretty obvious. When I was a child none of us kids in my family ever wore shoes in the summer, as long as we were right around the house, because it wasn't worth wasting good shoe leather and the money it took to buy it just to keep kids from getting cut feet, not when you could buy at least two or three days' worth of tobacco for what it would cost to buy a pair of shoes and there were six kids. Why, my father might have had to go without cigarettes a whole month at a time to keep us in shoes for the summer!

The area we lived in had regular neighborhoods, and even an elementary school, within walking distance, but my family lived on a dairy farm, and the milk my father delivered was raw milk, from herds certified disease-free. Nutritious, no doubt, and pleasant to think about, if you didn't have to live with it. But if you've ever walked barefoot through a cow pasture . . . well, the city dwellers' bucolic vision of sweet-smelling cows in a sweet-smelling field takes no thought at all for cow patties, nor for the fact that the cows don't eat the prickly pears unless someone burns the thorns off them. Walking through a cow pasture in Tarrant County, or most other parts of Texas, is walking through a field of shit and cactus.

· · · · ·

In other places, I suppose it is shit and thistles. Barren is an understatement. I expect your typical desert smells a lot better and has a lot fewer germs.

The year I was fourteen was the year our pastor had his heart attack, and for months he could not preach, could not get to church at all, and my father, as head of the board of elders, was up in the pulpit every Sunday morning, every Sunday night, every Wednesday night, telling other people how to live. He preached a series of sermons on the prophets, focusing for three weeks on the Book of Hosea, explaining how Hosea's marriage to a "daughter of whoredom" was intended to symbolize Israel's lusting after false gods. He was eloquent; some people who didn't normally attend our church came to listen. *But Hosea repeatedly forgave and God forgives, as many times as people will repent. That was the real message of the Book of Hosea, the message my father left out. The real sins are the sins people commit against people; God is too big to be harmed by human sin. "I will have mercy and not sacrifice." Which prophet taught that? My father would know—the words, and the source, but never the meaning. Never the meaning. Because the laws were given for the benefit of humans, and the laws forbid incest.*

I remember, too, that during that six months, because he didn't want to prepare but one sermon for Sunday, he used his Halley's Bible Commentary's discussion of Catholicism as the basis for a series of evening talks about the history of the papacy. He spent a lot of time talking about the horrible vices of the medieval popes, and that, too, many people came to hear. Catholicism still is not popular in most of what was the Old South, and most people are delighted to hear about the crimes of those they dislike.

But no amount of knowledge about the medieval popes or the sorrows of Hosea was sufficient to stop my father from sexually abusing his own daughter on Saturday night before stepping into the pulpit on Sunday morning. So indeed the snakes had pursued me even into church . . . Vaguely I remembered a hymn with a line in it, something about "Where is my refuge?" I had had none.

. . . . .

Neither had my sister, nor any of my brothers. My father didn't go to church at all the last twelve years of his life, after the song service in which he sang so loudly (in his admittedly splendid tenor voice) that one of my brothers, standing next to him with an earache, put his hands over his ears to shut out the piercing sound. Instantly my father grabbed my brother and marched him down the aisle and out the door, leaned him against a column, and proceeded in full view of an elder and two deacons to break three of my brother's ribs and knock out two of his front teeth. My father was voted out of the congregation that same day; my mother went on attending, trying to ignore the pitying stares of the other women until gradually people's attentions focused themselves on other things, and the board and congregation relented enough to allow my father, for my mother's sake, to be buried in the church-yard.

But while his children were young, none of us had a refuge.

Nor had Dusty, nor Sandy, I realized, as my thoughts veered away from my own past problems and those of my brothers and sister. Sandy had never had a refuge, and Dusty's refuge had van-ished when Sandy did. Now, if Doreen knew anything at all about what had been going on, she knew her refuge was gone.

But Dusty had been sixteen when she died. From what Sandy told me, it was reasonable to assume she had been molested for at least four years. What, then, could have precipitated her suicide *now*? She wasn't pregnant; we knew that. So far as we could tell the abuse hadn't escalated, as she was still at least technically virgin. So perhaps Sandy hadn't, as I thought I had understood her on Friday, been asking me why Dusty died. Perhaps what she had been asking was why Dusty died *now*, as opposed to some other time, and I—because of exhaustion, pain, fogginess from medication—hadn't understood.

But to find out why Dusty had died *now*, I would need a starting place, and that starting place would have to come at least partially from Sandy. Yes, of course Captain Millner had told me not to try

· · · · ·

167

to work on it, had told me there were plenty of people on it. But I had resources he didn't have; I had resources none of the people officially working on it—working on the disappearance of Doreen, that is, because the rest of the case was closed—had. I had Sandy Miller willing to talk with me.

And yes, I fully realized that Harry and Captain Millner were right that we could not do anything now to help Dusty. But if investigating Dusty's death would help to save Doreen, then it was worth doing. And surely nobody—including Dusty—would disagree with that.

Ignoring the fact that I was about as exhausted, about as groggy from medication, in about as much pain, as I had been Friday, I called Sandy and, of course, got her answering machine again. To that perky voice, I said, "This is Deb Ralston, and it's about noon on Tuesday. Please call me when you get the chance."

Then I and my rolling footstool went on into the living room, where Harry was sitting—somewhat grumpily, I deduced from his posture—at the computer table. He had a stack of reference books arranged beside the keyboard, and was trying to hold one of them open with another book while he typed from it. "I have a plastic cookbook holder that will keep that book open for you," I offered.

"If I wanted it I'd get it," he snarled.

"Sorr-ree," I said, and sat down on the couch. In deference to his obvious preoccupation, I did not turn on the television and begin to channel surf. I just sat.

"Sorry," he said, somewhat more calmly. "I'm just sick of this paper. And you've offered me your cookbook stand before and every time I tried to use it I knocked it over and wound up knocking stuff off the desk. But if I wasn't just so sick of this . . ." His voice trailed off into mumblings.

I could well believe it. Unlike most of the assigned papers for his MBA course, which ran five to seven pages and were at least half the time done in committees, this last paper was supposed to be fifty to seventy pages long. It was supposed to detail a real business

· · · · ·

problem, the way it was (or was not) solved, and ideas that if thought of at the time might have presented a better solution, and it was supposed to be based on real situations at Harry's place of employment. That assignment had necessitated a lot of trips to Bell Helicopter to talk to the decision makers Harry seldom met, and in fact would continue to seldom meet even after he did complete the MBA and get his promised managerial position. He had selected a situation involving the sale of Bell Long Ranger helicopters to Saudi Arabia. In fact, the problem had been solved quite expeditiously, and trying to come up with alternative, much less better, solutions was taxing Harry's imagination to the utmost. I had no idea what the book was that he was entering quotations from into the computer, but I suspected it had something to do with business customs of the Arab world.

I further suspected he was about at the end of his tether and did not need any suggestions, helpful or otherwise, from me until he finished what he was doing and had time to calm down.

The only problem with the couch, I decided as I rearranged myself for the tenth time in about two minutes, was that without Lori to bring me pillows I couldn't get myself into a comfortable place, and considering Harry's present mood it would be inadvisable to ask him to bring me pillows. Balancing on my rolling footstool, I went to the kitchen and got my milk shake out of the refrigerator; I would wait for the avocados until Lori was there to help. Grabbing the morning newspaper, which I hadn't read yet, I returned to the bedroom and began the task of trying to figure out how to read the paper while keeping my foot propped up. It was, I soon discovered, impossible without folding the newspaper into very small bundles. I certainly hoped Harry was through with it, because if he wasn't he was really going to be mad when he tried to read it later.

I had finished Ann Landers and was almost through with the comics—of course I read them before the front page, doesn't everybody?—when the telephone rang. Owing to the difficulty of

. . . . .

169

putting down the newspaper, disengaging my foot from the pile of pillows, and rolling over to get the telephone, I found Harry already speaking on the extension by the time I grabbed it. "She can't come in today," he was saying, quite firmly. "I already called and told somebody—"

"You told me," Rafe said, "and I don't want her to come in. I didn't figure she should have tried it yesterday. All I want to know is, does she mind if I give her phone number to Laura Washington."

"Who's Laura Washington?"

"Something I can handle over the phone," I said, finally managing to get a few words in edgewise.

If Laura Washington was upset enough to ask for my phone number at home, knowing I was sick—and Rafe surely must have told her that just in case she'd forgotten—then I didn't expect to have to wait long for her call. And I didn't; it was less than three minutes before the phone rang again.

"Thank you for letting me call you," Mrs. Washington said. "I know you're feeling poorly, and you're probably tired of me anyway, but I just don't know what to do."

"Let me know what's happening," I said. "Something else about Diane? Or the Bonandos again?"

"The Bonandos again," Mrs. Washington said, her voice sounding both grim and slightly frightened. "Our priest just left. That Bonando woman went and complained to him, and he's just warned us he doesn't want to hear any more of such carryings-on. But he won't tell us what she said, and since we saw you neither one of us has even *looked* at that girl. I mean, if she comes down the street David leaves the yard and comes in the house to give her time to pass by. I probably sound like that Mrs. Reddich, but I *know* David, and he's nothing at all like Emil Reddich. Deb, I don't mind telling you I'm to the point where this is scaring me. It hasn't been that long since a black man could get lynched in this town

. . . . .

with this kind of story going round, even if he hadn't done a living thing."

"We certainly won't let Mr. Washington get lynched," I said, "and I'm going to see what I can figure out to put a stop to it."

"I don't think it's just the girl," Mrs. Washington said. "I think she'd be okay, if that mother of hers would just let her alone. But she's keeping everything stirred up all the time—"

"I agree with you," I said. "I'll make some phone calls and see what I can do now. Let me have the priest's name and phone number."

The priest was Father Vincent, and it took me about half an hour of trying before I managed to reach him by telephone; apparently he was out making pastoral calls. "I'm Deb Ralston," I said, "and I'm the detective working on the situation between the Bonandos and the Washingtons."

"Oh, I wasn't aware that the police had been called in," he said. "I really think I could have dealt with it adequately—"

"I was called in before you were," I told him. "Mrs. Bonando came in to see me last week, and I talked with her and Janine and with both Mr. and Mrs. Washington at that time. Mrs. Washington telephoned me today, after you talked with the Washingtons. She's extremely distraught over the accusations, and I can't say that I blame her. Obviously, you can't tell me anything that was said to you confidentially, and I realize that, but it would be very helpful if you could answer a few questions for me."

"If I can." He sounded rather young, and not quite sure of himself.

"Do you know the Washingtons and the Bonandos well?" I asked.

"Yes, and to be perfectly honest I was quite astounded by this whole thing," he said.

"In what way?"

"Just that Mr. Washington would do such a thing as . . ."

. . . . .

"Such a thing as what?" I asked when he hesitated. "Because frankly, so far my investigation has not disclosed anything at all that Mr. Washington has done."

"Mrs. Bonando said . . ." He paused again, and then went on. "Perhaps you should know, because none of this was said under the seal of the confessional and it seemed, well, bizarre in the extreme. She said that the Washingtons have been approaching her daughter, but she seemed quite unable to define what she meant by 'approaching,' except that she said that in the past Mr. Washington had stood out in the front yard to watch Janine walk by, but for the last two days every time Janine goes by the Washingtons' house on her way to school, Mr. Washington runs in the house and watches her with binoculars."

"Has she actually seen the binoculars?" I asked.

"She says he draws the curtain and peeps through them, so of course she can't see the binoculars."

"Did Janine tell you that, or Janine's mother?"

"Mrs. Bonando. Janine's mother. She said Janine had come home from school yesterday very upset, and today when Janine walked to school she followed in the car so she could see what happened. She said Janine walked down the sidewalk and Mr. Washington was loitering in his yard, and as soon as Janine reached the block the Washingtons live on, Mr. Washington scurried inside. She could see the curtains move. She said she was quite certain he was watching Janine through binoculars, and then watching her as she drove past."

"Even if he was, that wouldn't be illegal," I pointed out. "And a man can scarcely be accused of loitering in his own yard. At present we have no evidence that he even owns a pair of binoculars, much less that he was using them to spy on Janine Bonando. She—Mrs. Bonando, I mean—hasn't told you anything else?"

"No, nothing."

"After a church service . . ." I hesitated. My ignorance of Catholicism is profound, so I was somewhat uncertain of anything

· · · · ·

at all about a mass. I tried again. "After a mass is completed, do you ever go out in the foyer?"

"Yes, I often do that."

"Have you ever seen Mr. Washington in the foyer speaking to teenagers? And if so, is it just the girls?"

"Yes, he's very friendly," Father Vincent said. "He speaks to both the boys and the girls."

"What sort of things does he say to them?"

"Asks them about their schoolwork. Sometimes he tells the girls their dresses are attractive, or the boys they have on a good-looking tie. Sometimes he asks them when they'll be graduating, and what they plan to take in college. If somebody's considering dropping out he tries to dissuade them, though of course they usually drop out of church before they drop out of school. He used to be a teacher in the public high school himself, you know."

"No, I didn't know that. I knew he was retired, but not what from. Of course, I knew she's a retired teacher."

"He started out in a black school, and then when the schools were integrated he fitted very well into a mixed school. Of course, I'm telling you what I've heard; I wasn't here then and in fact I'm probably younger than many of his students. He was a coach— head coach for track and field, and assistant coach for basketball and football. All boys' sports, of course. And he used to teach geography and civics."

"And there were never any complaints about him as a teacher?"

"Oh, no, in fact he won a citywide Teacher of the Year award one year, and I was here by the time that happened. His students were much taken with him; I'm told he was the kind of teacher who taught people to think. He's been retired about three years now, and I think he misses the boys and girls quite a lot. I've known many of his former students who have told me how much he had helped them, in personal matters as well as educational ones."

"So you would think it would be reasonable, if he saw a child

. . . . .

173

looking very lonely and upset, that he would try to say something friendly to her."

"Yes, of course. But as to making advances toward a child—and I gather that's what Mrs. Bonando meant by 'approaching'—well, I really could not believe that at all. But some of the most unexpected people do become child abusers, and I try to keep an open mind for the evil as well as the good, unpleasant as that may be for a parish minister."

"Watching for the evil is essential in your business as well as mine. But as I said, in this case I haven't seen any evidence that any abuse at all has occurred or is occurring. Mrs. Bonando came to the police department last week and talked with me. She told me the same thing she told you, that Mr. Washington was 'approaching' her daughter, and she was not able to define 'approaching' for me any more than she was for you. I went and talked with Janine, and she said that Mr. Washington had spoken to her several times in the foyer after mass, though she seemed unable to remember what he had said, and that he was in the yard when she went by on her way to and from school. Father Vincent, have you seen the Washingtons' yard?"

"Yes, I have."

"I have, too. How large would you say it is?"

A brief silence. Then he said, "Oh, quite a hundred thousand square feet. Very large, especially for this part of town."

"And what about its condition?"

"Very well kept. His roses are particularly fine."

"Do you know who does the yard work?"

"He does . . . I see what you mean. Of course it's reasonable, especially when the weather is this good, that he'd be in the yard working at the time when the children are coming home from school, and often when they're going to school."

"Exactly. I went and talked with the Washingtons. Mr. Washington agreed that he had spoken with Janine several times in the foyer. He said she seemed lonely and unhappy and he had hoped

. . . . .

to cheer her up. He said that when he was in the yard and she walked by he spoke to her, recognizing her from church and again noticing that she seemed lonely. He said she almost always walked alone, unlike the other children, who were generally walking in groups. He said that one day he was pruning his roses when she walked by, and he impulsively offered her a rose and she took off running. It was immediately after that day that Mrs. Bonando went to the police station. So what I'm seeing, Father Vincent, is not any type of inappropriate advances by Mr. Washington toward Janine Bonando, but rather the persecution of Mr. Washington by Mrs. Bonando on the basis of imaginary affronts to her daughter, whom she apparently keeps frightened to death. Does this scenario make sense to you?"

"It certainly makes more sense to me than the other scenario," Father Vincent said warmly. "The Washingtons have been model parishioners as long as I have been with this parish, but Mrs. Bonando seems constantly to be in some sort of stew or other, and most of them seem to be of her own making. Would you like me to speak to Mrs. Bonando?"

"If you think she'll listen to you, you might try," I said, "but I'm going to talk to somebody with some psychological background and see what we can do from the police department. Whether or not you speak to the Bonandos, it might help if you would let the Washingtons know you haven't automatically believed everything Mrs. Bonando says. Mrs. Washington is really quite frightened."

"I'll do that, of course," the priest said. "I . . . Well. This is really an odd situation."

I called Mrs. Bonando, then, as much to check in with her as anything else, and she said, "Well, I didn't call you."

"I know you didn't," I said. "I want you to tell me what, exactly, it was you told Father Vincent."

"Why should I tell you? You said you were going to stop it, and you didn't."

"What did you tell—"

. . . . .

175

"I told him what happened!" she shouted.

"Now tell me."

"Well, after you went over there, then he didn't talk to Janine no mo—anymore. But he went on looking at her. She told me when she went by the house he went in and then looked out at her through the curtains. And I went to see, and she was right. She came down the street, and he went in the house and then he looked out through the curtains with binoculars to watch her go by."

"Did you see the binoculars?"

"No, but they were there."

"How do you know they were there?"

"I don't have to see them to know they're there!" she said, and began to sob dryly.

"Mrs. Bonando," I said, "Mr. Washington has not broken any laws at all. He has not behaved in any improper manner toward your daughter. At this point, he has very strong grounds for a slander suit against you, and if he asked me what I thought, I would tend to advise him to pursue it."

"Everybody always takes the men's side!" she yelled. "I should have known, you're a cop, you're just like the men. Nobody ever believes what women say, everybody always believes the men, no woman is ever safe—"

"Mrs. Bonando," I said sharply, "I don't take the side of the men or the women. I take the side of justice. There is a vast quantity of child abuse, including sexual abuse, and I fight it every way I can. But your child has not been abused, at least not by David Washington, and your unwarranted accusations toward him amount to very cruel abuse."

She hung up. I sighed and dialed Susan Braun's clinic. I had about decided this was a psychiatric matter, not a police matter.

Susan was out of town for a convention and would not be back until Wednesday night.

Rats, I thought, and called Matilda Greenwood. She's not a

. . . . .

psychiatrist, but she's a psychologist, and she might very well be able to shed as much light on this complicated mess as Susan could. And unlike Susan, she was present and available.

"I'll need to rearrange a few appointments," she said, "but it won't take long. Give me an hour or so and I'll be there."

So I took a belated penicillin, another ibuprofen, and another pain pill, and of course went back to sleep. Just for a change I did not dream about snakes. In fact, to the best of my knowledge and memory I didn't dream about anything. I just slept.

. . . . .

$\mathcal{T}\varepsilon n$
. . . .

I HALFWAY WOKE up to hear Matilda, in the front room, telling Harry he looked like shit. "I feel like shit," he answered.

"How come?"

"A lot of stuff." Silence for a moment. I could picture Matilda's raised eyebrows, before Harry said, "I'm having to sleep on the couch because Deb's damn cast takes up half the bed."

"Awwww," Matilda teased, and Harry laughed.

"Okay," he said, "I'm being a jerk. It's only been three days. I just keep wondering how much longer, because the doctor said she'd have to wear the cast at least six weeks and maybe more, and I do sort of like to sleep with my wife once in a while." More silence, before he added, "She didn't say I had to sleep on the couch. But I know she's miserable, and I'm sort of a bed hog. Maybe when she gets to feeling better . . ."

"There, you're sounding more like yourself already," Matilda pointed out. "Is Deb asleep?"

"Yeah, you want me to wake her up? I know she wanted to talk with you, but—"

"Naah, let her sleep. I don't have anything else I have to do today, at least not before eight o'clock. I'll just read till she wakes up again."

Apparently my subconscious decided that that meant I didn't have to finish waking up now, because I dozed off again, waking when Lori tiptoed into my room to collect any dishes I might have

. . . . .

used since she had last inspected my room, after breakfast, which as usual she had eaten at our house. I sat up, and she offered, in about one minute, to rearrange my pillows, to make my bed, to get me some more ice, to get me a glass of milk, and to bring me a bowl of ice cream. I must have begun to look rather exasperated, because then she said, "I didn't mean to hassle you."

"You're not," I said. "I just feel cruddy. You're being very helpful." I got a good look at her then and realized she seemed tired, worried, and very unhappy. In an effort to cheer her, I said, "I can't remember—when is it your group has its show?"

"It's Hal's group," she said. "I don't like it." Her face began to tighten with the obvious effort to hold back tears, as she went on, "Deb, I can't sing as loud as they want me to. I've tried, and tried, and tried, and I just can't. I wish he'd get somebody else to sing. He's afraid I'd be jealous, but I wouldn't be. I can't do what I can't do, and that's that. But the show is Friday night. And it's going to be a complete disaster. Hal still thinks that by Friday night I can learn to sing loud."

"That must make you feel miserable," Matilda said, wandering into the bedroom.

Lori looked around at her and said, "Hi, Sister Eagle Feather."

"Not off duty, dear, not off duty," Matilda said. "Actually, I'm getting rather tired of being Sister Eagle Feather, if I could just think of a way out of it. But the spirits won't let me be, so I might as well use all the trappings. About the group . . ."

"It does. Make me miserable, I mean. And he keeps fiddling with the microphone, trying to make it sound like I'm singing louder when I'm not."

About that time a not quite coherent roar arose from Harry, along the basic lines of *why did you leave my tools in the garage,* and Hal yelled, "Because I'm not through with them yet!"

That was when Lori started crying, and it was only then—when she threw herself down on my bed and cuddled up to me to weep—that it dawned upon me that my illness, my immobiliza-

· · · · ·

tion, had brought back to her those horrible days after her mother's suicide, when she was still flat on her back in the hospital without the slightest idea of what she was going to do or where she was going to go, refusing to listen to reassurance from anybody but Hal. Of course she was frightened, I thought, even without knowing why, because although consciously she was perfectly aware that I had had only minor foot surgery, her subconscious was telling her over and over *if you lose this mother, too, what will you do?* Because the aunt with whom she nominally lived—she went there to sleep, and occasionally stayed to eat breakfast on nonschool days when Hal was on Scout trips or otherwise out of pocket—was cold, unloving, unwelcoming; she had made it clear that she had taken Lori in only because it was her duty, and the more time Lori spent elsewhere the better she liked it. And as I have said many times before, God help any child who is taken in because it was somebody's duty.

And yet I couldn't invite Lori to live with us, as much as I wanted to, because having Hal and Lori under the same roof would be far too explosive a situation, no matter how well meaning the two of them are. But once again I resolved that if Hal went on a mission—as theoretically all Mormon men do at nineteen, though only about two-thirds actually do it—then the day after Hal left for the Missionary Training Center in Provo, Utah, I would have Lori out of her aunt's house and installed in Hal's room for the next two years. I'd decide what to do at the end of those two years when the time came.

Meanwhile, as I was making those decisions, I was patting Lori on the shoulder and assuring her it was okay to be her. "No it's not!" she wept. "I'm a rotten person to be! My mother killed herself, and Aunt Jessie hates me, and—"

"Your mother was very mixed up," I said, "but you know she didn't hate you. As for Aunt Jessie, I don't know what's the matter with her, because I know you've done the best you could to get along with her, but whatever it is, it's her that's the problem, not

· · · · ·

180

you. And *I* certainly don't hate you. The only person I ever want you to be is the very best Lori you can possibly be, and you're managing that just fine. And don't worry if you can't sing loudly; that's certainly not the *sine qua non* of existence!"

"It is right now, for Hal!" she sobbed. "If his opening is a flop because I can't sing he'll be so mad at me—"

"If he's mad at anybody it ought to be himself, if he's expecting you to do something you can't do."

Behind Matilda, Harry and Hal were both crowding in. "I won't be mad at you, Lori, I promise!" Hal protested. "I know you can't sing loud, and I'm *trying* to find somebody who can!"

And Harry said, "Look, Lori, I'm not mad when the tools are being used, and even if I was I wouldn't be mad at you. I just thought Hal had forgotten and left them out there again, like he did last week."

Lori went on crying, and I went on patting her on the shoulder.

"I've got to go to a committee meeting," Harry said, sounding highly uncomfortable. That was another reason for me to be grateful his MBA school was nearly over; it had involved two years of near-constant committee meetings, as group members gathered to plot strategy on group assignments.

"I'll go work on the microphone some more," Hal said. "But look, Lori, I *don't* expect you to do anything you can't do, so don't worry about it."

As his steps receded through the living room, Lori said, "And you don't mind if I make a lot of noise in the morning?"

"You never make any noise at all in the morning," I said, astonished. "What in the world are you talking about?"

"Aunt Jessie says she doesn't care, because she's up anyway, but it's uncivilized for me to wake you at those ungodly hours."

I assumed that "those ungodly hours" had reference to the fact that Lori arose at five-thirty every morning for Hal to take her, in Harry's pickup truck, to early morning seminary, another of those interesting customs we discovered when Hal became a Mormon.

· · · · ·

They get back here about seven-fifteen, just in time to wolf down breakfast, which is usually cereal unless I've been feeling ambitious, and catch the school bus.

"If you did wake me, which you don't, I'd be awake anyway from Hal banging around," I pointed out logically. "Anyhow, I leave for work right after you leave for school, so obviously I've got to be up. And if I minded I'd let you know. So don't worry about it."

"And Aunt Jessie says I'm like a harpy, I always take and never give."

"You do a lot around here," I said. "You've picked up scads of the chores Becky and Vicky used to do when they were home. And I'm sure you'd do more for Aunt Jessie if she'd let you."

"She won't let me do *anything*! One time when she had a club meeting I thought I'd find *something* she didn't like to do, and I looked and looked and looked and finally noticed the oven hadn't been cleaned lately and I cleaned the oven and when she came home and saw it she said I was saying she was a bad housekeeper, and I wasn't, I was just trying to be nice, and—"

"You may clean my oven any time you want to," Matilda said. At that Lori laughed through her tears. Matilda added, "I'll bet Deb will let you clean hers, too. Let's see, Deb, who else do we know who wants a clean oven?"

"Aunt Jessie is a horse's rear end," I said, "and I wish I could think of a way to get Lori out of her clutches."

After a while Lori stopped crying, sat up, pushed her hair back from her face, and said, "Well, Lori makes an idiot of herself again."

"When did you do that?" Matilda asked, sounding highly interested.

"Right now. You saw me."

"I didn't see any such thing," Matilda said. "Did you, Deb?"

"No," I said. "I just saw a very upset young lady blowing off

. . . . .

182

steam, and that's something we all need to do every now and then. Anyway, Matilda, you haven't met Jessie Futrell."

"Who, I gather, is Aunt Jessie? That isn't but page one," Matilda said. "Page two is, I don't *want* to meet Jessie Futrell. Listen, Lori," she added, sitting down beside her on the bed—which made the bed sort of crowded—"people who don't cry or yell when they're upset are making themselves sick. Of course, so are people who cry or yell too much, but it looks to me like you cried just about exactly the right amount."

"How can you tell that?"

"Because you stopped, and now you're smiling." Matilda sat up and began to move her hands carefully around Lori's head, about eight inches out.

"What are you doing?" Lori asked.

"Smoothing your aura. Does it feel better?"

"I guess," Lori said, somewhat uncertainly. "I don't know how it's supposed to feel." She laughed a little bit and then said, "I guess I better go wash my face and then go see if I can help Hal."

After she departed, thoughtfully closing the door behind herself, Matilda—now half sitting, half lying, at the foot of my bed—said, "Now. Tell me what's going on."

I told her a lot more, probably, than I would have said if I hadn't been very nearly overmedicated. I told her about Dusty. About my sister. About the Washingtons and the Reddiches and everything else that was going on at work and at home, and about Harry's unaccountable edginess. "I've tried to ask him what's going on, and he either ignores me or yells at me," I said, "so I guess I'm going to have to just wait until he decides to tell me."

"I guess you are," Matilda agreed. "Sounds as if you have a lot more going on than anybody's likely to be comfortable trying to handle from the bed."

"Oh, I do," I agreed. "And right now what's really worrying me is, the little Reddich girl is probably home from school now, and

. . . . .

183

the mother probably went back to work, and I keep wondering, her daddy had been baby-sitting her after school, so has her mom been able to find anywhere else for her to go? Or is she at home alone? Or is her dad back over at the house?" I paused a minute. "That's one thing I can check out right now."

"Are you sure you want to?"

"I always tell people, if they call in something they thought was serious and it turns out not to be, I'd a heck of a lot rather they call me when they turn out not to need to than not call me when it turns out they needed to." I was dialing dispatch as I spoke. "Send a car by"—I gave the Reddich's address—"and see if everything's okay. There's a little girl who lives there, Diane Reddich. Insist on seeing her. Authority of Detective Deb Ralston. We had the little girl in the station today; we think her father's been molesting her. There's a court order for him to stay away, but I have a hunch he might be over there again. Either call me while the patrol officer's there or have the patrol officer call me from there."

By the time I hung up the phone, Matilda was inspecting my ice chest. "What have you got that's sweet?" she asked. "I had a client banging on my door early this morning, wanting me to consult the spirits for her, and after even as short a session as that I spend the rest of the day halfway shocky from low blood sugar. I've been living on Snickers bars today."

"Then no wonder you're blacking out," I said. "My doctor says if you've got low blood sugar you need protein, not sugar."

"I need protein *and* sugar," she replied. "Sugar for right now and protein for long-term."

"There's ice cream in the fridge," I said. "I would offer to get it for you, but—"

" 'But' is right," she replied. "I'll get it for myself. Want me to bring you some?"

"Yes, if you don't mind. But, Matilda, please, if you're feeling shocky, don't try to take off yet. I don't have enough friends I can spare any."

· · · · ·

184

She grinned at me. "That's our Deb, always worrying about everybody. I'm a big girl now, Mommy. I wouldn't dream of going any farther than to the refrigerator for the ice cream. Be right back."

After we were both settled down with chocolate fudge ripple ice cream, Matilda said, "I don't like the sound of this Reddich situation any more than you seem to. That court order you told me about isn't worth horse hockey. If he's got his wife as much under his thumb as it sounds to me like, she's not going to call anybody if he comes back in. What I want to know is, what's the mother been doing while all this stuff has been going on? Has she been out somewhere? Or has she been right there in the house? Because to start with at least, that kid had to be screaming. From what the doctor says, she might not be screaming now, but to start with—"

"I don't know," I said. "She works during the day; she told me she's done it all along, because they figured Diane was better off with her parents than a baby-sitter."

"And of course under normal situations she'd be right," Matilda agreed. "A lot of people do that, to stay close to the kids and save baby-sitting money at the same time, and most of the time it's just fine, but when you've got somebody with evil intent, it's like leaving the barn door open. But what I'm thinking now . . . I'm glad you sent that car over. Because if the kid is out of school now and he hasn't headed for work yet, but the mother is still at work . . ." She stopped. She didn't have to say anything else.

"If he's there, I wonder what he'll tell the patrol officer."

"He could be there ostensibly to get his clothes," Matilda said.

I grabbed for the phone again.

"What are you doing?" Matilda asked.

"Getting that car—Hello? This is Detective Ralston. Have you had any report from—Dammit, I didn't say send a car when you got a chance, I said send a car *now*. I don't *care* what the car is doing, if that one can't get over there send another one, but get somebody over there *right now*. There could be an assault in progress—No, I

. . . . .

can't go myself, I'm in bed recovering from surgery. Get somebody on over there. And let me know what happens."

While we waited for the call-back I chattered my head off—a combination of nerves and the medication that had reduced my inhibitions, I figured later. I told Matilda what the doctor had said. What the Washingtons had said. What the Bonandos had said. What the priest had said. She listened and said nothing. Although usually I appreciate her nonjudgmentalness, this time it was rather a relief when the telephone rang and I snatched at it.

"Detective Ralston?" said a young male voice on the other end. "I'm Officer Padgett. Your snitch was right; the father was here. At least if the father is Emil Reddich. He says he's just getting his clothes, and anyway there wouldn't be anybody to look after the child if he wasn't here, till the mama gets home from work. Sound right to you?"

I hadn't told anybody I had a snitch, but it was a logical supposition on Padgett's part. "That's him," I said. "Have you gotten a look at the girl?"

"That's affirmative. She's been crying, but I don't see any evidence of injury. Neither of them—father or daughter—will talk with me. What do you want me to do?"

"Get somebody over there from Juvenile to baby-sit until the mother gets home. Then arrest the father for violation of a court order."

"He says he doesn't know anything about a court order."

"He's lying," I said. "He was definitely notified. That I know."

"Who's got copies of the order?"

"He got one himself, Judge Franklin kept the court's copy, and the other was turned over to the mother in case she needed to show it to an officer."

"You've seen it, and you're sure he was notified?"

"Affirmative," I said.

"Ten foah," Padgett said. "Get somebody over here from Juve-

· · · · ·

nile to baby-sit until the mother gets home, then arrest the father for violation of court order, on the word of Detective Ralston."

"Affirmative."

"Will do."

He hung up, crisply, and I turned to Matilda. I didn't have to say anything. She said, "He was there."

"Obviously."

"Any idea what will come of this?"

"Depending on how long it takes him to find a bail bondsman, he'll be back out sometime between five P.M. and seven A.M. And most likely, he'll be right back over there again, and twice as mad as he was before, after a few hours in jail."

"Somebody's got to talk some sense into that social worker's head," Matilda said. "Or find another social worker. You'd think she'd know. Is she new?"

"No," I said, "just overly idealistic."

"A lot of people are. Sometimes I wish I hadn't decided to stick myself with being Sister Eagle Feather, because I'd love to have a conversation with that social worker and with whatever judge you get on the case, but my credibility would fall apart about the time somebody asked me what I do for a living."

"Tell them you write books," I suggested.

"Ri-i-i-ight," she said. "My dear, you don't make a living by writing books. At least not unless you're Janet Dailey. Look, what about getting Susan Braun up there?"

"She's unavailable till Wednesday night. Means we probably couldn't get her and the social worker together before Thursday at the earliest, and heaven knows what could happen to that poor kid by Thursday. Anyway, if the social worker won't believe the evidence of her own eyes and ears, what makes you think she'd believe you or Susan? And I don't know who's handling the case with me out of the office," I said bitterly. "There's at least one

· · · · ·

detective in the Sex Crimes Unit who's on the father's side. It drives me crazy to be stuck at home."

"I've been thinking about that, since you told me," Matilda said, "and I'm not sure that doctor is right. Oh, sure, you've got to keep your foot propped up, but you can do that anywhere there's room enough. If you could just go in like half a day at a time, that'd allow you to keep your hands on things and not worry yourself into a tailspin."

"That's what I think, too," I said, "but catch Harry letting me."

Matilda raised her eyebrows again. *"Letting* you?"

"Oh, you know what I mean! He's not going to lock the door and stand in front of it like a Victorian father, but Matilda, I can't drive right now."

"Well, if he won't take you, call me and I'll come get you," Matilda said, in a tone light enough that I could tell she didn't really think that was any kind of a solution at all. "Seriously, Harry knows you. He'll know perfectly well that you'll just worry yourself sick if you can't be in on things. Okay," she said now, briskly, "you called me over here to talk about this Washington and Bonando thing. So let's talk about it."

I told her again, in somewhat greater detail, and she nodded. "Can you get the Washingtons to come over here?" she asked.

"Now?"

"Sure. I'd like to talk with them."

"I don't know. Probably."

While I made the phone call, Matilda strolled out to the garage, where practice was in progress, and moments later I could hear Hal and Lori straightening the living room, or at least as much of it as they could straighten without risking misplacing any of Harry's catalogs, schoolbooks, reference books, and so forth. It had, of course, deteriorated sharply since my mother's cleaning spree; without me in charge, even Lori's occasional efforts at tidiness tended to go just so far and no farther.

It was nearly five by the time David and Laura Washington

. . . . .

arrived, and Matilda immediately parked Mr. Washington in the living room and wandered off into the backyard with Mrs. Washington. They must have talked for nearly an hour before they came back in the house and Matilda brought Mrs. Washington in to greet me. Then the Washingtons departed. Matilda, I noticed, looked extremely pleased with herself. "What did you find out?"

"I promised not to tell yet," she said, "but I think I know what's going on. How can I get in touch with your sergeant?"

I gave her Rafe's name and phone number, and then she said, "Do you have somebody appointed to make supper for you?"

I explained about supper, and she nodded. "Then I'll head on for home."

Manuel Rodriguez called about seven. Harry still wasn't home, so when Manuel asked if I could possibly come in tomorrow for just a couple of hours I didn't say no. I asked what was going on.

"The Super Glue rapist hit again," he said. "The victim is in the hospital, but they said they'll turn her loose tomorrow. They haven't got her mouth unglued yet, but she's been writing notes. Says tomorrow she wants to talk with a woman officer. Rafe said if you weren't up to it he'd get Margie to come up, but he'd kind of rather it be somebody who's worked in Sex Crimes before, and I already called to see if Chandra could make it and she thinks she's starting labor."

"Then I guess that leaves me, doesn't it?" I said. "Yeah, I'll be there. I don't guarantee what time."

An hour later the phone rang again, and I grabbed for it, hoping it was Harry explaining where he was, or Sandy Miller answering my message. It was Rhonda, and her voice was a little slurred. "Can I come over?" she demanded.

"By yourself?"

"Of course by myself, who else would be with me?"

"Did Mom say you could use her car?"

"D'ja think I was going to steal it?"

. . . . .

In view of the fact that she had done exactly that twice in the past, I didn't answer, and Rhonda said, "No, this truck driver buddy of mine, he said he'd drop me by and then come back and get me. You don't mind, do you? Because he already brought me to Fort Worth, and we're over in White Settlement."

It takes about ten minutes to drive from White Settlement to my house. I did not want any drunk person, and especially not Rhonda, at my house with me doped up with pain medicine and Harry out somewhere without explanation, but at the moment, feeling thoroughly guilty for not having protected her when we were children, I said okay.

I could tell when she came in the front door that she was even drunker than I had thought to start with. She fell over a chair that was nowhere in the direct line anybody should be walking from the front door to my bedroom, and I could see Hal and Lori staring at her, both clearly appalled and rather frightened. Hal pointed at the front door, and I nodded; moments later I heard my car start. I didn't know where they were going; wherever it was, it was better than being around here with Rhonda on a tear.

Rhonda found her way into my room and stood in the doorway long enough for me to see that she was barefoot, wearing very short blue jean cutoffs, frayed at the crotch, which was about where the hem would have fallen if they'd had a hem, and a white tank top, rather dirty. Then she slouched ungracefully into the chair. "Old bitch is drivin' me nuts," she said loudly.

"What old bitch is that?" I asked cautiously.

"*Mom,* who else do you think I mean? Do this, do that, take a bath, pick up your clothes, make up your bed, isn't it time to take your medicine now—like I was six years old. I can take a bath when I need to and I know when to take my medicine and if it's my room I'll pick up my clothes and make up my bed when I want to. I didn't ask to live with her! She ast me to. I'm on disability, 'cause I can't work no more, and that's not enough to pay for the apartment I had, but I could get a little room somewheres, but no,

. . . . .

she says, 'Honey, you're sick, you need to come home and live with me,' like that was ever my home!"

Rhonda had a point. After Dad's death Mom had, of course, moved away from the dairy where he had worked and we all had lived, and had got a little house in town, which she eventually managed to buy. But only the two youngest boys had ever lived there with her. To the rest of us, that never was home in even the broadest sense of the word.

"I mean," Rhonda went on, "when I was a kid she was a hopeless helpless wishy-washy wimp, but now she's grown up into Dragon Lady, and I'll tell you, I don't like it."

She had a point there, too. But she was clearly extremely intoxicated, and I didn't want her throwing up on my carpet. Vomit includes body fluids, and with two cats, everybody in the family always has cuts on their hands. "What have you been drinking?" I asked.

"Haven't been drinkin' nothing."

"Then what are you on?"

She laughed loudly, raucously. "Daddy's airplane glue. I been sniffin' it. Thought it would make me forget I'm gonna die. Didn't work."

"Daddy's dead."

"His airplane glue ain't. Deb, that room she's got me in, it's like a shrine to poor dear Daddy. She never threw *none* of his stuff away. His clothes, his shoes, his model airplanes and even the ones he never finished and the glue he was workin' on them with. Only thing she threw away was his feelthy peectures, the magazines and the movies both. But all the rest of it, it's right there. Deb, I tell you, I cain't sleep in that room, it stinks of Camel cigarettes and that awful green aftershave he used to use, I cain't remember its name, but it's like every time I close my eyes I expect to find the old buzzard in bed with me. I ast her to let me throw the stuff away—I think it's the clothes the smell is in—and she wouldn't hear of it. Deb, I cain't sleep in there, I cain't!"

· · · · ·

"I didn't realize that," I said. "I don't go over there very often, and I don't think I ever have gone into the back rooms. That's morbid—"

"Morbid! I wish morbid was all it was," Rhonda said bitterly. "It's like he was some sort of saint. Deb, I'm gettin' out of there, I'm gonna find somewheres else to live. And before you ask, no, I'm not askin' to live here."

That was just as well, though I had already begun mentally rearranging things and trying to think of a way to talk Harry into agreeing to the total disruption her presence would have made.

"I'd be willing to try," I said cautiously, "but I honestly don't think it would work."

"Oh, hell, I know that. I'd wreck your household on one of these sprees, and I have been drinkin' anyway. I sniffed the glue, but it just made me feel worse, and then I called Phil, and Phil, he don't care if I've got the virus 'cause he's got it, too, even if he's not showin' it yet. And no, he didn't catch it from me, says he caught it from some piece of tail at a truck stop, but wherever he got it, he got it. So we went and shared a fifth of vodka and made out in the cab of his truck, and then he said he'd drop me by here so I could say bye to you, 'cause I don't think I'll ever come back this way no more, and he'll pick me up in the mornin'."

"In the morning," I said faintly.

"Yeah, he's spendin' the night at one of those truck-driver motels, you know, with just the little cubicles, and he said I could sleep in his sleeper, but it's always too hot or too cold in the sleeper, and anyway, I've got where I'm scared to sleep alone. But I've got this friend in Denver and he's headed for Denver, said he'd take me along. Before I 'cided to come over here he was gonna pick me up in the mornin' at Mom's, but I already put all my clothes and stuff in his cab and Deb, I cain't sleep in that room no more, so you won't mind if I sleep on your couch, will you?"

Obviously it would do me no good at all to say that I would mind, and anyway I'd prefer that she sleep rather than throw up.

· · · · ·

So instead I said, "Rhonda, I hate for you to take off to Denver, you've got no family at all there. Why don't I talk with Mom about getting that stuff out of the room?"

"Never mind," she said, "I ain't gonna live with Mom no more. Should have had better sense than to try it, but I didn't know she'd turned into Dragon Lady. Deb, I cain't live there no more. And none of my brothers will even speak to me. I tried to call Jim a couple of days ago and he done hung up on me."

"Jim was mad at me and taking it out on you," I said. "He's probably over it now."

"Jim was mad at the world and always has been," she retorted. "Like nobody never peed on nobody but him."

"Look," I said, "if you'd just wait a couple of days. You don't want to make a hasty decision—"

"It's not a hasty decision," she said, sounding for a moment halfway sober. "Deb, look, I'm not blamin' you none. If I was you I wouldn't want me to live here neither. You got kids to raise, and anybody'd go crazy livin' with me. I sleep all day and watch TV all night and never put nothin' away. But when I had my place, at least it was my place, and not Mom naggin' me all the time like I was eight years old. Can I go sleep on the couch?"

"Sure, Rhonda," I said, "go sleep on the couch. But come in and talk with me again before you leave in the morning."

"Yeah," she said, and wavered toward the couch.

It was after midnight when Harry came in. The last straw, I thought—he'd been drinking, too. He wasn't quite drunk, but he was fortunate that nobody had stopped him on the way home. Of course I knew that he would have been at the Elks Lodge drinking with his buddies, not at a bar with a girl, but that didn't make me any happier. He came into the bedroom, waking me by turning on the light, and said thickly, "I see the couch is occupied."

"I'm sorry, Harry. She'll be leaving in the morning."

"I see. And in the meantime, where would you suggest I sleep?"

"There's room here—"

. . . . .

193

"Right. Like I want to wake up at two A.M. being bonked with your cast while you crawl over me to go to the bathroom."

I glared at him and said, "In that case, I would suggest the extra bed in Cameron's room. He's obviously not using it."

Harry wiped his hands across his face. "I must be losing my mind," he muttered. "I'd forgotten that bed was there. For some reason I was just remembering the crib."

I forebore to point out that we had removed the crib rails and replaced them with a standard bed frame, so the crib was now a youth bed. Instead, I asked, "Harry, if you'd just tell me what's the matter—"

"*Nothing*'s the matter," he answered. With a muttered and not fully coherent apology for waking me, he wandered off toward Cameron's room.

When I woke at seven, I was alone in the house. Hal, of course, had taken off for seminary, collecting Lori from her aunt's house, and Rhonda's truck driver must have picked her up. Before leaving, she had carefully straightened the couch, folded the blanket she had been using, and set the pillow on top of it. Harry, too, was gone; taped to his computer screen was a note: "Sorry I was such a jerk last night. I took the car, since Hal's got the truck. I'll have breakfast downtown—I've got some business to attend to. Don't know what time I'll be home."

Damn, I thought, *I forgot to tell him I'm going to work.* That, of course, meant that Hal would have to take me to town in the pickup truck, and getting in and out of the cab in my present situation might get a little bit hairy, especially since he would want to take Lori to school, and fitting him, me, and Lori—along with my cast—into the front of an old Ford pickup was going to be a tight squeeze.

It also meant that I would get to work on time, which was exactly what I did not want to do—ten o'clock, about the time the

. . . . .

victim was due to show up to make her statement, was more what I had in mind—and after I got there I was stuck unless I got somebody to take me home. I left a note for Harry, in case he got home fairly soon, but I wasn't exactly holding my breath.

· · · · ·

Eleven
. . . .

ACCORDING TO THE PAPERWORK on my desk, the Super Glue victim was one Michele Chaney, called "Michie" by her friends.

It was eight-fifteen; I had been bodily lifted into and out of the pickup truck, and this was one time I was grateful for a son who seemed to have topped out at six foot seven. (As most Koreans are rather short, we could only assume that the non-Korean side of Hal's genetic heritage must have been very, very tall.) After writing Hal an excuse for being late to school, which he was definitely going to be—Lori had decided to take the bus, because an excuse from me for her wouldn't carry much weight—I had headed on into the police station clutching my pillow and rode the elevator up to my floor, where I was pleased to find everybody out. That gave me the time I needed to arrange chairs so as to keep my foot propped up (fortunately I was in a corner near the door, so that nobody was likely to run into me) and then dive into my in-basket. It seemed astonishing that so much could have found its way into it in only one day.

I had just started on that when Roger came in. From the way he was dressed, I assumed he was on his way to court; he rummaged through his desk, got out a couple of pieces of paper, and tore back out again. Except for throwing a nasty look at me, he ignored me the whole time. That was fine with me. I ignored him right back.

Rafe came in then, to check his report basket and find out what

. . . . .

196

had happened since the last time he checked it, and I asked him about the Reddich case. "Nothing new," he said. "We've sent cars by to check several times, and the father's apparently now staying away like he's supposed to. But I don't trust the man for a second, and if that damned social worker doesn't get on the stick I'll find a judge who'll give us a court order to pick up that kid. It ticks me off, though. I've never before, in a situation like this, *needed* a court order; usually the child protection people do it on their own."

"Situations change," I said, "and there's been a lot of fuss in the papers about children taken from their parents without due process. I don't mind the due process; I just object when the due process takes so long, or when the social worker is so concerned with the parents' rights that the children get lost in the shuffle. There was that case a couple of years ago—"

"Yeah," he said. We both knew what case I meant. A retarded child, severely neglected and abused by parents who didn't understand how to cope with retardation and who detested the child for being so much trouble. The family kept moving, and child protection agencies in three states had started action but never got far enough to take the child from the home. It was in Fort Worth that the parents finally killed him.

"I've got to get back to court," Rafe added. "They're trying that Jackson rape case this morning, and I'm supposed to be in the witness room right now. I figure they won't get to me for another two hours, but you never know."

Once more alone, I resumed my alleged perusal of the contents of my in-basket. I have commented before, and will comment again, that if the city really expected any of us to read all the contents of a daily in-basket, they would have to find somebody else to do the detecting, as we'd be spending all our time reading. Being new to this squad, I didn't know yet whose basket things reached mine from and whose basket I could sneak things into, so I studied the initials to see who had already read most of the stuff and then transferred it all, after I had glanced at it and read what

. . . . .

seemed essential, into the in-basket of the person who hadn't initialed any of it. That, I am pleased to mention, was Roger Hales. Maybe if his in-basket was full enough to keep him busy he'd leave off hassling people for a while.

But I couldn't help worrying about Harry. Getting in after midnight, and almost drunk? Leaving again before seven? And he'd been so morose and withdrawn lately. I had asked him several times what was wrong, and he kept insisting nothing was wrong, which was patently untrue. I would have called Susan— as shrink, not just as friend—to ask what I could do that I hadn't already thought of, only she wouldn't be back in town until later this afternoon. So I called Matilda instead. She was up to her ears in genealogical research, and merely said robustly, "I'm sure he knows what he's doing."

"But *I* don't," I pointed out.

Matilda sighed. "I wasn't trained as a marriage counselor," she said, "and I've never been married. Maybe if I had, I would understand these things. All I can think of to say is, I'm sure when he's ready for you to know he'll tell you, but that's probably a highly unsatisfactory answer."

"It is, rather," I said. "But I suppose it's the only one there is to give."

By now it was almost ten o'clock, and when somebody from downstairs called to say that Michele Chaney was here to talk with me, I was more than ready for her to be brought up. A patrolman brought her into the squad room and looked around, apparently bewildered as to whom she was supposed to meet with. "Detective Ralston?" he called.

"I'm over here," I said. "Behind the door. Pardon my informality, Ms. Chaney, but as you can see—"

"Oh, yes," she answered, "I broke my foot skiing last winter, so I know how it is. You should have seen me getting home on the plane." She moved toward me, her abundant curly strawberry blond hair confined with a yellow terry cloth headband and her

. . . . .

body draped in an unattractive black maxiskirt and loose drab purple sweater, and sat down. Her mouth looked swollen and chafed, as did the area around her eyes. "Well," she said then, "I don't exactly know what you want me to say. By the way, please call me Michie."

"Fine," I said, "and you're welcome to call me Deb. Most people do. As to what to say—eventually we'll have to get down to specifics, but for now, it would help if you'll just sort of ramble, tell me what pops into your head about the whole thing. Especially anything you can think of that might possibly help us to identify him."

Ms. Chaney grimaced. "You know," she said, "I always thought, if I even thought about it all, that being raped would be the most awful thing that could happen, and nothing else surrounding it would matter at all, but I'm not sure now that was the worst of it. See, he hid in the back of my car and I didn't know it. He got in my car at the mall—"

"What mall was that?" I interrupted.

"Fort Worth Town Center," she said. "On Seminary Drive, you know. I'd gone to the mall to eat, because I'd had a perfectly lousy day, and then after supper I went to Dillard's to buy a new blouse, and the best I can figure out is he got my car open somehow, and I don't know how because I *always* lock my door and I have those flush door locks that you're not supposed to be able to get into with a coat hanger or anything like that. Do crooks have some way of getting them open anyway?"

"Pros do," I said. "Amateurs usually don't. You're sure you couldn't possibly have forgotten to lock it this one time?"

"Positive," she said. "I have this car, an Eagle, that you can lock all the doors from the front, and I always lock it when I get out."

"Then that's something to go on," I said. "Either he's worked around cars a lot, or he's no beginner."

"I thought there was a lot of this kind of thing going on," she said. "I mean, where the guy hides in the woman's car and all—"

. . . . .

199

"There is," I agreed. "But a rapist is an unusual kind of criminal, and most often they start off amateurs and they stay amateurs, in a lot of ways. Not many of them really study crime scientifically, the way, say, a forger would. But of course some of them do. And what you're saying tells me this one probably did."

"I see what you mean," she said. "I don't know, I thought they might be all like Ted Bundy, you know, who spent so much time figuring out exactly what to do without getting caught."

"Let's be glad they're not," I said. "Ted Bundy was extremely intelligent, which made him extremely dangerous. Most of them are . . . not of abnormally low intelligence, but not of abnormally high intelligence either. Which is fortunate for all of us."

"For sure," she said. "I'd rather be alive." She paused for a moment, shivered, wrapping her hands around her elbows and forearms as if it were January in the snow rather than March in a comfortable office, before continuing. "At least I think I would. Right now I really don't. But probably tomorrow . . . You don't want to hear all this."

"I want to hear whatever you can tell me," I said. "Whether it's relevant or not, if you need to say it. And truly, it will get better as time goes by." I couldn't honestly say that to all rape victims; some few go totally over the edge. But this woman seemed basically sound. She'd heal, given time and help.

After a brief hesitation, she began, "He rode all the way home with me without my even knowing; I guess he was lying down in the backseat or even the back floorboard. I've got an automatic garage door opener and I close it behind me after I'm in the garage, so once it's closed again I don't even *think* about prowlers. But then when I got out of the car, just after I unlocked the door from the garage into the kitchen, he was out of the car behind me with a knife, holding it to my neck. I mean, I didn't even *see* him get out of the car, he was just *there*, but that was the only way he could have gotten into my garage at just the right time, or even at all, I think."

. . . . .

"A lot of the door openers use the same frequencies," I suggested. "Some burglars drive up and down streets pushing door openers just watching to see which doors open."

"Mine has a code you have to enter, besides the frequency," she said. "It's supposed to be pretty secure. I'm . . . I've always been scared about things like this, because my best friend from high school was raped by a total stranger. And how would he have known which house had a woman living alone, if he did that? No, he had to have been in the car. I know because I had closed the door I got out of, the driver's front, and of course there was no reason for any other car door to be open, but when I looked at the car again, after the police helped me get loose from some of the glue—you did know he glued my mouth and eyes and all?"

I nodded, and she went on, "So I looked at the car as soon as I had got off as much of the glue as I could before they took me to the hospital—it wasn't as bad as he meant it to be, because I opened my eyes as wide as I could, after the glue was through being liquid so it wouldn't burn my eyes but before it really stuck, so I wasn't totally blinded by it—and when I looked at the car I saw the driver's side back door was standing open. So, to get back to what happened—there he was with the knife to my throat inside the garage with the door to the kitchen open, and he told me to go on in, and then he went in with me." She again wrapped her hands around her upper arms and torso. "And now I . . . it's like I'm scared all the time. My house feels dirty and my car feels dirty, and it's a *nice* house and car." She half laughed, very unhappily. "It's like there's no place at all I can go to feel clean and safe. And I can't even move because I bought the house and I can't afford house payments and rent both, but I feel so dirty there, like the whole place is contaminated. Does that sound nutty? I mean, I'm twenty-seven and I've lived on my own since I was nineteen and nothing like this ever happened to me before, so I must be overreacting."

"It certainly doesn't sound to me that you're overreacting," I

· · · · ·

replied. "A traumatic event like this causes very strong emotional reactions, and it's important to deal with them early in hopes of keeping them from getting worse."

"I'm not sure what you mean."

"Well—posttraumatic stress is normal. In some people, I forget the percentage, it goes on to turn into posttraumatic stress disorder, which is a really serious psychological condition. But most of the time the people that happens to are people who don't deal with the stress right after the trauma occurs, people who sort of try to sweep it under the rug and hope if they ignore it, it will go away. People, often, who keep telling themselves they're overreacting. And you were attacked yesterday. You spent the night in the hospital. You've been home, what, an hour or so?"

"Not even that," she said. "A friend drove me home to get some clothes, and I dressed and came right up here."

"So you've hardly had time to begin reacting. You might feel more comfortable if you find a psychologist or psychiatrist who can work with you for a month or two, to help you move through the trauma instead of trying to bury it." *And listen to me preach,* I thought wryly. Susan and Matilda, as well as my husband, my daughters, and my psychiatrist-to-be son-in-law, had been telling me for years I needed help to work through the trauma of the man I shotgunned—he was, of course, trying to shotgun me at the time—and I had been ignoring them.

"So you don't think I'm being stupid?" she said, still with her arms wrapped around her torso. "Because my friend Janet, the one that picked me up at the hospital and then brought me up here, she's waiting downstairs in the lobby, and I kept wanting to tell her over and over what had happened and she kept telling me to quit talking about it and put it out of my mind."

"That's the worst possible advice," I said. "And I'm serious. Of my two closest friends, one is a psychiatrist and one is a psychologist, and they both talk a lot about 'venting.' That means when you go through any kind of traumatic event, whether it's a rape or a

. . . . .

robbery or a car wreck or whatever, you need to talk about it as much as you feel you need to and maybe even a little more than you feel you need to. Because every time you talk about it you're defusing it a little bit more, you're getting rid of a little bit more of the stress."

She looked doubtful. "It seems to me it increases the stress, because every time I tell it I start crying and shaking all over again."

"That's all right," I said, "because if you weren't telling it, that crying and shaking would just be locked inside you."

"Well," she said, "I guess I get to tell it all again now. I hope you've got *lots* of Kleenex."

"A reasonable quantity," I said, getting out the box I always keep in the top right-hand desk drawer and putting it on the table. I'd had to move my own box; Chandra's was empty. "And please keep in mind that I really don't know what happened. All I know is that one of the men called me last night at home to tell me the Super Glue rapist had hit again and the victim—you—wanted to talk to a woman."

"I thought it would be a little easier," she said. "I mean . . . not that I think all men are rapists or anything like that, but some of them, you know, if you haven't screamed yourself hoarse and clawed your fingernails out and been beaten half to death, they don't think it was really rape. Not that that kind of attitude is limited to men, of course," she went on, half to herself. "Some women . . ." She shuddered deliberately, expressively, and looked at me.

"In general, people in the Sex Crimes Unit wouldn't tend to react that way," I said. "But I'm with you. If it were me I'd rather talk to a woman."

She took a deep breath. "All right," she said, "he got in the house. The fingerprint people came out last night to dust the house and car and everything, so I can start driving my car again as soon as I get the fingerprint powder cleaned out."

"You have any idea whether they got any prints?"

. . . . .

She shook her head. "I was gone to the hospital by then."

"Well, I'll check later and find out," I said.

"I wish you'd check now. I'd like to know, too."

"Okay." I turned to the computer terminal, punched in the case number, and checked the report from Ident. "A whole lot of the same prints, which they assume are yours. They'd like you to go down to Ident to be fingerprinted for elimination before you leave. One other print, on the plastic inside the back door on the driver's side."

"I remember he went around wiping things before he put the glue on my eyes," she said. "He got a dish towel and started wiping everything he could think of. Then he glued my eyelids so I couldn't see, or at least he figured I couldn't see, and he went on into the front room and from the sounds I think he went on wiping everything he could think of."

"When was the last time you had somebody in the backseat of your car?"

"I've never had anybody in the backseat of my car," she said. "I've only had it six weeks, and nobody's ever ridden in the back of it."

"So either it's the make-ready person at the dealership," I said, "or it's him. And only one print . . . Could be he missed that one spot, forgot he'd touched it."

"What happens now? With the print, I mean."

"Until very recently, not much of anything would happen," I said, "because although in a smaller department it might be possible to search a single print through the files, here we've got over a hundred thousand fingerprint cards, and a search like that would take years. But now there's a computerized system, and within a day or so, if he's on file anywhere in the area, they'll have him identified."

"And if he's not?"

"If he's not," I said, "then the best we can do with the print is

. . . . .

wait. Every so often they recheck old prints, in the hopes that the perps have been printed somewhere since the previous check. But in the meantime, we'll go on checking other things that don't depend on fingerprints." No need to tell her that all that checking had already been done repeatedly, after every time this rapist struck. "Okay, let's backtrack, because we've kind of got off sequence. You're in the garage and he's got a knife to your throat and he tells you to go on into the house. What then?"

"The garage door opens into the kitchen," she said, "and so we went on into the kitchen. Then he took the knife away from my throat and said, 'Don't try anything, because I can throw this a lot faster than you can scream. Nod if you understand me.' So I nodded, and he—"

"Did he touch anything in the kitchen?" I interrupted.

"No. He asked me to get him a glass of water, but then he told me to wrap a paper towel around the glass. He drank the water and then he put the paper towel in his pocket."

That was a lot of caution, I thought. Almost certainly he'd been fingerprinted; almost certainly he'd been caught once on fingerprints. A paper towel is so rough that the chances of getting a usable print from it approach nil, but either he wasn't aware of that statistic or he was taking no chances at all.

"So then," she said, "he told me to go to the bathroom and take a bath."

"That's weird," I commented. "Before this guy got started I don't think I ever heard of one doing that."

"And he sat on the toilet and watched me."

"At this point did you get a good look at him?"

"As good as I could," she said. "He had a ski mask on."

"What can you tell me? Any idea about height?"

"Oh, yes, he's about the same height I am."

"About five seven?"

She nodded. "Pretty slender. I don't really think he'd weigh as

· · · · ·

much as I do; if he didn't have that knife I could have fought him off, but I was scared to try to fight a knife. I keep thinking, now, I should have—"

"You did what seemed best at the time," I said. "Don't try to second-guess yourself. You do what you can do, and don't worry about anything else."

"I keep telling myself that."

"Keep on telling yourself that. Okay, he was about five seven, slender . . ." I paused.

"He had on the ski mask," she said, "but enough of his hair was visible that I'd say it was light brown. His eyes were blue. Let's see . . . He had on a long-sleeved shirt, white, you know, a dress shirt like you'd expect a man to wear a tie with, but the cuffs weren't buttoned and they were rolled up a couple of turns so I could see his arms were very hairy, black hair."

"Any rings?"

She shook her head. "No rings, no watch, nothing like that. Let's see, he had on dark blue pin-striped suit pants, and black shoes—lace-up, but they weren't shaped quite like ordinary men's shoes. I mean . . . I don't know how to say this."

I remained silent, and finally she went on, "Okay, most men's shoes are stitched kind of like oxfords, or else they don't have a visible seam on the toe at all. But his had a seam from the middle of the line where the tongue was sewed in that extended down the center of the toe to meet the center of the toe of the sole. Does that make sense?"

"It does to me," I said. "And you said the shoes were black?"

She nodded.

"Did you notice any special smell about him?"

"Like what?"

"Like anything. Like aftershave, cologne, any industrial smell that might suggest where he worked?"

She shook her head. "Uh-uh. If he smelled like anything, it was

. . . . .

soap. I guess that was it. He did smell like soap. Like he'd bathed just before he came after me." She laughed dryly, a small tense laugh. "Something different, huh? Like you said? A clean rapist? Maybe that was why he wanted me to be clean."

"I've known clean murderers," I agreed, "but I think a super-clean rapist is a new one on me. This one's done it every time, though. Okay, so after the bath . . ."

"He handed me a towel and told me to go into the bedroom."

"And he was still brandishing a knife all this time?"

"Yes, and . . . Do you have any idea how vulnerable it made me feel, him fully dressed and me wearing nothing but a towel? Even if he *hadn't* had the knife—"

"I have a pretty fair idea," I said, without seeing any need to go into details.

"Then . . . um . . . do I have to tell the rest?" Before I could answer she said, "I guess I do, don't I? Because you have to have all the information, not just part of it, for legalities if for nothing else. Okay, he . . . umm . . . he told me to undo his pants . . ."

"Did you notice anything at all about him at that time?"

"Like what? His pants had a hook-and-eye at the top and then a zipper, and I couldn't tell what brand of underwear he wore, and he hadn't been circumcised. And then he told me to suck his thing, you know, and not get any bright ideas about biting because if I did he'd kill me, and he kept the knife by the side of my throat the whole time, and I thought if, maybe, you know, his attention got distracted a little bit then I could grab for the knife, but before he was through he told me to stop and then he reached in his pocket and got out a condom and told me to put it on him, he told me he didn't know where I'd been before and he didn't want to catch anything from me, and then he told me to lie down and then, you know, he did it, and—Irish Spring!"

"What?"

"That's the soap he smelled like, Irish Spring. I used to go with

· · · · ·

a guy who used it. I guess now I'll never want to get anywhere near anybody using it." She reached for a Kleenex. I hadn't kept careful count, but I thought this was about her fifth.

"Will I ever stop remembering him when I smell it?" she asked, after wiping her eyes and blowing her nose.

"Probably not," I said. "I've got unpleasant connotations with it, too. There was this guy who was shot and put in the trunk of his car—this was while I was in Ident—and after they got the body out of the car I had to go through and process the car for fingerprints and collect evidence and everything, and he had all his luggage in the trunk, and there were three bars of Irish Spring in the luggage. That's been a good ten or twelve years ago, and I still can't stand the smell of it. My husband decided to try some a couple of years ago and I thought I'd throw up."

"That's a shame, you know?" she said. "I wish he'd been using something grungy. Irish Spring smells so *nice* to have such bad associations."

"I agree. For what it's worth."

"Now I guess you'd like me to go on telling you what happened."

"It would help." It would help a lot, I thought. I was tiring rapidly; a glance at the clock told me it was nearly eleven, and I had hoped to be able to get a ride home when people began wandering out for lunch.

"Okay, well, like I said, after he got through with all that *and* wiping things off, he got out this bottle of Super Glue and glued my mouth shut and then my vagina and then my eyelids last, and then he told me to stay on my bed for half an hour. That didn't make sense, him gluing my eyelids last, because I'd already seen him—"

"Unless he didn't want you to see him leave," I said thoughtfully. "Could he have used your phone to call somebody to come get him?"

"He did do that, and . . . Wait a minute," she said. "Wait a

. . . . .

208

minute. I thought he had picked me at random, but he couldn't have, because when he called he just said, 'Come get me.' He didn't give an address. He just said, 'Come get me.' That means he knew who I was. He got in my car at the mall, I'm sure of that, but he didn't pick it at random—he picked it because it was my car. He knows who I am." She started crying, then. "What am I going to do? He knows my car, he knows my house . . ."

"For what comfort it is, which probably isn't much," I said, "he hasn't gone back to any of the other victims."

"How many women has he attacked?"

I'd familiarized myself with the case files while I was waiting for her, so I could answer without having to look it up. "Seven," I said.

"In how long?"

"Just about four months. He's hitting every two weeks."

"*Exactly* every two weeks?"

"Not quite," I said, "but almost. There was one one-week interval, one three-week, one four-week. And always on Tuesday."

"And he hasn't been caught."

"There's been nothing to go on," I said. "We may get lucky this time. He's never left a fingerprint before. If that really is his . . ."

We talked a while longer. "What kind of work do you do?" I asked.

"I'm an accountant. A CPA."

"Do you work for a large firm?"

"No, just me. That's another problem. I'd planned, when I bought the house, to close my office and work out of my home. I've been trying it the last couple of weeks, to see how I liked it—moved my computer and everything. But now . . . I don't know if I could manage it now. Talk about a lousy day. And coming right after spending all day coping with the IRS—"

"The IRS?" I asked.

"Yeah, one of my clients had an audit. And he was in my home

. . . . .

office all day, him and the IRS agent, both of them yelling at one another, *and* the toilet overflowed and I had to call a plumber with all these people there, and then the water was cut off about an hour and my client went out for Cokes and came back with beer and got drunk. Why couldn't I have picked a *simple* job? Like defusing bombs?" She was crying again, but she was laughing through the tears. She'd be okay, I thought.

She didn't have much else to say. By the time she left, Rafe was back in, though nobody else was, and I asked him if he'd heard anything about Doreen Miller, if she'd been found. He told me she hadn't and assured me, as everybody else was assuring me, that she'd left on purpose and that she was surely all right. Who did he think he was talking to, I wondered. In the first place, it wasn't even his case, though everybody in the detective bureau was tracking it a little by now, and in the second place nobody had any way at all of knowing why Doreen had left. Maybe this reassurance tactic might work on Ms. Average Citizen, though I doubted it; it certainly wasn't working on me. I told him so, and he said, "Sorry. But, Deb, it's not doing any good for you to get so wound up."

"Never mind," I said resignedly, and changed the subject. "Let's compare notes again on the Super Glue rapist." We already knew that in all cases the perp had reportedly got into cars at shopping centers, but there was no one shopping center he always used. Instead, he'd hit just about every large shopping mall in Fort Worth, and had chosen one victim—his fourth—from the downtown library parking lot and one from a grocery store parking lot. In every case, the victim had an enclosed garage, often but not always with an automatic door opener, and in every case the rapist had not shown himself until the car was inside the garage, the garage door was closed, and the door to the house was open. In every case, the rapist had ordered the victim to bathe. And in every case, the glue had not been applied until after the victim had had every chance to see the rapist. In every case, the rapist had called

· · · · ·

somebody to come get him—which was odd, because rapists usually work alone.

And every one of the victims, including Michele Chaney, insisted he was clean and well-dressed, had a perfectly identifiable
voice, and she had never met him before—as least so far as she
could tell without seeing his face.

The victims did not live in the same neighborhood, did not shop
at the same stores, did not go to the same church, did not use the
same doctor or dentist, and did not buy gasoline at the same gas
station.

This, I discovered, was the first time a victim had commented
that she was sure the rapist had chosen her specifically, which was
a little odd, considering the telephone calls he'd made when he was
through. So what were his *exact* words in each telephone call? In
other cases had he given the address? Or had he always just said,
"Come get me"? Because if the latter was true, then every victim
had been selected. Rafe agreed with me, though how useful that
would be was questionable if we couldn't find how he had selected
the victims. We'd call them all again, we agreed. Rafe handed me
some names and telephone numbers and kept some for himself, and
we both started telephoning.

"Kathryn Purvis? This is Detective Deb Ralston . . ."

Thirteen telephone calls later—we had to call several places for
some women before we reached them—Rafe and I were able to
agree that five women were sure they had been personally selected,
one was sure she had been chosen at random, and one we still
hadn't reached. The one who was sure she had been chosen at
random was the first, and maybe that said something, too.

"Let me take you home now," Rafe said. "You're worn out. I
hated for you to have to come in today, but we really did need you.
Listen, though, if we call and you really feel like you can't make
it, say no. We can always get somebody else. Margie, maybe. She's
helped us out before."

. . . . .

"I'd rather be here than at home doing nothing," I said, "except I get so tired. It's frustrating."

"I know, when you've always been active. But we've all got to live in the world as it is, and sometimes it's a pretty lousy one. That girl—excuse me, that woman—would sure say so right now. She seemed a lot calmer than most of his victims."

"That was surface," I said. "She was falling apart."

"I'll go get my car now," he said, "and meet you in front."

He headed for the door. I had started to reach for the crutches I used coming and going but no other time, when the phone rang again. I grabbed it mechanically.

"This is Jean Bridger," a hesitant voice said. "I think somebody named Deb Ralston has been trying to call me—"

"I'm Deb Ralston," I said. "Just a minute." I yelled to Rafe to wait a minute, and started going over the same questions I'd gone over with the other women and getting about the same answers.

It was almost a throwaway line when she added, "I'd gone out to the mall to get something to eat. I'd had a perfectly lousy day, with the IRS auditing me—"

I said, "Yeah, I bet," and then it hit me. "The IRS?" I asked.

"Yeah, this perfectly hateful IRS agent, he questioned every-thing, even when I had the checks to prove what I was saying, and—"

"Hold on," I said, and yelled, "Rafe, you better hear this. We may have our connection."

"Okay," he said after he hung up, "we'll take it from there."

"Who will? When?" I demanded. "Everybody's busy. I can just stay a little while longer—"

"We'll take care of it," he repeated, glaring at me. "Nothing else is going to happen before next Tuesday anyway."

"I'm not sure of that."

"There's a thermometer around here somewhere. Am I going to have to get it and prove to you that you ought to be at home?" Or am I going to have to order you off the case? Do *not* go work on

. . . . .

212

it at home, you hear me? He paused, giving me time to reflect on how much like Captain Millner he was getting to sound. "And *now* I'll go get my car and meet you in front."

I got my crutches and headed downstairs. But before I left, I wrote down the names and telephone numbers of all eight victims, Michele Chaney and the seven who had gone before her.

Cheese. Crackers. Fruit. Ginger ale. Antibiotics. Pain medication. I was beginning to feel like a broken record. And I was *not* looking forward to another snake dream.

I didn't have another snake dream.

Instead, I had another tidal wave dream. It started as the previous one had: I was on the bluff overlooking the bay, and the waters began to recede farther and farther out, and the fathers sent the daughters out into the bay to gather eels. And as the daughters obediently put the great writhing eels into their baskets, the fathers backed away, up the bluff until they were out of my sight and out of reach of the tsunami, and then the water came crashing back.

But this time, the daughters rose up above the waters, without the baskets, without the eels, and they rode the water, swimming clean and healthy and laughing as waves continued to break over their heads, and this time I did not wake sweating and shaking, I woke feeling as cleansed as if I, like the children I saw, had been swimming in the warm, bright waters of a tropical bay.

I was in the living room when Harry came charging in, dressed better than I had seen him in months, grinning from ear to ear and carrying a bag of hamburgers, fries, and milk shakes. He stopped short. "What in the world are you doing?" he demanded.

"I'm watching Oprah Winfrey. You look great."

"I feel great. But you *never* watch daytime television."

"When am I ever home to watch daytime television?"

"And you're dressed?"

"I had to go to work this morning," I said.

· · · · ·

He didn't start yelling at me. But he didn't say anything, either. He just went and got a couple of TV trays and started sorting out hamburgers and shakes, before he finally said, "Deb, I love you, but there are times I think that when it comes to taking care of yourself, you haven't got the brains God gave a pregnant jackass."

A jackass is male. A parental jackass would be a father, not a mother. So there is no such thing as a pregnant jackass. I got the point.

After a while I said, "Harry, I really did have to go. They needed me."

"I don't doubt it. You always put other people's needs ahead of your own. Just once in your life, though, I wish you'd try putting yourself first."

I had to think that one through. But not right now.

. . . . .

Twelve

About three-thirty Sandy Miller called. "I've been in Austin," she said, "and I didn't check my answering machine because I was out of town and couldn't do anything about anything on it. What did you need? Because if it's about Doreen, I still don't have her."

"It's not about Doreen," I said resignedly. Remembering how fiercely Sandy had spoken of rescuing her sister, I could not believe that she would be that casual, that composed, if she didn't know perfectly well where Doreen was—and come to think of it, surely she'd have checked her answering machine if she'd gone out of town, with Doreen missing. So maybe everybody who'd been reassuring me was right; maybe Doreen had left on her own.

"Well, I'm going to be busy later, but I could come over now if you want."

Frankly, I didn't want, but I'd probably have to agree anyway. I knew that if I wanted any information from Sandy I'd have to play it her way. What I wasn't sure of was what information I wanted, and whether she had any information I could use anyway. First I had to figure out exactly what she had meant to ask me the first time she had come over. "We may be able to clear this up over the phone," I said. "You know, when you came to see me the other day, I was pretty foggy, and I've got to thinking that I may not have fully understood what you were getting at. I thought I understood that you were wondering why Dusty died at all, but maybe what you really were wondering was why Dusty chose *this particular time* to die. Am I right, or wrong?"

There was a long silence at the other end of the phone. Then Sandy said cautiously, "I think that was what I meant, yes. Finally, anyway. I started off thinking he'd killed her, and then I thought he'd done something, like made her pregnant, that would have made her want to die. But when you said neither of those, yes. I wondered, why now? Because nothing that had been going on could have been new, unless he'd developed new kinks that I didn't know about."

"If he had, do you think she would have told you?"

More silence. Then—"I don't think she would," Sandy said. "I think she would be too embarrassed to tell even me."

"Then come on over, and let's brainstorm a little. Unless you'd rather do it over the phone," I added hopefully.

"I'd rather keep my phone free," Sandy said. "And I've been doing more than brainstorming. I've been asking questions. I've been asking a lot of people a lot of questions."

"In Austin?"

A little bit of a laugh. "No, I was in Austin for another reason." She didn't spell it out, and I didn't ask. "Okay," she went on, "I just got back into town, and I'm still in the clothes I was driving in. Give me a little while to change and clean up. Is five o'clock okay?"

I assured her that it would be, and she hung up.

Five o'clock would have her arriving here after Hal got home, but of course so would anything else more than twenty minutes from now. I could only hope, without much expectation, that when Hal arrived he would arrive quietly, because Harry—not unexpectedly, given his condition the previous night and the time that he left in the morning—had gone, after devouring the hamburgers, to take a nap in Cameron's room.

I leaned over to open the ice chest and get out a piece of cheese. I'd have to get somebody to take the chest out and drain it, I noted;

· · · · ·

216

two-thirds of the ice was now water. But nothing that had to stay dry was wet, thanks to the tray at the top, so the situation wasn't critical. As soon as I got the cheese out I heard a thud on the desk and looked around. Rags was shying around the place where the tomato plant used to be, looking nervously at the empty corner of the desk. But she had progressed to the point that she no longer felt it necessary to sit and stare, particularly not when cheese was available. She glided lightly to the bed and again landed with a slight thud, this time right beside my left hand. I was sitting up, leaning on one of those molded cushions that gives one the feel of an armchair in bed, and Rags stepped delicately up onto the left arm of it, walked across behind me, walked down the right arm of it, and again stepped onto the bed. Only then did she visibly notice the cheese; I could almost hear her saying, "My goodness, I do believe that is cheese. Now, where in the world did that come from?"

Of course, I am a sucker. I wouldn't have so many animals if I were not. Just let a stray dog or cat knock on my door and say, "Now I live with you," and sure enough, I agree that it does. I shared the cheese with her. She ate delicately, as if condescending to accept an offering, although both she and I knew perfectly well that if I had not given her the cheese she would have been one angry feline. Then she curled into a tight C, closed her eyes and wrapped her tail around them, and began to purr.

With Harry asleep I was for all practical purposes alone in the house; I had time for some telephone calls. Michele Chaney, first, to ask whether she remembered the name of the IRS agent she'd coped with the day of the assault. "Oh, yes," she said wrathfully, "I never will forget his name, the nasty little twerp." She gave it to me, and I went on to the next call. And the next one. After that, I didn't need to call all seven, but I did anyway.

And then I sat back and thought. I was sure, now, and I could convince any law enforcement officer. But I hadn't a shred of evidence I could take into a courtroom, and I was in my bedroom,

. . . . .

unable to drive and forbidden even by Rafe Permut to do anything right now about this case. What to do next . . .

Finally I called Ident and asked for Irene Loukas. Irene, who recently took over as head of the section, listened with some interest. "Oh, yes," she said finally, "I can call in a few favors. Yes, I can get that, and furthermore I will enjoy it."

Satisfied, I opened the ice chest again. After drinking some more ginger ale and wondering why I had this sudden urge to fill myself with ginger ale when I hadn't wanted any for years, I rearranged the cushion and settled down for a little sleep myself, waking when Hal came galloping in and yelled from the living room, "Hi, Mom!"

"Hi, yourself," I answered, sitting up. "Will you come drain this ice chest and get me some more ice?"

"There's no more ice in the freezer," he said. "I noticed that last time—"

"Then why didn't you mention the fact then?"

"I dunno. Want me to take the truck and get some more ice?"

"Please do."

"You want me to drain the ice chest now, or when I get back?"

"When you get back," I replied resignedly, hearing Harry up moving around and grumbling to himself on the other side of the wall, in what used to be Hal's room but had become Cameron's room when we decided letting a toddler have a bedroom with a window onto the front yard was not the best possible idea and moved him into the middle bedroom, which had been Hal's. Hal in turn moved into the front bedroom, which had been his sisters' when they were both at home, it being slightly larger than the middle bedroom. That had been Cameron's room to start with because it was easier to insert a crib into an unoccupied room than to move all Hal's stuff. Harry and I, of course, have the back bedroom, with its own huge private bathroom.

I have sometimes questioned the architect's sanity in designing a two-bathroom house in which the bathroom intended to be

· · · · ·

shared by the children in the house is also the bathroom that would be used by guests. But then, I frequently question the sanity of the architect who designed this house, with a kitchen almost large enough for one person, if she is very small, in which three doors— the refrigerator door, the door to the garage, and the door to the (alleged) pantry, which will not hold the staples plus one week of groceries—open into the same space. The kitchen can't even be remodeled and expanded because it is too close to the property line.

Oh, well. It's the house we live in, and we certainly can't afford to sell it and move, not when housing costs have dropped so dramatically in this area that the house is now worth somewhat less than what we still owe on it.

Wednesday afternoon. I had been in this cast for less than a week, and already I felt as if I had lived in it forever. My knee was hideously sore from resting on the rolling footstool, even though I had padded the footstool thoroughly with towels, and my under-arms were sore from the crutches, even though I used them only when I had to go outdoors. I had become pretty adept at figuring out what clothes I could get on over the cast, and I had quit feeling naked when I went outdoors without my shoulder holster, which of course I could not wear when I was on crutches. I still obedi-ently carried my pistol, however; knowing this was coming, last week I had dug out my old uniform bag from the oblivion of my top closet shelf, where I had consigned it when I started using shoulder holsters.

Logically, everything was just fine. I was able to work at least part of the day, Lori (with Hal's reluctant help) was keeping my housework from piling up too much, and people from the church were bringing in supper. The one who was bringing it tonight had called yesterday to inquire whether I liked sausage and brown rice casserole. I'd never had it, and it sounded delicious. Whatever was bugging Harry apparently had cleared up. I had nothing to feel sorry for myself about. But the fact remained that I felt very sorry

. . . . .

for myself. My lack of portability wasn't just depressing; it was frightening. And that didn't really make a whole lot of sense.

Part of what was wrong with me was that I wanted my baby back. I had no intention of letting my mother keep him the whole time I was on crutches, and I expected I'd be able to manage him fairly soon. But, I realized, not quite yet.

I made my way into the living room and plopped down on the couch. "Would you like some ice cream?" Lori asked timidly.

That bothered me, too. Until recently, timidity was the last thing I would expect, or get, from Lori.

I am recovering from bone surgery. Obviously I need lots of calcium. Ice cream has calcium in it. Go on, Deb, justify your gluttony. "I would love some," I said. "What kind do we have?"

She investigated. "Chocolate fudge ripple and cherry vanilla. What do you want?"

"Some of each. What do you want?"

"I want some of each, too."

She handed me a bowl and spoon and joined me on the couch. "I was thinking," she said, and came to a dead halt.

"All right," I said encouragingly.

"About the people from the church bringing in food because you can't stand up long enough to cook right now."

"And?"

"If you'd write down what you want, I could go get the groceries and do the cooking. Or if you use that computer program Harry made, I could still do the cooking. Or even, if you didn't feel like it, I could plan the meals and order the groceries and do the cooking. I'm really a very good cook. I used to do a lot of the cooking, before Mom . . . you know. And I'm over here all the time anyway."

"That is a terrific idea," I said.

"Then you don't mind? Before you had your surgery I mentioned the idea to Aunt Jessie and she said it was presumptuous."

. . . . .

"Aunt Jessie is a jerk. The only time it's presumptuous to help somebody is if it's somebody who doesn't want to be helped."

Suddenly—but not totally unpredictably—Lori put down the ice cream and burst into tears. "Deb, I *hate* living with Aunt Jessie! She keeps telling me it's all my fault Mom shot herself and I ought to be dead, and she tells me I'm a slut for hanging around with Hal all the time, and she doesn't believe me when I tell her we *don't* do anything we shouldn't do, and she says my Social Security check doesn't begin to support me and she'd get rid of me in a minute except it would reflect on her if I wound up living on the street, and Hal says as soon as he's out of high school we'll get married but I don't want to get married until after he goes on his mission because I know he really wants to but he won't even put in his papers for it because he says if I stay living with Aunt Jessie it'll make me sick, and—"

"Aunt Jessie is a bitch. Hal is nineteen," I said. "He will be going on his mission very soon after he graduates from high school, which will be in two and a half months. We had planned at that time to see if we could arrange with Aunt Jessie for you to come live with us. If you think you could stand sharing a bedroom with Cameron, and it wouldn't be too difficult for you and Hal, you are welcome to move in at any time."

"I didn't mean—"

"I know you didn't. But I did. I rarely say anything I don't mean. Do I, Harry?"

Harry, who had walked out into the living room during that discussion, said, "No, she does not. Nor do I. Welcome home, my dear."

She was still hugging me when Hal, who of course hadn't heard a word of the discussion, parked the truck in the driveway, spoke briefly to the dog, and came through the front door with three bags of ice. I could see the signs of strain on his face as he went toward the garage to put two of the bags in the freezer. Of course, Lori

. . . . .

221

would have told him a lot more of the situation than she had me; and I should have realized he had something on his mind far more serious than his band's opening performance Friday night. "When does Aunt Jessie get home from work?" I asked.

Lori looked at her watch. "She's probably home now. She works seven to three."

"Dial the number, and hand me the phone," I said.

Hal came back in from the garage and stopped in the living room, a bag of ice on his shoulder, staring at me as I said, "This is Deb Ralston. I understand that having Lori live with you is causing a strain. My husband and I shall be delighted to have her move in with us at once . . . No, we do not consider it your duty. As we anticipate that she will one day be our daughter-in-law, we're sure it is far more our duty than yours . . . Not at all, we had intended for her to do so in a couple of months anyway, and we are overjoyed to have her sooner . . . Excellent. My husband will telephone our attorney to make the custody arrangements, and we should have papers for you to sign in a couple of days. In the meantime, the kids will be over shortly to get her clothing and other possessions, and they'll bring along a temporary form for you to sign . . . The Social Security, yes. I don't know what forms will be necessary. Our attorney will check on that, and of course we will be saving the money for her college or whatever other plans she makes in the future. No, I'm sure we can support her without it."

Sometime in the middle of the conversation Hal dropped the ice. "Are you kidding?" he yelled. "Lori's gonna come live with us?"

"Hush, your mother's on the phone," Harry said. "Of course she is."

He then walked over beside Hal, picked up the bag, and handed it back to Hal as I hung up the phone and said, "That bitch. Hand me a notebook, Lori. I've written enough search warrants and stuff in my life, I ought to know how to write a form for that mercenary

. . . . .

222

witch to sign that'll allow us to take care of school papers and medical stuff."

Harry turned the computer on. "I'll boot up the word processing program. It ought to be in triplicate."

"Is that enough?" I asked. "One for her to keep, one for the school, one for us. Is that enough, or do you think we should have one apiece for you and me?"

"One between us should be enough," he said. "We'll get Don to do it formally next week." Don is our older son-in-law, Vicky's husband, the one who's an attorney. "We should have done this months ago," Harry added, to Lori. "If I'd known she was blaming you . . ." He left the sentence unfinished. I hadn't realized he was as angry as I was, although we had already agreed to inviting Lori to move in as soon as possible.

"Hal," I said, "will you please attend to the ice chest. By the way, do you want to go on a mission?"

"Yeah, sure," he said, "if Lori's okay—"

"Then call the bishop at once. Lori tells me you should have put in your missionary papers weeks ago."

Hal was still looking dazed as he hung up from talking to the bishop, checked his pocket for the truck keys, and said, "Let's go," to Lori.

"There are multiple kinds of child abuse," I remarked to Harry, as the pickup truck backed out of the driveway. "Aunt Jessie's kind may be the meanest."

"They're all the meanest," he answered. "I couldn't figure out what was the matter with her; I wish we'd realized, or she'd told us sooner. I wonder how long it'll take us to get Lori back to normal."

Vicky was first, and she was over a year old when we got her. She had several dozen cuts and bruises and was infected with every kind of parasite you can name, and she was ten pounds underweight, which is a lot for a one-year-old. She didn't walk, or talk, until she was almost two. She was three years old, and just barely to the point of entirely normal—although

. . . . .

she didn't give up her bottle until she was four—when we got Becky. Becky was only four days old, but thanks to Rhonda's bad habits she'd been born addicted, and the first six months were pretty horrible. It was several years after that before we got Hal. He was six months old. He'd lived in an orphanage in Seoul, and his physical condition was fine, but he'd had a different person to care for him every shift, and it took forever to get him to bond. Cameron, of course, was born to us, and he was the only child we'd ever had who was completely healthy, physically and emotionally, to start with.

Now we had another walking wounded to deal with. That was all right. Nourishing a teenager is different from nourishing a baby, but we'd known Lori long enough to know what she was supposed to be like, and Lori already knew we love her.

"She'll be all right," I said, and Harry nodded.

They were still over there when the bishop, a fellow police officer, dropped Hal's papers by at four-fifteen. "I'm glad you're taking Lori," he said. "The poor kid's been falling apart, and I'd just about decided to ask the Relief Society president who she could find to take her."

"We'd have done it sooner," I said guiltily, "except I was worried about her and Hal being under the same roof."

"Normally you'd be right, of course," he said. "But they'll be okay. Hal and I have already had a long discussion on the matter. He'd been telling me he wanted to go on his mission but he couldn't stand to leave Lori in her present situation."

"I should have already told him we'd take her—"

"He thought you probably would. But he was worrying himself half to death. I'm glad it's straightened out now, but I'm sorry for the aunt. She's never in her life had anybody to love, or anybody who loved her, except her baby sister."

"Lori's mother?"

He nodded. "And when she had the chance—a hurt, vulnerable, child—she chose to be hateful instead of loving. Lori was willing

· · · · ·

224

to love her. But she wasn't willing to be loved. You know what? Hal doesn't know it yet, but over the next couple of years he's going to knock on a lot of doors of people just like Aunt Jessie. And what he'll find strange is that although most of them will slam the door in his face, some of them—just *because* he's a stranger they'll never have to see again if they don't want to—will invite him in, unload on him, and then actually listen to him. Uh . . . when we turn in these papers I turn in a recommendation with them. How would you feel about his being sent to a foreign country? Often— not always, but often—they decide to send someone like Hal to his country of origin. Would you be able to afford transportation to Korea for him, if that's what they decide on? The church will pay his way home, but normally the family pays the missionary's way out, and living expenses in a foreign country are sometimes higher."

We already knew we would be responsible for his living expenses, but I hadn't thought about transportation. I already had my mouth open to answer when Harry, standing behind me, said, "We can come up with the money. If we don't have it ourselves by then—and I think we will—he's got a brother-in-law who'd be honored to do it."

I was somewhat astonished; Harry, though no longer actively hostile to the church, still had given no impression of loving it. But he and the bishop chatted amiably for another couple of minutes before Harry returned to the computer. The bishop started to leave, and then turned again. "Uh . . . Lori's aunt never would consent for Lori to be baptized, and Lori's been pretty upset about that. Now that you've got custody . . ."

He left the question unfinished, and I said, "We won't have formal custody until sometime in the next month or two. I'll sign whatever you need then. It should be before Hal leaves for wherever he's going."

I expected him to point out next that it might be a little awkward for Hal to leave on a mission when neither of his parents were

· · · · ·

church members. He did not. He just walked down the sidewalk whistling, stopped to scratch Pat behind the ears, got in his car, and drove away.

I called Vicky and Becky to let them know what was going on. Vicky said, "That's great, Mom, I'll tell Don to call as soon as he gets home."

Becky couldn't come to the phone, which was answered by a teenage voice—a baby-sitter, I guessed; Becky often had baby-sitters to help even when she was home—who said she'd have Becky call back. Which she did a couple of minutes later. "No, not a babysitter," she said, "just a friend who's staying with us for a while."

That was nothing new, either; she and her husband, Olead, seemed lately to collect stray youngsters to the extent that sometimes I thought they should be licensed to run a safe house for runaways and throwaways. Olead would bring them home the way a man crossing a parking lot in the rain will impulsively pick up a throwaway kitten and put it in his pocket, and sometimes I was convinced Becky went out looking for them. They never seemed to stay long; sometimes they went back home and other times they moved on either into a recommended situation or on their own; but it seemed since they started the habit about six months ago there were always a few youngsters there. But I rarely met them—even though I was Becky's mother, I was still a cop to a runaway.

"I was in the bathroom," Becky went on. "Mom, why do I have to be *afternoon* sick? Morning sickness is bad enough, I guess, but I've never had it—just afternoon sickness."

I commiserated, but couldn't answer.

"Anyway, I'm glad Lori's moving in," she added. "The poor kid was a shipwreck last time I saw her."

Hal informed us that Aunt Jessie had signed, in total silence, the temporary custody forms we had made out, kept one copy, returned the other two to Lori, and said, "I'll thank you to leave your key when you finally depart."

. . . . .

226

She had not said another word, but had stared so steadily that Hal asked, "Do you want to inspect and make sure we're not taking anything of yours?"

She hadn't answered. She'd just gone on staring, balefully.

Using the pickup truck and the camper, the kids had managed to get everything of Lori's, including her bed, dresser, desk, and desk chair (some of which would have to be stashed in the garage for the time being), in one trip, carrying clothing and books out to the truck in garbage bags (mine, of course; they'd taken them along knowing they'd need them and not wanting to ask Aunt Jessie for hers) after they ran out of boxes. It was just as well they did manage in one trip, because neither of them wanted to make a second. As it was, Lori was in tears again just from the look on Aunt Jessie's face by the time they got through.

Hal was sitting at the kitchen table filling out the papers that the bishop had dropped by—he'd already brought to our attention that he would have to have both a medical and a dental checkup—and Lori was singing in a high, sweet, but very soft voice as she rearranged what had been Cameron's bedroom to make room for her possessions as well as his when Sandy arrived at five.

Harry went to the door to let her in; I'd forgotten to tell him she was coming, and he might have a word or two to say to me later about that—though he probably wouldn't, considering what had been going on—but he didn't let on. He just said, "Deb will want to talk with you in the bedroom, so why don't you wait a minute while she gets back there?"

"I know you talked with several of Dusty's friends," Sandy said. In dark copper-colored tailored slacks, an ivory tailored blouse, and oxblood leather lace-up shoes, she looked like an upper-class college student, and she was sitting straight, neatly, in the same chair Rhonda had sprawled in several times. "I talked with them again, and with some others you probably didn't know about. Nobody claimed to know anything, but they had that look. You know."

· · · · ·

"I know," I said. "You used to have it all the time."

She laughed lightly, that tinkling laughter I had assumed she must have for use when needed. "I probably did. I was keeping secrets. Mrs. Ralston, there *was* something strange going on. I'm sure of that, even if I don't know what. Some of Dad's friends still recognize me on the street. I thought, if it made sense to you, I'd call and talk with them."

"Tactfully, please. And I *do* wish you'd call me Deb. Everyone else does, and it makes me nervous when you don't."

She stretched, catlike, and returned to her original position. "Well, Deb, I am a *genius* at getting what I want out of men. And not just the way you think. If I get anything, I'll get whoever I get it from to call you directly, if that's okay."

"I should have known," Harry said resignedly. "What is it going to take to make you stay home in bed like the doctor said?"

"I'll go home early, if you'll go get me," I argued, "but Matilda is going up there this morning, and she thinks she can get this Bonando thing settled."

"And Captain Millner has okayed letting a trance medium use the squad room." His tone implied he didn't believe that for a minute.

"I didn't ask Captain Millner. I asked Rafe. And she's not just a trance medium, she's also a psychologist."

"Deb, *I* like Matilda just fine," Harry pointed out. "I'm just thinking of her possible effect on a jury."

"There is no earthly reason why this case should ever go to a jury."

"Since I don't even know what kind of case it is, I'll take your word for it," Harry replied. "But I'm going to take you to a restaurant and see to it you get a decent breakfast for once."

Until my health was at least halfway back to normal, I wasn't expected either to be on time or to stay till normal quitting time.

. . . . .

Hal and Lori had been up quite late moving furniture, had barely made it to seminary on time, and had breakfasted on Cheerios and Pop-Tarts, a combination I considered a tad contradictory, but then I am not a teenager. A restaurant breakfast sounded wonderful, and as soon as I saw the menu I felt like eating everything on it. My appetite was bouncing back, which was something in my favor.

When I arrived in the office, Matilda, in a very sharp business suit and three-inch heels, was sitting in a desk chair—Henry Tuckman's, I noticed, and wondered where Henry was—and Rafe was sitting on the corner of the desk beside her. Mrs. Bonando, looking extremely unhappy, was in a chair beside the desk, and Rafe was in midsentence. ". . . is a psychologist. Although she has no official connection with the police department, she frequently works with one of our detectives."

"Mrs. Ralston?" Mrs. Bonando asked.

"That is correct. One of the things that makes Mrs. Ralston an excellent officer is that she has the ability to use many unofficial resources efficiently, and Ms. Greenwood has been happy to be one of those resources. Obviously, I cannot require you to talk with her, but she spent some time yesterday talking with Mr. and Mrs. Washington, and I feel that if you are willing to talk with her equally frankly, we can clear this whole problem up very quickly. Now, when you talk with her nobody from the police department will be present, and Ms. Greenwood will not tell us what you say unless you consent, so you can speak as freely as you want to."

Mrs. Bonando looked around, furtively, the way a trapped animal looks around. Then, in an uncertain voice, she said, "All right."

After the door to the interview room closed behind them, Rafe stood up, walked toward the door, and saw me for the first time. "Thanks for the kudos," I said.

"Earned," he answered briefly. "Let's see, everybody's either in

. . . . .

229

court or out on one thing or another except Henry, and he's down in Ident. All you need to do is sit around here and keep the roof on. I've got to head back to court."

Good planning. But you know what they say about the best laid plans of mice and men. Approximately three minutes after Rafe departed, Henry Tuckman came in, looked around, and said, "Nobody here but you?"

"Nope."

"Then I need you to come with me. We've got an arrest to make."

I had to work hard to keep from smiling; I was pretty sure I knew what arrest. But I put on a careful show of reluctance. "Henry," I pointed out, "I'm on crutches. It'd take me five minutes to draw, and I couldn't put handcuffs on a mouse."

"He's not going to give us any trouble," Henry answered, "and I just want you there so there'll be somebody to testify I didn't give him any unnecessary trouble."

"Well, I guess I can manage that."

"I'll pull the car around in front."

In the detective car, I realized for the first time that Henry was grinning irrepressibly. "What's with you?" I asked.

"AFIS couldn't get us an ident on the Super Glue rapist."

"That's something to be pleased about?"

AFIS—the *A*utomatic *F*ingerprint *I*dentification *S*ystem—is one of the most important developments of all time for law enforcement. In its very first field test, in San Francisco, in a six-month period it cleared eighty-three homicides that otherwise would probably never have been cleared, and since then departments all over the country have used it to great advantage. The computer does not itself make the identification; rather, it kicks out up to ten possibles for the fingerprint technician to study. If the regional net any given police department is on cannot locate a match, the prints are then faxed to the FBI, which can do several

. . . . .

hundred single-print searches in a single night. Thus the ideal of making a single-print search through the huge FBI fingerprint files, previously no more than a dream, is now an everyday reality.

"AFIS didn't," Henry said, "but Irene did."

"Huh?"

"Somebody called Irene and told her several of the Super Glue rape victims had been audited by the IRS the day they were raped, and each time it was by the same auditor. So Irene called Washington and got a fingerprint card faxed down here, and we just got a hit."

"Who is he?" I asked, managing not to grin triumphantly. This was one nobody official would ever know I had cleared, but *I* knew. And sooner or later, if I knew Irene as well as I thought I did, she'd manage to let somebody in authority know, after enough time had elapsed so that nobody would be too worried that I had gone on working after being told to let it alone.

"One Mitchell Kennedy," Henry said. If possible, his grin widened. "Mitchell Kennedy is an IRS investigator."

"What?" I hoped that sounded astonished enough.

"You heard me," Henry said.

"I thought the IRS thing was a lead." I could get away with saying that, because Rafe knew I had developed the lead. "But I didn't think . . . because Michie Chaney said she couldn't recognize the voice . . ." That really did puzzle me.

"Lots of people use different voices for different situations," Henry said. "This one apparently does. After Irene told me, I called all the victims I could reach. Except for Michie Chaney, *every one of them* had just been investigated by the IRS, and of course she'd just been involved in an investigation. As you found out. Four of the six I reached, including Michie Chaney, remembered the IRS agent's name, and guess what, it was Mitchell Kennedy. Funny thing, some of them insisted they'd already told you that."

"Oops," I said. "I didn't know you would call them again."

. . . . .

He looked at me questioningly.

"Rafe told me to leave it alone," I said. "But I couldn't, Henry."

"So it was you who called Irene."

"Yeah," I confessed, "but I told her not to tell anybody. Because I don't want Rafe to get mad at me again."

"I doubt Rafe will be too mad," Henry said, grinning.

"So anyway, what happened next?" I asked.

"I called his office, and his office told me who he was hassling—excuse me, *investigating*—today. And I think—I really do think—that somebody in the middle of an IRS audit might be tickled to death to have the investigator arrested, don't you?"

"There is a certain poetic justice to it," I agreed, as Henry parked in front of a small printing company.

"And all things considered, you really ought to be in on the arrest," Henry added, as he held the door open for me and my crutches to enter.

There was no receptionist on duty, and he and I made our way somewhat carefully through a cluttered front room into an office where stacks of receipts and canceled checks were spread out on a desk and a table, and two men were talking earnestly. Both turned to look at us, and then the younger man returned to the clipboard on which he had been writing industriously. "What is it?" the older man, who looked about sixty, asked.

Henry displayed his identification, already present in his hand. "Police."

"Just what I need," the man said. "I've already got the IRS." He glared at me. "And who the hell are you?"

"I'm police, too," I said.

"Yeah, yeah, we got to be politically correct," the man said. "A black male cop, a white female cop. On crutches yet. I've already got the IRS. They only sent me one of them."

"So I heard," Henry said. "Mitchell Kennedy?"

The younger man turned again. "I'm Mitchell Kennedy," he

. . . . .

232

said politely. He was a clean-cut, well-dressed man, smelling of Irish Spring soap.

"Mitchell Kennedy, I'm Henry Tuckman of the Fort Worth Police Department, and you're under arrest for rape. You have the right to remain silent—"

Kennedy looked quite startled. Then he asked, "How did you find me?"

"Your habits got a little too regular," Tuckman told him. "And last time you left fingerprints."

"That's impossible," Kennedy said. "I always wipe my fingerprints off."

"You didn't Tuesday, in Michele Chaney's car." Tuckman said nothing to indicate that the uninvited statement Kennedy had just made would be admissable in court under the *res gestae* rule. "Do you wish to give up the right to remain silent?"

"I suppose so," Kennedy said, "as you couldn't possibly have located me otherwise. That's really quite annoying, I can't imagine how I came to miss . . ." He snapped his fingers. "That plastic strip on the back door. That's where it was, wasn't it? I *knew* I had missed something—but I really must finish my investigation here."

"I'm afraid someone else will have to finish that investigation," Tuckman said.

The older man leaned back. "You're arresting the IRS?" he asked incredulously.

"Only one member of it, I'm afraid," Tuckman said. "Someone else will probably be back."

"Oh, I'm sure they will," Kennedy said. "An audit of this importance cannot be left incomplete." He began to gather papers into his briefcase, and Henry, after glancing into the briefcase to be sure it contained no weapons, allowed him to do it and then took custody of the briefcase.

"Five hundred bucks," the business owner said. "Five hundred lousy bucks he wants to collect. I'd *give* him the money to get him out of my hair, but no, he says it can't be done that way."

. . . . .

233

"Due process must be followed," Kennedy said fussily. "These papers must be taken back—"

"I'm sure they must," Tuckman said, "and I'll be glad to release them to whoever comes to get them. If you're willing to talk with us, would you please just sign right here?" Normally he would have asked me to witness the signature, but instead he asked the business owner, who scrawled "Dale Calder" on the witness line with evident relish.

On the way to the car, Henry asked, "Why did you pick those particular women?"

"They thwarted my investigation to a really annoying degree," Kennedy said.

"Does that mean you couldn't figure out a way to make them cough up any more money?"

"Really, that is not my function," Kennedy said. "And to be perfectly honest, I suppose my superiors will be most annoyed with me. My task is merely to make sure their tax information was *correct*. But in each case I was quite certain these women were hiding something which they refused to divulge, and I felt it necessary to punish them."

"What was Michie Chaney hiding?" I asked.

"Nothing of her own, so far as I know," he said. "Although I haven't looked at her personal files yet; I met her only because I was investigating one of her clients. It was just . . . her name is so similar to mine."

"And why Tuesday?" Tuckman asked.

"What?"

"Why did you just hit on Tuesday?"

"Oh, I didn't, of course."

"But Tuesday's the only day we've gotten reports from," I said.

He looked at me as if I were simpleminded. "Tuesday is the day I usually come to Fort Worth," he explained. "Today was quite unusual."

. . . . .

"And why only women with garages? How did you know about the garages?" I asked.

His look was even more pitying. "I went to their houses for the audit," he pointed out, "and of course I would pick only houses with garages, for proper concealment. I knew they would go out to eat after I left—women always do, I don't know why they can't just cook at home, the lazy deceitful sluts—and I followed them, saw where they parked their cars, and then checked in at the closest motel, bathed, notified . . . my friend . . . that I would be continuing the investigation on into the evening, and then returned to their cars. I have a way of getting them open." He seemed quite pleased with himself.

"And you did that in other towns as well?" Tuckman asked.

"When it seemed appropriate."

Tuckman and I glanced at each other. Obviously we'd need to contact a lot of neighboring agencies—some of whom, we hoped, would have DNA if they didn't have fingerprints.

"An *accountant?*" Michie Chaney yelled over the phone. "I was raped by an *IRS* accountant? *Mitchell Kennedy?* That twerpy son of a bitch isn't even a CPA! If I'd known it was him I'd have broken his neck! What I'll do to him if I ever get my hands on him—!"

Across the room, Mitchell Kennedy was asking, "How soon do you think I'll be able to get out on bond?"

. . . . .

Thirteen

. . . .

WHEN WE HAD ARRIVED back at the police department with Mitchell Kennedy in tow, I had noticed the Washingtons sitting side by side in what were evidently the most comfortable chairs anybody could find to put them in. A priest, rather older than I had guessed from his voice if this was Father Vincent, was sitting near them, and Janine Bonando was at the back of the room, perched on the windowsill looking out the window in her usual slouching posture. She was—as only an adolescent can do it—elaborately not seeing either the Washingtons or Father Vincent. Neither Matilda nor Mrs. Bonando was in sight, and the door to the interview room was still closed, as it had been when I left.

I crossed the room to speak to the Washingtons. They introduced me to Father Vincent, who said little more than "Good morning" and indicated that he hoped this matter would soon be finally settled, as it was very distressing to all concerned. I said hello to Janine, who responded with a rather incoherent grunt that might or might not have been a greeting.

I didn't have much more time to talk with them because I had to go call Michie Chaney, and just after I hung up the telephone after speaking with her, Captain Millner came in with an expression on his face that clearly indicated, at least to me, that he was loaded for bear. "First chance I've had to read the reports on this Reddich situation," he said, sitting down beside me. "What's going on now?"

. . . . .

"So far as I can figure out, nothing," I answered, making no attempt to disguise my anger. "The social worker won't let anybody do anything on it. The child is still in the home, no warrants have been taken, and while he's theoretically staying out of the household, nobody around here believes he really will."

"Who's that social worker on the case? Constantine? What's the rest of her name?"

"Gayle Constantine."

"How long has she been a social worker?"

"I don't know," I said. "Long enough to know better, in my opinion. I've been seeing her around for several years. She told me once she has an MSW and some background working in an adoption agency. It's not that she doesn't care, I think; it's just that she *really* thinks you can teach fathers not to molest their daughters, and mothers to protect them. And that's not so. When neglect or abuse is due to ignorance, you can educate the problem away, at least some of the time. But not this kind of problem. And that's what she can't understand. I can see that keeping families together is great when it's reasonably possible, but sometimes it isn't."

"Where's Rafe?"

"In court."

"Do you know what he's doing about it?"

"He told Gayle if she didn't pick them up he'd get a court order and do it himself. I don't know how long a time he gave her to do it, though."

"I don't suppose you know whether she's talked with her superiors about this."

"No idea."

"Give me her phone number."

I did, with some relish. Captain Millner can sound rough when he's being extremely friendly; people who hear him talking to me, without knowing we're really quite good friends, are likely to call him things like "chauvinist pig," which doesn't happen to be the

. . . . .

case. When he's thoroughly ticked off—well. You don't want to be on the receiving end.

"Gayle Constantine . . . I don't care how busy she is. Tell her the head of the Fort Worth Police Department Detective Bureau wants to talk with her *right now* . . . Ms. Constantine, I'm Captain Millner, and I'm . . . Good. Glad you know who I am. I'm sure you're aware that no court order for pickup is needed when we have compelling physical evidence that a child's safety and possibly a child's life is at stake. *First* you pick up the child and *then* you get the court order. Now, listen good, because I'm only going to say this once. Either *you* go out to the school and pick up the Reddich child and get her up here, or *I* go out to the school and pick up the Reddich child and get her up here, and if I'm the one to do it, your supervisor is going to hear a whole lot more about it than she wants to hear and especially than you want her to hear. Once we get them here, *I'll* get whatever court order you think you need. But we'll worry about court orders *after* that little girl is in a safe foster home . . . The hell with keeping the family together! What does the son of a bitch have to do to get you to act, dismember her? I read the pediatrician's report . . . Her mother will be notified; I'll see to that, too . . . The hell with her clothes, we'll get them later or the county will buy her some clothes. Which would you rather have, a safe kid with nothing much to wear, or the best-dressed corpse in Tarrant County?"

I don't know what Gayle Constantine said, but when Captain Millner hung up the phone he was looking slightly pleased. "Until the kid gets here," he said, "I'll just stick around."

It was then that Matilda came out of the interview room, saw me, and said, "Oh, good, you're back. Can you come in here?"

"Sure," I said, with a quick glance at Captain Millner, and followed her in, closing the door behind me.

Mrs. Bonando had been crying. Her eyes were red and puffy, her nose was running, what was left of her makeup was smeared, and about half of the original contents of the Kleenex box on the

. . . . .

table before her was now in the trash can beside her. "You explain," she said to Matilda, her voice muffled by the tissue she held to her lips.

"Mrs. Bonando and I have had a long talk," Matilda said, "and she has some justification for her unreasonable attitude toward Mr. Washington. When she was nine years old, a friendly fatherly neighbor, who was in the same parish and went to mass the same time she did, began to molest her, and he continued to molest her until she was seventeen. Every time she tried to get out of going to visit him, her parents accused her of being heartless toward this poor lonely old man whose family were all dead. When she began to notice that Mr. Washington was behaving in a friendly, fatherly manner toward Janine, she was afraid that he would behave as her neighbor did toward her."

In a fresh burst of weeping, Mrs. Bonando said, "I didn't want her to get hurt! I was scared—"

"Of course you were," I said.

"He really didn't do anything," Mrs. Bonando said. "I mean, that was the point. I wanted to make sure he didn't have a *chance* to do anything. I mean, if you'd gone just on the way he acted with people around, you'd have thought the guy that *did that* to me was just the nicest man you'd ever want to meet. So I wanted to make sure Janine never got *close* enough for Mr. Washington to do anything. As for looking at her . . . I don't know, I still think he was looking at her. But Miss Greenwood said he was looking at her because he was sorry for her. I . . . Miss Greenwood says I've scared Janine so much she hasn't got any friends. I didn't mean to hurt her! I just didn't want—"

"Of course you didn't want her hurt," Matilda said. "But girls can learn to protect themselves without fencing out the universe. Deb, Mrs. Bonando has agreed to family counseling for her and Janine."

"But only if you'll do it," Mrs. Bonando said, her voice dreary. "I'd be scared of anybody else."

· · · · ·

239

"I really don't have a private practice," Matilda said, her tone suggesting she'd said it several times already.

"You've been saying you wanted one," I pointed out. "And I know you have the necessary licenses because I've seen them myself."

"All right," Matilda said, "but I'll want to meet with you and Janine in your own home instead of in my office."

Mrs. Bonando looked slightly startled. "Isn't that unusual?"

Matilda looked at me. I know she and I were both having the same mental picture: Janine and Mrs. Bonando climbing the rickety wooden outside stairs to Matilda's office-apartment combination (that Matilda grandiosely, and mockingly, called her workstead) over her spiritualist "church" that in fact served as a mental health agency for older people, mostly women, who would feel disgraced for life if they were seen going to psychiatrists or psychologists. "As Ms. Greenwood has not recently had a private practice," I said, "she isn't set up in a normal office. She's quite right. Meeting with you in your own home would be best."

"I guess I have to apologize to Mr. Washington, don't I?" Mrs. Bonando said, her thin voice continuing dreary and almost monotone.

"You don't have to," Matilda said, "but it would be kind."

"I better talk to Janine first . . . You tell her."

With Janine in the room, Matilda went through the whole recitation again. Janine slumped down in her chair; that was not, I had already observed, an unusual posture for her. "Well," she said. "Well, all the kids at school kept telling me Mr. Washington was real nice, that he helped a lot of people in trouble, and all that, but when Mom said . . ." She looked accusingly at her mother. "You *said* he wanted to . . ."

"I think now I was wrong," Mrs. Bonando said. She glanced quickly at Matilda. That was what Matilda wanted her to say, so she would say it. She wasn't sure, yet, that was what she really thought. It would take a lot more work, on Mrs. Bonando's part as well as

· · · · ·

Matilda's, before Mrs. Bonando was able to distinguish truth from falsehood in this kind of situation.

"So he *doesn't* want to." Janine demanded.

"No, he doesn't," I said. "Janine, Mr. Washington has been worried about you because you've seemed so lonely and unhappy. He's wanted to befriend you and to help you, just as he's befriended and helped many other teenagers in the last thirty years."

Matilda explained the whole thing yet again, this time to the priest, and then we all trooped out into the squad room, where the Washingtons were sitting, understandably tense.

Henry Tuckman was gone, with Mitchell Kennedy; presumably the IRS agent was now being booked, and would soon find out that after the string of rapes he had committed, getting bond would be more difficult than he seemed to think. (So, I suspected, would keeping his job. He was undoubtedly correct that his superiors would be displeased.)

The apologies that followed were more than a little strained, and the Washingtons looked more bewildered than reassured. Mrs. Bonando went on crying, twisting a tissue in nervous hands that tore the tissue to shreds and reached for another and another. She was still extremely frightened, I thought, for herself as well as Janine, and Janine had been too frightened—deliberately—by her mother to be able to come out of it immediately. But Father Vincent, who presumably had arrived with the Washingtons, departed with the Bonandos (and come to think of it, since she arrived in my absence, I hadn't the slightest idea when and how Janine had arrived), and the Washingtons remained seated while Captain Millner joined us to find out what was going on. "Now that the Bonandos are gone," Matilda said to Mr. Washington, "I have permission to tell you what the real situation was."

She went through the whole story once more, and both the Washingtons' faces told their reaction clearly. "That poor child," Mrs. Washington said, and it was unclear whether she meant mother or daughter.

· · · · ·

241

But Mr. Washington said, "Those poor children. Of course she frightened her daughter to death; she was nothing but a frightened child herself."

"I've got to go now," Matilda said, and turned to me. "Deb, I'm going to be sort of tied up the next two or three days."

"Take care of yourself," I said.

The Washingtons stayed to talk with me for another moment or two, and they had just begun to get out of their chairs when Gayle Constantine got off the elevator, passing Matilda, who got onto it, and came in with the little girl. Gayle paused, looking surprised. "Oh, hello, Mr. Washington, Mrs. Washington," she said. "I had just tried to telephone you. How on earth did you know to meet me here? Oh, the detectives must have called you, of course."

"We didn't . . . ," Mrs. Washington began, looking totally bewildered.

Gayle Constantine's voice rushed over her like a river in flood. "Your application as foster parents was approved this morning, just in time. We're so short of foster parents, and we've got this little girl—"

"I know Diane," Mrs. Washington said. "I . . . talked with her several days ago. Don't you remember?" Turning to her husband, she said, "You remember me telling you about the little Reddich girl, don't you?"

From his expression, I'd have guessed he didn't remember, but he smiled amiably and said, "Sure I remember."

"I saw you lots of days last year," Diane said, "on the playground, when I was in kiddiegarten. You substituted for the principal when she was having her baby."

"I remember that," Mrs. Washington said. "It was the middle of winter and there you were in those short skirts. I'd forgotten until just now."

"I told you I wanted to go live with you," Diane said forlornly, "and you told me I couldn't."

. . . . .

"But you didn't tell me why," Mrs. Washington said. "If you'd told me why—"

"Just *because*," Diane said.

"But I think maybe you can come live with us now," Mrs. Washington said. "If Mrs. Constantine . . ." She looked questioningly at the social worker.

"Yes, of course," Ms. Constantine answered. "I thought I had made that clear."

Groping for words that would be over Diane's head, I added to Mrs. Washington, "The girl's . . . um . . . immediate ancestors are probably both soon to be incarcerated—him definitely, for unlawful carnal knowledge of a minor, highly aggravated in nature, and her probably, for conspiracy to conceal a crime. You were absolutely right to notify us when you did. The . . . minor in question . . . is going to need long-term foster care. Ms. Constantine seems to feel that your home would be acceptable."

"*Highly* aggravated?" Mr. Washington asked, in a horrified voice, and I remembered we hadn't kept Mrs. Washington posted on the course of the investigation.

"Very highly," Ms. Constantine said.

Mrs. Washington's arms tightened around the little girl.

"I hadn't expected to see you here," Ms. Constantine repeated, "but I was trying to call you. I would have taken her to you later this afternoon, if you were willing to take her. The situation, which of course you know about, is quite complicated, and not all foster homes would be suitable. But if you feel you can handle—"

"Well, of course we can," Mrs. Washington said indignantly, and glanced at her husband. "We want to take Diane home, don't we?"

"That's why we asked to become foster parents," he said. "It doesn't matter how serious the situation is. We'll handle it." His confident tone stopped Ms. Constantine's dithering.

.   .   .   .   .

With obvious relief, Ms. Constantine said, "In that case—if you want—why don't you take her home now?"

"I'm glad you know something you do have the authority for," Captain Millner said.

"Mrs. Washington?" Diane said. "Can I really go home with you?"

"That you may." The astonished little face looked up and then immediately buried itself in Mrs. Washington's bosom again. "Well," Mrs. Washington said, looking at the top of the little head, "since you're going home with us now, you'd better call me something better than Mrs. Washington. Would you like to call me Auntie Laura?" She pronounced it *ahntie* rather than *antie*. "And here's Uncle David."

Looking at the girl's attire with some disapproval, Mr. Washington said, "I think we better go first thing and get you some slacks to play in. That skirt, uh, doesn't look very comfortable."

What it really looked, he had forborne to say, was indecently short, but Diane looked up at him and said, "Daddy won't let me wear slacks. You 'member, Mrs. . . . . Auntie Laura. I told you last year."

"How come?" Mrs. Washington said. "You didn't tell me that."

" 'Cause he says it's harder to get at my cunt in them."

Mrs. Washington closed her eyes briefly, said, "Oh, Lordy," and then reopened them and said vigorously, "Your daddy has taught you some bad things. 'Cunt' is not a pretty word. Can you say *vagina*? Say it with me, *vagina*."

Diane repeated 'vagina' rather loudly and agreed it was a prettier word, and then Mrs. Washington said, "And furthermore, until you're grown up and married, no man is *ever* supposed to touch your vagina unless he is a doctor and you're sick. And if somebody tries to touch your vagina, or any other part of your body that would be covered by a swimsuit, you come tell me or Uncle David and we'll put a stop to it right quick."

. . . . .

"You mean I don't have to—" There was joyous astonishment in Diane's voice.

"Auntie Laura *always* tells the truth," Mr. Washington said quietly. "So you remember that. And while you're gone with Auntie Laura to get some slacks," he added, "you be thinking real hard about whether you'd rather have a kitten or a puppy or maybe both. I've got to stay here and talk with this lady for a while, and then you and Auntie Laura will come back and get me."

"David," Mrs. Washington said, "why don't you just meet us at the ice skating rink, when you're ready?"

"Okay," he said, and watched the two leave the squad room. After the elevator door closed on them, he looked at me and said, "She's a baby. I can't imagine how anyone . . ." He faltered to a stop, shaking his head.

"That's right," I said. "She's a baby. Except she never has been allowed to be a baby. The best we can figure out, she's been treated as a whore since she was two or three years old."

"And the father did it."

"The father did it," Captain Millner said. "The reason we're charging the mother, too"—I got an approving look from him over that—"is because she had to have helped to cover it up. From the medical report, which I read this morning, her genitals are pretty well healed now, although they'll never be back to what should be normal, but to start with there had to be a lot of bleeding and infection. She couldn't possibly not have known."

David Washington shook his head again. "I don't understand stuff like that. I never did. How any human being could ever look at a child and even *want* to do something like that, much less actually do it . . . And so tiny. Did he *like* hearing her cry? Did he *like* hurting her? His own child? Or anybody else's, for that matter? It's gonna be a hard job, turn that one back into a child. It's been a while since we had children around the house. But we'll manage."

He went off with Ms. Constantine, and Captain Millner stood

．　．　．　．　．

up. "There, that didn't take so long. Now I'm going to make some phone calls and lean on a judge. I want that man behind bars."

That left me alone in the office, alone and more than ready to go home if I could find a ride. It had been quite a day, and maybe I'd stay home Friday and do what the doctor said for a change. After all, we had a satisfactory conclusion to the Washington-Bonando situation, the Reddich child was as well cared for now as possible, although it probably would be impossible for her ever really to get her childhood back, and the Super Glue rapist was under arrest—thanks to my bright idea. Of course I still didn't know where Doreen Miller was, or what had caused Dusty Miller's suicide, but I was satisfied that Sandy knew where Doreen was and was satisfied, and as long as Doreen was out of her father's reach, finding out why Dusty had died was not time critical.

I reached for the telephone to see whether I could locate Harry, and it rang. I picked it up. "Sex Crimes Unit."

"Deb, is that you?"

"Yes, Mom, it's me," I said resignedly. She sounded as if she had been crying. If so, I might be in for a long siege on the phone.

"Did you know Rhonda had left?"

"Yes, I did," I answered. "She spent the night with me before taking off for Denver."

"I just don't understand it," Mom wept. "I did everything I could for her. If I could just figure out why—"

"Do you really want me to tell you why?" I asked.

"I . . . Yes. If you know. Because if she gets sicker she might come back again, and I . . . I want her to . . . be able to stay, to *want* to stay, next time."

"Several things. First, you weren't treating her as an adult. Obviously, it's your house and you have a perfect right to decide how the general-use areas are to be used, but Rhonda's bedroom is Rhonda's bedroom, and if she wants to live in a mess, that's her business. And you don't have any right to tell her when to take a bath and when to take her medicine. Mom, she's nearly forty. She's

. . . . .

246

not fourteen. It's true that AIDS sometimes affects the brain, but you had no reason to suppose it had affected hers yet. That was the small thing. The big thing is, you were expecting her to use a room full of Dad's things—his clothes, his hobbies, his aftershave, even his cigarette smell—and she found that extremely distressing."

"Well," Mom said, no longer weeping, "I think it would be very heartless of me to just *throw away* my late husband's possessions."

"There are a lot of homeless men who would be very grateful for those clothes," I retorted, "and it's certainly far more heartless to expect a rape victim to sleep in what is in effect her rapist's bedroom."

"Debra! How can you say such things!"

"Because they're true and you know damn well they're true. And don't go crying to Jim about it and get him to call me again, because he knows I'm telling the truth, and I'm not going to apologize to you for that. Dad could have spent forty years in prison for what he did to Rhonda and me, and the least either of us has the right to expect is that we won't be called liars for telling the truth."

"Debra, I simply do not believe—"

"Why?" I interrupted.

"Debra—" She paused, then tried again. "From what Rhonda told me you're saying it happened about when you had tonsillitis for months, you remember, when they wouldn't take your tonsils out until you'd been well for two weeks and we couldn't keep you well for two weeks at a time? You remember, when you started hating oatmeal so much?"

"I never did like oatmeal," I said, far more harshly than I would have if we'd really been talking about oatmeal.

"Well, no, you didn't, but you always ate it before, and then all of a sudden you wouldn't and if we tried to make you eat it then you threw up. You remember that winter. You had fever so much you could have imagined just about anything."

. . . . .

Yes, I remembered the winter when I was twelve, when I lived from January to June on penicillin and aspirin and got down to about eighty-nine pounds because nothing I ate stayed eaten. I was certain, now, that the reason I was never able to shake the strep infection long enough for the doctor to do the surgery was that I was vomiting several times a day. And I knew I'd never tell my mother why I stopped eating oatmeal, what that slimy grayish goop that forms in cooked oatmeal felt like hitting the back of my throat at just past body temperature, and why by extension from that all food except very crisp things started turning my stomach.

Getting my tonsils out in June was heavenly. My father left me alone until September that year.

"Mom," I said, "I remember that winter. I remember the fever and the vomiting. But it didn't last from the time I was nine till the time I was nineteen. And Rhonda never did have tonsillitis. Face it, Mom, it happened. All of it. Rhonda was telling the truth—and probably not all the truth, just enough of it to get across to you what it was like for us."

You'd think she'd have shut up then. But so help me, she tried again.

"But if the same thing happened to both of you, and it's supposed to have caused Rhonda's . . . conduct . . . since then, then why hasn't the same thing happened to you? You're all right."

In that second, I realized why I was all right and Rhonda had fallen apart. "Because," I said, "Granddad was around when I was a kid. And Granddad treated me like a child. Granddad took me out in the front yard to look at the stars, and into the shop to play with the wood curls, and into the garden to pick the strawberries. He took me to the feed store and the hardware store and sometimes even the barbershop. When I was a child there was a man that I could relate to other than sexually or fearfully, even if it was for only a short time, and I met his friends and they, too, treated me as a child. But he died when I was seven. Rhonda was only two. I could remember him, I could remember how he and I were to

· · · · ·

each other, and Rhonda never could. So I wasn't taught first, and only, that I had to be sexy for men. I was taught first that I could be me around men, and Rhonda never learned that. The only man Rhonda was around until she entered junior high and started having male teachers was Dad, and except for rare occasions, like taking us to the library in the summer because the busses didn't run where we lived, he had two modes: sex or beatings. I had Grand-dad. Rhonda didn't. That's why I came out okay. That's why Rhonda didn't. But don't tell me you don't believe it, because you do believe it. You know I'm telling the truth. The fact is you don't *want* to believe it. But that's your problem. Not mine, and not Rhonda's. If you want Rhonda back, admit the truth, and get rid of that stuff in that bedroom. It was crazy to keep it anyway. Who do you think you are, Queen Victoria?"

Mom slammed the phone down. I sighed and reached out to push the button for an empty line, and the phone rang again. "I'd like to speak to Detective Ralston, please." The voice was male, and I guessed him to be in his fifties.

"I'm Detective Ralston," I answered.

"I'm Rodney Kilgore," he said. "I . . . Do you know Alexandra Miller?"

"Yes, I do."

"And you've been working on this thing about her sister?"

"I was assigned to the case," I said, which was perfectly true and said nothing about the fact that I'd also been pulled back off it, the powers that be having decreed that there was no case at all.

"I'd like, if you don't mind, to come in and talk with you tomorrow," he said. "Would ten o'clock be all right? I've got some spare time then and I'm having lunch downtown anyway."

I agreed to that, and this time successfully reached a telephone line, for all the good that didn't do. Harry wasn't home. In the end, I maneuvered myself down the hall to Captain Millner's office and asked if he would drive me home.

Which he did. And I took the occasion of a captive audience to

·   ·   ·   ·   ·

249

go on and tell him about what Sandy had told me, and about Rodney Kilgore coming in on Friday, and he listened and for once did not yell at me about trying to do too much. "Sounds as if there might really be something there," he said. "Did you tell this girl, Sandy, that it's not too late for her to make a case against him?"

"I did, and she's afraid her testimony might not be credible, in light of later events."

"I think I might want to have a talk with Miss Alexandra Miller. See if you can arrange that tomorrow," the captain said, and let me out at my house.

I'd just got out of my work clothes and into the shorts and tank top I was currently sleeping in, and poured myself a ginger ale, when the telephone rang again. When I leaned over to answer, a rough voice said, "My name's Phil. Phil Harkness. You don't know me, but your sister Rhonda left with me t'other day. See, I got some kind of bad news."

"Tell me," I said, visions of Rhonda in jail, Rhonda too drunk for anybody to control, Rhonda in any one or more of half a dozen idiotic situations dancing through my head.

"Rhonda's dead," he told me.

I sat straight up. "What?" I asked shakily. "What do you mean? She wasn't that sick—"

"No, ma'am, she wasn't that sick, not yet, and maybe it's better she did die this way, before she got that sick. See, last night about midnight I pulled into this big truck stop outside of Amarillo to gas up and get a bite to eat, and Rhonda, she was asleep in the camper, and she got up after I was already halfway to the restaurant, and I heard her call my name and I turned and looked behind me and I seen her. I can see her now, like a picture in my mind. She had on those denim short-short cutoffs she likes . . . liked . . . to wear, and a white tank top, and her hair all tousled 'cause she'd been asleep, and she was carryin' her sneakers in her hand like she wanted to wait and put them on in the light, her sneakers and that brown corduroy and leather bag, you know the one, and then this tractor-

. . . . .

250

tanker combination, he pulled in, and she was standing in the middle of the lane and his lights caught her like a rabbit in a jacklight. And she just stood there like a rabbit in a jacklight, him a-honkin' fit to kill but no way he could stop the rig in that distance, even as slow as he was going, and me trying to run toward her to get her out of the way and I knowed full well there wasn't no way I could reach her in time. I don't guess I ever will know whether she was like a rabbit, too scared to run, or whether she just—in that second—decided she'd run too far and she was too tired and this was the easiest way to get it over with. But when they found out she didn't have no insurance to cause trouble, the county mounties here, they said they would call it an accident. An', ma'am, I hope nobody minds, but I claimed the body for buryin' here, said we was married common-law. It ain't altogether a lie. I would have married her any time in the last ten years but she wouldn't have none of it, said she poisoned anybody she touched."

"So she's being buried in Amarillo, as Rhonda Harkness?" I asked faintly.

"Ma'am, she was buried this afternoon. We just had a graveside service, with nobody there but me and the trucker that hit her, and ma'am, I'm sorry for him, he was cryin' like a baby even if there wasn't no way he could have stopped. But I decided not to call you until after it was done with. She done told me—not after she was hit, they said she died instant and didn't feel nothing—but while we was drivin' we was talkin' about her goin' off to Colorado by herself, and she told me you was laid up, and there wasn't nobody else in the family she'd want at her buryin'. She said you was nice to her even if she did useta steal from you, and nobody else cared whether she lived or died. She . . . maybe she shouldn't of done it, but she told me what her ol' man did to you and her, and about her mom expectin' her to live in the room with all his clothes and stuff. That was . . . ma'am, that was pretty brutal, if you ask me."

"I agree," I said. "I . . . Would you mind sending me a copy of the death certificate?"

．　．　．　．　．

"Yes'm, I knowed you'd want it and I got one to mail soon's you give me your address. I . . . It don't mention the virus nowhere on it. Just said she died of being struck by a truck. So if you'll give me the address—"

I gave it to him and then said, "Thank you for letting me know." There didn't seem to be much else to say.

"You're welcome, ma'am," he said. "I guess I'll be going now. I still got a load of steel pipe to get into Colorado. Not much reason for doing it now, it don't seem like, but I still got to do it."

I hung up the phone, feeling numb, and rolled over and pulled two pillows over my head, and I was still there, still awake, when Harry came in.

He must have been able to tell from my posture something had hit me hard, because he sat down on the bed, put his hand on my arm, and said, "Honey, what is it?"

Without removing the pillow, I said, "Rhonda's dead."

"What happened?"

I told him, and finally, then, I could start crying.

"You called your mom yet?"

"No," I said, "and I don't want to. I really chewed her out this afternoon—"

"Did she have it coming?"

"Yes," I said, and started to explain, and balked, remembering the reason, which I could scarcely explain without explaining too many other things.

He took a deep breath. "Deb, would it help if I told you I overheard you and Rhonda talking the other day? I . . . I came home and saw Pat was locked in the front yard, so I went to open the side gate right under the bedroom window so he could get in the back, and heard what you and Rhonda were saying. It . . . threw me for a loop."

I rolled over to face him, scattering pillows in all directions and startling the cat, who I didn't realize had crawled in beside me. "I

. . . . .

heard the gate. That puzzled me, because I looked and there was nobody out there. That's why you've been acting so horrid."

"Yes. And I'm sorry. You had enough to worry about without me acting like an ass. But I . . . I had to think it through. I didn't know how to react. I . . . Remember, I knew him."

"Of course you knew him; we'd been married for years before he died."

"Right. Well, to be perfectly honest, I didn't like him. I never did like him. I tried to get along with him for your sake, but I never did like him. But if I'd guessed anything like that . . . Deb, I might have killed him."

"Which is one of the reasons why I never told you," I answered. "One of. Only one of. I . . . Harry, how was I supposed to know how you'd react? There've been men walk out on their wives over something like that, or treat them from then on like they were something that had crawled out from under a flat rock—"

"You didn't do anything," he said. "And I don't want to hear any more about it unless you want to tell me."

"I don't."

"All right. Then that's that. I won't ask. But I hope you can understand why I had a little adjusting to do. I . . . Probably you remembered it all along; I know there are some women who forget until something triggers the memory, but you—you don't forget things. So you remembered, didn't you?"

"I tried not to," I said slowly. "For years at a time I could avoid thinking about it very much, but then it would all fall over me again like a black cloud. No. I never forgot. I always knew."

"You knew it," he repeated, "and I didn't. I had to think."

"And get drunk."

"I hoped you didn't notice that," he said ruefully.

"I noticed."

"I only did it once. But . . . do you want to tell me, now, why you reamed out your mom?"

· · · · ·

I told him. He was silent for a long time, his hand absently rubbing my arm, staring off into space at a closed and curtained window, which I felt reasonably sure he wasn't seeing.

"I don't know what to say," he said finally. "That boggles the mind. Look, when my father died we packaged up all his things that nobody in the family had a use for and we sent it all off to the Salvation Army. I thought that was what everybody did. Even if he was the best husband and father in the world, there's no sense in creating a shrine to him, and even if she—willfully or not—didn't know this was going on, she certainly knew enough to know he was by no means the model male. Hell, *I'm* not the model male."

"You'll do," I said.

"But when I die, don't keep my clothes lying around."

"The feeling is mutual, if I die first. But, Harry, you know, I think that's why."

"Why what?"

"Why she keeps his stuff around. She can't look back at a lot of pleasant memories and say, well, I had this really terrific husband even if he did die before me. So she keeps all his stuff around so she can go and look at it and think, well, I really did have a husband, see, here's the proof."

"That's morbid," Harry said. "Do you want me to call her?"

"Do you want to?"

"No, but I don't want you to have to."

In the end, we chickened out. Neither of us called her. We called her pastor, and he promised to go over and notify her personally about Rhonda's death.

. . . . .

Fourteen
· · · · · · · · ·

I WANTED TO CALL MOM, after we'd given the pastor time enough to get over there, but Harry suggested I wait and give her a little time to settle down. "She'll call you when she's ready to talk," he said. He also pointed out that I hadn't taken my pain medication, and I was definitely showing that fact. I didn't want to take it, because I knew I'd go to sleep right after it—that was why I hadn't taken it at work—but he was right. If I didn't take it soon, I wasn't going to be capable of very coherent thinking.

But I didn't feel up to snake dreams *or* tidal wave dreams. So, of course, I had both. Nothing new—just the same old same old, to start with. But gradually the dream calmed down until all I could see was Rhonda as I had seen her last, only strangely different, Rhonda as she might have been if no evil had ever befallen her, and she was clean, swimming freely and laughing joyously as the waves broke over her head. I woke suddenly, startled and sweating—not shaking and sick with fear, as I usually woke from snake dreams, but sweating only because my fever (which I hadn't realized I had) had broken as I slept. I glanced at the clock. It was after five; Harry surely had left long since for school, and the kids should be home (and were; that was the sound of their practicing I heard from the garage). And Mom should have called me long ago.

I had assumed, of course, despite what Harry had said, that she would call me the minute the pastor—one Brother Hitt, a man in his early thirties, Brother Green having finally retired after about

· · · · ·

255

sixty years with the same church—left her alone. But apparently she wasn't going to. That meant I was going to have to call her, which to be perfectly honest I wasn't exactly looking forward to. So I would first take the time to go to the bathroom and douse my head under the detachable shower head before I called. The needles of hot water felt wonderful, and I knelt beside the bathtub, which I couldn't get into because of the cast, stripped off my sweaty clothes, showered my upper story, and used a washcloth on everything I couldn't get into the bathtub. I dried thoroughly then and put on talcum powder and clean dry clothes. I probably smelled a lot better now, I thought as I removed the wet towel I had first wrapped around my head and replaced it with a dry one, and I certainly felt better.

I crawled back into bed, got the phone into bed with me, propped myself up on that molded armchair pillow, and dialed. Mom didn't answer at first, and when she did she sounded out of breath.

"How are you?" I asked cautiously.

"I'm all right." She didn't sound all right. She'd been crying, and she was still crying.

"Look, Mom, I'm sorry I jumped all over you this afternoon—"

"Well, you shouldn't be," she retorted. "You were entirely right. I told Brother Hitt all about it, and he said that making a shrine to the dead is idolatry. He said that effectively by expecting Rhonda to sleep in there I was sacrificing the living to the dead. And I told him what you and Rhonda said, and he said that unless I had some strong evidence that it wasn't true I should believe you both, and he told me things like that are far more common than most people suspect, and then he asked me what evidence I had that it wasn't true and I didn't have any. I never thought about that before. None of it. About idolatry, and about seeing the truth. Brother Green never would tell me that. Even when they threw Ed out of the church, he told me I should respect my husband no

· · · · ·

matter what he had done, and he told the children we still had at home they should respect their father no matter what he had done. Like it was all right for God to be mad at him but not okay for you kids or me to be mad at him. Or even to say he was wrong."

She paused for breath, and I thought, *I can well believe that was what Brother Green said. But to do him justice, when he saw my father beating my brothers he saw only an excess of zeal toward discipline, and I'm sure that even in his wildest nightmares he could never have imagined that any man—and certainly not any man he knew—could treat his daughters the way our father treated us.*

"You want to know what my bishop said in a talk the other day?" I asked.

"What?" Mom is glad I'm going to some church, but would prefer I return to hers. Her voice sounded very odd.

"He said the best way to honor an unworthy parent is to try your best to be the kind of person you would have been if the parent had behaved the way he or she should have done. But you don't honor an unworthy parent by endorsing his actions, or imitating them."

"Oh," Mom said rather blankly, and went on talking. "You know what Brother Hitt told me?"

"No, what?"

"He said, 'Ye shall know the truth and the truth shall make you free.' That's in the Bible."

"I know," I said.

"Well, I know, too, but I didn't think it applied to things like this. But Brother Hitt said it does. He said I had kept myself enslaved to Ed's tyranny by refusing to know the truth, and I had tried to keep my children enslaved to Ed's tyranny, too. He said I had to decide to know the truth. And he's right. But I should have decided a long time ago. Because it's too late to help her now—"

"Her," of course, obviously meant Rhonda. "I dreamed about Rhonda," I interrupted.

"When?"

. . . . .

"Just now. I took some of the medicine for my foot, and went to sleep, and had this weird dream." I told her about it, emphasizing the way Rhonda looked at the end of the dream.

"That means something," she said.

"What?" I inquired.

"I don't know," she said. "But something."

A silence on the phone is twice as awkward as a silence in person, because each person is clearly expecting the other to say something. Finally I said, "Well—"

At almost the same time, Mom said, "Well—"

"You go ahead," I said.

"No, you go ahead," Mom said.

"I was just thinking about Rhonda," I said. "What's happened has happened, and there's no way of changing it. So there's no use any of us regretting ourselves to death. And it wasn't all Dad's fault for molesting her, or our fault for not protecting her. She made a lot of very bad decisions herself. The fact remains, though, that what's past is past and there's nothing to do about it now."

"But I should have admitted it," Mom said. "Brother Hitt told me so. It was wrong for me not to admit it. I didn't know it when it was happening, and I don't know how I could have known, but later, when you and Rhonda both told me, I should have admitted it then. As for protecting her, that was my duty, not yours; you were a child yourself. And I knew even then he beat all you kids horribly, and all I could think of to do was cry and say, 'Ed, don't.' And that time when he got thrown out of church—"

"Happened," I said. "It happened, and is past."

"But I'm still cleaning out this room. I've got a lot of bags in here. I'm taking all of Ed's stuff to Goodwill, so if any of you ever need to stay with me again—"

"I doubt any of us will. But cleaning the room—"

"And besides," she said, "I had Cameron sleeping with me while Rhonda was here, and now that Rhonda's gone, once I get this room totally clean—"

. . . . .

"He wets the bed sometimes," I reminded her. "You're lucky he hasn't done it already."

"I'll put a plastic undersheet on, then. And I think cleaning the room will be very good therapy for me."

She was still crying, had been crying throughout the conversation. But she was right: cleaning the room was good therapy, far better therapy than talking with me. So I let her go, and went into the living room to see what Hal and Lori were doing. As I should have guessed, even if I hadn't been able to hear them from the bedroom, they were still in the garage practicing for tomorrow night. German Measles or Chicken Pox or whatever the name of the band was; I was too foggy to remember right now. Hey Fever, that was it, with the misspelling deliberate.

It could have been worse; they could have still been trying to do heavy metal. But Lori, thank goodness, would never be a heavy metal singer, and they had decided, rightly I expect, that the market for country and western music was far greater around here than the market for heavy metal. And at least country music was slightly less depressing to listen to: instead of a message of "let's kill all the cops and have sex with all the girls" (I have, of course, cleaned up the heavy metal message slightly), its message is "I have a lousy job and my wife/husband doesn't love me and I'm going to a bar and drink away all my sorrows."

When I listen to what's on the radio now I think I must be getting old. It all sounds so sordid. What's wrong with Tennessee Ernie Ford? "Sixteen Tons" and "Big Bad John" (whoever it was who sang that, I don't think it was Tennessee Ernie), and "Purple People-Eater" and "Ting Tang Walla Walla Bing Bang," or maybe its name was "My Friend the Witch Doctor"? Well, on second thought, maybe the music when I was younger wasn't so sensible after all, but at least you could hear the words and they didn't make you want to go out and shoot yourself or somebody else. "Chantilly Lace" and "Teen Angel," and I was definitely feeling my age. "Itsy Bitsy Teeny Weeny Yellow Polka-Dot Bikini." And what

. . . . .

was that thing about the Nash Rambler that wouldn't go out of second gear? Rhonda ripped off my record of that and never would give it back. That and "Ebony Eyes" both. "Ebony Eyes" was the Everly Brothers, I think. What was that song when I was probably not much older than Cameron was now, something about "Constantinople (Now It's Istanbul)"—what a thing to make a song about, but people loved it. And "Wake Up, Little Susie." Nowadays I'd hate to think what Little Susie would be waking up from.

I get like this about once in six years, and this time it was pretty evident what had precipitated the mood.

"Cherry Pink and Apple Blossom White." That was one of Rhonda's favorites of my records; she played it over and over and over, when she was still a really little kid; I'm not even sure she was in school yet. And now Rhonda was dead and if I still drank beer I would undoubtedly be crying in it.

So many of those songs dated back to my preteens, some of them even before I had started to school. Why was it I couldn't remember the songs of my teens as well as I could the ones that came earlier? But I knew the answer to that . . . my mind had chosen to remember virtually nothing about my teens, including the music.

Lori was trying to sing "Stand by Your Man," but her voice was too thin. Other country and western songs have made it perfectly clear that some men aren't worth standing by. My father wasn't.

Enough of this, I told myself sternly, and forced myself to begin to think about supper.

The Relief Society president had been unwilling to hear of Lori, or anybody else in the family including Harry and Hal, trying to cook until a week after my surgery, so for the time being somebody from church was still bringing supper to us. That was probably just as well, as Hal, though he wouldn't admit it, probably would resent anything that would take Lori away from practice for very long. Harry would eat tonight on the way to school, so there was just Lori and Hal and me to feed.

I was, I noticed, falling into a pattern. When I took my pain

. . . . .

medicine it took it from fifteen to forty-five minutes to take effect, depending on how recently I had eaten, and then I fell into a very deep, dream-filled sleep for about half an hour. Apparently the pain medicine also did something about the fever, because I'd wake up with my hair as wet as if I had been showering. But once I woke, unless it was a time of day I'd normally be asleep, I was up for the next two or three hours, though my mind might be wandering quite a lot, as it clearly was now.

That would be good—being awake I mean, not letting my mind wander—if I had anything to do. But the supper was being brought in, and even if it wasn't, I couldn't stand up long enough to cook it. Hal and Lori—after Matilda's help that one day—were keeping the house reasonably clean, and even if they weren't, I couldn't clean it. The laundry was stacking up a little, but it would be all I could do to get myself through that mousehole of a kitchen into the front part of the garage where the washer was, much less get myself and a load of laundry there, so on Saturday Harry (which probably meant Hal, which probably meant Lori) would have to do that. And Cameron, of course, was still with Mom.

So the point was, I was awake with nothing to do. This is a distinctly unusual situation for me, and I was not finding it at all to my liking.

I turned the television on, channel surfed for a couple of minutes, turned it off again, got out my long-abandoned crocheting and decided within about two minutes that I didn't feel up to crocheting, went back to the bedroom and got the book I had been reading, decided I was not up to reading a book, tried the most recent grocery store magazine and found I was not up to it either, and went back to bed.

I knew what the problem was. The problem was that I wanted to have had one more conversation with Rhonda. She was drunk the last time I saw her. I had asked her to wake me up before she left, but she didn't. And now I wouldn't have another chance to talk with her. (*She is dead and gone, lady, she is dead and gone,* with

. . . . .

a tune to it, a thin reedy tune far better suited to Lori's voice than the Reba McEntire songs she was trying to belt out, and for a moment my mind groped for a source and then I thought of *Hamlet* as done by Mel Gibson, only I'm probably remembering it wrong.)

What the heck was the matter with me? Had I absentmindedly taken my pain medication twice? But the throbbing of my foot assured me that was not the case.

(But in one part of my mind, now, Doreen had become my sister. And Dusty had. And Sandy. And Diane. And Michie and every other girl and woman some ornery man had shat upon.)

I didn't know when I had started crying again, only that I was now, silently, with tears oozing between my closed eyelids, and with my eyes closed I cried myself to sleep. When Harry came in at midnight my supper was still sitting, neatly covered with plastic wrap, on the ice chest where Lori must have placed it. The house was quiet and dark, so presumably Hal and Lori had both gone to bed on time. "We had a little bit of a party after class was over," Harry said. "I started to call and let you know I'd be late, but I figured—well, hoped—you'd be asleep, so I decided not to call. Want some pizza?"

I could not think of much of anything I wanted less than I wanted cold pizza, unless maybe it was the cold chicken and noodle casserole beside my bed, and I told him so.

"Would you like me to go back out and get you a hamburger? Or maybe a milk shake?"

"Harry, it's midnight," I pointed out. "There's nothing I need enough for you to go out at this time of night to get it. You're treating me like an invalid."

"You are an invalid," he answered dryly. "You just won't admit it. Do you want *anything*?"

"I'm not enough of an invalid to send you to the store at midnight. And I don't know what I want. Yes I do. I want you to drain the ice chest and get me some more V-8."

"Do we have some more V-8?"

. . . . .

"How should I know? When is the last time I looked in the pantry?"

"You're recuperating," he said. "When people start getting this grouchy it means they're getting better."

"I'm not grouchy. I'm just . . ."

I hesitated, and he said, "Grouchy," and we both laughed.

"All right, I'm grouchy," I agreed. "But, Harry, I don't want another day like this again in my whole entire life."

"Do you still want the V-8?"

"Yeah."

In the end, he went down to Stop 'n Go to get me several cans of V-8. I drank one and promptly developed heartburn, which does not usually happen. After a handful of Tums and another pain pill and another penicillin, which I had forgotten earlier, I went back to sleep, leaving Harry—who certainly could not sleep in Cameron's room now that Lori was sleeping there—to change clothes in our bathroom and then make his bed on the couch.

Harry didn't even try to argue me out of going to work Friday morning. He just told me he was going back home and do the laundry after dropping me off, and I should call when I was ready for him to pick me up. "Only," he added, "it has to be before noon, because I've got some business to take care of after noon, and I don't know how long it's going to take, so you might have to get somebody else to bring you home."

Last time Harry did the laundry, which must have been about eight years ago, he put about ten times the right amount of bleach in the washer and it ate all the seams out of my newest slip. But this time there was no new slip in the laundry; come to think of it, there also was no bleach he could use, that being something I had left off my last grocery list. So I felt fairly safe in thanking him profusely and letting him do it.

Rodney Kilgore arrived on schedule, and I was ready for him. Rafe would have been ready also—I gather that he and Captain Millner had had a long talk this morning—but he had to go to

· · · · ·

court again. His case, whatever it was, might not have been taking an unusually long time overall, but it was certainly demanding an unusually large amount of his time. So we wound up with Captain Millner—rather unwillingly, as he felt he was usurping Rafe's direct authority over this unit—and me meeting with Kilgore. "I don't know how much good any of this is going to do you," Kilgore began by saying.

"Let us decide that," Captain Millner suggested.

"Well . . ." Kilgore glanced at both of us, uncertainly, as if unsure who he should be talking to. "I kindly grew up with Seth Miller, he lived just down the road from us when we was kids, and so I used to know the family pretty good after him and me was both grown and married. We used to go on picnics with them, go boating, that kind of thing. Don't know them as well now as I used to, since Seth went high-hat on us, but I used to know them real well. Maybe I better explain, I know I look like a roughneck" (he did; a roughneck, in case you don't know, is an oilfield laborer) "and that's how I started out, but I run my own business now. Drilling business. Small, but we've got enough wells producing that we've weathered the last ten years, an' that's more'n some of the big boys did. And look, I got kids of my own, and I think maybe I understand kids a little better than Seth ever did. So when Sandy went off the rails like she did, well, if it'd been a daughter of mine I'd have been upset, sure, I'd have been mighty upset, but I wouldn't have disowned her, the way Seth done. I'd have tried my best to keep a door open for her to come back. So I tried to stay friends with her, as much as I could. That wasn't much; I sort of had the feeling she didn't trust anybody male, but I'd hear from her maybe two, three times a year. But anyhow, yesterday Sandy called me and asked if I'd heard anything at all from Seth that sounded a little strange, either before or after Dusty . . . did what she did. I asked her what she meant, and she said anything about Seth going hunting or fishing and bringing along a female. And happened I had."

. . . . .

264

"What was it you heard?" I asked.

"Well . . . just . . . I don't know if it means anything or not, but there was this fishing trip planned."

He came to a halt again, and I said, "Okay."

"Me and about five other owners of small drilling businesses. Seth had rented a cabin up at Lake o' the Pines and we were all going up there for a week fishing, and Seth, he was gonna give us all the details of some new equipment he had while we was up there. He told us he'd have a 'sweet young thaing' there to cook for us. Said he'd gotten a cabin big enough we'd all have our own rooms, including the girl. So . . . well, we were having lunch together, at the Petroleum Club, and Seth said this, and then this other guy asked if she was for everybody. I . . . I'll tell you, ma'am, that kindly bothered me, because when I go fishing I go to catch fish and maybe knock back a little beer, play a little poker, but I don't go in for that funny stuff. But Seth, he swelled up like a pouter pigeon and said she was there to *cook* and *clean* and that was all. But he acted . . ." Kilgore paused and then said slowly, "He acted like she wasn't there just to cook and clean. He acted like a kid out of school, like he was putting something over on somebody. And you don't call somebody a 'sweet young thaing' unless . . . you know. I'll tell you the truth, ma'am, it kindly turned my stomach. So, anyhow, I told this to Sandy, and Sandy asked if he'd told who the girl was, and he hadn't. So then Sandy, she asked if I'd come in and tell it to you. So I have. And I hope it means something to you, ma'am, because it sure don't mean nothing to me."

"What would you say," I asked, "if I told you it was Dusty he planned to bring?"

"Dusty? Dusty Miller? His own daughter? Ma'am, he wouldn't have done that, not no way. Dusty, she wasn't but sixteen—"

"I know," I said.

"Take his own daughter out there with a bunch of drunk roughnecks? Ma'am, I can't believe that. Ain't nobody would be that low-down."

· · · · ·

265

But he kept looking at his big, gnarly hands spread out on the table. He wouldn't look at Captain Millner and me. So we kept waiting, and finally he said, in a voice so low as to be inaudible, "I'm lying. I believe Seth would be that low-down. He took Sandy on a hunting trip, one of those game reservations, you know, where they got game that isn't native to Texas, so it isn't controlled and you can shoot it all year round, and he took Sandy along to cook for him and a bunch of A-rabs. And it was right after that Sandy went off the rails, and I always figured it was one of those A-rabs done it to her the first time. But I thought, maybe that was a mistake, Seth taking her along. I mean, maybe because A-rabs, they don't usually drink, maybe he thought she'd be okay with them, but surely he wouldn't take Dusty along with a bunch of East Texas roughnecks. But I suppose he would. I just keep remembering . . ."

"Remembering what?" I asked, when his voice trailed off.

He looked up at me. "That thing that happened in Daingerfield a few years back. Remember it?"

I nodded, and Captain Millner said, "Vaguely. What about it?"

"Ex-schoolteacher went into a Baptist church, during services I mean, with his rifle and started shooting. Killed several people and hurt a bunch more. They said later—and I don't know how much of this is true and how much is something somebody dreamed up—but they said later he done it because he'd been . . . *using* . . . all his kids, and somebody in the church, the preacher or somebody else, was about to blow the whistle on him. I heard some people say he was just stressed out for no reason, and I heard other people say he'd just been a-beatin' his kids, like that was nothing, and was about to get in trouble about that, but I heard some people say he'd taken his daughters out fishing and hunting and used them like they was whores. Like I said, that's what I heard. I don't know how much of it's true. But . . . I just keep thinking. Seth would do that. Seth would do that."

. . . . .

266

"Go after a whole church congregation with a rifle?" Captain Millner asked in considerable surprise.

"That, too. But mainly I was thinking he'd . . . he'd do whatever he thought he could get away with. You'd have to . . . know Seth. See, his family wasn't just dirt poor, the way we was. They lived in total squalor, and it was like they didn't care. I mean, they still used an outhouse and didn't even cover it with morning glory. Seth, he made up his mind he was getting out of that world, and he did. But he wanted so bad to get out, it was like he decided whoever made the rules didn't mean the rules to cover him. He was gonna do whatever he had to do to get what he wanted. It wasn't altogether selfish—he wanted the best for Ellen and them kids—but they had to do exactly what he wanted and do it his way all the time, because he figured he'd figured the way out and nobody else's ideas mattered. And once he made up his mind about something, wasn't nobody ever going to change it for him. So, you're saying he . . . used his daughters. Yes, I can believe that. He figured womenfolk were there to take care of menfolk. Sewing, and cooking, and washing, and cleaning, and that, too. And the girls, once they weren't kids any longer, then they were womenfolk."

"So you wouldn't be surprised if I told you he'd been molesting Sandy and Dusty," I said.

He shook his head. "No, ma'am. I wouldn't be surprised. But I don't know he was doing it. I've done told you all I know."

And that was all he would say. We let him go with our thanks; there was nothing else to do and nothing else he could tell us.

I was sure, now, why Dusty had killed herself. But I was equally sure there was nothing official I could do about it. Even if I was right that Dusty had killed herself because she felt that she would go the same way Sandy did, Captain Millner pointed out correctly, there is no law that says a man cannot take his daughter to cook and clean for a group of his friends. There was absolutely no evidence

. . . . .

he had intended anything else, either for Sandy or Dusty; in fact, there was no real evidence he had intended to take Dusty with him at all. Because for all he'd told Kilgore, he could have been taking anybody young and female.

If I couldn't do anything officially, could I do anything unofficially? It wasn't a matter of revenge, I told myself, either for Dusty's death or for Sandy's wasted life, and I wasn't using Seth Miller to stand in for my own father, who was beyond the reach of anything anybody could do. No, it was far more important than revenge for anybody or anything. Because sooner or later, Doreen would have to go home. And I wanted her, unlike her sisters, unlike me and my sister, to have a safe home to go to.

I called Ellen Miller, Dusty's mother, and asked her if she could come down to the police station. "What for?" she asked, sounding more fretful than grief-stricken over Dusty or worried about Doreen. "Is this about Doreen? Have you found her?"

"No, we haven't found her," I said, "but the results of what I need to discuss with you might help to get her home again."

"Well, can you come here?" There was a whining note in her voice that set my teeth on edge.

"Mrs. Miller," I said, "I'm on crutches. I can't even walk, much less drive a car. No, I can't go there. Obviously, I can't force you to come here. But if you don't, I'm going to have a lot of mental questions as to why you won't."

Ultimately, as I had expected she would, she agreed to come in and said she'd arrive about noon. Ducky. It was only ten-thirty now, and I had been hoping to get away early enough that Harry could come get me; I didn't like having to look for a ride two days in a row. But in view of the fact that we couldn't make her come in, we had to accept her when we could get her.

"I still want Sandy up here," Captain Millner reminded me.

"One thing at a time," I said. "I know what I'm doing."

"I hope you do." He sounded unconvinced.

"Don't I usually?"

.   .   .   .   .

"That's true. Speaking of true, you lie a lot."

"What brought that on?"

"Telling that woman this discussion might help get Doreen home again."

"That's not a lie," I said. "That's the truth. It might help get Seth out of the house, whether it's into jail or not, and my guess is, once Seth is gone, Doreen will be back."

Ellen Miller was late. By the time she arrived, Rafe had returned from court, which wasn't supposed to resume again until 2 P.M., and Captain Millner and I had briefed him on the subject of the discussion. She came in looking as fretful as she had sounded; I was sure there was real grief there, for Dusty, and real worry, for Doreen, but she had succeeded in masking them. "What's this all about?" she demanded at once. "If you haven't found Doreen, what do you need to see me for?"

"We're still looking into Dusty's death," I said.

"What in the world for?" she burst out. "She jumped. You know that; you were there when it happened."

"I know she jumped," I agreed, "but haven't you ever wondered why she jumped?"

"*Wondered!*" she shouted. "I've asked myself that a hundred times a day ever since, why she did it! We gave her *everything!* Her clothing allowance alone was more than two thousand dollars a year, and you saw how her room was decorated, we let her pick out everything in there, and a private school—and her grades were perfect—and her friends were all so nice, not like those people where we used to live. There was no reason at all!"

I was sorry for her. I'd be sorry for anybody in this situation. But I still had to ask questions, and she wasn't going to like either the questions or the answers she would have to give, to herself if not to me. "Were you aware of that fishing trip Mr. Miller was planning?"

. . . . .

269

"Of course I knew!" she retorted. "You don't think he'd go off for a week without telling me, do you?"

"So you were aware that he intended Dusty to go with him?"

"Yes, of course. Dusty's . . . Dusty was a very fine cook, and he wanted—"

"Did *Dusty* want to go?"

"Well, no, not particularly. Some of her friends had other things they wanted to do that week, and she wanted to go with them. It was going to be spring break, you know. Not for the public schools—they'd already had theirs—but for her school. But as Seth said, with all he gave her, it wouldn't hurt for her to do what he wanted this once, and I had to agree. Of course, it wouldn't be *fun,* cleaning fish and cooking them, and making beds, but it certainly didn't amount to slave labor." Her voice was perfectly reasonable, but her hands betrayed her true feelings, as she twisted her wedding and engagement rings around and around her finger in a completely unconscious gesture.

"And you don't see any similarity at all between this and what happened to Sandy."

"I don't know what you're talking about. I don't have a daughter named Sandy."

"Your husband told you to say that?" I asked incredulously. "You do have a daughter named Sandy. Named Alexandra, that is, and called Sandy. I know her. I've known her for years."

"We . . . we disowned her. Her conduct . . . As to any similarity between her and Dusty, I don't know what you're talking about."

I leaned forward. "Mrs. Miller, you know exactly what I'm talking about. I'm talking about Seth Miller taking his oldest daughter on a hunting trip with six men, so she could cook and clean, and I'm talking about her coming back from that trip and running away and supporting herself by prostitution ever since. And I'm talking about what happened on that trip, and before that trip, to cause her to make that decision, and I'm talking about Dusty jumping out a window because dying was preferable to what

. . . . .

she was afraid she was heading into, which was the same life Sandy is living now."

"You don't have any right to say that." She was crying, now, and she pulled out an embroidered handkerchief to dab it to her eyes and then went on twisting the ring around her finger, holding the handkerchief in her right hand.

"But Seth had a right to sexually molest his daughters?"

"That's a lie!" She jumped to her feet, almost knocking over the table. "You have no right to say such terrible things!"

"You think back," I said. "You ask yourself how many times, in the last ten years, you've been away from home in the evening and Seth has been alone with his daughters. You ask yourself how many of those times Seth somehow managed to engineer your being gone and his being home with the girls. You ask yourself how many nights when you *were* at home Seth found an excuse to be in his daughters' rooms in the middle of the night with the door shut. And you ask yourself how happy the girls seemed the next day. Especially the oldest one at home at any given time."

"Seth never . . . Seth wouldn't . . . Look, you don't understand," she burst out. "We'd been poor so long . . . We both grew up poor, Seth and me, and we went together all the way through high school, and we *planned,* it was going to be different for us, we weren't going to live like that, and Seth told me if I'd do just what he wanted and help him all I could, one day we'd be rich, but when we got married, and when the kids came along, we were still poor. We didn't ever have anything. Then he got that wonderful job— but he had to *keep* it, and to do that he had to keep all those people happy. You just don't understand! I . . . When I was growing up there were all five of us kids all crowded into one bedroom, and then when we moved to a bigger house so we finally had three bedrooms, one for our parents and one for the boys and one for the girls, the bathroom roof leaked so bad in the winter you had to take a bath wearing a raincoat because there was an icy wind blowing down your back. And . . . you could get used to the smell and

. . . . .

271

having to rinse the glass three times if you got a drink at night so you wouldn't accidentally swallow a roach, and you could get used to mouse poop on the clean, folded sheets, but . . . You know what I never could get used to? None of the towels matched. I kept wondering, since they have to buy towels anyway, even if they can't afford to buy more than one at a time, why can't they at least buy them all the same *color* so they'll sort of match. I got where sometimes I thought I'd have *killed* just to have the towels match . . . Going on a camping trip and cooking for the hunters, that wasn't too much to ask, to help her daddy keep that real good job—a nice house, each girl had her own bedroom and even her own *bathroom* and no roaches and no mice and no leaky roof and all the towels in the whole house matched . . ."

Nice to know what your daughters are worth, I thought but did not say. Of course I was sympathetic. Nobody could help feeling for somebody coming out of that sort of situation. But decent house-keeping, and decent maintenance, could keep a house livable; proper planning could keep matching towels in the bathroom, without having to use—or sell—your daughters.

"You don't understand," she wailed again.

"I'm trying to," I said. "I can see you grew up in a lousy situation, and from what I hear, so did Seth. But you don't have to be rich to avoid that kind of life. Did you ever ask the girls whether they'd rather have fewer possessions and not be mo-lested?"

"It wasn't too much to ask . . . Nobody hurt them . . . It didn't hurt me when my—" She came to a dead halt.

But she'd said enough, and I reminded myself of the hostage syndrome—the victim who comes to side with the criminal. But no matter how bad Ellen Miller's childhood had been, no matter what Ellen Miller's hang-ups were, her remaining daughter—be-cause she'd lost Sandy, and Dusty was dead—had to be protected. "I see I'm going to have to get Sandy up here," I said to Captain Millner.

. . . . .

"I told you so," he answered. "While you're about it, get Seth Miller in here, too. I want to see what that son of a bitch looks like."

I was sorry for Ellen Miller, more so than I might have been if it hadn't been for the last incomplete sentence she blurted out. But I wasn't half as sorry for her as I was for her children. My mother had denied what happened. But my mother really didn't know. Ellen Miller, I was now convinced, did know. Did know, and out of her own covetousness as well as her own victimhood, had decided matching towels—and all the other appurtenances of gracious living—were more important.

I started making phone calls.

. . . . .

Fifteen

FRIDAY AFTERNOON AT 1:30, and the squad room was rather crowded. Rafe had managed to get himself excused from court for the rest of the day, on the grounds that he had pressing work in the office and if they did need him again—which nobody really expected—he could be there in fifteen minutes. Captain Millner had decided he was more interested in the Dusty Miller case than he had originally expected to be—his orders to me to stay out of it were by now totally discarded, if not quite forgotten—and he was sticking around. We'd got Sandy there, and kept Ellen Miller, and got Rodney Kilgore to come back, and we had Seth Miller present and stashed in an interrogation room—not a holding cell, because he hadn't been charged with anything and technically he was free to go at any time—but let's say the interrogation room was being well watched by a uniform officer, and if he decided to go anywhere he might find it wasn't a very good idea.

The first hour was a rerun as far as I was concerned, so I was mainly an onlooker. But Rafe hadn't heard any of it firsthand, and Captain Millner had heard only part of it. We talked to Rodney Kilgore first; he basically repeated the same story, neither augmenting it nor removing anything from it, and then Captain Millner let him go again. There was no reason for keeping him, and we'd decided we didn't—at least now—want Seth Miller to know which one of his friends had snitched.

We talked with Ellen Miller next; there were no surprises there

. . . . .

either. She cried; she denied any possibility of wrongdoing; and she asked to go home. Captain Millner suggested she wait a while, and sent her to sit out in the squad room.

Then we got to Sandy. They asked her a lot of questions: what *exactly* did your father do, did Dusty know what happened when you went to cook for the hunting party, did Dusty know your present occupation, how did Dusty feel about that?

Sandy was patient, but it was pretty evident that despite her present occupation she was extremely embarrassed by the questions. Her father had not raped her; he had insisted on hand to genital and mouth to genital contact (and that was how she put it), with her on both the giving and the receiving end. Yes, Dusty knew what had happened when Sandy went to cook for the hunting party. Dusty knew Sandy was a prostitute and she considered prostitution disgusting.

"What did you tell your father when you left?" Rafe asked.

"You mean when I moved out? I didn't tell him anything, face-to-face," Sandy said. "He'd beaten me up before, claiming it was for my own good—he *always* claimed things were for my own good. Why should I ask for it again? But I left him a note."

"What was in the note? I'm not trying to pry into your personal affairs," Rafe said, "but we need to know—"

"I know," Sandy said evenly. "What was in the note . . . I just told him that I was tired of being his free whore, and if I had to do it anyway I might as well get paid for it. I told him one of his Arab friends had paid for my getaway. I told him not to bother to look for me, because he'd never get me back. And I told him I was armed and if he tried to come after me I'd kill him."

"Were you armed?" Captain Millner asked.

"Well, if you consider a butcher knife armament."

"Would you have killed him?"

"I'd have tried," Sandy said. "He wasn't going to get me back. I'd made up my mind to that."

"Did Dusty know about the note?" Rafe asked.

. . . . .

Sandy sighed. "The note I wrote? Yes, I told her about it, and I asked her if she wanted to go with me. Thing is, he—my father—didn't mess around with me until after, you know, I started having periods. Dusty had started by then, and I figured he'd start on her when I left. So like I said, I tried to get her to go with me. But Dusty was scared. Please try to understand what I'm saying. Dusty was scared. Dusty . . . wanted things pleasant. Dusty wanted the road paved, and a paved road and a pleasant ride is what you don't ever get around my father. All through life, if things didn't work out for me, I'd fight back . . . and you don't think I'm going to stay in this shit business from now on, do you? I've got better sense than that. I was just . . . working my way through school, and I'm through with school now. After I dropped out of high school I went and got a GED and then I went into Tarrant County Junior College and then I transferred over to Arlington, majoring in accounting. I was down in Austin earlier this week"—here she smiled at me—"to pass my CPA exam. I'm starting a new job next month, after I take a little vacation, and yes, my employer knows my past history. Little Sandy's through getting screwed, by my old man or anybody else. I'm a fighter, you see? I land on my feet.

"But Dusty, she wanted everything to be just right. She wanted to make straight A's in school and she wanted to be on the drill team and she wanted to have pretty pastel clothes and she wanted to have the right friends and she wasn't . . . willing, or maybe I should say able, to fight for any of it. If things didn't go my way I'd fight. If things didn't go her way she'd cry. I was angry. She was scared. So to her, it was like life went schizoid. The Dusty that got good grades and was on the drill team and in the National Honor Society was the real Dusty, and the Dusty at ten o'clock at night with her daddy in bed with her, well, that wasn't Dusty at all. And she could make herself pretend that, and make herself believe that, because nobody but she and Daddy knew about it. And me, of course, but I didn't count because that was a part of her sister that didn't exist for her, any more than that part of her existed. And

· · · · ·

Mom, but she didn't count either because she never admitted she knew, so we could pretend she didn't, at least Dusty could. But here's what I think. I think when Daddy said he was going to take her on that fishing trip, well, there were people we *knew* who were going to be on that trip. If it'd just been like me, Arabs, or somebody from South America or Scotland or whatever, I don't think it would have flipped her out. She'd have been terrified, but she'd have gone meekly and done what Daddy said. But people we *knew* . . . And Daddy could hide it from Mom, at least enough to satisfy everybody in the family, though like I said, if you ask me I think Mom does know about it. But we all knew what he was like when he was drunk. He'd think he was being inconspicuous, and he was about as inconspicuous as an elephant in a tutu. So people would know. Rodney Kilgore would know. Ray Garcia would know. People we *knew* would know. And she couldn't face that."

She looked at me. "Deb," she said, "I know you think she jumped because she was afraid she was going to be like me, and become a whore. But I don't think that was why. I think she jumped because she just couldn't stand to have anybody *know* what her daddy thought of her. I think . . ." She looked down at her long, well-manicured fingers on the table. "You ask me, Dusty didn't die when she jumped out that window. Dusty started to die when she realized—and I kept it from her as long as I could, until it got to the point I knew I had to leave 'cause if I stayed I'd wind up killing the old man—that she and Doreen and I were no more to him than a piece of ass. And she finished dying when she found out he didn't really care if his friends knew about it. What happened after that was just the icing on the cake. But she was already dead, long before she jumped out that window."

"Didn't either of you try to get it across to your father how this was affecting you?" Rafe asked.

Sandy stared at him incredulously and laughed, a harsh, almost frightening, laugh. "You've got to be kidding," she said. "We told him. I told him. Dusty told him. Not together, because telling him

. . . . .

277

together might be admitting it was really happening and Dusty couldn't handle that. But he knew how we felt. He couldn't not know. You've got somebody sucking you off and crying and vomiting, you know how they feel. He knew, and he didn't care. As far as he was concerned, we were overreacting. He wasn't doing anything to us. He was just educating us, and it was for our own good. I wish I had a dollar for every time he's told me he wasn't doing anything to me. He really, honestly, believes that unless the hymen is punctured it doesn't count. So no, he didn't care, and he still doesn't care. You have a look at him. You won't see him caring about what happened to me, or what happened to Dusty, or what might be happening to Doreen, on account of that. If he pays for clothes, for a nice place to live, for the food on the table, if he sees to it his kids get an education, then he's done his part and his kids *owe* him what he wants. So you won't see a man sorry he's outraged his daughters' maidenly modesty. What you'll see is a bull ape pissed off because part of his harem has vanished. All he's got left right now is Mom, because Dusty's dead and Doreen . . . is gone. He's a horny gorilla who can't get laid by more than one person right now unless he actually goes out and pays for it, and he's going to be as antsy as if he were in a cage. But care? No. He doesn't care."

"I don't understand that," Rafe said, half to himself.

Captain Millner rose, briskly. "Thank God you aren't able to," he replied. "Miss Miller, thank you for coming in. I'd appreciate it if you'd wait, in case we need to talk with you again. Would you like us to leave you in here, so that you don't have to see your father, or would you rather go out in the main office?"

"I don't care about seeing my father," she said, "but I'd just as soon sit in here."

Rafe, Captain Millner, and I all moved to the other interview room. Seth Miller looked up when we came in. "Just what is this all about?" he demanded. "The person who called me at my office and suggested I come here was quite incoherent."

. . . . .

278

The person who called him was Captain Millner. And Captain Millner—who is *never* incoherent—seated himself quietly and began the conversation. "You asked what this is all about. Just what do *you* think this is all about?"

"I assume it has something to do with my runaway child. You've found her and are ready to return her to my care."

"We haven't found her," Captain Millner replied, "and if we had found her I would see to it that she was *not* returned to your care. Now, listen to me and listen good. You are suspected of the crime of unlawful carnal knowledge of a minor. You are not under arrest at this time. You have the right to remain silent . . . Do you wish to give up these rights?"

"I don't have any secrets," Miller said, with that smirk that is totally familiar to all law enforcement officers, the smirk that says "I'm getting away with it and there's nothing you can do about it." He signed where Rafe pointed on the Miranda release.

Then Captain Millner leaned back in his chair and crossed his arms across his chest. "Tell me about Sandy."

"Sandy?" Miller sounded coolly amused, detached.

"Sandy. Your oldest daughter. The one you like to pretend doesn't exist anymore. She exists. We've heard her version. Now we'd like to hear yours."

"Sandy is a prostitute, a drug addict, and a liar."

"Sandy is no longer a prostitute, has never been a drug addict, and is not a liar," Captain Millner replied. "She is a CPA. Drug addicts are pretty easy to spot, and I've been around enough liars that I'm fair-to-middling good at spotting them, too."

"If she told you she's a CPA—"

"We're not talking about her past," Captain Millner said. "We're talking about now. At this time Alexandra Miller is a CPA. I agree that at one time she was a prostitute; she has never denied that. To the best of my knowledge, she has never been either a drug addict or a liar. Deb, you've known her for years, what about it?"

. . . . .

279

"She used to use marijuana some," I said, "but never enough to be called an addict, and there's some question as to whether marijuana is addictive at all. She used to smoke cigarettes, and of course that's addictive"—I smiled sweetly at Seth Miller, who was chewing on a cigar Rafe had forbidden him to light—"but she's quit even that." I didn't explain how I knew, but the fact is that since nobody in my family smokes, I can spot the smell on the clothes of a smoker even if he or she doesn't light up in front of me. "She's never been a liar to my knowledge; she's far more likely to tell very inconvenient truths."

Miller sighed, elaborately. "So you want to hear my side of the story. I fail to see any rhyme or reason to this, but I'll play along; I'd hate for you good officers to consider me uncooperative. I'm sure that according to her side of the story I'm the ogre of the universe. I've provided for my family well—better than anybody ever provided for me when I was a child. I fed her well, housed her well, bought her nice clothes—"

"A well-fed, well-housed, well-dressed slave is still a slave," Captain Millner said harshly. "Never mind her house and food and clothes."

"*Slave?*" Miller asked, eyebrows raised. "Is that what she told you? I have *never* expected anything unreasonable from any of my children. I love and cherish my children. Yes, I expect a lot from them, but I give a lot to them. It is true that I took her on a hunting trip. I was entertaining some extremely important business clients from out of the country, and it was essential that all go well; as you know, the oil industry is in a severe depression and has been for some time, and I sell oil field equipment. If I could make that sale, it would be enough to support the family for a year. I took her along to act as hostess, to do a little cooking and housekeeping, and I certainly don't consider that slavery. At some point during the trip, and I don't know exactly when, she developed an unfortunate . . . liaison . . . with one of my guests, who I gather paid her well.

. . . . .

By the time the trip was over, she had the idiotic notion that she could get off on her own, out from under my authority, and continue to make that kind of money. I believe that later, when things did not go to suit her, she decided that her poor choices were my fault."

"Prior to that hunting trip, what kind of relationship did you have with your daughter?"

"It was strained," he said. "Some adolescents . . .."

"How do you think your molestation of her contributed to that strained relationship?" I asked.

He looked at me. "I have no idea what you mean," he said, and clamped his jaw down on the cigar. But he waited a fraction of a second too long to say it, and for just that fraction of a second a beast was looking out of his eyes. Rodney Kilgore was right. This man wouldn't think twice about killing, if he had any reason to want to and to think he could get away with it, and I wondered, with a sudden chill, whether Sandy really knew where Doreen was or just thought she did.

"Don't you?" Captain Millner said. "Well, try this one on, then. Didn't you think it was a little unwise to take an adolescent girl along on an otherwise stag hunting trip?"

Miller adjusted his tie, carefully. "In retrospect, perhaps it was a little ill-advised. But I had no reason to suspect that a gently nurtured young woman would react as she did."

"So after she reacted that way, you decided to take your second daughter on a stag fishing trip?" Rafe asked.

"In return for the food, clothing, education, and nurturing I provide, I have a right to my daughters' services," Miller said, "so long as it does not interfere with their schoolwork or their church activities."

"What kind of services?" Captain Millner asked. "Do you just use your daughters yourself, or do you ever lend them to your friends?"

. . . . .

"Certainly I would never lend—"

"Why did you tell your friends you were bringing a 'sweet young thaing' to the fishing trip?" I asked.

We hadn't told him about Rodney Kilgore or let the two see each other, and I had a hunch from his reaction that he wasn't expecting that question. But he recovered fast. "Why shouldn't I call her that? Didn't your father ever call you a 'sweet young thaing'?"

"Yes, my father was a lot like you," I said.

Captain Millner glanced at me, quickly, when I said that, and then returned his attention to Seth Miller. "What do you think most men around here mean when they call someone a 'sweet young thaing'?"

"I haven't asked them."

"Isn't there usually a connotation, in those words, of sexual availability?" Rafe asked.

"There might be," Miller said.

"What about those bruises in Dusty's perineal area, and the yeast infection she had?" Captain Millner asked.

"Teenagers will experiment, of course. That has nothing to do with their parents—"

Rafe stood up and spoke rather loudly, as if Miller were having trouble hearing. "I don't believe you," he said. "You drove one of your daughters into prostitution, one into suicide, and one into hiding, and you don't have any remorse whatever?"

"What for?" Miller asked. "I didn't harm them. I provided them with the best of everything in this world, and all I expected of them was obedience. If they misunderstood what I did, that was their problem. Sandy was virgin until she went to bed with that . . . Arab. Dusty died a virgin."

"So did the daughter of Bernarda Alba," I said *sotto voce,* but nobody heard me.

"My intention was to discipline them and educate them," Miller went on. "I wanted them, when they married, to be responsible

. . . . .

282

women, able to keep house, manage a budget, serve as graceful hostesses, and satisfy their husbands and know how to know what they wanted themselves. My mother wrecked my father's life and her children's lives by being unable to do any of those things, and my wife had to learn every bit of it after she and I were married, to the great detriment of our marital relationship, particularly considering that some of it she has been quite unable to learn. I myself am a self-made man. I was determined my daughters would know all they needed to know *before* they were married. I did no harm to them whatsoever, and if they thought my discipline was too harsh, that was their problem. I never harmed them, and if they were truthful they would tell you that themselves. Anything that happened, they enjoyed. They might have changed their minds later, but at the time they enjoyed it, and believe me, I can tell. So . . . remorse? I'll say it again. What for? I didn't do anything to harm them."

"I have a lot of respect for a hard worker," Captain Millner said. "I have a lot of respect for anybody who can rise above the hand fate deals him. If you'd stopped there you'd have no problems. But you've put yourself above the laws of the state, above the laws of morality, and above the laws of common decency. Nobody—your wife, your daughters, the people in this room—owes you any respect now. Had you started . . . educating . . . Doreen yet?"

Again Miller adjusted his tie. "Not yet," he said pleasantly. "Except in very minor ways. And if you think you're going to take anything I have said into a courtroom, think again. There is no law that says a man may not educate or discipline his children."

"That depends on what he's educating them in and how he's disciplining them. Where do you think Doreen is?"

"She's like my other daughters, ungrateful for all I've given her and done for her. I don't know where she is."

"How much did Doreen know about the way you . . . educated . . . Sandy and Dusty?" Rafe asked, and I knew then that he and Captain Millner were wondering the same thing I was.

· · · · ·

283

"She knew as much as she needed to."

"What is that supposed to mean?" Rafe demanded.

"Take it however you want to."

"Here's how I'm taking it," Captain Millner said, standing with one foot on a chair, towering over Miller. "I'm taking it that Doreen did know what you'd done to your other two daughters. Maybe you had already started on her. And unlike Sandy, who just wanted to get out, and Dusty, who killed herself over it, she threatened to call the police. And you wanted to make sure she never had the chance. So you killed her, and you put the body somewhere you think we'll never find it. How does that scenario sound to you?"

"You're crazy," Miller said. The contempt in his voice sounded real; it didn't sound like a veil for anger or fear.

"Am I? We'll see. Stay here," Millner said. His voice was soft, but anybody who knew him would know that he was in a towering rage. Rafe and I followed him back into the other interview room, where Sandy was sitting composedly. Millner sat down across the table from her and said, "You're going to have to help us."

"How?" Sandy said.

"First thing, tell us the honest-to-God truth. Do you know where Doreen is? I'm not asking you to identify the location, just tell me whether you know where she is."

Sandy studied his face for a long moment and then visibly made up her mind. "Yes, I know."

"When's last time you spoke with her?"

"This morning, over the phone."

"Does your father know where she is?"

"No."

"You're sure of that?"

"I'm sure." Her eyes slid over to look at me. "And he couldn't get at her if he did know. She's safe."

"Then that's out," Millner said cryptically. "Okay, listen. In Texas, there is no statute of limitations on unlawful carnal knowl-

· · · · ·

284

edge of a minor. If the daughter is willing to testify, even twenty years later, the state will make a case. He's not going to admit to anything. He honestly doesn't think he did anything wrong. Your mother won't admit to anything. From what you tell us, as well as what he tells us, there will be no physical evidence whatever. That means that unless we can find Doreen and get her to testify, the only way we're going to be able to make sure Doreen is safe from him is to make a case against him for what he did to you and make it stick. Are you willing to testify?"

"Yes," Sandy said, "but will the court believe me?"

"You're a more convincing witness than he is," Captain Millner said. "He's got the kind of arrogance that pisses off juries. I can't tell you for sure we'll get a conviction. Nobody can. Juries are unpredictable. But it's worth trying. If you're willing."

"I'm willing."

"Thing is, even if we don't get a conviction we'll embarrass the heck out of him, and maybe serve notice that he can't get away with a repeat performance."

"Do you think that'll stop him?" Sandy asked.

"No. So we're going for a conviction. If you're ready to fight."

"I'm ready."

"Then you go sit down at the typewriter with Detective Ralston and she'll put together an arrest warrant. Deb, while you're about it, make one for that son of a bitch Reddich and his wife. Just one on Miller so far, until we find out what Doreen knows and whether she'll testify. I don't think we'd be able to prove anything on Dusty, and I don't think we can prove the mother knew anything. Rafe, you want to be the arresting officer, or want me to?"

"Let Deb do it," Rafe said. "On Miller, that is. I'll arrest on Reddich, because we may have to go looking for him. But you better take the warrants to get them signed. I have to stay where the court can find me, and frankly, I don't trust Roger on this one."

As Sandy and I conferred over the typewriter, I could see Roger

·   ·   ·   ·   ·

Hales and Wayne Harris talking together quietly. I was not at all surprised at the looks expressive of—to say the least—extreme dislike that Roger cast in my direction. But I knew he'd keep quiet while there were civilians in the squad room. He wouldn't dare raise sand until only cops were left.

It took half an hour to make out the warrants, another half hour to find a judge and get them signed. Miller had already come out twice announcing he was going to leave, and each time he'd been dissuaded by the patrol officer we had watching the interview room, the first time with a polite suggestion that Mr. Miller might like to call his attorney, the second time a little more forcefully, with the explanation that Mr. Miller could call his attorney or not, precisely as he chose, but he wasn't going anywhere. Each time Miller said he didn't need an attorney.

When Captain Millner came back with the warrants, the three of us went together into the interview room. With the warrant in my hand, I said, "Seth Miller, I'm placing you under arrest for the crime of—"

He came over the table at me, reaching for my throat, screaming, "You fucking bitch, all you bitches are just alike—frigid ball-busting man-haters—"

I was in no shape to move fast, but I saw Rafe and Captain Millner heading for him from both sides of me. Rafe is small, but the captain is bigger even than Seth, and despite the protestations of the defense attorneys in the Rodney King assault trial, it does not take billy clubs to control somebody large, violent, and potentially dangerous. I simply dropped to the floor and scuttled out of the way, back into a corner, until the struggling was over and Seth Miller was handcuffed. "Assault on a police officer," Captain Millner said in a very pleased voice. "In front of two other officers. That'll add a year or two to your sentence. Deb, are you okay?"

"I'm fine," I said, getting cautiously to my feet and wishing I'd brought my pain pills with me instead of leaving them by my bed.

· · · · ·

I'd struck the entire length of the incision hard against a chair leg, and I was definitely feeling the results.

"I was startled," Miller said, yet again straightening his tie, which this time really needed straightening. "Any jury will understand that."

"I'm sure they will," Rafe said, and called the patrol officer to take the man away.

When the rest of us went back out into the squad room, Sandy Miller was sitting beside her mother, talking quietly as her mother cried. She glanced up at me. "I've told her Doreen's just fine," she said, "but I still don't think she ought to go home."

Captain Millner sat down. "You're right," he said, "and since you can get in touch with her, please tell her to stay exactly where she is. Have her give me a call, and I'll make arrangements to get her into foster care or, if she prefers, arrange to have the place where she is declared an appropriate foster home, if that's possible. You can't take her, Miss Miller, and I hope you understand that."

"I don't have her," Sandy said.

"Mrs. Miller, you need to be aware that almost certainly your husband will be able to get out on bond," he went on. "He will be angry, and he will probably be dangerous. I would advise you either to get a peace bond against him that will keep him away from you, or to go somewhere where he can't find you."

"I can't do that," she said gloomily. "I promised—for better or worse—and he's really a good man, you just don't understand . . . Besides, if I try to get away and he finds me, he'll kill me."

Captain Millner and I exchanged glances; obviously our definition of a good man differed sharply from that of Ellen Miller. "On your own head be it," Captain Millner said. "You'd be a lot better off trying to get away than sitting around meekly waiting to be killed, but I can't make you do it. Thank you for coming, Miss Miller. Please keep me informed as to where you can be located."

"I will. Right now I'm going to take my mother home. I'll get

. . . . .

somebody to bring me back later and get her car home. She's not up to driving."

"What about your daddy's car?" Ellen Miller asked.

"We'll get it home later, too. Come on now . . ."

Roger Hales was coming to a boil, and the elevator door hadn't more than closed on the two women before he was screaming at me, in almost exactly the same words Seth Miller had used. "You bitches all stick together," he shouted. "Two fathers—two decent men, pressured beyond endurance by seductive little whores— both of them locked up, while everybody coddles the little whores. Where's your compassion for *them*? Don't *they* have any rights? That Seth Miller, he's worked fucking hard to get everything he's got, and got nothing but ingratitude for it. I'm telling you, and I don't care what anybody says, there never was a woman yet screwed when she didn't want to be, without she tried like hell to fight him off. Right, Wayne?"

Wayne Harris, behind him, said, "Roger, I still don't know if—"

"You hear all this crap about child molestation, well, I'm telling you, it *doesn't happen!*" Roger went on wrathfully. "The little broads ask for it. If they didn't want it they'd say no, or they'd tell somebody, or they'd fight—"

"Did I ask for it?" I screamed, the self-control that had kept me quiet all the time we talked with Seth Miller finally snapping. "My father started molesting me when I was nine years old, and all I knew to do was cry. Tell somebody? Who are they supposed to tell? When the people who are supposed to protect you are the very ones who attack you, who do you tell, Roger? Who's going to come and save you when you're nine years old and your daddy is standing beside your bed at ten o'clock at night waking you up and saying 'Suck it'? Have you ever seen a picture of me when I was nine, Roger? With freckles all over my face and my hair in

· · · · ·

braids and my mouth and nose and eyes looking like I was five instead of nine? But to my father that was sexy, because I was female, and because I was female, I didn't have the right to say no. And fight? How well do you think a nine-year-old can fight a grown man? And if she's got bruises on her butt three hundred and sixty-five days a year because his idea of discipline is a doubled belt, she's damn well not going to try. So I couldn't say no. I didn't have the right. And neither did Rhonda. My father drove my sister into prostitution just like Seth Miller drove Sandy into prostitution, only Rhonda didn't have the sense Sandy had, Rhonda didn't get out of it, and Rhonda was buried yesterday! My only sister was buried yesterday, and I don't care what it said on her death certificate, my father murdered her, just the same way Seth Miller murdered Dusty. My father murdered her when he killed her spirit!"

"Bullshit!" Roger yelled. "Yeah, that's what I say, bullshit! A little screwing never hurt anybody—"

"Hales, empty your desk and get out of here," Captain Millner said in a very quiet, totally emotionless voice. "You're on administrative leave until we find out if Uniform Division has a place for you."

"I'll be glad to get out of here," Roger said. "Damn whiny broads all the time, begging to be fucked and crying when they get it—"

"Never mind cleaning your desk," Rafe said, equally quietly. "We'll send the stuff after you. Get out now."

"Who are you gonna get to replace me? Minnie Mouse?"

"Deb, what's the name of that officer you said kept his head the day that Dusty died?" Captain Millner asked me.

"Woodall. I don't remember his first name; I'll have to check."

"Think he'd work out here?"

Roger Hales was standing with his mouth open, as I said, "I think he probably would. He seemed pretty sensitive as well as sensible."

. . . . .

289

"How does he sound to you, Rafe?" Captain Millner went on.

"I haven't met him, but if Deb thinks he'll work out we'll sure give it a shot."

"Just like that, I'm out?" Roger yelled. "Over some little cunts—"

"Just like that, you're out," Rafe said wearily. "And if you don't get your ass on the elevator, I may make a case against you myself, for disturbing the peace."

"Deb, if you'd told me something like that had happened to you, I wouldn't have put you in that unit," Captain Millner said. We were in his private office, which he uses about once in a million years for anything other than chewing somebody out.

"If frogs had wings they wouldn't bump their tails when they hop," I retorted, staring at the top of Millner's cluttered desk, hearing the sullen anger in my voice.

"I'm not a frog. I'm your friend. I hope."

I took a deep breath. "If something like that had happened to you, would you want to go tell the universe?"

"I'm not the universe. Anyway you just *did* tell the universe, at least the universe you work in. You think I've never before in my life met anybody something like this happened to? You think none of them are my friends? Well, guess again. I figure—since men and women who've been harmed are drawn either to situations in which they can continue to be victims or to situations that let them defend themselves—at least one out of every three policewomen in this or any other police department, one out of every five or six policemen, has been hit by a sex crime at least once. I know of some, and I'm not going to tell you their names because I don't have the right to."

"If I could just understand why," I said, half to myself. "I guess with some of these men, somebody, at some time, convinced them it was really okay, convinced them incest isn't really harmful to

. . . . .

anybody, convinced them it was really okay to seek their own gratification even if their children are crying, screaming, vomiting. My father wore religion like a garment to cover his nakedness, the same way Seth Miller wears his financial success."

Captain Millner nodded. "We've seen Miller's reasoning. About your father, maybe it was partly that he was trying to conceal his evil, from himself as well as everybody else, and maybe, do you suppose he tried to be religious in the hopes of finding the strength to overcome his evil?"

"Not him," I said. "He couldn't have been trying to overcome it. He didn't recognize or admit it existed."

"So far as you know," Captain Millner said, very softly.

I looked at him, and a picture flashed into my mind—my father, only a few months before he died, clothing his stooped, wizened body in a clean jumpsuit and going off to an Easter service in another church because the church he still recognized as his wouldn't let him in. Without realizing I was going to, I burst into tears. Captain Millner didn't say anything, he just slid a Kleenex box over to me, and after a while I choked out, "Well, everybody's been telling me I needed to get counseling; I guess now I've *really* got to get it."

"Yes, you do," Captain Millner said soberly. "Because . . . You know the Bible pretty well, don't you?"

"I guess."

He went on looking at me.

"All right," I said. "All right, yes, I know the scriptures pretty well."

"The fathers have eaten sour grapes and the children's teeth are set on edge. Just remind yourself, Deb, that thing about the sins of the fathers being visited on the children isn't a threat; it's a statement of fact. Your father's sins—as you said a while ago—killed your sister, this long afterward, and your father's sins are still eating you. Deb, you don't need that kind of visit."

· · · · ·

291

I grinned a little through my tears and said, "You're right. I don't. Okay, I promise. I'll call Susan and see who she recommends, and I'll talk with my bishop."

He didn't reply to that, but I knew he wouldn't. As an ardent member of the Church of Christ, he was less than crazy about the Mormons. But he wouldn't say that to me, at least not right now, though he'd go on, as he had been doing for the last seven years, inviting me to his church on the average of once a week.

"Deb—I'm sorry," he went on. "I should have known you wouldn't refuse a transfer if you didn't have a good reason. So I'll put you back into Major Case and, let's see, I can go on and move Margie up from Juvenile—"

"No," I said.

"What?"

"No, I'll stay here till Chandra gets back," I said. "It's just . . . I didn't want to stay in this unit unless I could do some good. And I guess—maybe—I'm doing some good after all."

"You are. But Deb—"

"Yeah?"

"You don't have to do it all yourself. We've got a whole police department here. You don't need this. I'm putting you back in Major Cases. We were going to pull Margie in here anyway, and now is as good a time as any."

. . . . .

$\varepsilon\ p\ i\ \ell\ o\ g\ u\ \varepsilon$

I WAS TRYING to decide who to ask to take me home when Harry called. "I've been out at Bell," he said, with barely concealed excitement in his voice, "and I just thought I'd see if you were ready for me to pick you up." I assured him I was, and said I would meet him in the front lobby.

Bell, when he says it that way, has nothing to do with telephones. It's the helicopter firm he's worked for ever since he got out of the Marines, and is presently on medical leave from. Or was on medical leave from. Because when he picked me up he was wearing his finest suit, grinning from ear to ear, and somehow I wasn't surprised when he told me he'd be going back to work Monday morning. "You've got your job back?" I asked rather stupidly.

"Nope," he answered, and waited a second or two to see what I'd ask. When I didn't ask anything, he said, "I've got a promotion. Ten thousand dollars a year worth of promotion."

"Wow," I said, and we proceeded home in comfortable silence.

We could hear Hal's band—the whole thing, this time, not just Lori and Hal and a tape recorder—before we stopped the car. My son-in-law Olead's van was parked in front of the house, and I deduced without much difficulty that he'd been roped into hauling the whole kit and caboodle over to wherever it was Hal was doing the show. An unfamiliar red Miata was parked near it, and I assumed that must belong to one of the other people in the band.

. . . . .

As we approached the house, we could hear an unfamiliar voice inside the garage belting out "I Am Woman." And then, joyfully, I realized it wasn't an unfamiliar voice at all—it was Lori. Our old Lori back again, not the quivering mass of fright who had crept around the house for months, but the old Lori who almost never walked anywhere because it was more fun to run, who kicked a murderer in the ribs almost exactly three years ago in New Mexico.

When we got in, we found they had an audience. Sandy Miller was saying, "There, I knew you could do it, it's all in breathing right."

My daughter Becky was sitting on an improvised bench with Olead, holding her youngest child so far, with the other two sitting on the floor staring big-eyed at the drums. And beside her was Doreen Miller. The vaguely familiar voice that had answered the phone that day . . . I should have realized. But so many teenagers are in and out there that I never once thought of Doreen.

They all saw me practically simultaneously, and Becky stood up and said, "I've had her all along. Mom. I was sorry not to tell you, but I was afraid, with your job, you'd have to send her back, and I couldn't—"

"Of course you couldn't," I agreed, and turned to Lori. "Surely that's not all of the show! Let's hear more."

So we heard more, as they rehearsed the whole thing straight through from beginning to end and then began to rush drums and keyboards and music stands into the back of Olead's van.

I watched Hal bustling around with a checklist and boundless energy, seeing to it everything was put in the right place, and wondered where my scatterbrained boy had gone. He'd got lost, somewhere between Lori's accident and her recovery, and except for occasional relapses he wasn't coming back anymore. Now— quite suddenly, in my mind's eye—I could really see Hal, in a dark suit with his hair combed and that little plastic nametag that will say "Elder Ralston," spending two years away from Lori, away from Harry and me, away from his sisters and brother and nieces and

. . . . .

294

nephews, because he recognized a duty to God. As an adult, he wouldn't be at all like my father; he'd say a lot less, but he'd do immeasurably better.

Love, that's the big thing, I thought, sitting on the footlocker one of my daughters many years ago had covered with stickers of animals and birds and flowers, sitting comfortably with my back leaning against Harry's side, thinking about my older son. Half Korean, half who-knows-what (but tall, very tall), Hal had been abandoned by his birth mother, and he could have grown up like those heartbreaking Romanian children we all have seen on television, swaying back and forth in a crib covered with feces. He'd learned to love because we loved him before we ever saw him and went right on loving him in spite of all his shenanigans . . . and the bishops loved him, and his Young Men's leaders, and his Scout leaders, and his seminary teachers . . . and that truck driver loved Rhonda even if she was too badly bruised to accept his love . . . and the Washingtons loved Diane Reddich enough to completely rearrange their lives to make room for her . . . *God is love . . . We love Him because He first loved us . . . Love one another . . .*

"Honey, are you asleep?" Harry asked gently.

"Uh-uh," I said, and blinked, and realized we were alone in the garage. "Well, maybe I was."

"Take you out to dinner?" Harry asked.

"Umm . . . let me think about it . . . Harry?"

"Yup?"

"You know how I'm always remembering stuff they made me memorize in school and it didn't make any sense to me then but now it does?"

"I remember." He sounded rueful. I could understand why. Quoting things at length is one of my minor bad habits.

"Well, there's this thing that starts out 'The quality of mercy is not strained; it droppeth as the gentle rain from heaven' or something like that, and the teacher told us that 'strained' meant 're-

. . . . .

strained.' And I've been thinking about that, and it's not quite right."

"What do you mean?" Harry asked patiently.

"Mercy might drop as the gentle rain from heaven," I said, "but people do their best all the time to restrain it. This guy today . . ." I started telling him, and then veered off. "Oh, never mind, it's too nasty to think about. Anyhow, when people get out of the way, there's always this little angle of mercy left over . . . Everybody's been so nice to us—the Relief Society bringing in supper. You know what the Relief Society motto is?"

"Uh-uh."

" 'Charity never faileth.' Charity in the Bible means love, you know, not people giving people things."

"Uh-huh," Harry said, sounding as if he was the one going to sleep now.

"And we didn't ask Lori to come live with us to be nice. We love Lori."

"Right." He sounded a little more awake.

"I wish I was as nice as that truck driver who buried Rhonda. Or as nice as the Washingtons."

"Huh?" Harry sat straight up, dislodging me. "My dear, you are as nice—and as loving, which I think is what you mean—as that truck driver, and the Washingtons. A little bull-headed and impulsive maybe, but—"

"Gee, thanks. All right, I am. And you're bull-headed, too, and altogether too secretive—but I love you anyway."

His reply was quite satisfactory.

Two hours later dispatch called. "Can you come in? The TCU rapist is at it again."

"I'm on sick leave," I said, "and I'm back out of the Sex Crimes Unit anyway. You'll have to get somebody else."

I could hear a little rustling of papers. "Oh, that's right, Manuel Rodriguez is next on rotation. I've got you marked off sick . . .

· · · · ·

296

Chandra had her baby; it's a boy . . . Let's see, Roger Hales is marked off permanently . . . Calvin Woodall put in with a question mark . . . What on earth are you guys doing in the Rape Squad?"

"It's the Sex Crimes Unit," I said, "and they're, um, reorganizing. But count me out. You've got a whole police department there."

Harry didn't say anything after I hung up—probably he didn't dare, for fear I'd immediately change my mind—but he looked very approving. "You sure you don't want to go out to dinner?"

"Then we'd have to put our clothes back on, and I don't have the energy. Maybe if we just sent out for pizza—or what's that Chinese place that delivers? No, I forgot, we don't have to. One of the sisters is bringing us supper. I guess you had better dress, to get the door."

I dreamed, later, about children swimming, girls and boys together, and the girl who had been strangled by her mother in my dream was swimming, and Lori was swimming, and Diane Reddich and the Washingtons, and Sandy and Dusty and Doreen Miller, and the truck driver I'd never seen but who had a pleasant, rugged face, and my sister Rhonda, and Oprah Winfrey, and Captain Millner, and Rafe, and of course Harry and I were swimming, too, in a bright, glistening, shining, warm bay, and later, much later, my father came, and Seth Miller, and Emil Reddich, and then more and more and more people, until everybody I knew and everybody I didn't know was there, and there was nobody angry or threatening, nobody giving wrongful orders. Only the water and the sunshine and all the clean, happy children swimming.

. . . . .

Author's Note

. . . .

LIKE AS MANY as one in four American women, and about one in seven American men, I—along with several of my siblings—was a sexually and otherwise abused child. By the time I was emotionally ready to discuss the matter, both of my parents were dead, so the type of confrontational techniques psychiatrists recommend were not possible. But I want to mention here that my brothers and cousins, as well as my husband and children, rallied to my emotional support, and my bishop located a self-help group for me that has been wonderful. However, I know other women who have been further assaulted by having their assailants years later look them in the eye and deny that anything ever happened, and have had their entire families deny that anything happened and accuse the women of trying to cause trouble. I urge any of my readers who recognize themselves anywhere in these pages to ask for help. Whether or not you can afford a psychiatrist or a psychologist, help is available. And I could not possibly have written this book without the emotional support not only of my family but also of my extended sisters from all over the Wasatch Front who meet with me on Tuesday night.

To anyone who reads this book and is presently an abused child, I urge you to talk with your teacher, your counselor, or the police and get help at once. No matter what anyone may have told you, you do *not* deserve what's happening to you, and nobody—no matter what he may insist—has the right to do such things.

. . . . .